D0267761

BALLI
KAUR JASWAL

THE UNLIKELY ADVENTURES OF THE SHERGILL SISTERS

HarperCollinsPublishers

HarperCollins*Publishers*
1 London Bridge Street
London SE1 9GF

www.harpercollins.co.uk

Published by HarperCollins*Publishers* 2019
1

Copyright © Balli Kaur Jaswal 2019

Balli Kaur Jaswal asserts the moral right to
be identified as the author of this work

A catalogue record for this book
is available from the British Library

HB ISBN: 978-0-00-820993-3
TPB ISBN: 978-0-00-820994-0

This novel is entirely a work of fiction.
The names, characters and incidents portrayed in it are
the work of the author's imagination. Any resemblance to
actual persons, living or dead, events or localities is
entirely coincidental.

Set in Perpetua by Palimpsest Book Production Ltd, Falkirk, Stirlingshire

Printed and bound in Great Britain by
Printed and bound by CPI Group (UK) Ltd, Croydon CR0 4YY

All rights reserved. No part of this publication may be
reproduced, stored in a retrieval system, or transmitted,
in any form or by any means, electronic, mechanical,
photocopying, recording or otherwise, without the prior
permission of the publishers.

MIX
Paper from
responsible sources
FSC C007454

This book is produced from independently certified FSC™ paper
to ensure responsible forest management.

For more information visit: **www.harpercollins.co.uk/green**

For Asher

SCOTTISH BORDERS LIBRARY SERVICES	
010302764	
Bertrams	10/06/2019
	£14.99

Prologue

My dearest children,

If you are reading this, you know the end has finally come for me. I hope that our final moments together were peaceful and that I had a chance to tell each of you how much I love you. If not, I hope that you know how much you have enriched my life. I am so very proud of each of you and the individual paths you have trekked in this world. I am blessed to have been witness to your triumphs and challenges, your heartaches and your successes. Guiding you from infancy to adulthood allowed me to live life over and over again, and in this way, I feel that I have stepped into so many worlds in the course of my brief stay in this universe.

There are matters to be discussed of course, involving the will and my estate, but these will come later. I trust that the lawyers will discuss the inheritance and the division of property and assets with you after the other formalities are taken care of. If you would like to be informed ahead of time, please see the attached.

Please take care of yourselves and each other. Make time, not just on special occasions, to come together and enrich your bond as a family. I have learned that the most important thing in life is that we show appreciation to our loved ones. Remember that nothing matters more than this.

This was the letter that Sita Kaur Shergill overheard the old woman in the next bed dictating over the phone. A few times, her voice quavered and she had to pause to sigh and sniffle. Sita had turned down the volume on her television to listen to the part about the lawyers – she was most interested in what this woman was leaving to her children, but 'the attached' was not available on this side of the partition. She had seen the children on their visits – two middle-aged sons who were possibly twins with vastly different diets and a handsome blonde woman who always repeated the same soothing words, 'We're here, Mum. We're here.' They often arrived separately but left together, squeezing each other's shoulders and making light conversation about parking spaces or the declining quality of the hospital canteen's coffee.

Sita pressed the buzzer on her remote control and when the nurse arrived, she requested a pen and piece of paper. These were the earliest hours of the morning, before visitors were allowed. It was the best time to think about dying. The pain encompassed her entire body, radiating from her toes to her temples and vibrating in her bones. Despite the morphine, the pain was always visible – she saw it edging in the shadows of her vision on the best days and wringing her frail body like a towel on the worst. Today she was feeling strong enough to sit up; the letter from the woman in the next bed had motivated her, and by some miracle, the nurses attended to her request within the minute.

My dearest daughters, she began. She stopped and frowned. When had she ever addressed her children as dears? She crossed out the line and began again. *To Rajni, Jezmeen and Shirina.* There – a command for their attention. She used to stand at the foot of the stairs and shout all three names even if she only wanted one of them to come down; she could always find something for the other two to do once they arrived. It only worked for a while, then Jezmeen started calling back: 'WHICH ONE OF US SPECIFICALLY?'

To Rajni, Jezmeen and Shirina:
By now, I am dead. It is just as well because I've had enough of this ghastly life – all this working and suffering and trying to take care of

myself for no bloody reason. Please enjoy your health while you have it because once your body betrays you, no comforts in the world will make up for your loss.

No, she couldn't leave them with that. It was too honest. If these were her last words, they'd never forgive her. She folded the sheet and set it on her side table, weighing it down with the pen, and then she closed her eyes. How did she want to be remembered? She had been a wife, a mother, a widow and a grandmother. Sikh funerals didn't include eulogies, so her daughters would be spared the task of scraping together a list of her meagre achievements. On some days, she thought she knew which of her daughters would remember her least kindly and on better days, she assured herself that all of them would at least agree that she had tried her very best.

Sita pressed the button to call for the nurse again. It took a while this time, but eventually the rail-thin girl with the tattoos and half her head shaved arrived. She was not as friendly as the Jamaican nurse who sometimes squeezed Sita's hand and said, 'You rest now,' but she smiled when Sita asked her: 'How old are you?'

'I'm twenty-seven,' she replied. There were zig-zag patterns shaved into the sides of the girl's scalp. Sita wondered what man found this sort of thing attractive.

'Have you ever been to India?' she asked.

'No,' the nurse said, a bit regretfully, which pleased Sita.

'If your mother asked you to do something for her, no matter what it was, would you do it?' she asked.

The nurse slid Sita's table down the bed so she could tug at the edge of the blanket, which was bunched up by her feet. Her fingers grazed the knuckles of Sita's toes. 'Of course I would,' she said. 'Now, is there something you need, because—'

'What's your religion?' Sita asked.

Her question was met with narrowed eyes. 'I do believe that's a very personal question to ask.'

Sita frowned. There was a reason she liked the Jamaican nurse better. She wore a thin gold cross that hung just beneath the V-neck of her scrubs. 'Ho, Lord,' she wheezed quietly, stretching her back at the end of a long shift.

'Can you hand me my pen and paper, please?' Sita asked. As the girl reached into the drawer next to the bed, Sita's heart leapt into her throat. *Not there!*

'It's right there, on the table,' Sita snapped, pointing at the table, now out of her reach. Although the nurse was unlikely to pluck Sita's jewellery pouch from where it was nestled between a prayer book and her mobile phone charger, Sita had lived long enough to know that you could never be too careful. The girl moved the table back and then left, probably to grumble and tell the other nurses that they were right, old Mrs Shergill needed to cark it already. Last week, Rajni had stormed into the nurses' station and told them off for leaving Sita shivering during a particularly agonizing episode. 'I don't care if she's already got a blanket, get her another one,' Rajni nearly shouted, making Sita want to weep with gratitude and also chastise her daughter for making a scene.

The pain was inching into her body now, and she could sense that it was going to be a bad day. Her daughters would visit this afternoon – hopefully all three of them, since Rajni had called Shirina and informed her to fly over at once when it appeared that Sita's remaining days were down to single digits. She had to write this letter before the strength leached out of her.

To Rajni, Jezmeen and Shirina:

If you remember correctly, when I was first diagnosed with cancer, I wanted to go to India to do a pilgrimage to honour the principles of our great Gurus. You and the doctors convinced me that this was a bad idea because my health was already so fragile, but I think it would have enriched my spirit, if not my physical condition.

I am attaching a list of the places that I would like you to visit on my behalf, after I am gone. They are in Delhi, Amritsar and beyond.

The whole journey will take a week. You should go together and do all the tasks as instructed: seva, to serve others and preserve your humility; a ritual sarovar bath, for cleansing and protecting your soul from ailments; and a trek to the high peaks of spirituality, to feel appreciation for that body which carries you in this life. I would also like my ashes to be scattered in India.

There are also some places I'd like you to visit because I won't have the chance to do so. Simple pleasures, like watching the sunrise at India Gate, and sharing a humble dinner together. I will outline the itinerary in more detail on the next page. Please do this for me. It will be a way of completing my journey in this world and continuing yours.

Love,

Your mother, Sita Kaur Shergill.

Sita's vision began to blur as she read over the letter. There it was, the searing sensation in her bones. She squeezed her eyes shut and clutched the sides of her mattress. There was only so much morphine the nurses could administer in a day and no legal dose seemed to be enough to wash it all away. 'We're here, Mum, we're here,' she imagined her daughters saying, just like the blonde woman, as she presented the letter to them. Their faces would be awash with tears and they would take each other's hands, united for once.

As the wave of pain subsided, Sita picked up her pen again and turned over the sheet to work on the itinerary. Agony was quickly replaced by nostalgia – Sita's memories of India were stronger than ever. An end-of-life counsellor named Russ who visited last week said that it was common to remember the past vividly as death approached. 'Think of it as a transition,' Russ had said. 'You are finishing one stage and entering another.' Recalling those words, Sita considered her daughters' journey to India. She would insist that they do this – no excuses, no backing out. It was a comfort to know that while they returned to her origins, she would be busy entering the afterlife. Who knew how long it would take to adjust to her new surroundings there, make friends, find out how the coffee machine worked?

What if Devinder had also ended up in this new place? She had decades of catching up to do with her late husband, after she'd finished telling him off for leaving so suddenly.

Thoughts and memories of those early years of marriage and having children flooded Sita's mind, reducing all remaining traces of pain to a dull ache that settled in her chest. Those were chaotic days – learning to be a wife and a mother, running a household and adjusting to life in a new country. When she finally got the hang of it all, her husband died. There was only a small fraction of Sita's lifespan when her family was whole. She scribbled more items onto the itinerary. Her last trip to India had been nearly thirty years ago. In his explanation of the stages of grief, Russ had said that some people experienced an intense desire to turn back time. Although Sita prided herself on being too pragmatic for such wishes, she also hoped that her daughters found India just as she had left it.

There was something else Sita wanted to tell her daughters. It was a confession of sorts, for something she made up her mind to do after Russ left her bedside. She would have to find a suitable moment to tell them. It was not appropriate to write it down; she'd have to lower her voice and prompt her daughters to gather closer. They'd dismiss her at first, of course. 'Mum, don't be silly,' Rajni or Shirina would say. 'You're kidding, right?' Jezmeen would retort, because to Jezmeen, nothing was real, not even on a woman's deathbed. Then they'd begin to protest, telling her she didn't know what she was saying. That was by far the most frustrating thing about being terminally ill – everybody thought she was thinking through a haze of fear, a desperate need to cling to life. But death was the most certain thing in the world. To prove to her daughters that she was indeed being serious, she'd tell them to open the drawer and take out the jewellery pouch. Have a look inside. You see? Now, please don't argue with your mother.

Chapter One

I would prefer that you take this journey during a cooler time of the year, but since Rajni can only travel during school holidays, you will need to go to India in July/August. Book your tickets and hotels quickly — I know my last trip to India was well over twenty years ago, but the last-minute bookings were very expensive.

Rajni was not built for fainting spells. Moments after Anil told her about the girlfriend, she considered pretending to faint, but she knew she'd throw her arms out at the last minute to break the fall. Nobody took a woman seriously if she staged her own collapses. A feigned faint, ha-ha.

So she stared at Anil as simple mathematical sums populated her mind:

$36 - 18 = 18$

The girlfriend was 18 years older than Anil.

$36 \div 18 = 2$

The girlfriend was exactly twice Anil's age.

$43 - 36 = 7$

The girlfriend was only seven years younger than Rajni herself.

This last fact made her light-headed. The overpowering smell of half-eaten fish wasn't helping. For dinner, she had baked three pieces of salmon because Omega Threes were supposed to make everybody live to a hundred. This girlfriend of Anil's, did she know about the nutritional benefits of Omega Threes? Probably not.

'Mum, come on,' said Anil. All Rajni could do was shake her head. No, no, no. Tonight was supposed to be special: their last dinner together before she went off to India. If Anil had chosen this occasion to tell them about his girlfriend, then she was supposed to be . . . well, a *girl*. Somebody who called her Mrs Chadha and whose parents regarded Anil with a reasonable amount of suspicion until he won them over with good manners and clean fingernails.

Anil turned to Kabir. 'Dad,' he said in a slightly desperate way that made it clear to Rajni that they had already discussed this matter without her. Guilt rippled across Kabir's expression. He stole a glance at Rajni.

'You knew about this?' Rajni asked Kabir. 'For how long?'

Kabir had thin lips, which almost vanished when he was unhappy. 'He came to me this morning,' he said. 'You were packing for your trip and I didn't want to disturb you.'

Dinner time – morning = a whole day.

Rajni fixed Kabir with the kind of stare usually reserved for naughty students called into her office. 'And how do you feel about this? Care to share your opinion?'

'Obviously, I'm concerned, but Anil is old enough now to make his own decisions.'

'Concerned? Concerned is how you feel about old Mrs Willis next door when she's struggling to put her bins out. This is our son, Kabir. He finished Sixth Form mere weeks ago and now he tells us he wants to move in with a woman twice his age!' Where did Anil even meet a thirty-six-year-old? A horrifying thought struck her. 'She wasn't a teacher of yours, was she?'

'God, no,' Anil said. Rajni let out a sigh. Thank goodness. She had always worried about Cass Finchley, a music teacher who swayed too suggestively on the edge of the dance floor while chaperoning school formals.

Kabir cleared his throat. 'Anil, your mother and I just know you have a bright future ahead of you. We don't want you squandering it on some . . . fling.'

'It's not a fling,' Anil said. 'We're serious about each other.'

'I'm sure you feel that way now, but there will be problems, son.' Rajni used to find it touching when Kabir called Anil 'son'. It was old-fashioned and charming and it brought a rush of warmth to her heart. Now he said the word like he was losing grip on its meaning.

'There's nothing we can't work out, innit?' Anil said.

'Nothing?' Rajni echoed.

Anil shrugged. 'We've got the same cultural background. We get each other. People are always saying that's the main thing.'

'You're from completely different generations. She's a grown woman. You're a boy! You might as well be from different planets.'

'Nothing,' Anil repeated tersely. With his jaw clenched like this, he looked so much like Kabir that Rajni wanted to suspend the argument and run for her camera. They say photos of the first-born child always outnumber those of subsequent children. As Anil was their first-and-only born, Rajni documented him thoroughly with no fears of sibling inequality. Their home was a shrine to Anil's childhood: portraits and finger paintings, pencil marks on the wall charting his growth over the years.

Crises about Anil's future were becoming an annual milestone. Last summer's fight had been about Anil's declaration that he wasn't going to apply to university – he wanted to be done with education after completing Sixth Form. 'They don't teach you nothing you can't learn on the internet these days, don't they?' Anil said. Rajni, head spinning from all the double negatives she had spent a lifetime correcting in her son, had left the room. When she returned, Kabir said he would talk some sense into Anil. It took months, but they finally arrived at a compromise: Anil would apply to university, but he could defer for a gap year. He was supposed to get a job during that time (his parents' hope being that the gap year would help him to recognize the limitations of being without a degree), but then his grandmother had died and left him a small inheritance, turning the gap year into a paid holiday.

'Think about this for a moment then, Anil,' Kabir said. 'She's surely at an age where she wants to settle down.'

'That's why we're planning on moving in together.'

'But do you realize what this entails? For her?'

Anil clutched the back of the dining chair in front of him. His news had brought them to their feet, standing before their unfinished meals. A scaly whiff from the salmon hit Rajni in the nostrils again. She picked up the plates and brought them to the kitchen.

'I understand exactly what Davina wants,' Anil was saying. As Rajni tipped the scraps into the bin, she had an uninvited image of her son tumbling around in bed with an experienced woman. *Stop it,* she ordered her mind. She looked around the kitchen for something, anything, to focus on. There was a leaflet on the counter from the Jehovah's Witnesses who came by yesterday evening. They were such a bother but she found it impossible to shut the door on their faces – those pallid cheeks and impressively starched shirt collars. 'I'm busy at the moment but perhaps you can leave behind some literature,' she had offered as a consolation for not wanting to be saved, even though the leaflet would find its way to the bin within a day or two. *ALL SUFFERING IS SOON TO END*, declared the header over a painting of a sunny green meadow. How nice to be so certain. The words brought Rajni only a brief shot of relief before she returned to reality.

'A woman at that stage in her life is looking for a long-term partner,' Kabir was saying to Anil.

'This isn't some kinda *phrase*, Dad.' He meant 'phase'. Rajni was too upset to correct him but she kept a mental note to educate him on the difference later.

'Son, listen for a moment. I'm saying that Davina probably has bigger, more permanent plans.'

Rajni rushed back into the living room. 'Tick-tock!' she cried, startling her family. 'That's what everyone says to a woman in her mid-thirties whether she wants children or not. "Have one before it's too late."' (In her case: 'Have another one, you're not just having one, are you? Finish what you started! Give the poor boy a sibling.' As if she and Kabir didn't try and try until sex became another routine household task like doing the laundry or paying the water bill.)

'Yes,' Kabir said. 'Societal pressures. They're bigger than you think, Anil, especially for adults.'

'Look, the only person pressuring me is you. Davina and me are just fine.'

'So if she wanted a baby tomorrow it would be okay? You'd give up all that travelling, your nights out with mates?' Kabir asked.

That ought to give him a fright, Rajni thought, noting the swell of unease on Anil's face. He'd been plotting his European holiday: skiing in Bulgaria; island-hopping in Greece; God-knows-what in Amsterdam.

'I would. I am going to give it all up,' Anil said quietly. He gripped the chair.

The room became still. Anil bit his lower lip and looked at his knuckles, which had turned white.

Kabir stared at him. 'What are you saying?'

'I am going to give it all up for her,' Anil repeated.

'Son?'

'Mum. Dad. It's not a big deal, alright? You have to promise not to overreact.'

The edges of the room began to blur and the floor tilted slightly. Rajni heard Kabir gently saying, 'Okay, we promise. Now what is it?'

'Davina's pregnant,' Anil said.

And then Rajni fainted.

The customer had seen a video online about how bronze highlighter could be used to take ten pounds off her face. 'The girl just sweeps this brush across her face and suddenly she has cheekbones,' she gushed.

'Those videos are very helpful,' Jezmeen agreed. 'Lots of useful tips.' Especially useful for a person like her, who had no experience doing make-up professionally. After being suspended from her job as a host on *DisasterTube*, one of the studio make-up artists had given Jezmeen the lead on this job. It was temporary, Jezmeen kept reminding herself. Everything would blow over, and she'd find another role soon. The last time Jezmeen checked online, the number of views on her video had hit 788, which was hardly viral, but her agent Cameron still believed they had to be cautious.

'Lie low. Wait for the dust to settle,' he had urged her. There was no end to his supply of banal encouragements whenever they spoke – 'Take some time for yourself,' was another favourite which roughly translated to: 'Take the least humiliating job offer thrown your way and we'll just have to wait for the anonymous masses on the internet to decide your fate.'

'Are you going to use highlighter on me, then?' Stella asked.

'I've got other plans for you,' Jezmeen said warmly. Starting with matching a more appropriate foundation to Stella's skin tone. At the moment, she was less 'Youthful Summer Glow' and more 'Fell Asleep in the Tanning Bed'.

As Jezmeen rubbed a wipe across Stella's cheeks, she had a distinct sense of déjà vu. In another time in her life, Rajni used to apply make-up on her while she struggled to sit still and not turn to the mirror to see her reflection. Jezmeen remembered doing the same for Mum on the morning of Shirina's wedding. The bridal make-up artist had chosen a deep-purple eye shadow and insisted on a crayon-thick line for Mum's eyelids. Mum was horrified. 'I can't go to the temple like this,' she'd gasped. 'People will say . . .' She didn't finish that sentence; she rarely did. It was bad enough that people would say anything. 'Jezmeen, get me some tissues,' Mum had commanded. Helping to clean the make-up off Mum's skin, Jezmeen had noticed the looseness of her cheeks, and the way her eyelids folded, and she vowed never to let herself grow old.

Jezmeen's phone buzzed on the counter. 'Excuse me, Stella,' Jezmeen said, leaning over to see the screen. Message from Rajni. She ignored it. Rajni was likely panicking about the trip and asking everyone if they had taken their tetanus shots, or something similarly hysterical.

'I'm going to use this primer on you,' Jezmeen said. She showed Stella the bottle. 'It's a great base which keeps your make-up on for much longer during the day.' Her phone buzzed again.

'I'm so sorry,' Jezmeen said. She shot a glare at her phone.

'No worries, love. Your boyfriend must be anxious about you,' Stella said.

Ha! If only there were an anxious boyfriend, or a boyfriend at all. Her last relationship had ended more disastrously than Stella could probably imagine.

'Oh no, that's my sister,' Jezmeen said. 'We're going on a trip to India on Thursday and she's probably just reminding me to pack sunscreen or something.'

'A holiday! Just the two of you?'

'The three of us. Our youngest sister's flying there from Australia.'

'That's lovely,' Stella said.

People always said this when Jezmeen mentioned having two sisters. Lovely. Cosy teas and long chats. Some sort of unbreakable bond. Stella's smile was so bright that Jezmeen didn't want to tell her how much she was dreading this trip with uppity Rajni and irritatingly perfect Shirina.

'We're going there for our mum,' Jezmeen explained. 'She passed away last November and we're doing a pilgrimage in her memory and scattering her ashes there.'

'Oh, that's beautiful. What a tribute,' Stella breathed. She reached out and clasped Jezmeen's hand. Now Stella probably had an image of three dutiful daughters in matching loose white robes solemnly making their way up a misty mountain as they took turns carrying an urn filled with ashes. Again, inaccurate. Pilgrimages weren't even a requirement of their religion (she had done some quick Googling on Sikhism, and sent all the links to Rajni as part of her continuing campaign to oppose everything her older sister wanted them to do), but after the cancer treatments stopped working, Mum had turned to all kinds of holy remedies. There were rituals she had been too weak to do, places she had been unable to visit for the last time, so her daughters were tasked with completing the journey. Jezmeen noticed that Mum had sneaked in a few itinerary items that involved the sisters simply spending time together, probably because she knew they wouldn't bother to make the time otherwise. As far as Jezmeen saw it, this trip was less about spirituality and more about Mum forcing them to travel together.

This time Jezmeen's phone rang. 'For fuck's sakes,' she muttered.

'Just answer it, darling. It could be important.'

'Thank you, Stella.' Jezmeen picked up the phone. 'Rajni, I'm in the middle of work.'

'Did you see my messages? You'll have to find your own way to the airport. Something came up at home last night and . . . I just have some things to deal with. Kabir's driving me there directly.'

'Alright. Is that it?'

'Yes.' Rajni hesitated. 'What time do you plan on leaving?'

'I'll be at Heathrow two hours before we fly, Rajni, don't you worry about it.'

'You're still at work?'

'Yes, and I have to get back to work. Bye now!'

Rajni had started saying something when Jezmeen hung up. She put the phone on 'silent' and turned back to Stella. 'Now, I'll be using two different concealers because we're really working with two different shades of irregularities here.'

'Do I mix these?' Stella asked.

'No, we're using this one for under your eyes and this one for those blemishes on your chin.' Jezmeen held up each bottle. While Stella inspected them, Jezmeen glanced at her phone. She had a funny feeling. Why did it matter to Rajni that she was still at work now if she was only flying out on Thursday?

'I might need to write these down,' Stella said, rummaging through her purse. 'Otherwise, I'll forget which one goes where.'

'Here you go,' Jezmeen said, handing her a pencil and a card with a face drawn on it. 'Just draw an arrow to the eye area and write "Nude Secret 19".'

Stella had careful penmanship. 'Darling, you have such a lovely manner, has anyone ever told you that?'

Jezmeen smiled, surprised. 'Thank you.'

'I must take your name card. Do you do private sessions as well? My daughter's looking for a good make-up artist for her wedding. It's only next spring, but good services get booked up so quickly.'

Jezmeen's smile faltered. Next spring! Her stomach contracted at the thought of still working at a make-up counter. No, no, it wasn't possible. She was lying low and taking time for herself while the dust settled. People would move on. But Cameron said it wasn't necessarily about her. 'There's a lack of roles for Indian actresses to begin with,' he'd explained. 'And directors can't really afford any bad PR if they're taking a chance on somebody new. So there's just a lot working against you at the moment.' What he avoided saying was that there was one Polly Mishra already. He knew that Jezmeen balked at the frequent comparisons between herself and that actress, who had overshadowed Jezmeen's career as soon as she arrived on the scene.

While Stella labelled her card, Jezmeen stole a look at her phone. Three missed calls from Rajni in the last two minutes and a message:

'You DO realize that we're flying out tonight right?'

Jezmeen's heart stopped. She nearly dropped her phone. She texted Rajni back:

'YES of course I know. Just finishing up and leaving straight from work.'

How the hell had this happened? It was Thursday they were supposed to leave, not Tuesday. She had a vague memory of a conversation with Rajni about finding a cheaper flight for Thursday. 'It's at two a.m. though,' Rajni had said. 'I guess that's alright.' And something in her tone annoyed Jezmeen, so she had said, 'Not all of us have school holidays, you know.' Rajni *had* booked the Tuesday flight, then.

Or had Jezmeen just imagined Rajni giving in? Sometimes she had entire conversations with Rajni in her mind. She used to do this with Mum too – it was easier than fighting out loud. In the fantasy arguments, Jezmeen always emerged the winner, with the other person apologizing and sometimes even grovelling for forgiveness. They were leaving tonight, then. They were leaving tonight! She would have to call the manager and tell her something had come up – this could count for a family emergency.

'What's the primer called?' Stella asked.

'It's just primer,' Jezmeen replied. *Shit, shit, shit.* She didn't even know where her suitcase was.

'Oh dear,' Stella murmured as the pointy end of her pencil punctured the card.

Oh dear indeed.

At Melbourne Airport, an elderly Indian couple were being seen off by their extended family. Shirina watched them move like a swarm of bees to the departure gate. 'Do you think they're returning home? Or going back to visit?' Shirina asked.

Sehaj shrugged. 'Doesn't make a difference. They all have to go through the same gate.' He was busy scrolling through his phone. Shirina glanced at his screen. Numbers and graphs. Work stuff, he'd mutter if she asked what was keeping him so busy.

'They look like they're going to visit. What do you think?' Shirina asked, focusing on the family.

'Don't know,' Sehaj muttered.

'I'm just trying to make conversation,' Shirina said. Sehaj seemed to remember himself then. He put the phone aside and tucked a stray hair behind her ear. 'Sorry,' he murmured, pressing his lips to her temple.

Shirina let her head sink into his chest. Finally, in this bustling international airport terminal, a small chance at intimacy before she left. The past couple of days had been filled with tense silences. She shut her eyes. Sehaj's shirt smelled like a mix of cologne and that fabric softener his mother had recommended. Her life as a married woman smelled like pressed linens; it was the first thing she had noticed when she moved into the joint family home three years ago. His fingers stroked her hair. She thought she might start to cry, so she twisted away from him and then she felt a heavy weight rolling over her foot.

'Ow,' she said, drawing her foot back. It was a suitcase. The woman dragging it didn't notice. She trotted off towards the gate in stilettos that looked like they were stabbing the ground with each step she took.

'I'd say they live here and they're going back for a holiday,' Sehaj said, nodding at the elderly couple. 'The family's too cheerful.'

'Why would all their kids and grandkids be seeing them off then?' Shirina wondered aloud.

'Long trip, maybe?' Sehaj asked. 'They might have a home there where they spend a few months out of the year.'

These were a few good months to spend away from Melbourne. Every day, boulders of grey cloud rolled across the skies and showered the city with icy rain. Nobody in England thought it got cold in Australia; even Shirina refused to believe it until she married Sehaj and came here. Now, whenever the news reported heatwaves in July in Europe, Shirina looked out the window at the slick wet roads and the tree branches bowing under the force of heavy wind and she thought, *How is that possible?*

'How about them?' Sehaj asked. He nodded at two young men. 'Brothers? Best friends?'

'Best friends,' Shirina said, delighted that they were playing this game again. On their honeymoon, stranded in the airport due to a snowstorm in Istanbul (another city Shirina did not expect to have winter, let alone snowstorms), they had passed the time making up stories about strangers. Two and a half years wasn't such a long time ago, but Shirina felt she needed to remind Sehaj of that carefree period in their lives.

'Do you remember finally getting on that flight from Istanbul and sitting behind the Hollywood Spy Couple?' Shirina asked.

Sehaj's eyes lit up with recognition. 'The ones who looked like movie stars and couldn't keep their hands off each other?' They had kissed and snuggled the entire flight – honeymooners, Shirina and Sehaj decided, although those two put other newlyweds to shame with their public caresses and sighs. Then, just before the plane landed, they moved to two empty seats on opposite rows and they disembarked separately. Shirina and Sehaj watched them step into different lines at Customs and

17

then part ways without even acknowledging each other, the woman heading to the Underground, the man staying behind at Baggage Claim.

'Definitely spies,' Sehaj said. He liked his Cold War-era thrillers.

Shirina checked the time. She needed to go soon. New destinations and boarding times winked on the Departures screen. There were flights going to Berlin and Jakarta, Pretoria and Chicago – from where Shirina was standing, it was possible to go anywhere. This thought electrified her. It was like sitting in front of the laptop screen again, scrolling through profiles of eligible men, each one a window to a new future.

Sehaj's body went tense, and her own stomach tightened. He looked like he was ready to say something.

'I'd better get in there,' Shirina said. 'I told Jezmeen I'd get her some Duty Free stuff.' It was a small, imperfect lie – when was the last time she and Jezmeen spoke? If Jezmeen needed something, she probably wouldn't tell her.

'Okay then,' Sehaj said. He seemed distracted by his thoughts. They stood up and he took her bag. The Indian family was still hovering at the Departure gate and the elderly couple weren't within view from here. 'Excuse us,' Sehaj said. The Indians didn't budge. 'Excuse us,' he said again, this time with more force. They shifted a little bit, their conversation too engrossing to follow any orders.

'Come on, people, it's an airport. Get out of the way,' Sehaj said. This caught their attention. Shirina took his hand but he pulled away and elbowed through the crowd. 'Sorry,' she murmured, her head down, but she was annoyed at the family as well. Now her pleasant moment with Sehaj was gone.

Shirina hugged her husband, hoping that this would dissolve his anger. His body was still stiff. 'I'm sorry, Sej,' Shirina said. *How do some married couples fight all the time?* she wondered. It was hard enough trying to get through this one conflict. Apologizing made her feel better. Even though she hadn't done anything wrong, she was sorry for the situation.

Then Sehaj took something from his pocket. Shirina recognized the stationery – that stiff cream-coloured card, premier quality – and his

18

mother's handwriting. Shirina took in the name and address and stared at Sehaj.

'You can't come back unless you do this,' Sehaj said, pressing the card into Shirina's hand. He didn't give her any time to respond before he walked off and disappeared into the crowd.

Chapter Two

Day One: Arrival in Delhi

Be patient. India is not going to be like London. The pollution and the bustling crowds will overwhelm you immediately. You girls always joked that I talked too loudly, and I turned everything into chaos. When you enter India, I want you to think about how it felt to leave this place and go somewhere as orderly as Britain, with ruler-straight rows of houses and trains that run on time. I also want you to understand how hard it was for me, adjusting to all of that quiet.

Rajni's headache was returning, like fingers pressing against her skull. This newly built boutique hotel in Karol Bagh with its patio dining was far removed from the chaos of Delhi that they experienced on the journey from the airport – the hustling luggage handlers, the cab driver that dived into oncoming traffic to overtake his lane, the girls in tattered T-shirts that hung to their knees, dodging rickshaws and potholes with babies propped on their tiny hips. It had been a relief to finally arrive at the King's Paradise Hotel in one piece, but a glance around the lobby during check-in confirmed that the pictures on the booking website had been aspirational – the door-men's shoes left prints in the thin layer of plaster dust on the floor and there was some loud, clanging construction going on upstairs. The owner was putting finishing touches on the place, the staff explained as if their apologetic smiles could mask the strong smell of varnish that made Rajni's head throb. They promised, however, that the hotel café was 'one hundred per cent ready'.

The minute they sat down, Jezmeen began making fun of the menu. She pointed at a list of indulgent summer beverage offerings: *an iced vanilla mango smoothie topped with whipped cream and seasonal fruits.* 'Isn't that just a fancy mango lassi?' Jezmeen mused. 'Look at this one – *an iced turmeric latte sprinkled with cinnamon and coconut shavings.* That's just haldi doodh with ice and some toppings, isn't it?'

'It sounds pretty good to me,' Rajni said. She couldn't believe she had complained about the warmer weather in London last week when it only hit 27 degrees. It was close to 40 here, a furious heat that seemed to demand an apology. If Mum wanted them to appreciate Britain, mission accomplished.

Jezmeen continued to read the menu aloud: '*King's Paradise Hotel Café is a true crossroads between the traditions of the East and the modern comforts of the West.*' She rolled her eyes. 'So it's for people who want to say they've been to India without having eaten the food or experienced the culture authentically.'

'Could you not do that?' Rajni said. She was annoyed enough with the hotel's false advertising. 'If I picked some three-star hotel with monkeys shitting in the lobby for the sake of authenticity, I'd never hear the end of it from you and Shirina.' She only added 'and Shirina' to soften the blow. They both knew Shirina never complained about anything.

Jezmeen ignored her and held up the menu. 'Our monkeys are very well trained not to shit in the lobby. They have their own toilets made of fair-trade ceramic by local artists and they wipe their own arses with organic cotton tissues hand woven by blind Himalayan nuns,' she drawled.

'Shut up,' Rajni said but it felt good to smile. All through the flight, she didn't stop replaying Anil's revelation and its aftermath: the panic that seized his face as she collapsed; the lack of remorse once she recovered. 'You're being melodramatic,' he'd cried, and it sounded so familiar that

Rajni wondered if she'd fainted herself into a time warp where she was arguing with Mum. There had been a shouting match before Anil finally stormed out the door. Rajni and Kabir spent all of the next day fretting over his future. Anil finally returned about twenty minutes before they left for the airport, and he said, 'Nothing's going to come between us, right?' For a moment, Rajni thought he was talking about their family. She nearly cried with relief. Then, as Anil began packing up his things, she understood.

Rajni felt the panic rising in her stomach again. Her son would soon have a new family with his thirty-six-year-old girlfriend. She pressed a hand to her chest and took a sharp breath.

'Everything alright?' Jezmeen asked.

'Fine,' Rajni said. Thank goodness for this trip. Let Kabir talk some sense into their son — she had done all she could (mostly fainting and shouting) to no avail. She looked past the hotel's walled-in patio, where the foggy sky began. In the distance, a poorly tuned chorus of car horns pierced the atmosphere. The air smelled like burned rubber. Delhi. It couldn't be helped, Rajni supposed, although she wouldn't mind putting more mayhem at arm's length for a while. She had no desire to go out into the city, not after her last trip here with Mum. '*I know my last trip to India was well over twenty years ago, but the last-minute bookings were very expensive*' — in that part of the letter, Rajni could hear Mum's pointed tone. It took her years to recover her losses from that trip, and an even longer time to forgive Rajni for what happened.

There was a young European couple in the pool. The deep-golden curlicues of a recent mehndi pattern showed strongly on the woman's pale hands as they cut through the water, a postcard picture of holiday tranquillity.

Rajni pulled copies of the trip itinerary from her bag. She had typed up Mum's letter and made duplicates for Shirina and Jezmeen. Perhaps it was overkill — Jezmeen's expression told her as much — but she had gone ahead and highlighted the activities according to three categories: Spiritual, Tourism and Sentimental.

'Was your laminating machine broken?' Jezmeen asked dryly, flapping the paper at Rajni.

As a matter of fact, it was, but Rajni didn't say so. 'I thought we'd look this over together.'

'Shouldn't we wait till Shirina wakes up from her nap? She might have some suggestions.'

'Mum set the itinerary,' Rajni reminded Jezmeen. 'It's not like there's any discussion or negotiating involved.'

'I'm sure we can tweak it a little.'

Rajni stared at Jezmeen. No, they could not 'tweak it a little'. This tendency to apply her own interpretation to Mum's wishes had nearly got them all into massive trouble recently – had Jezmeen forgotten? No. Jezmeen matched her with an even look. She knew what she was doing; insisting that she was right.

'Jesmeen, I think you're missing the point—'

'Can you call me Jezmeen, please?' Jezmeen looked stricken all of a sudden. 'With a zed? I changed it legally two years ago and you're still the only person who calls me Jesmeen.'

'I'll try to remember,' Rajni replied but she didn't think she'd try too hard. She loved the name Jesmeen; Mum had let her choose it. It was the sort of privilege that came with being eleven when your younger sister was born. Two years ago, Jezmeen had gone through some crisis over turning thirty and sent out an email to close friends and family saying that she was legally changing her name. Rajni hadn't paid too much attention – Jezmeen thrived on theatrical announcements – so she was surprised when Jezmeen followed through with it. What difference did one letter make? Rajni wondered, but she didn't need to hear an explanation from Jezmeen, with all of the accompanying eye-rolling and pouting and the you-just-don't-get-it looks.

Rajni pointed to the itinerary, her finger resting on the header, *The Golden Temple, Amritsar*. 'If the purpose of this trip is to do a pilgrimage for Mum, then we're following this itinerary,' she tried again.

'I get that, but I think there's room to be flexible if, say, we don't want to spend too much time in one place or we decide we want an extra day somewhere.'

'It's not that kind of trip,' Rajni insisted.

Jezmeen plucked the sunglasses off her head and adjusted them on the bridge of her nose. She turned away so only her profile was visible to Rajni – those angular cheekbones, that small mole just at the top corner of her lip. The last time Rajni had stared so intently at her sister was at Mum's funeral, when the bruise on Jezmeen's cheek was just healing. There were no traces of it now.

'We'll have lots of quality time together, the three of us,' Rajni added. Hearing the false cheer in her voice, she was grateful that she couldn't fully catch Jezmeen's reaction. They all needed to sit together and talk about what happened in Mum's final hours – a calm and healing discussion now that they had some distance from all of it. Kabir had warned Rajni that it was naïve to think reconciliation would be so easy, but she reckoned it was all in the atmosphere. The banks of the gently rippling waters surrounding the Golden Temple in Amritsar were much more conducive to open-heart conversation than a Pret A Manger in London – and how often were the three sisters in the same place now that Shirina had moved to Australia? Rajni was determined that they could make peace and move on.

'You know, pilgrimages aren't even a requirement of the Sikh religion,' Jezmeen said.

'I'm aware of that,' Rajni replied calmly. Jezmeen was not going to get under her skin. Of all people, Rajni knew the futility of rituals. She had been a teenager when Dad died and Mum began performing little ceremonies to improve their family's fate. Rajni thought that luck and fate were one and the same – Dad's death had been unlucky, but Mum saw connections to a greater plan that needed adjusting.

A waiter appeared at their table. He was young, with glossy gelled hair spiked upwards and a nametag that read 'Tarun'. He probably didn't think Rajni noticed his eyes lingering on the line of cleavage that ran into Jezmeen's tight tank top.

'I'll have an avocado lime and cilantro smoothie, please,' she said. Jezmeen made eye contact with Tarun and smiled.

'Madam, I'm so very sorry but this drink is unavailable,' he said.

'Okay then,' Rajni said, opening the menu. 'I'll have the . . . oh, this looks nice. The peach and strawberry daiquiri.'

Tarun looked embarrassed. 'Madam, we don't have any strawberries at the moment.'

'That's alright,' Jezmeen cooed. Honestly, did she have to be such a flirt?

Rajni scanned the menu. 'Here. This one.' She pointed at the description that Jezmeen had been making fun of earlier. Below it, there was a picture of the iced vanilla mango smoothie with whipped cream and seasonal fruits. 'I'll have one. Jezmeen, you want one?'

'No thanks,' Jezmeen said. 'I'll just have a cup of chai.'

He smiled brightly at Jezmeen. 'We have chai. So Madam, I repeat your order: one chai, one vanilla mango smoothie.' He strutted off before Rajni could ask about the selection of seasonal fruit.

Rajni made another attempt with the itinerary. 'It's an early start tomorrow if we're going to do the morning seva at Bangla Sahib,' Rajni said.

Jezmeen did not respond. She was staring intently at her phone all of a sudden, her features scrunched in concentration. Moments later, she relaxed, but she continued to steal glimpses of the screen. 'Are you connected?' Rajni asked. 'They still haven't confirmed my account yet.' The staff at the mobile phone kiosk in the airport had assured Rajni it would take less than ten minutes to verify her details, but here they were, nearly two hours later, and she still didn't have any data.

'I'm using the hotel's WiFi,' Jezmeen said. 'So what are we doing tomorrow?'

'We'll cook and serve langar.' It was the foremost thing on Mum's itinerary, not that she could expect Jezmeen to have read it.

'So Mum sent us to India to wash dishes,' Jezmeen said. She looked up from her phone. 'She must have taken some joy putting that task in the itinerary – make my daughters do housework like good girls.'

'Men volunteer in the kitchen too,' Rajni reminded her.

'But when they go home, they get to put their feet up, don't they?'

Rajni thought of Kabir and Anil sitting in their twin recliners watching football while she flitted around them, sometimes still wearing her blazer and work shoes. 'Mmm,' she said, which was her standard reply when she agreed but didn't want to.

Her phone buzzed on the table. It was a message:

'MRS RAJNI SHERGILL CHADHA. WELCOME TO INDIA. YOU HAVE SIGNED UP FOR 2 MB OF DATA AND FREE CALLS WITHIN INDIA. PLEASE CALL THIS NUMBER TO CONFIRM YOUR IDENTITY.'

'Finally,' she said.

After keying in her birth date and the special pin code, Rajni was connected to an operator who asked her for one last confirmation of her identity. 'Your father's name, Ma'am.' Until she agreed to make this trip to India, Rajni hadn't mentioned Dad's name in years, but everybody here needed to know. The visa forms asked for his name; the customs officer required her to confirm it before letting her past the gates, and now she couldn't register for a temporary mobile phone account without saying whose daughter she was. It didn't matter that he'd been dead since she was a teenager. 'Devinder Singh Shergill,' she said. The operator processed this information and after a series of clicks and rapid typing, pronounced her connected.

'When you and Shirina get your phones sorted, there's an app that you should download,' Rajni said. 'FindMe. It uses the GPS to keep track of each other's movements. I've used it on school trips.' Supposedly it used up lots of data but it had saved Rajni from losing other people's children, so the disadvantages were greatly outweighed by the benefits.

Jezmeen stared at her nails and picked at a cuticle with her teeth. 'Why do we need that?' she asked. 'We're going to be together all the time anyway.' She made it sound like a prison sentence.

'It's a big country,' Rajni replied. 'A big, unpredictable country. It's easy to get lost here.'

'Isn't that the point of coming to India?' Jezmeen asked, nodding at the

European couple in the pool. They were both floating on their backs now and gently flipping their toes. 'To get lost? And then find ourselves again?'

Oh, you want to argue. This was what Mum would say if any of them were being contrary – it was a warning against proceeding any further with their case, whether it was extending a curfew or picking a quarrel for the sake of it, which was Jezmeen's speciality. Rajni had to bite her tongue to keep from saying the same thing to Anil whenever he questioned her.

Jezmeen waved to somebody in the distance. 'Hey, sleepyhead.'

Shirina entered the foyer wearing a brilliant turquoise caftan and white espadrille sandals that criss-crossed her slender ankles. It was the other women in the café who turned to stare. That was the difference between her two sisters, Rajni observed. Men looked at Jezmeen and hungered after her long legs; women took note of the details that assembled petite Shirina like a doll – the shiny shoulder-length hair, the bracelet that matched the bag.

And that ring! Rajni couldn't help staring as if it was the first time she'd noticed it. Had Shirina's diamond got bigger? Her white-gold wedding band sparkled as well, but the diamond engagement ring looked like something you saw on the news after a successful archaeological dig. *Tacky,* she'd thought immediately after seeing it the first time, even though she knew just how many carats it was worth. Shirina hadn't said anything, of course; Rajni had looked up 'huge diamond ring' on the internet and trawled through pictures until she found one that matched, and then looked up its value. If it was true that a man spent three months' salary on the engagement ring, then Sehaj was making very good money indeed – but then, they all knew that already. The heir to one of Australia's largest family-owned property businesses was not going to skimp on accessories for his fiancée.

'All caught up on your sleep?' Jezmeen asked.

'I'm getting there,' Shirina said. As she settled at the table, Rajni noticed dark circles under her eyes. 'Nice hotel, Raj,' Shirina said, looking around. 'It's pretty quiet here.'

'I'm so glad somebody appreciates my efforts,' Rajni said, giving Jezmeen a pointed look.

'That's a lovely dress,' Jezmeen said but Rajni noticed her studying Shirina as well. There was a small slump in her shoulders that the bright caftan could not disguise.

'Thanks,' Shirina said. 'I'm afraid it takes me a while to get over the jet lag, so if I sneak off for another nap, don't mind me.'

'As long as you're up at the crack of dawn tomorrow to serve at the temple,' Jezmeen said.

'That early?' Shirina asked.

'She's exaggerating,' Rajni said. 'We'll get up when we get up.'

'Okay,' said Shirina.

'No later than nine though,' Rajni added. 'So how's it all going, Shirina? You've been so quiet on Facebook.'

'I don't really do social media any more,' Shirina said with a shrug.

Being a school principal, Rajni wasn't crazy about it either but she used it to keep up with old friends and she found that Shirina had suddenly stopped posting pictures and status updates. Her last activity was a condolence message on her wall from an old classmate dated the day after Mum's funeral. 'How's work?'

'It's good,' Shirina said quickly. 'Very busy lately. I'm glad to have some time off.'

'Oh,' Rajni said. That explained the dark circles then. She waited for Shirina to say more but she was leaning towards Jezmeen and staring right at her chest.

'Is that a new tattoo, Jez?' Shirina asked.

Jezmeen grinned and nodded. She pulled down the neck of her tank top to reveal a black letter Z with vines and tiny flowers woven through it. *For heaven's sakes,* Rajni thought. 'I'd been thinking about getting it ever since I made the name change official, but I didn't know where to get it.'

'"Where" as in the tattoo parlour or "where" on your body?' Shirina asked.

'Where on my body,' Jezmeen said. 'I didn't want it to be too obvious, like on my forearm or something. Then I thought about some really secret places, like my inner thigh, but I wanted it to be a little more visible than that.'

'Ouch. Inner thigh,' Shirina said, wincing.

'I like this spot,' Jezmeen said. She kept her neckline low. Rajni couldn't help herself.

'You need to be a little careful, Jezmeen,' she said. She knew what she sounded like and she didn't care.

'Oh, the instruments were all sterile. This was the same guy who did my first two tats.'

'I mean, you need to be careful about . . .' Rajni began to gesture at Jezmeen's blouse and ended up waving at her whole outfit.

Jezmeen looked amused. 'You don't think I only packed shorts and bikini tops for this trip, do you? It's Delhi. Supposedly we're in India for religious reasons. I've got other clothes.'

'I should hope so,' Rajni said.

Shirina picked up the menu. 'Hmm, these juices look refreshing.' She waved over the waiter. He came bounding back.

'Hello again, Tarun,' Jezmeen said, flashing him a warm smile. Her tattoo was on full display and — Rajni was sure she did this just to spite her — she leaned forward slightly, exposing the deep line of her cleavage.

'I'll have the mint, green apple and carrot detox juice, please,' Shirina said.

'Madam, so sorry but unfortunately, we don't have any carrots at the moment,' Tarun said.

'Just the green apple on its own would be fine,' Shirina said.

Tarun looked very troubled. 'I must apologize, Madam, but we are out of all fruits at the moment.'

Which meant Rajni's mango smoothie with seasonal fruits would be made of what, exactly? 'What do you have then?' Rajni snapped. She handed him the menu. 'Go on. Point it out for me.'

Tarun nodded at the menu, his features squeezed as if she'd challenged him to conjure all of the missing menu items. The look of concentration on his face made Rajni momentarily ache for Anil. It had been a while since she'd seen him so vulnerable. Something happened around the time he became a teenager, when his whole existence suddenly depended upon appearing tough and streetwise. After Rajni reluctantly conceded to letting

Anil take his gap year to work, she couldn't help pointing out that his regular outfits of hoodies and baggy pants weren't going to impress any employers. 'If they can't except my authentic self, then I ain't excepting their job offer,' Anil replied. 'Accept!' Rajni had snapped, and walked off as Anil scowled and muttered, 'It's what I said, though.'

'Madam, I really don't know what to tell you—' Tarun said.

'It's really alright, Tarun,' Jezmeen said. 'It's not your fault.'

Tarun uttered another apology and scrambled away. 'Really Raj, did you have to scold him like that?' Jezmeen asked.

'I'm sorry, but when I'm given a menu, I expect items I can actually order, not a wish list.'

'He's doing his best,' Jezmeen said. 'We're in India. Adjust your expectations. You can't throw your weight around like some colonial returnee. Nobody puts up with that nonsense any more.'

'You think you can just blend in with everyone here? I'd like to see you try to walk outside wearing that outfit and all that make-up and showing off that tattoo.'

There. It was done. She couldn't even create one day of peace with Jezmeen. 'I don't need another mother on my bloody case!' Jezmeen used to shout when she was a teenager. *Mother.* Jezmeen always said this word like a foul word was supposed to come after it.

Shirina had a talent for taking herself out of these arguments. Rajni had noticed her training her eyes on the couple in the pool as they splashed each other playfully. Now, she picked up the itinerary. 'Why don't we talk about tomorrow?' she suggested.

'Yes, why don't we?' Jezmeen said. She took the itinerary from Shirina and studied it. Rajni knew it by heart, she had studied it so many times. 'I was really hoping to take a side trip, but I guess that's not on the schedule.'

Rajni sighed. 'Where exactly were you planning on going, Jezmeen?'

'There's a music festival in Goa and then I thought I'd get a city fix in Bombay after getting through all these holy places. There are tons of cheap flights to the South.'

I'll get to Vitosha Mountain in Bulgaria for skiing season and then spend a few days in Sofia. Anil and Jezmeen were alike in this funny way. They talked about places they hadn't been to with such familiarity and confidence.

Like when Anil said, *I'm going to give it all up for her.* A shudder went through Rajni. What a fool, she kept on saying to Kabir. What a stupid fool our son turned out to be. They had spent all of Anil's life trying to steer him towards a steady future, giving him every opportunity at success. *More opportunities than children with siblings,* Rajni and Kabir told each other over the years, a salve for the pain of being unable to have any more kids. Anil had all of their resources and attention. And although Rajni didn't always understand her son – why, for example, did he insist on being from the streets when he grew up in a lovely Victorian terrace in North London? – she never expected his path to diverge this far from her expectations.

'I'm afraid my plans have changed slightly as well,' Shirina said. She pointed to the final item on the itinerary – the trek to Hemkund Sahib, where they were meant to scatter Mum's ashes in Lokpal Lake. 'I was going to email you about it but I thought it would be better to tell you in person.'

'Tell us what?' Rajni asked.

Shirina took in a deep breath. 'It's really a last-minute thing. Sehaj's family – the extended family in Punjab – they haven't met me yet. I agreed ages ago to visit their village at the end of July.'

Rajni stared at Shirina. Was she really telling them now that she would be skipping out on the most important part of the pilgrimage? The mountain trek would be the most strenuous part of their journey. Rajni hadn't sent her sisters multiple links to websites about preventing Acute Mountain Sickness for Shirina to just opt out of going altogether.

'I'm very sorry,' Shirina said.

'This is a crucial part of the journey, though. I've kept Mum's ashes all this time and brought them to India so we could carry out her wishes. Can't Sehaj's family see you a few days later?' Rajni asked.

'They're a huge family, people have already made plans to travel down. If I change the dates at the last minute, it'll look bad.'

The last minute? Plans for this trip had been in the works since Mum's death in November. Rajni saw an opportunity to lecture Shirina on priorities — she had missed her chance when Shirina returned to Australia so quickly after the funeral. But Shirina lowered her eyes, as if expecting to be scolded.

Rajni glanced at Jezmeen. There wasn't much Rajni and Jezmeen agreed on, but Shirina's marriage to Sehaj had united them, if only in a cursory way. They shared little observations about how Shirina had disappeared into her role. In that first year, every time Rajni sent a message to check in with Shirina, the replies were about Sehaj and his extended family — new business ventures, celebrations of other marriages. Jezmeen also reported to Rajni that she noticed Shirina had taken down all pictures of herself on social media in any skirts above the knee, or at parties where cocktail glasses and beer bottles were visible.

It was surprising, because although Shirina had always been obliging, she had never really struck Rajni as an aspiring conservative Indian trophy wife. In university, Shirina had been ambitious enough to do summer internships at PR firms where she wanted to work one day, and after graduation, she landed a good job, earning a salary in her own right. Rajni knew that all sorts of women chose the arranged-marriage route these days, not just the traditional ones who wanted to keep house and have babies right away, yet Sehaj's wealth seemed to have bought a certain acquiescence from Shirina. *'The ring would have cost him six digits,'* Rajni had confirmed to Jezmeen in a single-line email when Shirina got engaged, to which Jezmeen had responded, *'OMG SERIOUSLY?'* Rajni was hoping to catch Jezmeen's attention for another *Can you believe this?* moment, but Jezmeen was busy staring at her phone again. She thumbed urgently at the screen, her lips moving as she read something quietly to herself. Rajni was tempted to pluck the phone from Jezmeen's hands and toss it into the pool.

'Madam, your orders.' Tarun arrived with a tray and two drinks that looked nothing like the pictures. 'Thank you very much,' Shirina said, clearing the itinerary from the table. Rajni took a sip of her smoothie. It was a mango lassi and it was sickeningly sweet, like drinking pure syrup. The rapid fire of a drill went off in the lobby, rattling her nerves.

'Anything else I can get you, Madam?' Tarun asked tentatively.

Yes. I'd like to fast forward to the end of this trip, please, Rajni wanted to say. Being a wife and mother was complicated enough. She didn't want to be a daughter and a sister as well. *I'd like this week to be over as soon as possible.* Tarun wouldn't be able to grant this request but there was nothing new about that.

Chapter Three

Day Two: Gurdwara Bangla Sahib

If the doctors had let me travel to just one place, it would be to this holy shrine to honour the memory of our eighth Guru, Guru Harkrishan. He was invited to stay here as a guest when it was the magnificent bungalow of a Rajput prince. During our Guru's time here, an epidemic of smallpox and cholera swept over Delhi. Instead of resting in the comfort and safety of the bungalow, he went out to bring food and medicine to the suffering.

You will spend the morning serving others by working in the Gurdwara Bangla Sahib kitchen. Think about what this place once was and what it continues to represent — a home and a place of healing. It's a symbol of selflessness, sacrifice and service. If only I could get there, I know I'd be better.

Jezmeen woke up the next morning to a *ping!* and she lunged for her phone, nearly knocking over the bedside lamp. She had set up a Google alert for searches of her name to keep track of what people were saying about her. So far, nobody had made the connection between the host of *DisasterTube* and the security footage from the Feng Shui restaurant in Soho showing a woman going berserk and causing more expensive property damage than she could imagine. Jezmeen still maintained she was acting in self-defence, although she knew that the video didn't show the scale of the threat to her.

The alert that came up this morning was similar to those that had popped up yesterday while she was sitting by the pool with her sisters – somebody describing a clip he had seen on *DisasterTube*, and criticizing Jezmeen's introduction of it. 'Somebody tell Jezmeen Shergill to shut up already. God, she's annoying!' Yesterday's alert had been kinder: an entertainment feature on celebrities who could be twins. There were the usual comparisons between Jezmeen and Polly Mishra, although this writer did refer to Jezmeen as a 'fun and fabulous TV host' and Polly as simply an 'actress'. Was that a subtle snub at Polly? Jezmeen hoped so.

God, she's annoying. Jezmeen knew better than to let comments from strangers online bother her, but she found herself clicking on that guy's profile and searching for comments that he'd posted on other videos. It took a few minutes, but eventually she found another criticism. 'Are we supposed to believe that this guy did it all without the help of steroids – LOL gimme a break,' he'd posted under a video of a bodybuilder showcasing an impressive lifting routine using household objects. He was a serial troll, then. At least he wasn't one of those guys who sent around a petition to get Jezmeen and Polly Mishra to have a naked boxing match. Those sorts of things cropped up every now and then. Outside the Tube station a few weeks ago, a man approached Jezmeen cautiously, saying, 'I hope you don't mind me saying, but you look a lot like Polly Mishra.' Jezmeen had flashed him a gracious smile and said, 'Yes, people say I look like her.' It was the deep-set eyes and the sharp cheekbones, she'd been told. She and Polly Mishra also both wore their shoulder-length hair loose and slightly wavy, although Jezmeen distinguished herself with caramel highlights. The man replied, 'Oh, I'm glad you're not offended. I met her once and when I told her she looked like Jezmeen Shergill, she was very annoyed.'

Screw Polly Mishra, Jezmeen thought. She swung her legs over the side of the bed and sprang up with more enthusiasm than intended. Her head swam to cope with the sudden rush of blood and the room went dark momentarily. Gripping the bedside table, Jezmeen was taken back to the days of her hypochondria phase. Every minor glitch in her system had been a potential symptom of impending death. Could she be blamed? Dad's death had been so careless and simple – he had slipped in the shower and hit his head, then carried on with his day. If he had gone to the doctor, a scan would have revealed the dangerous blood clot that resulted from the impact and killed him on the walk to his car after work several days later. Needless to say, Jezmeen was very careful when walking on slippery surfaces. But there was only so much she could do about inheriting weak, sickly genes from Mum. After Mum's cancer diagnosis, Jezmeen had made multiple mammogram appointments, which she was then forced to cancel because she was informed that she was abusing the National Health Service.

After her shower, Jezmeen got dressed and went down to the lobby. Shirina and Rajni weren't there yet, so Jezmeen stepped out for a moment into the haze of Delhi. The air was dense with noise and movement and the summer heat bore into her skin immediately. Horns blared incessantly here and the air was thick with dust. But this was also a city where a person could disappear – a thrilling possibility. In a frank evaluation of her career prospects after her contract wasn't renewed, Jezmeen had considered packing up and moving to India because she had a chance of anonymity here, or at least starting over. But what did starting over mean? She had spent years flitting from one audition to another, landing only minor parts in commercials and extra roles in *EastEnders*. Her small chance at national visibility had arrived only nine months ago and then she had blown it over one moment of foolishness; there could be another decade of proving herself all over again.

The dizzying maze of shops, traffic and tea stands that made up Karol Bagh market was just around the corner. The King's Paradise Hotel was tucked away at the end of a service alley. Next door, a row of crumbling shop houses sat obscured behind tangled telephone wires and crisscrossed bamboo scaffolding. A stray dog with jutting ribs crouched under a parked van to seek shade. One of the alley walls was adorned with fading pictures of Hindu goddesses, under a sign saying, '*Do not disrespect.*' Jezmeen wondered if images of these deities really did anything to deter men from pissing on the walls, as they were intended. Judging from the acrid whiff of urine in the air, probably not.

A valet with gel-slicked hair approached her and asked if she needed a taxi. 'In a moment,' Jezmeen said, looking over her shoulder. Rajni was coming out of the lift, wearing beige linen pants and a flowy silk blouse which matched the scarf wrapped loosely around her neck for covering her head later.

'Where is Shirina?' Jezmeen asked. She self-consciously smoothed out the wrinkles in her own cotton kameez top. How did Rajni have the patience to press and iron everything, even on holiday?

'She was still asleep when I called her room,' Rajni said.

'Must be the jet lag again,' Jezmeen said.

The punishing heat burned through Jezmeen's clothes. They returned to the lobby and sank into the plush sofas. The air bore the potent smell of disinfectant. At the reception desk, a woman wearing a red blazer held the phone to her ear. 'This is your wake-up call, sir,' she said and then she nodded and replaced the receiver.

'Did you sleep well?' Rajni asked.

'A few hours,' Jezmeen said. 'You?'

'I never sleep well in hotels.'

The television screen mounted on the wall flashed brightly. It was the morning news but the presenter only took up a small square on the screen. Banner ads rolled across the length of the screen and neon columns showed the latest stock market figures. It was like watching a casino machine.

'I was watching one of those sing-along shows on TV last night,' Jezmeen said. 'Mum loved those.'

'Mum and Dad used to watch them together,' Rajni said. 'Dad would hum along and Mum would shush him for ruining the song.'

Jezmeen smiled. 'I think I remember that.' It was hard to know which early memories were hers and which were constructed by Rajni's recollections but she thought she could hear Dad's off-key humming. She was only five years old when he died, and sometimes she envied Rajni for having known Dad for so many more years. Jezmeen longed to say things like, 'I got my laugh from my father,' or 'My father used to say that.' A sense of legacy would help her feel less lost, especially now that Mum was gone too.

'I do the same thing now when those shows come on,' Rajni said.

'You hum along?'

'I shush Kabir.'

No surprise there. 'And does Anil watch as well?'

'He did when he was little. Now he pops in his earphones and just watches whatever he wants on the iPad.'

That sounded like Anil – hypnotized by a world beyond his parents' living room. Since he hit adolescence, Jezmeen had only seen about three emotions register on her nephew's face: sullen, bored and enthralled (but only by whatever was on his phone). His intrigue factor had spiked only briefly over the weekend when she spotted him skulking around the perfume counter at the mall. Excited that he might have a girlfriend (and at the prospect of torturing Rajni with the info), Jezmeen had waited for him to leave before sidling up to the counter girl to get the scoop. 'He wanted something mature,' she sighed, throwing a sorrowful look at the Sugar N Spice line for teen girls. Jezmeen was disappointed too. All of that anticipation and Anil turned out to be buying a gift for his mother, whose birthday was next month.

'Should we call Shirina again or something?' Jezmeen asked. 'She might have gone back to sleep.'

'Give her ten minutes,' Rajni said. She glanced towards the hotel lifts. 'Do you think it's weird that she didn't tell us about visiting Sehaj's family till yesterday?'

Jezmeen shrugged. 'Maybe she got the dates confused. It sounds like she's been really busy.'

Rajni frowned. She didn't look satisfied with this response, and truthfully, neither was Jezmeen, but it seemed that Shirina had become another casualty to marriage, like so many other women Jezmeen knew.

Appointments were never set in stone and they often brought their partners along to dinner at the last minute.

'Is it just me, or does she look . . . different?' Rajni asked.

'She's gained weight, hasn't she?' Jezmeen said. She wanted to sound concerned but she could hear the glee in her voice. *Shame on you,* a voice scolded Jezmeen.

'I was thinking more about those dark circles under her eyes. She looks worn out.' There was pleasure in Rajni's tone as well. Jezmeen decided it couldn't be helped. All their lives, Shirina never had a blemish – on her face or her character. If they had to be petty to find one – or two! – so be it.

'I feel bad,' Jezmeen said anyway. 'Maybe something's going on.' That would certainly be interesting. After a lifetime of meeting parental expectations, Shirina was long overdue for a crisis. Develop a pill addiction. Join a cult. Something. It would certainly take the pressure off Jezmeen to be the default family screw-up.

'I gained a bit of weight in the year after I got married as well,' Rajni said. 'If anything, it's good to see some meat on her bones again. She was so skinny for her wedding. Near the end, she was on a steady diet of leaves and broth.'

Rajni had a point. Shirina had been a little obsessed with her figure. 'I remember going over to Mum's to help decorate the house for the wedding a couple of days before Sehaj's relatives arrived. She'd bought all those fairy lights, which took ages to put up and we lost track of time and ordered pizza. Shirina ate one slice and then went to the gym for two hours,' Jezmeen recalled. She had admired and secretly envied Shirina's discipline. At an audition the next day, Jezmeen had to suck in her tummy to prevent the casting director from seeing the paunch created by her six slices. She didn't get the role.

'She'd tell us if she was pregnant, wouldn't she?' Rajni asked.

'Shirina's quite private about her life these days,' Jezmeen reminded Rajni. Shirina hadn't told them anything about searching for an arranged marriage online. She never even mentioned her courtship with Sehaj – all six months of it – until he came to London to meet her in person and proposed on their second date. Everything happened quickly from that point and nobody objected because Sehaj was such a catch – good-looking, wealthy, and from a respected family. Then she said yes, and moved all the way to Australia. If that wasn't an effort to keep her distance from her family, Jezmeen didn't know what was.

'That's not something she'd keep from us though,' Rajni said.

'Probably not, but I don't think we're necessarily the first to know about things with Shirina.' *Were we ever?* Jezmeen wondered. For as long as she could remember, Shirina had preferred to keep her thoughts and emotions closely guarded. Next to her, Jezmeen always felt like she was exaggerating whenever she expressed her (admittedly wide and varied range of) emotions.

'I wish it weren't like that,' Rajni replied.

Jezmeen shrugged. 'It's her choice,' she said, although she had been hurt when Shirina announced her engagement. Why didn't she even tell Jezmeen she was seeing someone?

'It's a shame if we can't communicate. I'd like to think we can talk about things with each other.'

Jezmeen noticed that Rajni had turned to face her and was giving her a Meaningful Look. *Oh, don't you dare,* she thought. They were not going to talk about Mum in the same space as speculating over Shirina's weight gain. In fact, Jezmeen was determined to not discuss Mum's final moments with anyone, least of all Rajni.

'The weight gain is probably just a post-wedding thing,' Jezmeen said. She made a deliberate shift towards the television screen and stared intently at it. The flashing graphics gave her an instant headache but at least Rajni couldn't try to engage her in any more conversation. The newscaster wore a grim expression, which belied the brilliant hues of her sari and the ticker speeding across the screen announcing the engagement of two Bollywood stars.

When Shirina finally joined them in the lobby at 8.30 a.m., Jezmeen noticed the dark circles under her eyes were gone. Her lips shone with pink gloss and a touch of rouge, which brightened up her face. She was the only one of them wearing a traditional salwar-kameez, with her long hair also pulled back in a bun. The weight gain was still there though, a roundness in her cheeks that actually made her look – Jezmeen felt a twinge of jealousy – a little bit prettier.

It was a short distance from the hotel to the Gurdwara Bangla Sahib but the roads were already clogged with traffic by the time they left the hotel. The taxi could only inch along the wide boulevard under the Karol Bagh Metro bridge. The driver's window was rolled down, letting in the sound of every puttering engine and trilling horn. People dodged around vehicles, taking their chances every time there was a pause in traffic. Heat shimmered atop the silver surfaces of street vendors' carts as the taxi crawled along. Shirina's mouth watered when she caught a whiff of pakoras being deep-fried in bubbling oil.

On the taxi's dashboard, a multicoloured row of miniature plastic deities created a shrine to Hinduism. It looked like the dashboard of that taxi Shirina had taken home from after-work drinks in Melbourne one night, except it was populated with icons and symbols from all religions, plus one Pokémon bobblehead. Too much wine on an empty stomach had made Shirina chatty that night.

'Do these guys join forces to protect you?' she'd asked the driver.

'Yes,' he said with a laugh. 'More religions, more power.'

'What's your actual religion then?'

'I'm Muslim,' he said. 'From Somalia. You?'

'Sikh,' Shirina replied. 'From Britain by way of India.' She spotted a small card bearing Guru Nanak's picture between a miniature Buddha and a little Arabic scroll on the dashboard and pointed him out. 'He's one of mine,' she said. 'My mum always said just think of God as your father but that's wrong, I think.' The words just kept tumbling out of her mouth. 'My father died when I was just two.'

The outburst was met with silence. 'Sorry,' she mumbled.

The driver waited until he reached a traffic light before turning around, his warm, kind eyes meeting Shirina's. 'It's okay,' he said. 'In my car, you have countless blessings.'

Now Shirina focused her attention on the sprawl of Delhi. Shops were stacked like uneven bricks with shouting block-lettered signs: ENGLISH LANGUAGE INSTITUTE; ALIYAH'S BEAUTY SCHOOL; ICCS TECH SOLUTIONS. Simpler services took place under the Karol Bagh Metro tracks – a barber arranged his tools on a low wooden stool and beckoned his first customer from a small crowd of men; a pair of toddlers, naked from the waist down, their limbs coated in soot, helped their mother sort through a pile of plastic bottles.

The road ahead narrowed and widened inexplicably, its borders determined by the debris that spilled out onto the edges – benches from chai stalls, a rusty abandoned wheelbarrow overflowing with rubbish. Rising behind them was a skyline of anaemic pink and beige buildings. The potholed surfaces of the road made Shirina jostle with her sisters in the back seat. A few times, she caught the driver looking at their reflections in the rear-view mirror and she realized his eyes were tracking the movements of their jiggling breasts.

'Not obvious at all, mate,' Jezmeen muttered but she shifted to occupy more space in the mirror.

'You know what you're supposed to say to put them in their place, right?' Rajni said to Shirina. '"Don't you have a sister? Don't you have a mother?"' Hearing these English words, the driver focused back on the road. 'See? It works.'

'So it's our job to summon a woman the men own in some way?' Jezmeen retorted.

This thought occurred to Shirina too but she suppressed it, knowing that this type of argument belonged in a different place. It was the sort of thing her friend Lauren from work would say. The driver's eyes locked with Shirina's. She adjusted her dupatta so it concealed her chest. An easy solution. Nothing needed to be said.

Worshippers and tourists were already milling about outside the gurdwara when they pulled up. 'Water, water, cold cold water,' called a man pushing a cart full of plastic bottles. Taut muscles bulged through the sheen of sweat on his skinny calves. A marbled walkway led the sisters away from the tangle of cars and people on the street. The temple was tiered and white like a wedding cake, finished with golden caramel on the domes. Nearby, the water of the sarovar rippled gently, catching flecks of sunlight.

First they had to deposit their shoes at a counter, which they swapped for metal tags. Then they returned to the gurdwara's entrance and stepped in a shallow trough to clean their feet. They climbed the carpeted stairs and shuffled along with the crowd into the prayer hall. Ceiling fans and chandeliers dangled from the hall's roof and the floor was covered in soft red carpet. At the centre was an elaborate golden trellis, its patterns delicate like embroidery. Three men sat cross-legged there, thumping on tablas and singing holy hymns. The *Guru Granth Sahib* lay open on a gilded platform, its pages framed by a thick garland of marigolds. Shirina found a small space to bow, touch her head to the floor and then slip her small tithing into the bank.

Pushing herself to her feet again, Shirina felt the discomfort of her padded body. This weight gain gave her an imbalance she was unused to. She stumbled slightly, and recovered. She sneaked a look at Jezmeen and Rajni to see if they had noticed, but they were pressing their own foreheads to the floor and making their donations. Hopefully she was concealing it well enough but if anybody asked, she'd say, 'Just a bit of winter weight. I need to cut back.' She'd laugh and look embarrassed so they'd know she was trying and hopefully, they would know to drop the subject. The other day, she had made the mistake of opening her wedding album again and afterwards, she was unable to look at herself in the mirror, saddened by her fuller cheeks and her collarbone fading behind a new layer of skin.

Shirina had wanted to dive into those photographs and make her wedding day come to life again. As soon as she and Rajni and Jezmeen found a place to sit, she closed her eyes and little snapshots of the ceremony rushed into her consciousness. Her hennaed feet poking out from under a full lengha skirt that floated as she stepped closer to the altar; the walk around the Holy Book with Sehaj as their guests looked on approvingly. Peering out from under her heavily jewelled dupatta, she had been so pleased to see the abundance of her husband's guests – cousins, uncles, nephews, aunties, two sets of grandparents. They had flown a long way to see the firstborn son of the family get married, and when she presented herself in those glorious bridal adornments, she felt as if she had earned her place. She couldn't help comparing them to her own threadbare family – a smattering of distant relatives, her widowed mother, two sisters, always bickering, never just *listening* to one another. 'Do your family members get along?' she'd asked Sehaj after they met on the Sikh matrimonial website and arranged a phone call. 'We rarely argue,' he'd replied. 'What's that like?' she'd asked. He thought she was joking. He told her that he had always had a good relationship with his mother. 'After my father died when I was sixteen, my mother and I became even closer,' he said.

That was when Shirina decided she wanted to keep getting to know Sehaj. She reminded herself not to get her hopes up; there were countless stories on the arranged marriage message boards about men being nothing like the pictures and personas they presented online. During the next conversation, she asked if they could do a video call, and she was both relieved and thrilled to see that Sehaj's handsome profile photo had not been altered or taken ten years ago during a fitter phase – there was not so much as a receding hairline to distinguish the live person on her screen from the one in the picture on her Successful Matches list on the matrimonial site. Not wanting to seem desperate though, Shirina waited for Sehaj to initiate the first in-person meeting. After a few months of chatting on the phone, he finally said he wanted to come to London to see her. Again, Shirina was relieved to see that Sehaj was real, and just as much a gentleman as he was on the phone. He opened doors for her, kissed her lightly on the cheek at the end of their first date, and told her he was looking forward to seeing her again.

At one point, Shirina was bold enough to ask how Sehaj was still single. He was certainly the most eligible bachelor on the matrimonial site, and his membership had been active for a year before Shirina came along. 'There were other girls,' Sehaj shrugged. 'But they balked at the idea of living with my mother. I can't compromise on that though. She's family, and that's what I'm here for – if I don't look after her, who will?' Shirina thought it was sweet. She only met her mother-in-law for the first time at the wedding ceremony. Mother had pressed her palms to Shirina's cheeks so lovingly, and said, 'You are our daughter now.'

Shirina opened her eyes. The hall was filled with people she didn't know and her disappointment at being thrown back into the present was profound. She looked at her hands and noticed the flesh of her ring finger bulging around her gold wedding band. It was heat that made her fingers swell but she wiggled the ring, struggling at the knot of her knuckle. It was a relief that it came loose eventually, but she quickly pushed it back on. The men at the altar thumped the heels of their hands rapidly against the tight skins of their tablas. Each beat had an echo that bounced across the walls.

The memory that had surfaced in the cab was niggling at Shirina, filling the spaces between musical notes. She wished she knew how to pray but it was too late to learn now – it was like getting in touch with a neglected friend just to request a favour. And what could she pray for? That night had been her fault – for drinking so much, for stumbling up the driveway, for making the driver so concerned that he threw on his brakes and followed her. 'You're okay, one step at a time,' he said, just a pace behind her, his hands hovering at her waist, braced for a fall but not actually touching her. She had struggled to find her keys so he reached into her bag to help her. She remembered leaning towards him, just to rest her head on his chest for a moment because she could fall asleep right there. The bag was squished between them. 'Hey,' the driver said with a nervous laugh. 'Wake up.' Then the door opened anyway.

'Shirina,' Jezmeen whispered. 'Are those guys looking at us?' Shirina followed her gaze and saw a group of young men sitting cross-legged and staring at them, their lips twitching into smiles. 'They are, aren't they?'

'They're looking at you,' Shirina said, which was true but it was also what Jezmeen wanted to hear. Shirina adjusted her dupatta again, this time so it obscured her profile.

'Do you think people here would mistake me for Polly Mishra?' Jezmeen wondered aloud. 'Or does that happen more in the UK because there are so few Indian women on television?'

'You do look alike,' Shirina said.

'That's the problem,' Jezmeen said with a sigh. 'There can only be one actress with our looks. She's had better luck than me, getting such a great break with *The Boathouse.*'

Sure, luck had some small role to play in Polly's success but Shirina had watched several episodes of *The Boathouse* and thought Polly was brilliant in it. She knew better than to say this to Jezmeen, who was sensitive about the whole rivalry. She had once read a celebrity blog site referring to Jezmeen as 'the poor man's Polly Mishra'.

Jezmeen was considering something now. 'Do you think, if I went up to those guys now and pretended to be Polly, they'd know the difference?'

'Jezmeen, this isn't the place to be impersonating actresses,' Rajni said.

'What *is* a place to be impersonating actresses, Rajni? I'm curious.'

'People come here to worship,' Rajni reminded her.

'Does it matter?' Jezmeen asked.

'Of course it matters.'

'We're not exactly sitting here praying. I've spent the past ten minutes mentally revising my Christmas party invitation list.'

'It's July,' Rajni said accusingly.

The guy in the middle said something to his friend and grinned. He took out his phone and pointed it at Jezmeen. The flash went off. 'Now that's just rude,' Jezmeen said. She sprang to her feet and marched across the prayer hall. 'Oh my god,' Shirina said. She glanced at the bearded granthi serenely reading from the Holy Book, his cadence as hypnotic as a gentle tide. Now would be a good time to take up prayer.

Rajni went after Jezmeen, muttering something about inappropriate behaviour in the temple. One of the tabla players looked up and met eyes with Shirina. She gave him an apologetic smile. He shut his eyes, tipped his face towards the ceiling, and let out a string of melodic drumbeats. She got up and followed her sisters.

'Hello there,' Jezmeen said when they approached the men. She smiled sweetly. 'I noticed you took a picture of me and I thought you might like a close-up.'

The men exchanged looks and two of them were suddenly sheepish. Shirina noticed that they were younger than she'd thought – just boys. One had the patchy beginnings of a beard on his bony chin and the other was wearing a *Star Wars* T-shirt.

'So?' Jezmeen pressed. She placed one hand on her hip. 'Let's not be shy now.'

People were beginning to stare. Shirina tugged her sister's sleeve. 'Jezmeen, this is embarrassing.'

'Jezmeen Shergill,' one boy said. He was the one wearing the *Star Wars* shirt. 'So it is you.'

His British accent took Shirina by surprise. Jezmeen said nothing. The boy kept watching her, a slow grin spreading on his face. His friends were hiding their smiles behind their hands. The tabla thumped like a heartbeat.

'Yes, that's me,' Jezmeen said. 'Just because I'm on television, it doesn't give you the right—'

'I'm a huge fan,' the boy continued.

Shirina caught the boy with the patchy facial hair discreetly pulling his phone from his pocket. When he noticed her looking, he dropped his hands.

'Really?' Jezmeen asked.

The smirk on *Star Wars* boy's face made Shirina nervous.

'Can we get a photo with you?' he asked.

Rajni poked her head between them. 'She's not Polly Mishra.'

'They know, Rajni,' Jezmeen said. 'He said my name. Are you boys fans of the show? Here, let's take a quick selfie together, and—'

The boys began to snicker and nudge each other again. 'Do it,' *Star Wars* boy whispered to the boy with patchy facial hair.

The boy let out a theatrical sigh. 'Oh, Jezmeen Shergill,' he said, 'I was *dying* to meet you.' And then he stuck out his tongue, crossed his eyes and flapped his hands. The other boys collapsed into laughter.

What the hell was he doing? Shirina stared at the boys, forgetting for a moment where they were and how much disruption they were creating. The boys scrambled to their feet and out of the hall. Jezmeen's face was ashen.

'You alright?' Shirina asked, still puzzled. She reached out but Jezmeen's shoulder flinched at her touch. Jezmeen turned away, pulling her phone from her bag and tapping away rapidly.

'I wonder where their parents are,' Rajni remarked, looking over her shoulder at the boys. 'I'd like to have a word with them.'

'Just drop it,' Jezmeen said, not looking up from her phone.

'They're obviously here on holidays with family – you'd think their parents brought them here to get some spiritual enlightenment, not sit around—'

'I said, "drop it",' Jezmeen said. Her eyes were blazing. 'Oh my god,' she whispered. 'A hundred thousand.'

It meant nothing to Shirina. She looked at Rajni, who looked just as perplexed.

They stood for a while in tense silence. A pair of women walked past, looking at them curiously. Shirina was conscious of the scene they were probably presenting to passers-by – three sisters at an impasse in a terrible family argument.

'Why don't we just start our work at the langar hall?' Shirina suggested brightly, eager to dismantle this tableau.

'I'll join you both in a few minutes,' Jezmeen said. Shirina and Rajni watched as she turned around and pushed her way out through the stream of people entering the prayer hall.

'Should one of us follow her?' Shirina asked.

Rajni shook her head and sighed. 'It's Jezmeen,' she said. A sufficient explanation for Shirina. Jezmeen existed in her own sphere, and trying to understand her crises was like walking late into a house party where all the other guests had already become friends. Over the past few years,

Shirina's sense of solitude had grown more profound as Jezmeen chased auditions and pined to be noticed. Sometimes she forgot that they used to talk to each other more, because every conversation that Shirina could recall having with Jezmeen in adulthood was about Jezmeen: what she was doing, where she was going, what she wanted. Jezmeen never really thought about the consequences of her actions for other people. They were a long way now from when they'd been little girls, staying up so late into the night playing and chatting that Mum more or less gave up on setting a proper bedtime. When was the last time Shirina went breathless from giggling with Jezmeen? *You two, knock it off and go to bed now,* Rajni would call from downstairs, so much sterner and scarier than Mum. They would pretend to oblige, reducing their voices to whispers, which inevitably became louder until Rajni marched up the stairs to tell them off again.

This wasn't a good start to their journey. Mum believed that whatever happened in the morning set the tone for the rest of the day – all of her rituals were completed by the time the sun rose. If Mum were here, she wouldn't be happy. The morning wasn't even over and they were already down to two.

The langar hall throbbed with the same noise and energy of a Delhi street, but the scene was surprisingly organized. People sat on the floor in rows and ate with their hands from metal trays. Servers roamed up and down the lines, refilling plates with rotis and ladlefuls of dal. 'Of course you already know that in the Sikh religion, we believe in serving food to anybody who comes to the temple, regardless of their creed, gender or income,' Mum had written in her letter, after explaining the significance of this temple. 'They don't have to worship here. They don't have to offer any services, or money. This is a very good system, and one that helped our family after your father died.'

Shirina was aware of the temple's welfare from the meals that Mum used to bring home from the morning service, usually at times when the cupboards were bare. 'We're still okay,' Mum would say, looking at a full plate before her. Her tone was never convincing enough. Shirina would look at the plate and see the thinness of the roti, the watery dal, and sense that there was only so much charity they could ask for.

Shirina and Rajni entered a wide back kitchen, which bustled with activity. Along one wall, enormous steel pots were being stirred slowly by young turbaned men with ladles the size and shape of oars. In the corner, a cluster of older women kneaded balls of dough. The serving line was being set up and there were young children pushing for a chance to put out the plates.

Rajni wandered off to the vegetable counter and, with a few quick nods and smiles with the other women there, she was handed a knife, a chopping board and a tubful of carrots. Shirina considered her options more carefully. There was a counter dedicated to roti-making but those women were experts – just look at how they were flattening the dough into such perfect circles with the flick of their wrists. They were deep in conversation as well; Shirina would be intruding. She almost turned a full circle considering her options before she felt somebody gripping her by the shoulders. She turned around to see a small elderly woman standing before her.

'Looking for something to do? Can you take my place kneading dough for a while? Young thing like you would do a faster job than these.' The woman held up her hands and showed Shirina her curled arthritic fingers. Shirina felt a pang of sadness, remembering the way Mum clutched the edges of her letter, her voice shaking slightly as she read it to them. Grief came to her like a series of aftershocks – every time she thought she had moved on, something new reminded her of Mum.

Shirina thought some introductions might be needed but as soon as they saw her approaching, the women shifted and a space opened up for her. She drove the heel of her palm into the dough and then ran her knuckles over it and repeated this motion until the dough was soft and smooth. Then she started a fresh batch, combining the water and flour in a steel bowl. The fingers on one hand became sticky, so she switched to the other. Around her, pots crashed and voices shot into the air. The other women's chatter blended with the commotion. It was enough distraction, she thought at first, but as her motions quickly settled into a routine, the spaces between the noises began to open wide.

It had been quiet like this in the moment Shirina's mother-in-law opened the door to find her resting her head against the taxi driver's chest. Mother had stood stiffly in the doorway, arms crossed over her chest as the driver apologetically explained that he was just making sure she got home safely. 'Thank you,' she said to the driver, before pulling Shirina into the house and shutting the door. 'Get upstairs,' she ordered.

The morning after, her skull still throbbing from the wine, she had joined Sehaj and his mother at the breakfast table. Sehaj gave her a terse smile and Mother didn't even look at her. Shirina sat still, unsure of what to do. In her family, disagreements were shouted out until voices went hoarse. Here, nobody said anything. So this was what Sehaj meant when he said that his family rarely fought. Shirina opened her mouth to say how sorry she was but nothing came out. She realized how scared she was of doing the wrong thing again. When Mother did finally speak, it was to announce that she was going back to bed. The silent treatment lasted all weekend until Mother announced she had a doctor's appointment the following Friday afternoon. 'You will drive me there,' she said, and Shirina was so grateful that Mother was speaking to her again, that she cancelled a meeting and took half a day off work. She wanted to make sure she was on time to pick Mother up and bring her home as well.

In the folded printout from a website about Sikhism that Rajni had read last night, there was a quote about the simplicity of service leading to meditative thoughts. She was supposed to feel a sense of oneness with others and herself, so that her mind was free to focus on the present.

The work was certainly simple. Rajni chopped carrots into a pile until it threatened to topple over the edges of the board. Then she swept it into a big bowl and carried it to the station where a vegetarian curry was bubbling in a pot the size of a small bathtub.

She'd repeated this process a dozen times but the pinch in her shoulder interrupted any meditative thoughts. Then there was the pulsing pain just behind her eyes, now a constant presence. She had been unable to sleep last night from a combination of jet leg and flashes of acute anxiety about becoming a grandmother at forty-three. She cast a look at the gathering of older women kneading dough next to Shirina. *They* were grandmothers – dupattas tucked behind ears, backs stooped towards their work. She straightened her own posture and checked the time. Kabir would be fast asleep on his stomach with one leg thrown over the empty side of the bed.

The steam from the row of pots made beads of sweat prickle on Rajni's forehead. How many hours of service did one need to contribute in order to feel closer to God? It had only been about an hour and she already needed a break. She nodded to the women she was working with and as she moved towards the door she glanced over her shoulder at Shirina, quietly kneading dough, and Jezmeen, who had eventually returned and was elbow-deep in soap suds at the industrial sink.

Stepping out of the kitchen, Rajni expected to feel an instant release, but the langar hall was packed now. She pushed through the crowds, carefully tiptoeing past cups of tea that lined a narrow serving aisle. The fresh air and the sight of an unbroken blue sky above, when she finally descended the stairs, was gratifying. The grounds outside were a welcoming open space, with patterned tiled floors and long stretches of maroon carpet creating paths for worshippers between the low-domed buildings. Rajni walked up to the sarovar, a large pool at the temple's entrance. The water rippled from the movements of bathing worshippers, breaking Rajni's reflection. She pulled her short hair back and even through the movement of the water, she could see how much she looked like Mum these days – the sharp chin and dark eyebrows. Even when she smiled, she appeared stern and disapproving, or so her students said.

At the edge of the pool, a woman lowered her feet into the water, a small wave sweeping up to darken the border of her salwar. An elderly man wearing only a dhoti around his waist stood in the centre of the pool, bending his knees to reach down and scoop the water in his hands and pour it over his head. As it cascaded down his neck and shoulders, he tipped his head up to the sky and smiled beatifically. Plump orange fish cut their paths through the water, their tails flickering like faulty bulbs. With unexpected grace, the man folded at his hips to gather more water. Then he brought his cupped hands to his lips and drank.

Rajni flinched. She didn't mean to, it was an involuntary response to the man ingesting water that others were bathing in. Pissing in as well – surely the peaceful grin spreading on that child's face was not from a spiritual release?

The bathing was unnecessary, although Mum had told and re-told Rajni the story of her name and its roots in holy waters many times. Bibi Rajni, a woman married off to a leper, had remained devoted to her husband, carting him around in a wheelbarrow. One afternoon, he went to take a bath in the sarovar outside the Golden Temple in Amritsar and miraculously, his leprosy was cured. 'Remember your namesake,' was Mum's favourite character-building advice. The result was a childhood spent making tenuous allegorical connections (maybe being Asian was like having a terrible disease and she had to wash in the local pool so the girls on the bus didn't declare her street Paki Zone?).

Rajni and her sisters were expected to bathe in holy water once they got to the Golden Temple. It was one of those pilgrimage duties that Mum had stipulated, preceding a quote about bathing in God's immortal nectar that did not further clarify the difference between nectar and water, nor the figurative nature of this instruction. The power of metaphor was largely lost on Mum anyway. She had wanted physical proof of the presence of God when her symptoms first appeared, as if she could already sense the dire diagnosis. Wanting to help, Rajni had printed glossy pictures of all ten Gurus and pasted them around the house, which became a shrine of its own. Kirtan songs floated through the hallways, choral and sorrowful. Incense and birdseed and fruit platter offerings became commonplace. It was all too reminiscent of the days after Dad died, when superstitions and rituals became Mum's insurance policy against further misfortune.

In the hospital as well, everything was done in the spirit of making Mum more comfortable when they knew that a painful end was upon her. *Do whatever she wants* had been Rajni's mantra since returning from her last trip to India, and now it was even more pertinent because denying Mum any hope was akin to torture. Rajni even began feeling guilty for resisting Mum years back, when she tried to prescribe religious rituals and herbal remedies for her fertility problems. 'I'm telling you, it worked for me. After eleven years of thinking I couldn't have any more children, out came Jezmeen and then Shirina three years after her,' Mum insisted. Unable to deter Mum, Rajni finally resorted to the humiliating revelation that she and Kabir had stopped trying – stopped having sex altogether, in fact. The last thing Mum said on the matter was: 'Well, at least you've got a son. At least you don't have to worry like I did, with three daughters.'

At least that.

Rajni looked down at the water and took a small step towards it. Her feet were still bare and as they made contact with the small puddles that other pilgrims had left on their way out, she felt some relief. The water was cool and it protected her soles from the sunbaked tiles. She took another step, and then another. Now her toes were touching the murky water. The ghostly bodies of fish curved and shot off. The man who had drunk the water was now taking slow strides across the length of the pool, his knees lifting high like a soldier. Rajni remained on the edges for a long time, the heat prompting her to inch closer and closer until her entire feet were submerged. She closed her eyes. Spots of light darted across the darkness and then eventually, they faded. The din of traffic – those angry, insistent horns – could be heard in the distance. A child's high-pitched squeal rang out, shattering Rajni's inner calm before she even began to summon it. She sighed and opened her eyes.

She didn't want to be here. Especially not now, with everything happening at home, but also not ever. India did not suit her and not least because of the memories it evoked – physically, her body rebelled against the country: an itch from the soot-filled air was beginning in her throat, the bumpy car rides made her stomach turn and a bout of indigestion was inevitable, no matter how staunchly she abstained from potentially contaminated food. Jezmeen and Shirina didn't understand Rajni's aversion to India because by the time they came of age, a wave of multicultural pride was sweeping over England and all of a sudden, it was trendy to have an ethnic background. While Rajni had waited by the radio with her finger poised over the deck to record her favourite *Top of the Pops* song, Jezmeen's speakers played Hindi song remixes. At fifteen, Rajni had spent Saturday afternoons dancing frantically at those nightclubs which opened in the daytime for Asian kids whose parents wouldn't let them out at night, while Shirina's twenty-fifth year saw her gladly uploading her picture onto a Sikh matrimonial website. Rajni had done her best to pave the way for her little sisters to be more English, and instead they went ahead and embraced their culture, proving Mum's point that Rajni had no business having an identity crisis in the first place.

There were other reasons behind Rajni's complicated history with this country, reasons she could not explain to Jezmeen and Shirina. When they were planning this trip, Jezmeen had wondered aloud at why they never visited India when they were growing up. 'Mum couldn't afford it,' Rajni reminded her. 'Single mother with three kids? There was no way she could make that trip.' The steep price of a holiday had always been a convenient excuse, and it stopped her sisters from asking any other questions. *I can never go back there,* Mum had cried one afternoon when Rajni was sixteen, and despite knowing better, she couldn't help feeling that this was her fault. She still felt responsible for Mum's banishment from her family.

In the rippled water, Rajni's reflection was distorted. Her chin multiplied and overlapped, and her cheeks sagged. She withdrew her feet from the water. The sight of her pruned toes filled her with sorrow as she remembered Mum's bare feet poking out from under her blanket at the hospital. Her slow and laboured breaths were painful to listen to. 'Why isn't she wearing any socks?' Rajni had demanded of the nurses, who scurried around the foot of the bed, eventually finding Mum's socks. Rajni dismissed them from the room and she rolled the socks onto Mum's feet herself.

Her skin was ice cold to the touch, and Rajni had massaged her feet gently, hoping to ease those hard, heaving breaths. She had pressed her hands into Mum's bony heels and high arches until her own shoulders ached. She had waited for something divine to come from all this effort, all this wishing, but it didn't.

Chapter Four

Purity of heart, soul and mind are all important for achieving spiritual healing. You should not be intoxicated at any point during this journey. Please try to refrain from drinking alcohol while in India. Please also dress modestly and be respectful to the culture. I happen to know of a very good tailor in Karol Bagh market — Madhuri Fashions — if you want something stylish but also suitable for this journey.

That part of Mum's letter was definitely aimed at Jezmeen. She noted the word 'try' and congratulated herself for not drinking until she was back in her hotel room after their morning of service in the temple. Jezmeen opened the fridge door and surveyed the mini-bar. This tiny bottle of Grey Goose fit in her palm, so she was only sinning a little bit. She twisted off the cap, opened her mouth and tipped the contents down her gullet. The current crisis definitely warranted morning boozing.

Don't Google yourself. The voice in her head was Cameron's — he had just sent her an email, urgently asking her to call him. *'Too late,'* she had replied after the incident with the teenage boys earlier. *'I already saw it.'* She was screwed. The video had gone viral, and she had been identified. The internet was screaming with laughter over the irony of Jezmeen Shergill — the host of a television show which poked fun at people being caught doing embarrassing things on video – being caught doing something so embarrassing on video.

Cameron had warned Jezmeen that things would happen rapidly, but she could not have anticipated this. In the few hours since it had caught fire, there were mentions of her name on blogs, trolling comments, a particularly nasty thread on the National Geographic nature preservation forum and of course, there was the video. The first thing that came up when you searched for her name used to be TELEVISION HOST (to distinguish her from a paediatric dentist named Jezmeen Shergill in Birmingham). Now it was: TELEVISION HOST JEZMEEN SHERGILL BRUTALLY MURDERS ENDANGERED ANIMAL.

Needless to say, Jezmeen had compulsively typed her name into Google every few minutes today, while she was supposed to be doing seva. She was aware of Rajni watching and disapproving as she tapped away on her phone. Now she sat in the hotel, watching her notoriety multiply in the search result count. Another email from Cameron popped up: SERIOUSLY. DON'T GOOGLE YOURSELF. Easy for him to warn her against it; she'd searched for his name once and found only three hits. One, his earnest and suited LinkedIn picture from at least a decade ago (he had hair then), gave the impression that his early career was in real estate or insurance brokering.

'Oh God,' Jezmeen uttered aloud into the empty room. Her Wikipedia page – previously only consisting of a short paragraph outlining her modest career achievements – had been updated. The most objective account of Jezmeen's incident was headed 'Arowana Fish Controversy'.

On July 7th, 2018, Shergill was dining in Feng Shui restaurant in South London when she became involved in an altercation with her dining partner.

Feng Shui, which boasts a ten-foot aquarium, hosts its own rare Albino Arowana fish (valued at £35,000). The fish is known to be very sensitive to conflict and is prone to hurting itself when it is provoked or aggravated. The argument between Shergill and her partner took place near the aquarium, despite numerous attempts from the restaurant owners to ask them to respect the fish and move the argument outside. Onlookers reported that after the restaurant owner tried to steer Shergill away from the aquarium, she slammed her hand against the glass, causing the fish great distress. It leaped out of the water and onto the floor, where Shergill kicked it repeatedly.

This was the most objective version of events? It was lacking in some key details. For starters, the 'dining partner' had been Jezmeen's boyfriend, Mark. Jezmeen had mistakenly thought that reservations at Feng Shui meant a proposal. She hadn't allowed herself to consider the possibility that he might be breaking up with her. 'You just don't seem very happy with yourself,' he'd said.

'But my mum just died. I'm dealing with a lot,' Jezmeen protested. It was an understatement, because Jezmeen couldn't put in words how she felt about Mum's death. The thought of death in general had always made Jezmeen desperately want to rewind time, even when she was little. After Dad died, she found it comforting to pretend he was just in hiding for a while, until Mum told her to knock it off. Mum's death was still unreal to her. She was too old for fantasies of Mum's absence being temporary, which was where alcohol certainly helped.

Mark shook his head. 'It's been like this for a long time,' he said sadly, glancing pointedly at the bottle of wine, which had inched towards Jezmeen's side of the table.

And did the restaurant owner really attempt to 'steer' Jezmeen away? Try, 'grabbed her by the shoulders, leaving her no choice but to flail in self-defence, *accidentally* knocking on the aquarium.' Also, she did not think that the restaurant owner was serious when he told her that the fish – a bloated, miserable old thing – was 'emotionally vulnerable'. Those had been his words. It was only after the whole incident blew up that Jezmeen learned about the endangered Arowana fish and indeed its sensitive nature. Part of the reason there was so much interest in the incident was because although Arowanas were rumoured to be capable of putting themselves out of misery by flipping out of their tanks, nobody had actually captured it on video before. When Jezmeen and the restaurant owner started arguing, onlookers began filming, thinking they were just witnessing an entertaining tantrum. Now the death of the fish was taking on a life of its own.

Jezmeen sank back into the bed. She could feel the vodka working now – she had hardly eaten anything all day. After finding out that her video had gone viral, she had to return to the langar hall and wash old breakfast plates, which ruined what little appetite she had. Across the room, the dresser mirror presented an unflattering reflection, but not an unfamiliar one. If she clicked on Images, there'd be a few good headshots but even more stills from the videos: her brief and modest celebrity would turn into infamy now. She hadn't been on television long enough to have a solid reputation to fall back on – she was an up-and-coming entertainment figure once, and Fish Slayer forevermore.

Jezmeen scrolled to the bottom of the Wikipedia page where her few acting roles were listed. Before she landed the *DisasterTube* hosting role, she had been a waitress on *EastEnders* – recurring for three episodes – and a receptionist in a television movie based on a real-life scandal in a London investment bank. Several other roles hadn't made it to this résumé, though, and for the sake of beefing up her filmography, Jezmeen considered adding them. She had been a non-speaking extra in a few things, and what about that black-and-white student film she helped to direct ages ago? Then again, Jezmeen was grateful that some roles never made it to her page, like the short film for an amusement park in Taiwan, which people watched before getting on a rather racist *Arabian Nights*-themed ride. Never again, Jezmeen had vowed, after prancing around in that belly-dancer outfit and imploring roller-coaster riders to save her from her impending marriage to a cruel, moustached king. Then there were the countless runners-up, speaking parts that would have set her up for more opportunities, if she'd got them. 'Second in line to be considered for Barista #2 in a romantic comedy starring Hugh Grant.' 'Was told voice too husky to narrate commercial for major adult nappy brand.' (Initially, Jezmeen thought the director was complimenting her when he said, '"Ultra-absorbent" doesn't usually sound so suggestive.') Nobody looking at this page would know how Jezmeen Shergill almost became famous before killing that fish and clearly deserved another chance.

Jezmeen needed a distraction from reading about herself on the internet, or there was a risk of polishing off all of the mini-bar's offerings before dinner time. She glanced at her open suitcase. In her haste to catch her flight from London at the last minute, she had thrown together a lot of clothes that really weren't suitable for Delhi – the only appropriate bits were that long, mothball-scented cotton top she'd worn today, bought by Mum from a market in West London years ago, and her one pair of jeans which didn't have fashionable rips in them. *Please dress modestly.* Mum had found a way to lecture her about her skimpy clothing from beyond the grave. That was why Jezmeen bristled when Rajni told her off for revealing too much skin yesterday – it was enough to hear it from Mum's letter. Even though Jezmeen didn't want to admit that her mother and sister were right, she really needed a more modest wardrobe than tank tops and cut-off denim shorts for this trip.

Jezmeen picked up the phone and dialled Rajni's room number according to the instructions. The response was a siren-like dial tone. She pressed 0 for the operator.

'Hi, how do I call another room?' she asked when the receptionist picked up.

'You dial their room number,' she said in a tone that suggested Jezmeen was very thick.

'I tried that . . . Never mind. Thanks,' she said. After hanging up, she tried Shirina and by some miracle, got connected.

'Hello,' Shirina said.

'Hey, it's me. Want to do some shopping at the market?'

'Okay. Where's Rajni?'

'Didn't have luck calling her. I'll knock on her door,' Jezmeen said.

They hung up. Jezmeen did a quick check in the mirror and ran her fingers through her hair. Brushing it wouldn't help much against the gritty air once they got outside.

Rajni's room was at the end of the hall on Jezmeen's floor. She knocked and waited, then knocked again. Eventually, there was a voice at the door. 'Yes?'

'Raj, it's Jezmeen. Open up.'

The door opened a crack through which Jezmeen could see one reddish eye. 'I was napping,' Rajni croaked.

'Shirina and I are going shopping. You coming?'

'Uh . . . no thanks. I'm going to stay in.'

'Come on, Rajni. You have to see some of India while you're here. You don't have to just do what Mum stated in her letter.' Jezmeen thought about it. 'In fact, this is a great way to honour her memory. Mum loved a bargain and never understood why I bought clothes from High Street stores when they sold every type of knock-off at the flea markets she loved going to.'

It was a joke, but Rajni's reaction didn't change. 'I think I'm coming down with something,' she said.

Jezmeen sighed. She tried to sympathize – after all, during her para-noia stage, she had driven herself to A&E over a chest pain that turned out to be nothing but a reflux reaction to some salsa. But Rajni's aver-sion to India was so . . . wimpy. Ever since their pilgrimage plans were confirmed, Rajni had made a regular habit of forwarding cautionary articles. *'Make sure you bring hand sanitizer from home – not sure if we can trust the local brands!'* read one subject line. *'HAVE YOU SEEN THIS?'* read another. The email contained links to a story about a bridge that had collapsed in a rural northern town. Rajni's India was a land of disasters.

'We'll go ahead then,' Jezmeen said. 'Hope you get better soon.' Rajni sniffed loudly, mumbled her thanks and shut the door. Jezmeen stood there for a moment, contemplating her choices. Leave it or not? She knocked again. Rajni opened the door widely this time. Her eyes were puffy. It was clear that she'd been crying.

'Oh, Raj. I'm sorry,' Jezmeen stuttered. 'I didn't think . . .'

Rajni shut the door in her face.

Jezmeen stood in the hallway, stunned. She had never seen Rajni crying, not even during Mum's funeral. Her eyes had been bloodshot but it was clear that she had taken the time to cry in private before the ceremony. Did Rajni also blink sometimes and see Mum leaning over the edge of her bed, reaching for her jewellery case? Jezmeen woke abruptly some nights because that moment played back in her dreams, the details slightly different each time. Her subconscious exchanged the pale-pink colour of the hospital-room curtains for a cheery yellow and moved the dresser a few inches away, so Mum struggled to reach it and gave up. But even when Jezmeen was aware she was dreaming, she could never wake up before Mum died. That conclusion repeated itself in an infinite loop.

Jezmeen knocked on the door. 'Raj?' *You can talk to me,* she was about to say, but could she? She didn't know how they'd begin to talk about Mum's death and she suspected she knew how it would end – yet another fight.

Bargaining required no shortage of confidence. You had to be assured that you were in the right from the start, and willing to walk away from the item because pride was more important than purchase. This was why Shirina tried not to get too attached to anything she saw at the market – she didn't want to get into an argument like Jezmeen was having right now, which was verging on violence.

'You're expecting me to pay that much for these cheap chappal? Look at the workmanship. Look at these threads poking out.' Jezmeen waved a shoe in the shopkeeper's face. Rhinestones marched a path along overlapping plastic straps towards a shimmering plastic gem set in the centre. 'Cut the price in half and we'll talk.'

'In half?' the shopkeeper screeched. Shirina realized immediately that she'd underestimated him. He rolled up his sleeves as if listing the shoes' attributes was just as physically demanding as making them. Jezmeen did not look intimidated. As they continued to argue, the centrepiece came loose from the sandal and plopped to the dusty ground between them.

'We're done,' Jezmeen declared triumphantly, throwing her hands up and washing them clean of the sandals. She took Shirina's hand and led her to another stall. It was like being children again, except Jezmeen had always left Shirina trailing far behind. She held on tight. This was not a place where she wanted to get lost. The market bustled with chaos and it was full of men wandering in packs, their eyes sometimes connecting with Shirina's, at which point she hastily looked away. A stray dog with a ladder of ribs showing through his dingy fur weaved between two parked motorbikes at the side of the road. The row of shops seemed to stretch for miles, and where it ended, the main road was choked in peak-hour madness. She and Jezmeen had walked here, their feet traversing pavements that whittled into slivers and then vanished altogether, only to appear once more a few moments later.

'Honestly, they were bloody ugly shoes, weren't they?' Jezmeen muttered to Shirina.

'Why waste all that effort bargaining then?' Shirina asked.

'Sharpening my skills,' Jezmeen said. 'Look around. There's so much to buy.'

It was overwhelming – the columns of sari fabric and their dizzying brocade patterns, entire wall displays of glittering bangles in every possible shade. In a magazine, Shirina had once seen a sari made up entirely of tiny squares of every colour. Every single shade and variation in existence. It was beautiful and novel, but also functional, the designer's write-up explained. Women could wear the sari on their next trip to the tailor and pick out the exact colour they wanted from this wearable palette.

'I do need a pair of cheap sandals though,' Jezmeen said. 'I don't mind if they're a little gaudy, although those were just hideous. I need a decoy for the temple.'

Shirina smiled. She remembered shoe decoys from when they were young. It was always wise to wear your least expensive shoes to the gurdwara lest they get 'lost' or swiped from the cubbies outside. But they had to be presentable as well – tattered old Converse runners did not complete the Punjabi ensemble.

'Italian leather,' Shirina said, in a high-pitched imitation of their child-hood friend, Sharanjeet Kaur.

'Custom-fitted with a one-of-a-kind in-sole,' Jezmeen replied in a matching pitch.

'Designed by our personal cobbler.'

Jezmeen and Shirina both laughed. This was how they used to be, kicking each other under the covers and listening out for Rajni's footsteps. It was when Jezmeen started getting them into too much trouble that they started drifting apart. The first time Shirina told Sehaj she had sisters, she expected him to ask her what they were like, but he didn't really want to know about them. He was an only child, and she envied his untethered existence. For Shirina, at least until she stopped following Jezmeen around, having a sister meant being complicit in schemes and being seen as part of a pair rather than an individual.

'I wonder what Sharanjeet is up to these days,' Jezmeen said. 'What a bloody snob. Marries a rich guy and all of a sudden she's name-dropping her designer at your wedding and talking about her holiday house in the South of France. And that fuss she made after the ceremony when she couldn't find their shoes right away, like we had stolen them. Wasn't that long ago that she was a restaurant hostess.'

'I don't think she came to the wedding for me,' Shirina said. 'She wanted to rub shoulders with Sehaj's family.' Shirina had been surprised at Sharanjeet's appearance at all of her wedding events. A childhood friend who had disappeared once she got married, she was eager to reconnect with Shirina when she discovered whose family she was marrying into.

'Have you stayed in touch since then?' Jezmeen asked.

Shirina shook her head. 'I know she named her daughter Chanel,' she said.

Jezmeen rolled her eyes. 'I saw pictures of Chanel on her Instagram account. I think Sharanjeet blocked me at some point, though. I haven't seen anything from her in ages.'

'I'm sure it's all really superficial anyway.' Shirina said this with a shrug, as if she had lost track of Sharanjeet as well. She didn't want Jezmeen knowing that although she appeared inactive on social media, she still logged in to look up people like Sharanjeet, who publicized every inch of her privileged life. There were snapshots of designer bags and posed 'deep-thinking' pictures on the golden sands of Mediterranean beaches. The chorus of comments from Sharanjeet's friends and followers was openly envious and admiring. With nobody questioning what Sharanjeet's life was really like, Shirina felt petty doing so. Surely there were days when she fought with her husband or spent the afternoon simply waiting for the plumber to show up to fix the leaky tap was that driving her mad – but her pictures presented a life so unspoiled that Shirina didn't mind only believing in this version of it.

'You know who else recently had a baby?' Jezmeen said as they followed the current of the crowd. 'Auntie Roopi's daughter. She added me on Facebook recently.'

'Our old neighbour, Auntie Roopi?'

'Yup, from across the street. We stayed with her one summer, but you're probably too little to remember that. She had a cat that you desperately wanted to bring back to our house.'

Shirina vaguely recalled this cat, and the scent of channa masala bubbling on a stove in a kitchen that was bigger than theirs. She remembered going to Auntie Roopi's house sometimes but didn't remember living there. 'Why did we stay with her?'

'Mum and Rajni went to India together. It was shortly after Dad died. I think they were gone for about a month.'

An image was beginning to surface: tickling competitions with Jezmeen and the cat: the cat flicking its tail at their ankles while they struggled to keep straight faces. Shirina was about four or five, and they were over at Auntie Roopi's, having lunch. Auntie Roopi let them watch cartoons while she bustled around the house with a vacuum cleaner. At one point, she crossed the living room, blocking the television for a moment while she peered through the curtains. 'Your Mum's still away,' she said. 'You can stay for dinner.' But Mum was home all day, and the curtains of their house were always drawn, so Auntie Roopi was just saying that for their benefit.

Shirina and Jezmeen came home eventually to find Mum lying in bed, in the same place she'd been when they left. Rajni had told them off afterwards for upsetting Mum, and said to Jezmeen, 'I expect better behaviour from you from now on.'

It seemed that Jezmeen was remembering the same thing, because she said, 'Rajni was so strict with us when we were little.'

With you, Shirina thought. She learned it was better to avoid trouble after that incident, even if it meant also avoiding Jezmeen. 'I suppose she was just helping Mum,' Shirina said. 'She probably felt she needed to help raise us since Dad wasn't around.'

'Oh sure, lots of things had to change after Dad died,' Jezmeen said. 'But she used to be more fun. You wouldn't know it now, but Rajni was cool. She had this stash of sparkly eye shadows and bold lipsticks – the sort of thing Mum probably wouldn't let her wear, because I remember she always kept it hidden and didn't tell me where it was. She used to put it on me sometimes, and we'd dance around in her room. I was probably four years old then.'

It didn't sound like the Rajni that Shirina knew, and she was surprised to hear Jezmeen remember her this way. 'What changed?'

Jezmeen shrugged. 'I don't know. Dad's death, maybe? She and Mum fought a lot after that. There was also a visit from Dad's older brother before that, and that sparked a couple of arguments. They went to India the summer after Dad died. I remember she was really quiet when she came back from India with Mum and then soon after that, she was taking charge and being Sergeant Rajni – all about following the rules. And I have been resisting her ever since.'

Jezmeen said this with some pride, but any mention of Shirina's childhood, especially the teenage years, called to mind the sound of her sisters shouting. The arguments were so hostile and belligerent on both sides that it always felt as if the walls of their house were on the verge of collapsing. She had never fought with Rajni or Mum like that. She certainly refrained from taking every piece of bait her mother-in-law dangled before her; it was easier to say yes than to fight every battle. Life was so much more complicated if you always had to win. She recalled an Instagram post of Sharanjeet's from Christmas last year – mulled wine, a stack of presents wrapped with gold ribbons and the soft glow of a fire in the background. *Baby, it's cold outside, but my love knows just how to keep me warm,* the caption read, followed by a litany of hashtags: #winter #fireplace #mulledwine #xmascountdown #love #family #pressies #tiffanys #besthusband-ever #besthubbyever #spoiled #butimworthit. Shirina had read the caption over and over again. Painstaking selection of filters enhanced the picture so she could almost hear the firewood crackling gently. Shirina had been so absorbed in the world of Sharanjeet's life that she only vaguely registered Mother talking behind her. *Look at me when I talk to you,* Mother snapped, plucking the phone from her hand. It gave Shirina a small fright, because she hadn't realized the conversation wasn't over. Later, she told Sehaj about it, who frowned and said, 'I'll talk to her.'

'Ah, there it is. Madhuri Fashions,' Jezmeen said, nodding at a stall with magazine cut-outs pasted on its walls above a sewing machine. An elderly man stooped over the machine, tiny gold-framed spectacles perched on the tip of his nose. For his sake, Shirina hoped that the bargaining process would be reasonable. 'I'll be in there,' she said, pointing to the bookshop next door.

Books were crammed into every space, making them impossible to remove. When a title caught Shirina's eye, she extracted it with her finger-nails. 'Yes,' the bookshop owner said. 'Very good story.'

'You've read this?' she asked. It seemed unlikely. The title – *Mister Right Now* – was in raised pink lettering and didn't exactly shout this man as its demographic.

'I've read them all,' he said.

Well, that was impossible. There were too many books here for one person to have read in a lifetime. There were books in German and some in Scandinavian languages too, left here by tourists probably. His earnest-ness was admirable though. Probably sensing that Shirina didn't believe him, he started pointing to the spines of books and giving her a brief synopsis of each.

'Very bad man starts a corrupt business. Mafia bosses turn against him. He becomes very good man.

'This one: a family moves into a new house after the father loses his job and they find out it is haunted.

'A scientist starts a research station in some faraway country and spends thirty years there trying to find out what happened to his lost love.'

Shirina was amazed until she realized she had no way of verifying his claim. She nodded. 'Okay, okay,' she said, signalling with a wave that she had given up doubting him.

'Buy a book and I will also give you a numerology reading,' the man said, pointing at a little sign next to his cash box. 'When is your birthday?'

'May 10th, 1990,' Shirina said.

He repeated the date and tapped rapidly on a calculator. 'Your life path number is seven,' he said. 'Seven is a good number.'

'Oh,' Shirina said. She waited for more, but he returned to the shelves and began smoothing out the stacks by jamming the spines of books even further in. 'What does seven mean?' she asked. She had never had a numerology reading before – they were like horoscopes, worded to suit every person in some way. But horoscopes were intriguing sometimes. The recognition of herself was thrilling.

'For that, you must pay,' the man said.

Shirina almost laughed. She reached into her purse and wondered if the man knew how lucky she was that Jezmeen wasn't here. Once he took the money from her, he ducked back behind the counter again and opened up a slim silver laptop. Shirina's eyes followed its path of cables across the floor where they tangled and disappeared behind a cotton sheet nailed to a ceiling beam, serving as a curtain. The man waited, staring intently at his screen and then went to that back room. He appeared moments later with a printout.

'This is all the information about number seven,' he said.

Great. So she had just paid for a Google search. His face did not betray any acknowledgement that he had ripped her off. The ink was still damp on the paper; he took care to hand it to her on two flat hands, like a platter. Some words jumped out immediately at Shirina: 'sympathy', 'responsibility'. Then this sentence:

The number seven represents a person who will do anything to keep her family together. She keeps the peace and maintains harmony in situations of conflict.

This was why Shirina only read horoscopes once in a while in *Cosmo* or in the newspaper. If she subscribed regularly, their relevance became diluted. She saved them up and enjoyed the surprise of reading a description that matched her situation profoundly. The day before leaving Melbourne for Delhi, she had searched for her horoscope online – just one, she told herself, because it defeated the purpose to select the best of ten predictions.

You are at a crossroads but the power to make a decision is completely within your control. Consider the needs of your loved ones during this delicate time.

Words written so clearly that she could almost hear them.

Next door, Jezmeen was patiently standing with her arms stretched out while a silver-haired woman looped a measuring tape around her chest. 'I'm getting a blouse made,' she said when she saw Shirina.

'They'll be able to sew it that quickly?' Shirina asked. They were only in Delhi for another day.

'Yeah, I think that's why Mum recommended this shop. She did like it when things could be done quickly. Hang on—' She looked down. The woman was pressing the measuring tape to her collarbone, far above the neckline of the blouse in the picture. 'I want it to look like that blouse,' Jezmeen said, nodding at a picture on the wall. She sliced her hand across her chest to show exactly where the neckline should be. 'And sleeveless, please. It's too hot for anything else.'

The woman looked at her husband, who rose from a stool behind the counter. 'Madam, we can do this neckline only.'

'What do you mean?'

'This is a decent neckline. You walk around in Delhi with anything lower, there will be trouble. You must also have sleeves.'

'Yes, trouble,' Jezmeen muttered to Shirina. 'Mass erections. A city-wide catastrophe.'

Shirina didn't think a decent neckline was such a bad idea though. Her own blouse buttoned up at the neck and hung loosely around her waist. She had given away a lot of her sleeveless clothes to the Salvation Army a few months after moving to Australia, when it became clear that Mother didn't approve of them. The four-seasons-in-a-day weather in Melbourne was so unpredictable anyway that Shirina didn't have much use for anything that revealed her arms.

The measuring tape dangled from the crook of the woman's elbow. 'You want the order, or you want to cancel?' she asked impatiently.

'If I told you I wasn't going to wear this blouse in India, would you make it the way I want it? I'm going back to London.'

The woman shook her head with certainty while her husband retreated behind a small cabinet. He produced a clear plastic folder. It bulged with pieces of paper sticking out. Shirina patted the numerology paper in her pocket, relieved it was still there. It seemed that in the disarray of this market, there was no designated place for anything, and her printout fortune could very easily disappear into a stack of paper.

'You see what I have done,' the man said. His cheeks shone with pride as he presented the open folder to Jezmeen. Shirina wasn't sure which he was prouder of – his work, or his cataloguing of it. On each left-hand page, there was a glossy picture cut out from a magazine, usually a Western woman. On each right-hand page, there was his corresponding version – a tailored copy of the dress or skirt or blouse, with adjustments made for 'decency'. Necklines were raised from chest to throat. Skirt hems dropped below the knees. Waists were so generous that the dresses hung loose and forlorn like potato sacks.

'Decent,' the wife said, nodding her approval at the folder. 'If we made these clothes exactly to the specifications on the models, people would complain.'

'I won't complain,' Jezmeen said. 'Honestly, I'd just like an exact copy of that blouse over there.'

The woman screwed her eyes at Jezmeen. 'You'll wear it with what? Jeans?'

'Yes.'

'Then the hemline needs to be longer. Needs to cover this area.' She made a vague gesture at her lower half.

'You know, I could go to any other stall around here. I chose you because you came highly recommended by my . . .' Jezmeen's voice trailed off. 'By Mum,' she said to Shirina. 'She knew these people would try to make me a blouse with the fitting of a bed sheet.'

'You think so?' Shirina asked.

'I'm sure of it,' Jezmeen said. 'It's her final attempt.' She had a rueful smile on her face but Shirina caught something else too – a brief shadow over her expression. 'This is probably one of the ways she wanted me to "start taking more responsibility".' Jezmeen put air quotes around Mum's words. Shirina didn't know exactly what Mum had said, but it clearly bothered Jezmeen.

'Can't you just make it exactly the same?' Jezmeen pleaded. 'We won't tell anybody, if that's what you're worried about.'

They shook their heads.

'You can return my deposit then,' Jezmeen said.

The man and his wife exchanged a quick look. 'Deposit is non-refundable,' they both said in unison.

Shirina stepped out of the stall just as the arguing began. She surveyed the shops once again, disappointed that she'd return to the hotel empty-handed. There was just nothing she wanted enough to fight for. Behind her, Jezmeen was accusing the shopkeepers of swindling her. Shirina wandered back to the first shop with the hideous shoes. She supposed she needed a pair of decoy sandals herself. 'Two hundred rupees?' she asked, quoting Jezmeen's final price from their earlier bargaining.

The shopkeeper shook his head and quoted a price that was triple the amount. After all, she was an entirely new customer.

She remembered her friend Lauren encouraging her to fight back. 'You have to stand up for yourself,' Lauren said. It was after the taxi driver incident, when it was decided that Shirina should not go out for after-work drinks any more. '*Beti*, it's for your own good,' Mother had said. After that weekend of silent treatment from Mother, Shirina gulped down the words like a tonic.

On Monday when she returned to work, Shirina had told Lauren the whole story. She just wanted to share her shame with somebody — *Oh my god, we were so drunk on Friday. Can you believe what I did?* But Lauren looked more worried than amused when Shirina got to the part about Mother ignoring her. 'She's talking to me now though,' Shirina assured Lauren.

'Did she admit she was overreacting?' Lauren asked. 'And did your husband grow a pair of balls and tell his mother to butt out of his life?'

Shirina was surprised. Lauren seemed to be the only person in the office who understood when another co-worker made a joke about Shirina and Sehaj still living with parents. 'It's cultural, isn't it?' Lauren had said, shooting the guy a dirty look.

'Come out for drinks this week,' Lauren continued. 'She can't stop you from having a good time.'

'I have other plans,' Shirina said apologetically. Then the following week, and the week after that, she came up with new excuses. One day, Lauren cornered her in the break room and asked in a low voice if everything was alright at home. 'Everything's fine,' Shirina said but Lauren was not convinced.

'Tell your mother-in-law that you're an adult,' Lauren said. 'You're missing out on opportunities to socialize, and that's something we do at the pub. This is Australia, tell her that.'

But Shirina didn't mind going home for the evening, sitting with Sehaj, who told her she just had to humour his mother. 'She's traditional, you're not going to change her ways,' he said. Shirina sensed that his conversation with Mother about minding her personal space hadn't gone very far. She tried not to let it bother her, reminding herself that she liked being a wife and a daughter. While Jezmeen was busy fighting every battle, Shirina was walking away with a pair of shoes – what did it matter that she paid three times more than she wanted?

Chapter Five

Evenings: Share your meals together. I cannot remember the last time I saw the three of you at the same table. Don't take for granted that there will always be time to do this in the future. Make conversation with each other. Don't turn everything into a disagreement.

The curries arrived first, brimming and still bubbling in small steel bowls. The waiter carefully arranged them around the table, announcing the name of each dish: fish kadai, lamb tikka, bhaigan baratha. Rajni tried to ignore the ring of oil orbiting around each dish. When Mum commanded them to have a meal together, she probably pictured a cosy table in some local eatery, not one of the restaurants shortlisted from the Zagat's guide. But Rajni was determined to avoid food poisoning on this journey, and the presence of online reviews from Western tourists assured her that this was the right choice.

'Do you think we ordered too much?' she asked as the waiter returned to the kitchen. There were still the pilaf rice and naan to come, and she was already eyeing some items on the dessert menu. *Make conversation with each other.* Shirina opened her mouth for a moment and then closed it. Seconds later, her face twisted to suppress a yawn. 'Excuse me,' she whispered. Jezmeen was glued to her phone again. She tapped furiously, squinting at the screen. Rajni felt too tired to reprimand her again. In the taxi on the way here, she had peered over Jezmeen's shoulder to try to see what was so captivating, but Jezmeen had noticed right away and hunched over the screen to block Rajni's view.

'I think it's enough food,' Shirina said. She picked up the serving spoon and scooped two generous servings of lamb tikka onto her plate. Rajni glanced at Jezmeen, careful to be discreet about it in case Shirina noticed. *Do you see how much she's eating?* Jezmeen carried on staring at her phone.

At the next table, a woman with long, manicured nails was being very particular about her order. 'I can't have any dairy. Not even a drop,' she announced. 'It's just a disaster we'd all rather avoid.'

'Oh, me too. These things start to kick in with age, don't they?' her partner replied. 'I used to eat all manner of street food as well, but last week, that kebab nearly ended my life.'

Rajni felt her appetite waning. Why did people have to talk so competitively about the different causes of their indigestion? In moments, the inevitable 'paleo' and 'gluten-free' would enter the conversation. 'In my day, we just ate everything and didn't have so many opinions about it,' Mum had said to Rajni when she witnessed their neighbour whacking a pecan cookie out of her son's hands. 'I think he's allergic to nuts, Mum,' Rajni had said. 'If he had grown up in my village in India, he'd be so grateful for a cookie, he'd forget about being allergic,' Mum had retorted. Rajni had stayed silent, recognizing yet another version of Mum's 'England has spoiled you' rhetoric. After the cancer diagnosis, she followed the same line of questioning: 'Nobody used to have cancer, and now it's everywhere,' Mum said. Mum truly thought that living in England had changed the composition of her body.

Jezmeen sighed and chucked her phone into her purse. 'It's over,' she said.

'What's over?' Shirina asked. She speared a hunk of lamb with her fork and put it in her mouth. 'Oh, this is delicious.'

'My career. It's done.'

'Should we wait for the naan?' Rajni asked.

'Don't you care?' Jezmeen asked. She looked hurt. 'I just said *my career is over.*'

Had it really started? No, that was not a nice question to ask, although Rajni could see it printed on Shirina's face as well. Jezmeen had been whining about the shoddy state of her career since it began. 'It's a tough industry,' Rajni said by way of consolation.

Jezmeen let out a heavy sigh. 'I guess I might as well tell you,' she said. 'You'll find out anyway.'

She took her phone out of her purse and tapped once on it. A black-and-white video appeared. It was surveillance footage from a restaurant, probably one of the videos that Jezmeen presented on her show. Rajni watched with little interest; the waiter was returning now with a platter of steaming rice pilaf and a huge bowl of crispy golden naan. They had definitely ordered too much.

Shirina gasped. 'Oh, that's horrible,' she said. 'What's wrong with people?' She shook her head. Rajni turned her attention to the screen to find a woman kicking something – was that a large fish? It was difficult to tell.

Then she remembered the boys from the temple this afternoon. The boy who stuck out his tongue and pretended to choke. She leaned closer and squinted at the screen. 'Goodness, Jezmeen, is that you?'

Jezmeen nodded miserably. 'This was the first video that came out. Some animal rights activists managed to get some high-definition footage last night, and it's everywhere now. I didn't mean to knock on the glass. Obviously, I was upset. The video doesn't show the whole situation.'

The whole situation probably involved more alcohol than Jezmeen would admit to having had. Rajni wondered if Anil was aware of the video. She peered at her own screen. No calls or messages from him. He probably hadn't seen it then.

'Do your producers know?' Shirina asked.

Jezmeen nodded. 'I was at the end of my contract with the show anyway – they've chosen not to renew me.'

At some point, you had to be realistic. This was what Mum had said to Rajni once, when Jezmeen came up in conversation: you had to accept that you weren't going to be a famous star. 'Don't tell her that, please,'

Rajni said to Mum. She knew it would crush Jezmeen, even though she had to admit she didn't think Jezmeen would ever become a star. Not that Jezmeen wasn't talented, she just wasn't wanted. Now Polly Mishra, there was an actress whom people wanted. Rajni, Kabir and Anil had binge-watched an entire season of *The Boathouse* one winter weekend while sleet gathered on their windowsill. They had intentions to pace themselves, but the cliff-hanger at the end of the first episode was so good that they had allowed themselves one more, and then another, and then it was dinner time and they ordered a pizza delivery so they could continue watching.

Rajni longed for the cosy and peaceful indulgence of that afternoon now. As the air became chillier, they had huddled together, excitedly sharing their predictions about the following episodes. Rajni couldn't recall another time when she and Anil shared the same interests.

'They're saying it's because of this incident,' Jezmeen was telling Shirina. 'But I think they want to go with a more mainstream host.' She put 'main-stream' in air quotes. 'Somebody white would appeal to a wider audience.' Shirina nodded along sympathetically. Rajni didn't think that those *DisasterTube* clips of people injuring their crotches in various ways needed a wider audience.

'It was self-defence,' Jezmeen continued. 'He could have bitten me. What if he was poisonous?'

'I don't think Arowanas are poisonous,' Shirina said. 'They're just really sensitive. There was this article in *National Geographic* about animals which are capable of intense and complex emotions. Those fish actually experience distress.'

Jezmeen groaned. 'Now you make me feel even worse.'

'Sorry.'

'It's not just the issue of the video going viral either. I have to pay the restaurant back for the damage.'

'How much do you owe them?' Rajni asked.

'Thirty-five thousand pounds,' Jezmeen said.

'*What?*'

'They're pretty expensive,' Shirina said. 'One of Sehaj's clients has an

Arowana. He bought it from a fish farm in Singapore for a quarter of a million US dollars.'

'Are they very exotic-looking?' Rajni asked, reaching for the basket of naan. 'Or do they bring good luck?'

'Evidently not,' Jezmeen retorted. 'They just flop about the house, feeling complex emotions and then when somebody knocks on the door, they commit suicide.'

Rajni hesitated. It was the wrong thing to say, and Jezmeen knew it – she bit her lip as if she wished she could take back the words. Their eyes met and they both glanced at Shirina. She had stopped chewing and was reaching slowly for a glass of water. They were all thinking about the same thing. Rajni felt a rush of irritation with Mum for ordering them to converse with each other. *Now look at what you've done*, she thought.

In the middle of the night, Rajni woke to the sound of tentative scratching. Somebody was in her room. She bolted out of bed and hastily wrapped the bed sheet around her body. 'Excuse me?' she squeaked, not sure if this was an effective way to deter a sex pest. She glanced at her suitcase, quickly taking stock of what valuables she had. Her passport was in the safe, thankfully, but the canister of ashes was in plain view. Then she realized it was only valuable to herself – what would a thief want with an old woman's remains? Taking a small step towards the door, she thought she heard the scratching behind her, louder now. There was a ripping sound. She spun around in time to see the curtains come crashing down from the window.

'Fucking fuck fuck,' she said, jumping on the spot with her fists balled up tightly. The sheet fell away from her body and pooled around her ankles. It took a moment for the relief to seep in, and for her to process what had happened – the curtain, fastened to the rod at the top of the window by a Velcro strip, had slowly become unstuck throughout the night. Rajni picked it up and carried it to the desk in the corner of the room. How cheap were all these furnishings? She half expected the hotel to actually be made of paper – she'd lean on a wall and the whole place would crumple.

No chance of getting back to sleep now. Rajni picked up the phone from her dresser and sent Kabir a chat message – it was around nine o'clock in England and he'd be slumped in front of the TV after work.

'How are you?'

'Good,' he replied. *'How was first day of pilgrimage?'*

Rajni shrugged at the phone. What was there to tell him? She didn't manage to get through the first day of honouring Mum without thinking of those final, ugly moments. She had been tempted to skip that dinner with her sisters because she knew how draining it would be to engage with them, and she was proven right. She should have chosen room service instead – probably delivered by young, terrified Tarun from the café – but eating alone was no better. It would make her think of all the things that she and Mum had left unsaid. She wasn't sure she could get through the rest of the trip without unwelcome reminders of her last trip to India with Mum.

'Don't know how to describe,' she wrote. As soon as she sent the message, she realized that she sounded like a person in awe, as if all that carrot-chopping in the temple kitchen had filled her spiritual voids. She was about to clarify when Kabir sent another message.

'Managed to have a chat with Anil today.'

Rajni pressed the CALL symbol on her chat screen. Kabir's voice stretched into a million syllables, distorted by distance and a poor internet connection.

'Heeeeeelllllloooooooooooo?'

He sounded like a dying robot. 'Kabir,' Rajni said. 'Kabir?'

'HEEEEEEEEEEEEEEEEEELLLLLOOOOOOOOOOO.'

She held the phone away from her ear and waited for the connection to adjust. She had called Shirina in Australia once using this service as well, and halfway through the call, the echo had been so strong that she became annoyed with her own voice for interrupting her.

There was silence on the line. 'Kabir,' Rajni said. 'Can you hear me?'

A static-filled pause and then his voice came through in one piece. 'Yes.'

'So what did Anil say?'

Kabir's sigh sounded like a roar. Long-distance phone calls were not for subtlety, Rajni realized when she called Shirina to tell her about Mum's diagnosis. You had to be quick and direct to avoid the message being jumbled by a poor connection.

'I didn't have much time to talk with him – he just came by to get more of his things. He's staying at Davina's flat until they find a more permanent place to move into together. I'm not sure what we're expecting him to say or do, Rajni.'

'You said you'd handle it,' Rajni pointed out.

'This situation though – it's irreversible.'

'Kabir, you can't tell me that you're taking care of matters and then backtrack like this,' Rajni said.

'I meant that I would try to convince Anil to continue his education, not abandon his child.'

Rajni wasn't sure if that was a catch in his voice or the connection dropping. Either way, the word 'child' made her want to retch. Anil *was* a child. He was not supposed to be having one.

'How sure are we that this child is his?'

'I asked him that,' Kabir said. 'He's positive. He and Davina have been together for almost three months. She's six weeks along now – it's not like she got pregnant with another man and then hunted down some naïve young man with a small inheritance to support her.'

'So she says,' Rajni replied. 'Why should we believe her?'

'I suppose Anil really trusts her.'

'Did you ask Anil? Did you ask him if he's certain?'

'I didn't. I'm trying not to upset him.'

'*Trying not to upset him?*' The words burst out of Rajni's mouth. She was aware that the walls were paper-thin and that she had probably woken her neighbours on both sides. 'Our son's about to ruin his life and you're worried about sparing his feelings?'

'I don't think questioning the baby's paternity is the right way to go,' Kabir said. 'Let's assume it's his.'

Rajni remained tight-lipped. Kabir continued, 'I know it's difficult to accept, Rajni, but he'll need our support. He doesn't know the first thing about raising the child. Remember what a steep learning curve it was for us? We were only a couple of years older than him, if you think about it.'

'We were in our twenties and we had jobs. We were married and the same bloody age too,' Rajni corrected Kabir. She felt light-headed. 'But Kabir, you're saying . . . you're saying that this is it? They're going through with this?'

'It will be very hard,' Kabir said. 'But they've made the decision, and from the looks of things—'

'There's money,' Rajni said. She shut her eyes as she said this. She couldn't believe what she was resorting to.

'Money for what?'

'For – oh, don't make me say it, Kabir.'

It was Kabir's turn to go quiet. The background filled with a faint hum that made Rajni long for London – one long, peaceful note.

'What is this really about, Rajni?' Kabir asked. She hated it whenever he asked that question, usually at the peak of an argument, usually an argument about Anil. Because it always came to the answer that was sitting on the tip of Rajni's tongue now. *What will people say?* She refused to say it. She had spent the whole day with Mum on her mind; she was not going to become her.

'Forget it. Let's just talk about something else,' Rajni said with a sigh.

'Good idea,' Kabir said. 'What's going on with Jezmeen? I've heard there's some video going viral of her torturing an endangered animal?'

'Kicking a fish,' Rajni corrected.

'Is it for real? Or just a publicity stunt for that show she's on?'

'It's real,' Rajni said. 'She has to pay the restaurant back for the fish.' It occurred to her that Kabir hadn't actually seen the video. 'How did you find out?'

'Anil told me it's all over his social media. He called me the minute he saw it.'

'That's nice,' Rajni said. She felt her heart catching in her throat. 'Because he hasn't been in touch with me.'

'Can you blame him?' Kabir asked.

'That's not fair,' Rajni said. 'I'm worried about him.'

'Why do you say that as if I'm not worried about him too?'

'Because you're willing to let him ruin his future, Kabir. You're too soft on him. You've always been too easy-going, and look what it's led to.'

'Rajni, Anil has made a decision. It is irreversible.'

'It's not necessarily,' Rajni said. 'Maybe if we paid her to get rid of the baby and just get out of Anil's life, he could start over.'

'You of all people should think about whether you want something like that on your conscience,' Kabir said.

His words sucked the breath right out of her. She nearly dropped the phone. The internet connection was weakening again, and Kabir's immediate apology sounded like it was coming from underwater. At the small, crackling sound of static that took his words apart again, Rajni decided they had a poor connection and cut off the phone.

Chapter Six

Day Three: Sunrise at India Gate

By this time, you girls are probably annoyed with me for making you get up early each day but a sunrise is something that you shouldn't take for granted. India Gate is the best place to view the sunrise in Delhi. Just once, for me, stand still and watch a new day beginning. Think of all the new days you have left, and reflect on how you will choose to spend them.

There was a folded note on the floor between the door and the bathroom. In her bleary still-waking-up state, Jezmeen spotted it but could not summon the energy to get out of bed to pick it up. 'What is it?' she mumbled into the empty room. Then she caught a whiff of her putrid breath.

'Ah, shit,' she said, sinking back to bed. She rolled to her side and patted around for her phone to check the time. Now she could guess what the note said and who had written it. She had foggy recollections (she thought they were dreams) of being woken by knocking this morning, answering the door, and fabricating a very believable food-poisoning story. The 'I can't keep anything down' portion of the story was based on real events anyway. 'I'll join you guys later. I know how to get there,' she'd said with what she assumed was a confident smile. She now realized that one whiff of hangover fire had probably been enough to send her sisters scuttling down the hallway. She could bet anything that the note contained some chastisement on how poorly she had managed to impersonate a sober person.

An empty bottle of wine had rolled across the television console and remained precariously on its edge. Jezmeen appreciated that her dwindling bank account stretched much further here than in London. It made last night's room-service orders seem sensible and almost thrifty. She had spotted a bottle shop on the way back from the market last night but it was dank and shadowy and when she approached, a line of men lifted their eyes to meet hers and she lost her nerve.

Years ago, she'd read a news article about an Indian politician encouraging beatings of women who drank in bars. In response, women all over the country sent pieces of pink underwear to the politician's office and flooded his email inbox with images of the same. To this day, the politician's name could not withstand an internet search without hundreds of pictures of lacy pink thongs popping up on the screen. Jezmeen had been thinking about this as she drank straight from the bottle and searched for images of herself last night, pleasure mixing with punishment. It probably explained why she had the oddest dreams of the Arowana fish wearing pink bikini bottoms.

Jezmeen sat up and let her head adjust. She didn't remember finishing the whole bottle but the fog of this hangover was evidence enough. It was a slow and arduous walk to the door, where she picked up and unfolded the note:

We're at India Gate. You can join us if you feel like it — Rajni and Shirina.

Not as bad as she expected, although she could practically hear Rajni's self-importance in the straight edges and sharp points of her print.

It was close to noon. So she had missed the sunrise. Surely she could make it up somehow. There were sunrises every day. She could even go to India Gate now and it would be almost the same, wouldn't it? There was no reason Mum's letter had to be followed so exactly.

Jezmeen took a long shower, letting the steam clear her blocked sinuses. She stepped out feeling instantly better – hangover turnaround was a skill that many people underestimated. It enabled her to have a few too many once in a while and still wake up (albeit a little late for worship) and go about the rest of her day. 'Some people call that functional alcoholism,' Mark had said to her once with a grin. That dimple-studded grin. He had gone from teasing her lightly to giving her a pointed look every time she poured another glass. She knew she had been drinking more since Mum's death but didn't everybody grieve in their own ways?

Jezmeen got dressed and stepped out of the hotel, descending into the mob of people, rickshaws, stray animals, shoe-shiners, students. A scooter honked behind her and as it passed, the driver leaned towards Jezmeen. 'So sexy,' he hissed, like it was meant to insult her. 'Fuck off,' she retorted, but the blare of engines and the shouts of street vendors drowned out her voice anyway. She wove her way through Karol Bagh market, her head tipped up as if just keeping it above water. Her eyes were trained on the mammoth bridge at the end of this street, where the Metro ran above the city, unobstructed by the mayhem on the ground.

Where were the women? Jezmeen wondered. It wasn't her first time noticing that Delhi was a city of men, but walking alone made it all the more obvious. Men ran the textile shops, unspooling rivers of sari fabrics across the wide expanses of their counters. The jewellers held out delicate earrings between their thick, calloused fingers. Men clustered at the chai stand outside a small college building, clutching textbooks to their chests. They walked past and deliberately bumped shoulders or dipped their mouths to Jezmeen's ears, sometimes singing lines from Hindi songs, sometimes muttering filth. Whenever Jezmeen did spot a woman, her face reflected the hardness that Jezmeen realized was in her own expression.

She was already a bit worn by the time she elbowed her way up to the Metro station. Traffic hollered and screeched below her but the noises rose up and followed her towards the platform. From the bridge, she had the best view of Hanuman, the Monkey God, a gigantic statue that towered over the link road and made miniatures of the buildings and trees below it. His hands came together at his chest and his tail curled to the top of his head. Jezmeen couldn't stop staring but it was the sheer size of the statue rather than its spiritual meaning that captivated her. She wondered how long it took to build something of such scale, and if the builders had intended to make him loom over the city like this, the cars and bicycles skirting around below in a ring of disorder. She supposed it gave a reminder of how small she was, how insignificant, but walking along a crowded Delhi market street already gave her that message loud and clear.

Inside the station, the rush of people followed a slightly more ordered pace under the bright fluorescent lights. Central Secretariat station was only a few stops away, with a change.

A faded pink arrow on the sleek tiled floor indicated where the female-only carriage would line up with the platform. Jezmeen followed the arrow and found herself in the presence of a large group of women. It occurred to her that this was the first time since coming to India that she had seen so many women. A pair wearing kurti tops over stylish tight jeans were deep in conversation. Snippets of chatter filled the air.

'I mean, it's selfish, don't you think?'

'Not if she didn't agree first, but these companies do that kind of thing.'

'She didn't sign a contract or what?'

'They're saying it's void because she joined after the fact . . .'

Jezmeen's gaze wandered over the other women standing alone. Many were staring at their mobile phones, their lips curling into small smiles as their messages appeared. A middle-aged lady wearing a sari dragged a shopping trolley behind her. Plastic bags poked out of the grilles. When the train arrived, she hauled her goods into it, shooting a weary look at the others who piled past her.

Being in the carriage was such a relief after the short walk to the station. Her memory drifted back to their first day in India, when Rajni warned her about the effect her revealing clothing would have. But why did the women have to be sequestered like this just because the men couldn't control themselves?

The train glided into the next station and the doors slid open. Young women – students, Jezmeen thought – piled into the carriage and something changed in the atmosphere. Their voices trilled and they called out to each other. The other women looked up and shifted, some turning up the volumes on their phones. Many of these new passengers were wearing matching T-shirts. Jezmeen struggled to read the print across their chests in the crowded carriage, but from eavesdropping, it seemed they were headed to India Gate too, for some sort of event.

A girl in a tight purple T-shirt and ears studded in tiny rings stepped back as the train jostled, her foot landing on Jezmeen's. She tossed her head back and said 'Sorry,' and then her eyes lingered. There was a flash of recognition in them. She whispered to a friend standing next to her, who shot Jezmeen a glance as well. Jezmeen began to feel queasy – what if they knew her from the video? She could hear the snickers of those nasty boys from the temple. She pulled her sunglasses out of her bag and popped them on. Behind these wide tinted lenses, she was a little less recognizable.

When the train arrived at their destination, the T-shirted women poured out and the others who weren't with them dispersed, hurrying along to their lives. This loosening of the crowd allowed Jezmeen to see what was written on their backs: 'WOMEN'S RIGHTS MARCH'.

She could see the writing on their placards as well now: 'NO BODY DESERVES THIS' and 'END RAPE CULTURE, SAVE OUR CULTURE'.

The woman in the purple T-shirt turned to look at Jezmeen again. The corners of her lips turned up in a small smile. 'Are you . . . Polly Mishra?'

Jezmeen nodded miserably before she realized that the girl had said the wrong name.

'I knew it!' The girl's face brightened and she thumped her friend on the arm. 'I told you it's really her. Polly Mishra!'

Her friend grinned. 'Oh shit,' she said. 'Who got you?'

'Hmm?' Jezmeen asked.

'Was it Sunayana? She's always pulling surprises like this. Last year, she got Priyanka Chopra to send a tweet about our Slut Shame Walk.'

Jezmeen shook her head. She wanted to tell them that they had the wrong person, that she was not Polly Mishra. But she hesitated for a moment, suspended in the fantasy of being somebody else for the day. (What was Polly Mishra doing right now? Whatever it was, she was certainly having an easier time than Jezmeen these days.) Then the girl in the purple T-shirt let out a hoot. Her noise attracted the attention of the other marchers. 'Ladies, listen up,' she cried, linking arms with Jezmeen. 'Polly Mishra is here, and she's joining us for the march!'

A cheer went through the crowd. Jezmeen made sure to keep her sunglasses on. Bashfulness was the way to play this whole identity-stealing thing. There was too much attention on her otherwise, and somebody would out her. The tide of women carried her along to the station's exit. The girl in the purple T-shirt introduced herself as Sneha. 'I'm one of the organizers,' she explained. 'This is Anjuli,' she said, nodding at the girl who was next to her. 'She went to high school with the victim.'

'The victim?' Jezmeen asked.

Sneha looked at her. 'Haven't you been paying attention to the news?'

Sure, Jezmeen thought with shame. She'd been clicking obsessively on her own name and looking for any headlines, any blog posts or tweets that kept her relevant and afloat in the online world.

'No,' Jezmeen said. 'But I'm almost afraid to ask.' It had to be another gang rape, she realized, something horrific enough to inspire this sort of turnout.

'A twenty-year-old was violently attacked by a man in a bazaar last week,' Anjuli said. 'She was trying on clothes in the fitting room when he barged his way in. His brother and another shopkeeper held her down—' Anjuli had a delicate face and wide eyes that glistened with anger. Her voice choked on the last words.

Jezmeen's own eyes became hot with tears. After the bus gang rape in Delhi that made international headlines, she had followed the protests, the wave of feminism that swept across India – students marching, lighting candles, staging sit-ins. *We've had enough,* was the message from these teeming masses of bodies showing their support for the victim and their anger for the injustice. But the reporting afterwards stoked her rage to a point where it burned out and she became disillusioned. The rapists' lawyers had defended their clients by saying that the girl had enticed them by being out at night. A vocal counter-protest group insisted that not all men were rapists and that 'rape culture' was a gross generalization. And there were more rapes. Either they were reported more, or they were happening more – the difference didn't matter much to Jezmeen because they were still happening.

Fear struck Jezmeen's chest as she thought about her own trip to the market with Shirina yesterday. 'I'm with you,' Jezmeen said. 'I'm here to give my support.' Anjuli nodded and took her hand.

They descended the station's steps and emerged into the grimy summer atmosphere. Jezmeen squinted against the sunlight and followed the women towards India Gate. Its grand arc was triumphant against the blank, white canvas of cloudless sky. Visitors moved in small masses – the retiree Westerners with tall socks and bulky cameras hanging from their necks, the fresh-faced Indian couples grinning at their phones propped up on selfie sticks. Vendors wove between them, peddling balloons and cheap battery-operated helicopters and bubble wands.

'So I guess you're in India anyway for some kind of publicity event?' Anjuli asked as they pushed against the burning heat towards the gate.

'I'm here on a holiday of sorts,' Jezmeen said.

'Alone?' Anjuli asked.

'With family,' Jezmeen said.

'For how long?' Anjuli asked.

'I'm only in Delhi till tomorrow morning, then we're off to Amritsar,' Jezmeen said. 'We're visiting the Golden Temple.'

'It's divine,' Anjuli said with a smile. 'You go to a place like that and you wonder why the whole world can't be a sanctuary. We're obviously capable of peace, but only in designated sites.'

The women began to assemble as they arrived in the square's centre. It wasn't clear where or how the protest would start, but Jezmeen had a feeling she'd know when it began. The tourists and other people seemed aware that something was about to happen. They dispersed with some curiosity and perhaps a little bit of fear? Jezmeen intended to stay back and watch but Anjuli grabbed her hand and with surprising force, pulled her into the centre of the circle. A black duffle bag was resting at her feet. She pulled out a flat piece of wood that unfolded into a stand, giving her just enough height to be noticed. The stand gave her confidence. Jezmeen could see her shoulders squaring, her eyes shining. Sneha handed her a loudspeaker and it began.

'WHAT DID SHE DO?' Anjuli's voice burst across the air. 'SHE WAS JUST SHOPPING IN JANPATH MARKET FOR AN OUTFIT.'

Jezmeen surveyed the crowd – the other women were captivated. They nodded as Anjuli recited statistics of sexual harassment claims and gang rape incidents. She went backwards in chronological order, from the present day to the 2012 bus gang rape that started these protests. 'THESE ARE ONLY THE HIGHLIGHTED INCIDENTS,' she shouted. 'THESE ARE ONLY THE REPORTED INCIDENTS. WHO KNOWS WHAT ELSE IS HAPPENING, WHO KNOWS WHEN IT WILL STOP?'

A chant began amongst the women: 'When will it stop?' Sneha led them, pumping her fist into the air. 'When will it stop?' Jezmeen found herself saying the words too, her shouts blending with the collective chants so she could no longer hear herself, only this powerful united voice. She looked past the crowd, expecting to see people watching them, joining in, but disappointingly, India continued around them. The traffic crawled, the vendors courted customers, the tourists skirted the edges of the protest, some taking pictures, others maintaining a safe distance.

It was Sneha's turn now. She stood up on the stand and started reciting statistics – 875 women to 1,000 men in Haryana, she shouted. A girl waved a cardboard sign that said 'NO MORE FEMALE FETICIDE'. Honour killings were still happening in rural parts of the country – two girls held a banner high: 'THERE'S NO HONOUR IN KILLING'. The protest seemed to be for all manner of women's rights in India, and there was so much to fight for. It felt a bit overwhelming, like India itself. Jezmeen felt queasy looking at a placard displaying the bruised and bloodied faces of two village women who had been sentenced to a beating by a tribal court, for adultery. Next to their faces were images of Hindu goddesses, their faces covered in bruises and cuts to make them look like battered women – 'RESPECT ALL WOMEN THE SAME WAY' was scrawled across the top. The tall girl carrying the sign held it high so it could be seen beyond the crowd.

'And we have an international spokesperson here today. Polly Mishra, star of *The Boathouse* series in the UK, is here to tell us about how violence against women must stop.'

All heads turned to Jezmeen. Sneha was beckoning her to the stand. The crowd parted slightly to let her through. Her heart quickened for some reason. She never got nervous before auditions or experienced stage fright – just a squeeze of anxiety, which she quelled with promises of a drink afterwards. *Just behave yourself,* she told her gut, *and there will be rewards.* But she was nervous now. She realized that she hadn't spoken as herself in a very long time.

The crowd was silent as Jezmeen took the loudspeaker. What could she say? There was a sea of expectant faces but they seemed to know every-thing already – Sneha had given them the statistics and they lived it every day, didn't they? The teasing on the streets, the checking of their own outfits to see if they might be too arousing, the phone calls to their parents to let them know where they were, the clutching fear when they boarded a bus at night.

'Your experience is more valuable than my words would be,' Jezmeen began. 'You women do more battle just walking out your door in one day than I have to do in one year in London.' She shook her head. The words were not coming out the right way. It sounded a little bit like she was chastising them for not living in a place that was better for women.

The crowd seemed to shuffle with restlessness. Jezmeen could hear the car horns and vendors' shouts in the distance. 'When will it stop?' she asked. 'When do we decide it's enough? Do we keep shouting while the rest of India moves on? Do our words mean anything to all these people continu-ing their daily lives?' She made a great sweeping motion to include everyone.

Now they were interested. From where Jezmeen was standing, she noticed a ripple of excitement, as visible as an electric current, travelling through the crowd. The women holding signs straightened their arms to pitch them higher. Anjuli smiled and nodded.

'We're telling each other about the injustice, but we already know, don't we? We're living it,' Jezmeen said, her anger gathering momentum. 'Tell them!'

Heads began to turn. The women who started on the outer edges of the crowd were suddenly at its forefront – it was like those dreaded primary school games where everybody lined up and the one at the back was announced the leader. 'Tell them!' somebody shouted. 'Tell them!' This became the resounding chant of the protest, as the women turned their attention on the spectators. Tourists began to nervously put their cameras away and the clusters of people who had stopped in their tracks to watch the women were beginning to disperse. Only one group of onlookers remained rooted in place – men, very much like the ones that Jezmeen encountered on her walk to the station earlier. Scattered on the periphery of the protest, they were suddenly more visible than the rest of the crowd because of their stillness. She had not even noticed them when she and the women arrived, but of course, they were not organized. There was no counter-protest planned, but now that the women were turning towards them, they were afraid, and they found each other somehow.

First it was just a pair of men, who pointed at the women. A few more men joined in, jeering and calling out. They walked towards the crowd, chests puffed out, but their movements were slow and hesitant. The women outnumbered the men, and they knew it.

'Tell them!' One woman shouted, pumping her fist into the air. Jezmeen nodded and joined the chorus. The gaining momentum of this protest was exhilarating – her voice grew hoarse and her skin was slick with sweat but she didn't want to stop fighting.

'Tell them!' The girl holding the bruised goddess sign threw her arms high into the air. The images caught the attention of the men. Suddenly, they were walking faster and shouting louder. Jezmeen wasn't afraid until she noticed more men coming in from other directions. One of them pointed right at the sign, his cheeks red with fury.

Jezmeen couldn't understand the men's words because there was no unity in their response – they hadn't had time to prepare, after all. But later, she realized she was wrong. Of course they had time to prepare. For years now, women's protests had been taking place at India Gate and on message boards online, at dinner tables and college campuses. The responses on these men's faces, now full of rage that topped the fiery glares of the women, had been building up for years.

'Hey everyone!' Jezmeen shouted. She wanted to call for the crowd to calm down but then it surged like a wave, carrying her along with it. She tripped on another woman's leg and felt her blouse being grabbed, the fabric ripping loose. In the spaces between, she saw several men running up to the crowd, shouting – they were police officers. The angry mob of men didn't run away. They shouted and pointed to the women, who shouted back. To Jezmeen's shock, an officer raised his hand in a threat to hit one of the shouting girls. It was Anjuli, with bared teeth.

As the officers began working their way through the crowd, suddenly they were on top of Jezmeen. 'Wait,' she said. 'I'm a British citiz—' It was too late. The cops swooped in and led her away.

Oh my god. Oh my god.

Somebody was whispering those words. Jezmeen's shoulder throbbed from the forceful way the policemen had pinned down her arms and clapped the handcuffs on, even though she hadn't resisted. Her knees were trembling, and as the van jerked and lurched through the slow-flowing traffic, she felt her stomach churning. The van seemed filled beyond its capacity. Jezmeen could feel the humidity of other breaths all around her. The windows of the van were caged and criss-crossed with wires so Jezmeen had no sense of where they were, or how far they had gone from India Gate. Outside, it had been such a blindingly bright day, but this gauzy view threw the city into muted, frightening shadows.

Oh my god, oh my god.

If Jezmeen knew who was saying that, she'd try to assure her. You were exercising your right to free speech, there's nothing wrong with that. The police came racing in because they wanted to keep the conflict from getting out of hand. The men who wanted to start a riot were probably arrested as well. She didn't know if any of this was true, but she was too scared to consider the alternative.

A girl let out a loud, ragged sob when the van came to a final stop. Everybody heard it – Jezmeen sensed the heads turning, instinctively searching for the noise. The fear was palpable; without being able to see or know where exactly they were, they were terrified. They waited for a long time in the darkness of that van before the door rolled open and an officer barked at them to come out. Jezmeen struggled to scoot her way to the door, then crouch and negotiate the step without being able to grasp anything for balance. Once her feet touched the ground, she could feel the tremor in her knees. An officer called out and moments later, the black gates leading to the station yawned open.

The women were made to line up and then file into Tilak Marg Police Station, a low white-brick building that sat behind concrete barricades. Police officers in khaki uniforms and berets milled outside, their rifles slung casually across their waists. Jezmeen avoided eye contact with them, focusing instead on walking as steadily as possible.

Oh my god, oh my god.

Who was saying that? Jezmeen understood the sentiment: she felt as if somebody had pressed 'pause' on her day while she was addressing the crowd less than an hour ago, and hit 'play' on a nightmare instead. Had any of the women expected this?

In the station, things moved quickly. All the women lined up at the front desk and gave their names and details to an officer who recorded them by hand in a logbook. They were asked to surrender their possessions – purses, phones and jewellery – in large Ziploc bags which were passed down from the front of the line. Jezmeen got to the front of the line before she had to give up her phone. 'Am I able to call my consulate?' she asked. Even her voice sounded foreign to her here. 'I'm a British citizen.'

The officer looked up. He had thick eyebrows and a moustache that nearly covered his top lip. 'Name?' he asked.

'Jezmeen Shergill,' she said, her voice more level than she felt inside. She heard a ripple of murmurs from the women behind her as they realized she wasn't Polly Mishra.

'Quiet,' the officer called over Jezmeen's shoulder. 'Your passport?'

'I don't have it,' she said. 'It's back in my hotel. I've got a picture of it on my phone though.'

Static and muffled commands burst from the transistor radio on the officer's desk. He picked up his walkie-talkie and muttered something back. 'Could I just use my phone for a minute? I could get the picture from there.'

The officer nodded and returned to his call. Jezmeen took out her phone and went straight to her Contacts list. Rajni. She sent her a text in all caps:

'RAJ I'M IN JAIL NOT A JOKE SEND HELP PLEASE. TILAK MARG POLICE STATION. CALL CONSULATE.'

She pressed send and shot a look at the officer. He waved her over to one side and called up the next woman in line. Jezmeen found her passport page in an email she had sent to herself when she was applying for her Indian visa. She showed it to the officer, who took a long time scrutinizing the page and recording all the details before asking for the rest of her possessions to be placed in the Ziploc bag. Then he called out to another officer, who said, 'Come with me.'

Entering the hallway, Jezmeen felt the tremor in her legs again. Only when the officer told her to hurry up did she realize she was walking in tiny steps, as if afraid of what might be around the corner. *Oh my god, oh my god.* The officer showed her to a small room with a flat wooden bench. There were six more women in this room — all of the girls who had been in line before Jezmeen, and more to come. How would they possibly fit them all in here?

'You want to go to the toilet, you have to call for one of the female officers to bring you,' he said, perhaps noticing the way that Jezmeen was shifting her feet. She didn't have to go to the toilet though; she was trying to keep her legs from going numb with fear. 'Do you know how long—' She didn't get to finish her question before the officer turned his back and walked away.

Oh my god, oh my god.

Jezmeen realized that the voice was hers.

Once Shirina entered the air-conditioned café, she never wanted to leave. She was slightly embarrassed at how poorly she had taken to the heat this morning, to the sun beating down on her face and the sweat making her hair stick in curlicues to the back of her neck. She had been the one to suggest heading to the nearest shopping mall after their morning of watching the sunrise at India Gate. They didn't even make it far enough to get to the mall, stopping the driver once they spotted this café in a strip of upscale boutiques and restaurants of Khan Market.

'I want the most iced drink they have,' Rajni said, staring at the menu. 'In fact, I'd pay just to have a tall cup of ice to rub on my forehead.'

Shirina ordered a crushed-ice fruit drink and found a pair of plush armchairs by the window. Again, as she sank into the seat, she was so relieved to be sitting that she thought she might never rise again. She closed her eyes and saw patterns of light dancing around in the darkness.

At India Gate, she and Rajni had walked quietly among the early-bird tourists to find the best spot to catch the sun. They batted away the young boys who tried to sell them flimsy plastic toys and selfie sticks, and the ice-cream vendor who rattled off a list of flavours from a lopsided cart. Behind him stood the grand war memorial with the names of fallen soldiers inscribed into sandstone. There was an air of solemnity to the place, even as the city had already begun to stir. Mum had been right about the sunrise here being spectacular – the shifting hues of pink and orange, the wings of black kites swiftly crossing that canvas of changing light, the shimmering sun emerging triumphant despite the haze of the city. Shirina had thought of this item on the itinerary as Mum's simplest and easiest request but as she watched the day begin, she couldn't help thinking about Mum's last moments. Had she written this letter knowing that she would die before the sun came up the next day?

The coffee machine whirred behind the counter nearby. It was normal to feel depleted by the heat; in a way, the sun was a good thing – it gave Shirina an excuse to return to her air-conditioned hotel room, sink beneath the cool sheets, and do nothing for the rest of the day.

Rajni returned and set down her iced coffee on the table. Beads of condensation speckled the plastic cup and dripped onto the table's surface, forming a perfect ring. She took a sip from her straw and sighed, shutting her eyes. She looked the perfect picture of peace until she voiced her thoughts:

'I wonder what the hell Jezmeen is up to.'

Shirina had no doubt that Jezmeen had found her own way to occupy her time today. She didn't want to return to the subject of Jezmeen's truancy again. All the way in the taxi, Rajni had fumed. 'What is wrong with her?' she had asked, not looking for a response.

'Let's just forget about it,' Shirina said. For different reasons, she had been annoyed with Jezmeen as well. *She really should know better than to drink like that. It's disrespectful,* she'd said to Rajni, but she was over it now – the heat had compressed her anger into something small and manageable. This morning, Jezmeen's bloodshot eyes and the stench of stale wine on her breath had reminded Shirina of what her mother-in-law must have seen when she opened the door that night and found her slouched against the taxi driver. She was angry at Jezmeen for making the same mistake over and over again. Surely one time was enough? It was for Shirina.

There was a tapping sound on the glass window. Shirina turned to see a man dressed in slacks which were frayed at the hems and a dress shirt missing buttons. His skin was caked in soot. She met his eyes, two grey, watery pools, and turned away. Within moments, a barista hurried out to the pavement to shoo him away. Shirina watched him slowly shuffle to another shop entrance where a security guard held his palm up in a stern rejection. If he kept on wandering like this, trying his luck, he'd surely reach a place of some charity – a Sikh temple perhaps.

'Do you think they eventually get shooed away from the gurdwara if they keep showing up, day after day?' Shirina asked.

'That's not how it's supposed to be,' Rajni replied, watching the man as well. 'But I haven't noticed many beggars at the temple, even though the city's teeming with them.'

Inside and outside. The boundary between the temple and the rest of the world – and what was permissible in both spaces – had become a bit clearer to Shirina today. Yesterday, still under the fog of jet lag and fatigue, she hadn't noticed so much that people were kinder and gentler within the temple walls, more considerate under God's supervision. They fell into line and waited patiently for their food. They greeted each other with respectful nods. It was at India Gate this morning that she noticed all of these structures dissolving into the chaos of Delhi. Men roamed in hungry packs and whispered 'hello' in a way that made it sound like a threat. She and Rajni had held their bags in front of them, aware of how vulnerable they were to being snatched.

Shirina sipped her cool drink and watched well-heeled customers lining up at the counter, repeating their orders over the hissing milk steamer. There was a young couple sitting at the next table. Shirina knew they were newlyweds because the woman's forearm was nearly completely covered in glittering red bangles. Shirina wondered how she navigated Delhi's wobbling paths in those spiked heels and then realized that she probably never walked anywhere in them. Outside the café, where the begging man had been standing before, now there was a clear view of the car park and its rows of big, expensive cars.

The couple must have noticed Shirina staring – they stared back, and Shirina felt her face flushing with embarrassment. It wasn't her first time being caught looking at other couples; she often watched other men and women together and wondered if they were doing something that she and Sehaj should be doing. It was probably an arranged marriage thing, even though she and Sehaj had got to know each other online before setting the wedding date. There was some insecurity with wondering how to behave spontaneously. *Is this what couples do?* she wondered all the time, using other people as reference points. At one point, she became quite addicted to reruns of American sitcoms that featured meddling in-laws. She was relieved to make light of the petty arguments and the disparaging remarks about the daughter-in-law's cooking. In recent months, whenever Mother criticized her, Shirina was able to smile along to the laugh track that played in her mind.

Shirina looked away and took another long sip of her drink. The shock of the ice made her head throb. 'New bride,' Rajni said, nodding at the woman. 'I never wore mine.'

'Why not?' Shirina asked.

'They don't really go with a blazer and a pencil skirt.'

The bangles were incongruous with the woman's slick denim jeans and tight black tank top, but people here would understand that she was announcing her status as a new bride, rather than over-accessorizing. *People here would understand.* Shirina felt relief at that thought. It would be nice, not explaining her culture. 'I wore mine,' she said. 'All twenty-one days.' Each time somebody on the train or in the supermarket gave her a curious look for wearing such ornate jewellery with her everyday clothes, she wished they knew she had a reason for doing so.

Rajni looked surprised. 'Really?' She didn't ask why, but Shirina heard it anyway. She could practically see the question mark hanging in the air. It was the same when she told her sisters that she'd arranged her own marriage through a matrimonial website. *Why?* They itched to ask. How would she have explained wanting a new beginning – a definition of 'family' that was wholesome and content – without insulting them? She didn't really think she'd find what she was looking for so quickly, but once she registered and created her profile, she saw that there were abundant opportunities to become somebody new. From London to Bangkok to Nairobi to Wellington, there was the thrill of clicking on each potential husband, and the excitement of knowing that she was shaping her own fate. The thrill returned to her every time she saw her bangles.

'I was sad to take them off,' Shirina said. 'I could have worn them for much longer.'

'Mum was not pleased that I didn't wear mine,' Rajni said. 'She was also annoyed that my mehndi faded so quickly, because that's supposed to be bad luck.'

Shirina knew that superstition well from all the online discussions. If your mehndi faded quickly, you would have a cruel mother-in-law. Modern brides joked about it and posted pictures of their stained hands on the arranged marriage forum. *Very accurate – the woman can't stand my cooking,* one woman posted, with a picture of her faded hands. *Lemon, Sugar and Water!* was the title of that thread, inspired by the mixture that brides sprinkled on their hands to keep their mehndi colour strong.

'My mehndi stayed dark for a really long time,' Shirina said. She couldn't help feeling a bit proud. She didn't even have to use the lemon mixture.

'There are millions of these little sayings about your fate as a married woman,' Rajni said. 'I remember all this confusion over which foot I used to step into the house first, because it would determine the course of my relationship with my husband. First I stepped in with my right foot and half the room cried out that I was supposed to use my left. I switched to the left foot and the other half of the room said it was wrong.'

'What happens if you use the wrong foot?'

Rajni shrugged. 'Who knows? It's just one of those superstitions that doesn't mean anything. The happiness of a marriage isn't dictated by such arbitrary things. You would know. It's work.'

Since Shirina got engaged, she noticed that Rajni liked giving her marriage advice. It was one thing they finally had in common, and in Jezmeen's absence, they were free to discuss their husbands without making her feel left out. Sometimes she opened her emails to find links to articles recommended by Rajni in her inbox: *10 Things That Married Couples Should Say to Each Other* and *Secrets to a Happy Marriage – Advice from Three Couples Married Over 50 years*. Shirina usually skimmed them, then waited an appropriate amount of time so it would seem like she had paid close attention, and replied, 'This is great!' or 'Loved this – so true!'

'Believe me,' Rajni continued. 'When you've been married as long as I have, you'll understand. Do you remember that article I sent you about crazy things that couples can do to keep their marriage alive?'

'Yeah,' Shirina said. 'I think I stopped reading after wife-swapping came up.'

'That was one of the suggestions?' Rajni asked.

'Don't you read the articles you send me?'

'I read the first couple of tips. One of them was, "Don't talk to each other for forty-eight hours." A vow of silence, so you can appreciate each other without conversation.'

'How did that work for you?'

'I heard every other sound, and it drove me bananas. Kabir's breathing, his phone pinging with notifications. I think we were only four hours into the silence thing when I told him I'd had enough.'

Shirina forced a smile. She was all too familiar with the feeling of being encased in silence in her marriage. *Four hours? Try four days.*

'Well, I'm relieved that you weren't suggesting that Sehaj and I become swingers,' she said.

'Oh, don't be so quick to dismiss those wife-swapping parties,' Rajni said.

Shirina raised an eyebrow. Schoolteacher Rajni and accountant Kabir, a pair of swingers? She almost began to laugh at the thought, then she noticed Rajni peering over her drink, looking a bit offended. 'Sorry,' Shirina said. 'I knew there were parties like that in the Indian community in London, I just didn't really . . .'

'You didn't believe they were for real? Me neither,' Rajni said. 'Until I was invited to one.'

'Really? When? By whom?' Shirina couldn't contain her surprise. At the next table, the couple looked up sharply. She ducked out of their view.

'A friend,' Rajni said. 'Meenakshi – remember her from my wedding? Oh, you wouldn't, of course. You were so young. We're still good friends. Her younger daughter was born about two weeks after Anil. They used to have play dates together.' Rajni looked wistful. 'I thought Anil and Sahiba would make a fine couple one day.'

'There's still a chance,' Shirina said. Rajni cleared her throat. 'Hmm, yes,' she said, taking a sip of her drink. 'Anyway, Meenakshi was the one who told me about these holiday houses that Punjabi families book together over the summer. It all looks very innocent but in the evening, when the kids are all tucked away in bed, there's an agreement between the adults to exchange partners.'

It sounded very organized. Shirina wondered if there was a roster involved, or if everyone was just agreeable to moving from person to person like playing a game of musical chairs. 'Were you ever tempted?' Shirina asked. 'To see what it was like?'

Rajni shuddered. 'I couldn't imagine switching partners so casually and then going back to my husband after that. Surely the aftermath would be awkward? Not to mention seeing those other people in daylight again.'

'I would think so,' Shirina said.

'Meenakshi said it did wonders for her sex life though. I listened to her stories. They were pretty wild.' Rajni smiled. 'I'll admit, it made me a bit curious, because things had . . . stagnated a bit.'

'That's pretty normal though, isn't it?' Shirina asked. She was careful to sound casual.

'They say a sexless marriage is when you have it less than five times in a year,' Rajni said. 'We had it more times than that.'

Six? Ten? Rajni wasn't going to give an exact number of course, but Shirina could also picture her discovering the minimum number on a therapist's webpage and aiming to surpass it to break the threshold and be safe.

'Sexless marriage,' Shirina said. 'You're basically roommates then.' She measured the incredulity in her tone. *This is not something that would happen to me.*

'It's easy to go a while without it,' Rajni said. 'You're young newlyweds now, so it seems impossible, but life does get in the way. Plus we'd been trying for another child for years and it seemed like all the fun had gone out of it.'

'What did Kabir think of the suggestion?'

'He wasn't keen,' Rajni said. 'Neither was I. Meenakshi didn't mention it again. I think she was a little embarrassed afterwards. I suppose she was quite convinced that I'd say yes. But you wouldn't believe who brought it up again.'

'Who?' Shirina asked.

'Mum,' Rajni said.

'No,' Shirina said firmly. 'Now you're just making things up.'

'I wish I was. I'm serious. Mum told me to look into it.'

'How would Mum even know about these things?'

'That was my first question too,' Rajni said. 'It turned out that she only had a vague idea of what went on, but somebody had told her that there were parties in East London that married couples credited for spicing up their love lives.'

'She didn't know what they actually did?' Shirina asked.

'Not really,' Rajni said. 'Sometimes I wonder if she thought it was a big prayer circle. All these couples just sitting around and wishing for the spark to reignite.'

Shirina laughed at the image. There was a contemplative look on Rajni's face. 'We quarrelled over it,' she recalled.

'You and Kabir?'

'Me and Mum. I was annoyed with her for suggesting that we needed help. I only confided that we weren't having much sex any more because she wouldn't stop pestering me about having another child. Another son, I should say. Mum had this recipe for some vile concoction of fenugreek tea mixed with soaked dates and herbs. She swore by it, and even said I was more likely to conceive a boy that way. Obviously it didn't quite work for her.'

'Really?' Shirina asked. Rajni raised her eyes to hers, so she quickly followed up with, 'How did the argument end then? Did Mum just give up talking about it?'

'It took her a while. I decided to focus on my career to take my mind off it all, but when I told her I was going for a principal-track position, she said, "Your family isn't complete yet. Don't wait too long or there will be a big gap between Anil and his sibling," like I wasn't aware of how weird it was to be an adult and have a younger sister in primary school.'

Rajni's face was flushed, as if she was still in the throes of the argument. It was strange seeing her so worked up about Mum, when that was usually Jezmeen's department. Shirina could only remember Jezmeen's constant fights with Mum – everything had to be challenged, from curfews to what subjects she took in school to how much she wanted to spend at the hair salon. Shirina always situated herself at the periphery of those memories because that was how it was – Shirina at the edge of the room, keeping her distance from conflict, Shirina finding something else to do so she wouldn't get embroiled in a battle of wills between Jezmeen and Mum or Jezmeen and Rajni. The fact of her existence always made her guilty. Mum and Dad had wanted a boy. Shirina had been their last-ditch attempt at having a son. This, Shirina knew because Mum had told her. 'We didn't *need* another girl, but God decides these things.' In Mum's voice, the unmistakable sadness at God's plans for her family.

'So how did things get better then? With you and Kabir?' Shirina asked.

'They just sort of picked back up again once we stopped trying so hard. The doctor told us there wouldn't be any more children and it more or less lifted the pressure.'

'Mum never really talked to me about sex,' Shirina said. It seemed that by the time Shirina became a teenager, Mum had run out of steam. It was as if she had loaded all her advice onto the eldest and hoped it would trickle down somehow. Some things worked in this way – Shirina didn't have to question issues like curfews and the proper ways to dress and talk; the examples were laid out for her in what Rajni did to please Mum and what Jezmeen did to rebel. The only time Mum alluded to sex was to tell Shirina that she should have children sooner rather than later. 'Have sons,' she'd said, perhaps knowing what Shirina's mother-in-law was like.

'It was the first time she was really open with me,' Rajni said. 'I was surprised but I also didn't want to continue the conversation much further. She started going into that whole yarn about "keeping your husband interested, otherwise you'll lose him," and it put me off the conversation totally. It's not all up to us, is it? I had a job and a son to raise and here's Mum telling me I have to be a sex goddess as well, or I'd risk my husband leaving me. It was so old-fashioned.'

Shirina felt a familiar urge to defend Mum's values. She had done the same whenever she and Lauren from work discussed their personal lives. 'My mother-in-law thinks I should grow my hair out a bit more,' Shirina once told her. The response was a raised eyebrow. 'Do *you* want to grow your hair out?' Lauren had asked. 'Of course *I* want to grow it out as well,' Shirina had replied. Lauren did not look convinced. There were many conversations like this, Lauren's tone growing more exasperated and patronizing. Shirina decided not to tell Lauren she was quitting until she handed in her notice and word got around. 'Is she making you quit?' Lauren asked, cornering Shirina in the break room. Her voice was full of concern but Shirina didn't want to hear it. She didn't need to be rescued. She had written the resignation letter herself, providing no explanations because the Laurens of the world would never understand.

'Do you think Mum would have had an easier time if she had sons?' Shirina asked. 'Do you think she would have been happier?'

The question seemed to pain Rajni. She looked out the window and didn't answer Shirina's question.

Silence fell between them and the roar of the coffee grinder filled the gap. Shirina wondered if she should offer up some detail of her own married life to complete the exchange, but what could she share? She and Sehaj hadn't touched each other in a while but their circumstances were complicated, not that there was any need to talk about her married life with anybody, even her sisters. Especially her sisters.

Rajni looked as if she was about to say something when she suddenly jolted a bit in her seat and looked into her bag. She put her coffee down and picked up her phone. A moment passed and then she gasped and showed Shirina her screen. Before Shirina could read the message, Rajni said: 'It's Jezmeen. She's been arrested.'

Chapter Seven

Please look out for each other in Delhi. It's a busy city, and female travellers have to be more careful. Keep your eye on your belongings all the time, and don't draw too much attention to yourselves.

The police station was humming with activity when Rajni and Shirina arrived. They were shuttled through various checkpoints and patted down by female officers behind curtains to protect their modesty, before being led to a waiting room. Fluorescent lamps flickered on the ceiling even though there was still plenty of daylight outside, but there were no windows here. The air was sticky and the floor felt grimy under Rajni's sandals.

She dialled the British consulate phone number again. At this point, she could practically recite the list of pre-recorded menu options. *For opening hours, press 1. For visa status, press 2. For travel advisories and warnings, press 3.* There was no specific option for bailing family members out of Indian jails. She tried again to press 4 for 'urgent assistance', but the phone rang for a minute before disconnecting.

'I'm going to kill her,' Rajni muttered, tossing her phone into her bag. Shirina gave her hand a squeeze. *No, you're not,* she was probably thinking, but the rage Rajni felt in her fingertips was stronger than anybody realized. She didn't know exactly what Jezmeen had done to get arrested, but Rajni was certain that it was avoidable. Deliberate. Of course Jezmeen would

107

sabotage this trip. From the start, this had been her mission. She wasn't interested in the pilgrimage, in honouring Mum – why would she be? All she cared about was herself and settling scores. As these thoughts charged through Rajni's mind, she could see them hashing it out right there in the police station. *You think I want to be here?* Rajni wanted to scream. *You think I wouldn't rather be at home dealing with my own family's crisis instead of fighting with you on a tour across Northern India?*

A uniformed officer sat slouched at a desk near the entrance of the waiting room, the buttons of his shirt about to pop from the strain of his burgeoning belly. He flipped through files listlessly and called a few names. When nobody responded, he shut his file, picked up an empty glass mug and disappeared into the back room.

'Lovely,' Rajni said to Shirina. 'We're going to have to wait till chai break is finished.'

'It could be a while,' Shirina said, nodding to the door. More people were pouring in and crowding their space. Was there any place in India that wasn't teeming with people? Rajni had a new appreciation for the spacious hall of the gurdwara yesterday, and the wide boulevard they had walked along this morning. She wondered what Jezmeen's jail cell was like, and she felt an acute pang of fear for her sister, packed with strangers in a cramped and dimly lit room. Rajni's only point of reference for the image was those news documentaries that aired on TV back home about naïve British holidaymakers trapped in some drug or human trafficking ring and jailed in unimaginable conditions in Cambodia or Nigeria. She did not think she'd have the stamina to be like their families, shuttling back and forth to visit their incarcerated children and attend their court hearings. With a renewed sense of urgency, Rajni took her phone out of her purse and tried the consulate again. As she sat through the menu options once more, the officer returned with a steaming cup of tea and a spring in his step. He picked up a fresh stack of folders, and called out a few names. There weren't many parents here, Rajni noticed. Only one silver-haired man wearing a pressed suit and expensive-looking leather shoes stepped up to the desk. He and the officer exchanged a few grave words and then he was given a stack of forms to complete. Rajni groaned. Forms, more forms. They would be doing endless paperwork until it was time to return to England. The phone continued to ring.

'Jezmeen Shergill?' the officer called.

'Yes,' Rajni said, leaping from her seat with surprise like she'd just won a bingo tournament. Shirina followed her. 'We're here for Jezmeen Shergill. Is she alright? Where is she?'

The officer was busy reading from his file. 'You are the closest relative?'

'I'm her sister. We're here on holiday – from England,' Rajni said. The phone had rung out again. If the consulate wasn't going to answer her calls, then maybe she should just start announcing her citizenship and seeing if it had any clout. 'We're British citizens,' Rajni said. The officer did not look impressed but he did make some notes in his file. Then he picked up his glass and took a long, deliberate sip.

'Do you think . . .' Rajni whispered to Shirina. 'Do you think he wants some – you know?'

Shirina's expression was blank. She clearly did not know what Rajni was hinting at.

'How much do you think he's after?' Rajni tried again. 'You know, like, money. A B.R.I.B.E.'

The officer cast them a sidelong glance.

'He can spell, Rajni,' Shirina said.

'Right,' Rajni said. 'Shit.'

'Also, I don't think it works like that,' Shirina whispered back. 'I don't think anybody asks for money in these situations. You just sort of . . . work it out.'

'Sure, but there's a ballpark figure, isn't there?'

'You mean like a market rate?' Shirina asked. 'How am I supposed to know what that would be?'

Clearly, they were already terrible at this. Rajni didn't even have that much money in her purse. She'd have to negotiate slyly and then run out to an ATM machine. That wasn't right, was it? In the movies, everybody just slickly slipped money into each other's palms. Or was that just for valets so they didn't ding up your car?

'Can you tell me what she's been charged with?' Rajni asked the officer. 'Please?'

The officer squinted at his files. It was unclear whether he'd heard her. Rajni was about to ask again, when she felt somebody tapping on her shoulder. She turned to see the silver-haired man. 'It's better not to ask too many questions. You'll agitate them,' he said gently.

'It's just – we have no information, and we're here on holiday and . . .' Rajni felt the tears building up. *Mum's going to kill me,* she used to think every time Jezmeen got into trouble. She could picture Mum right now, arms crossed over her chest and shaking her head, asking, 'Why weren't you watching her?'

'Let me ask,' the man said. As he leaned towards the officer, Rajni wondered why it made any difference when he asked the same question, but the officer seemed to bend to his authority. It was either because he was a man or because he was the type of man who wore expensive leather shoes. They chatted in such low voices that Rajni wasn't able to catch everything that they said but at one point, the officer nearly cracked a smile.

The man turned to Rajni. She noticed the crinkles at the corners of his eyes were like Kabir's. 'It seems that your sister was rounded up with the same group that my daughter was in. The protest at India Gate.'

'A protest?' Shirina asked. She and Rajni exchanged a look. It sounded like a mistake. 'What kind of protest?'

'A women's rights march,' the man said. 'It got violent, and the police did a sweeping arrest of protestors that she got caught up in.'

'How violent?' Rajni asked.

'I don't know,' the man said. Then he dropped his voice to a whisper. 'I'm sure it was nothing serious, just a scuffle. The police use these scare tactics sometimes to deter the girls from protesting again.'

'Do they work?'

'You tell me,' the man said. 'It's my third visit to a station to get Parvana out of trouble this year.'

'Oh.' Rajni didn't know what to say. She was caught between extending her sympathies for having such a troublesome daughter and wanting to commend him for remaining so calm.

The officer handed over a clipboard of forms. 'Have a seat,' the man said, gesturing at an empty spot on the bench. 'My name is Hari, by the way.'

They all shook hands and introduced themselves. 'She's going to be okay, right?' Rajni asked. 'She's not going to stay here?'

'What did she tell you over the phone?' Hari asked.

'It wasn't a call but a text,' Rajni said. 'All it said was where she was being held.'

'Unfortunately, there isn't much they can tell us either. It's a waiting game.'

Looking up from her forms, Rajni stared at the door, trying to imagine what was beyond it. A row of jail cells with iron bars, and Jezmeen crammed in with the other women she was rounded up with?

'She'll be fine,' Shirina said, as if reading Rajni's thoughts. 'Of all three of us, Jezmeen's the most likely to survive a situation like this.'

Shirina looked like she needed some comforting herself. She looked very tired and on the way here, she had asked the driver to pull over because she needed to throw up. The driver had pulled over and the nausea abated. 'Probably something I ate,' Shirina had said weakly. Now sweat plastered her hair to her forehead and her eyes were bloodshot. The lack of ventilation in this room wasn't helping. The air here was stale and it smelled of sweat.

Rajni was sure she remembered this police station – the smells, the sounds, the fear. She remembered flickering lights, the beady-eyed officers, and the suffocating feeling of being in the wrong place. Of course, she knew it was unlikely that this was the same station she had walked into all those years ago. There were many other stations in Delhi. But the panic that was rising in her throat, that sense of feeling trapped and desperate to get home, of wanting but being unable to leave, made her feel like a teenager again.

To distract herself, Rajni concentrated on filling in the forms as quickly as possible. Next to her Hari took his glasses off. He pinched the bridge of his nose and shut his eyes. 'Are you alright?' she asked him, her pen still going rapidly.

'I just don't know when this will stop,' he said. 'My daughter – she's a college student. She gets so fired up that she puts herself in all kinds of danger.'

'My sister is like that too, except she's old enough to know better,' Rajni said.

'How old is she?'

'Thirty-two,' Rajni said. She put her pen down and looked at Hari. 'She's well past the age where I should be called upon to bail her out of trouble.'

'So it doesn't stop then?' Hari asked, a smile curling at the edges of his lips.

'You tell me,' Rajni said. 'I have a son entering university this year.' Yes, in some alternate reality, Anil was going to do exactly what she wanted. Rajni could only deal with one catastrophe at a time, so for the purposes of this conversation, she was not going to be a grandmother in a few months. 'I can't believe you've done this more than once,' she said to Hari.

'Last time, I vowed that I wouldn't. I told Parvana she'd have to find her own way out. But when she called to tell me where she was . . .' he sighed. 'There are all-women police stations, you know. I knew this wasn't one of them. I couldn't just leave her here, no matter how angry I was.'

Rajni looked around. The clicking of computer keys. The ringing of phones. The creaking fan mounted on the wall like a hunter's prize, slowly turning as if surveying the room and finding it very disappointing.

'No, I couldn't either,' she admitted. 'I could punch Jezmeen though.'

Shirina looked up sharply. Rajni immediately felt guilty for saying this. She had hit Jezmeen in the hospital that day, just before Mum died. She flexed her fingers and thought about how the feeling in her knuckles went numb after she'd hit Jezmeen, and she had wondered if it was a physical or emotional reaction.

'Have you tried calling your consulate?' Hari asked.

'Didn't get an answer,' Rajni said.

'Must be lots of Britons causing trouble in India today then,' he said.

'We're a rowdy lot,' Rajni quipped.

'Not my impression at all,' Hari said. 'Except when the football is on.'

'Thank you for doing this,' Rajni said. 'You really don't need to be comforting me when your daughter's in the same situation.'

Hari shrugged. 'It's not a situation that you share with many people. When Parvana was younger and got into trouble in school, my wife refused to talk to the other parents in the principal's office. She insisted that we weren't like them.'

Rajni nodded. 'I know that feeling.' She remembered seeing the bruise on Jezmeen's cheek at Mum's funeral and thinking with outrage: Who did that to my little sister? Before remembering that it was her.

A fresh worry struck Rajni now. 'So if this isn't an all-women's station . . . ?'

'There aren't men in the cells,' Hari said.

'But the officers?' *Do you know what could have happened to you?* Mum had shouted at Rajni. How naïve she was, to think that she could walk into a police station in the middle of the night, a teenage girl with teased hair and heavy make-up, and assume she would be safe. Her other option was to keep walking on the street though, and that was far more dangerous. What hurt most was Mum's fury. Rajni was trembling when she finally came home, and Mum had no words of comfort for her, only anger. That was the only reason Rajni had shouted back. It happened in a blink, and everything changed.

'You can think about all the possibilities,' Hari said gently. 'But they'll just drive you mad with worry. As of now, we know she's getting out in a few hours and we can only hope they won't change their minds. Let's just focus on that.' Rajni stared at him, unable to stop worrying. 'Breathe,' he said. 'I'm stepping out for a cigarette break, and then I'll try to talk to the officers again.'

Rajni swallowed and nodded. She shut her eyes and tried to picture a soothing landscape. She had taken an anxiety seminar once, and found the mindfulness and meditation chants only useful for as long as it took her to start making lists of how many minutes she was going to be mindful every day, because it wasn't that difficult, and it could change her brain chemistry. Then she piled on a new exercise routine and general tips on being a better person, and soon, she was overwhelmed by all her self-improvement plans and not being mindful at all, which led to more anxiety.

She opened her eyes and noticed that Shirina's eyes were closed. She was taking in deep breaths, but they didn't seem meditative. 'Are you okay?' she asked.

Shirina kept her eyes shut and nodded. 'Just my stomach again,' she said. There was a sheen of sweat on her face and her cheeks were flushed. Rajni looked up at the slow wall-mounted fan as it turned its head towards them. 'You might need some air,' she said. She felt bad for taking Shirina along with her now, but she had been afraid to go to the police station alone.

'I'll be fine,' Shirina said. She opened her eyes. The smile she gave Rajni was strained. Once again, Rajni found herself wondering what was going on with Shirina. Food poisoning and jet lag aside, she seemed troubled since she arrived in India. *I don't have to worry about you too, do I?* Rajni didn't have the capacity to take on another sister's problems, not right now anyway. She told herself she'd get to it later.

Rajni looked around. Without Hari, she felt even more vulnerable. The station was full of men – visitors, officers. The few women among them were on the sidelines like Rajni and Shirina. The officer at the front desk had only listened when Hari spoke.

'Should I cancel our train tickets for tomorrow? The hotel booking in Amritsar?' Rajni asked. 'Should we just call off the whole thing and go back to England once Jezmeen's released? Why are we here? What the hell are we doing?'

She realized she sounded a bit hysterical. The police officer behind the desk shot her a look, and then began rummaging through his files. Shirina looked nervous. *Breathe . . .*

Rajni closed her eyes and immediately saw Mum. It was impossible not to think of her now, in this place. Mum was sitting on her hospital bed, her face screwed in concentration as another wave of pain coursed through her body. Rajni tried to shake away the image – she was supposed to focus on calming thoughts – but Mum stubbornly remained. Her face looked younger and she had fewer white hairs. Rajni tried to cast her mind's eye to the window – maybe there was a view of some soothing greenery – but Mum moved with her. Even when Rajni pictured an empty white room, there was the younger version of Mum. She was packing their suitcases for a trip to India, to bring some sense into her eldest daughter. No nightclubs, no cigarettes, no bad influences. Just three weeks of learning about her culture and spending time with family. Mum was determined that Rajni would return to London a good girl.

'Raj,' Shirina said, nudging her in the ribs.

Her eyes flew open. As if Rajni had conjured Jezmeen, there she was, framed by the doorway behind the officer's desk. The officer who had looked up at Rajni was standing next to Jezmeen. She didn't see them waving at her. She was led to the front desk and given some forms to sign. Rajni watched as Jezmeen gave them a quick glance before scrawling her signature. Her gaze roamed the room until it rested on Rajni, on her feet. Just before Jezmeen walked out to greet them, Rajni felt the numbness returning to her knuckles and she fought to press her arms to her sides. She could easily punch her sister again. *What the hell were you thinking?* Mum had shouted at Rajni all those years ago, and Rajni, still terrified, had said something she would never be able to take back.

Chapter Eight

Day Four: Delhi to Amritsar

This journey will take you from India's capital city to Punjab, our ancestral state. Look out the windows and take in the landscape. Listen to the conversations around you. Watch people rejoicing as they rush to meet their relatives on the platforms of those smaller stops along the way. There's no greater show of love and faith than travelling a long distance for somebody.

The journey from Delhi to Amritsar was supposed to start and end with food. This was how Mum had always described the train rides to Punjab, and although Jezmeen had never taken the trip herself, her memory had absorbed Mum's stories so they became her own foggy recollections. She had images of an endless supply of pakoras and samosas, the paper cups of steaming-hot tea and the flat squares of Indian sweets.

They were pulling out of the station now. She looked out the window as the train picked up pace. Beyond the tracks, the sun burned fiercely, its image wavering behind the train's fumes. Mothers ushered their children ahead of them on a slow walk along the tracks. Mountains of garbage glittered behind clusters of boxy houses that appeared like Lego structures, extensions jammed together, jutting out. The train's pace picked up as the landscape widened before them. Once they had moved beyond the outskirts of Delhi, the greenery became more consistent, the houses further apart. Jezmeen stared at one home, painted bright orange and with a satellite dish sitting on the rooftop like a trophy, and she had a longing to be inert, lazing the day away instead of hurtling towards their history.

What a relief it was to be leaving Delhi. Just the movement of the train made Jezmeen grateful that she was out of that jail cell, even though her time spent there had been mercifully short. Last night, she had hardly slept. She kept replaying the moment of her arrest over in her mind, still shocked at what had transpired. In the early hours of the morning, she went into the bathroom with the intention of taking a shower but the sight of the small space made her remember the cell crammed with bodies, and she returned to bed.

Her stomach growled. She hadn't eaten breakfast – they had had to check out of the hotel too early to make their way to the train station, and although she had been tempted to stop at a roadside stall to get some fresh pani puris, a death glare from Rajni had silenced her. Jezmeen sneaked a look at her now. She was staring straight ahead and hadn't said anything to Jezmeen since her release. Not a word. *Don't you want to know if I'm okay?* Jezmeen was tempted to ask. She had felt very sorry for herself sitting in that jail cell, though she counted herself among the fortunate ones who hadn't been hauled off for questioning. The police eventually realized that the cell was overcrowded even with those women taken away, and they began releasing the ones who hadn't been directly involved in the organizing. Jezmeen was certain she would be there for ages but they let her go early. Her passport might have had something to do with it; also the fact that some of the women in the cell still thought she was Polly Mishra and kept referring to her as such, to the intrigue of passing officers. The women who learned Jezmeen's real identity simply ignored her, their thoughts probably too occupied with their current crisis.

Rajni's terse silence had followed them back to the hotel, where Jezmeen attempted to explain herself. 'I didn't—' She got that much out before Rajni raised her hand like a wall. 'I don't want to hear it,' she said. 'Let's just get the rest of this trip over with and then we can go back to our lives.' Her anger vibrated through her like an electric current and her fists were clenched at her sides.

The stretches of lush green land were becoming longer. Untamed stalks of grass rustled in the morning breeze, and on the dusty horizon, Jezmeen could see the sun hovering over a small hill of trees. The windows rattled as another train passed in the opposite direction. Cattle-class passengers clung to the railings in the open entrances. Jezmeen wondered what became of the other girls who had been arrested with her. Who could she ask? What could she do about it anyway? Her empty stomach made a mournful moan.

'Do you know if she booked our tickets with a meal service?' Jezmeen whispered to Shirina, careful that Rajni didn't hear.

'I expect so,' Shirina said. 'It's an eight-hour journey.'

In the seat in front of Shirina, a toddler was standing and peering at them through sweeping black lashes. 'What a cutie,' Jezmeen said with a smile. The toddler grinned back. Jezmeen waved with both her hands. The toddler clapped and disappeared behind her seat only to pop up again, this time trying to get Shirina's attention.

'Hello darling,' Rajni said from her seat near the window, but the toddler paid her no mind. 'Didi,' she said to Shirina, addressing her as 'sister', stretching out her arms to touch her. She appeared to be attracted to the bright-pink tunic which brought out a glow in Shirina's cheeks. 'She likes you,' Jezmeen remarked.

Shirina looked up from her book only briefly before returning to it. Not a terrible strategy, Jezmeen decided. As cute as the little girl was, there was a limit to how much amusement she could reasonably provide for eight hours. She pulled a few funny faces and then ignored the little girl, who found another passenger to amuse her soon enough.

The smell of deep-fried onion bhajis drifted down the aisle and made Jezmeen's mouth water. She craned her neck, expecting to see a food cart being pushed down the aisle, but the smell was coming from the seats ahead of them. Several generations of one family were travelling in the same carriage as them, and they had begun unpacking their snacks.

A flask of tea was passed around. Somebody split open a samosa and the steam unfurled in the air, carrying the smell of spiced potatoes to Jezmeen's nostrils.

She had a strong memory then, of being young and sitting on a kitchen stool while Mum bustled about. Mustard seeds popped and crackled in sizzling oil in the frying pan and the stove-top kettle whistled. Mum's expression was far from the serene look of Indian housewives in the drama series – her eyes were pained and her skin taut with worry. Jezmeen had just asked her to take her and Shirina shopping. *We need new socks,* she'd said, snapping the loose elastic on her socks to prove her point. *Your socks are fine,* Mum had said, refusing to look at them. Jezmeen took a closer look at the family occupying all those rows ahead of them. The men were loud and their presence most obvious, standing in the aisles and hollering out to each other. The women talked while juggling their children, their conversation often interrupted by the laughs and calls of their husbands and brothers.

The meal service, when it finally arrived, was a disappointing contrast to the abundant home-cooked fare of the extended family – two soggy potato fritters and a Tetra-pack of lassi – but Jezmeen devoured it. Yesterday, fear had cancelled her appetite. She believed that she might languish in an Indian jail cell forever.

Shirina hadn't touched her meal. She looked a bit repulsed by it. The toddler was slowly rising again, this time with a floppy-eared stuffed bunny as an offering.

'Are you going to eat yours?' Jezmeen asked. Shirina shook her head and pushed the tray to Jezmeen. She tore through the meal gratefully.

One of the men in the family was telling a joke. Jezmeen didn't catch the whole thing, but the punchline only elicited a few weak laughs. 'Oh, come on,' he thundered. 'Don't you all get it?'

'We get it. It's just a lame joke,' a woman replied. There was more laughter at this, and a few claps.

The man grinned. 'Darling, when we were engaged, you always laughed at my jokes.'

A few members of the family began to hoot. 'Calm down, we're in a public place,' shouted another man, who didn't seem to think that shouting in public was inappropriate.

'It's a different thing, *nah*, being engaged and being married?' countered another woman. 'After marriage, you hear the same jokes, over and over again. They stop being funny.'

'It's a good thing we're headed to the village then,' called the first man. 'I can always exchange you for another wife.'

The women's scoffing and eye-rolling responses showed their disapproval but they said nothing and returned to their circle for conversation.

'Didi?' the little girl pleaded. She waved her bunny. Shirina folded the page of her book into a corner and shut it. With one hand, she tugged the bunny's ears. The toddler giggled and yanked back her toy.

Jezmeen looked over at Rajni, who was staring out the window. Open fields and paddies came into view. The train crossed over a lake that ran like a bright vein through the yellow-green grassland. Jezmeen wished she had had the chance to come to India during her childhood. Imagine summers spent journeying with extended family members, sharing histories over pakoras while the train brought them to their origins. The carriage shuddered against the steel surface of the bridge and the family's laughter exploded, amplifying the sisters' own silence. The little girl giggled as her mother pulled her back into her seat. 'You'll fall, darling,' she said. 'Don't bother other people.' Through the gap between the seats, she flashed an apologetic smile at Shirina.

Jezmeen couldn't take the quiet any more. This was not how they did things. Rajni's eyes were shut and she was taking deep, long breaths. As she let out a breath, she looked like a deflating balloon. Jezmeen reached out and jabbed her hard in the arm.

'OUCH. What the hell, Jezmeen?'

'I have a few things to say to you.'

Shirina, sandwiched between them, pressed her back against her chair.

'I'm busy at the moment,' Rajni said.

'Doing what? You're sitting on a train, literally doing nothing. I can see you.'

'I'm practising mindful breathing,' Rajni said. 'Or I was, until you rudely interrupted me. Now I have to start again.'

'If you can't multitask breathing with conversation, you're doing something wrong,' Jezmeen informed Rajni.

'I'm not getting into another argument with you about mindfulness, the benefits of which are evidenced in multiple studies – OUCH. STOP PINCHING ME.'

'Shirina, exchange seats with me,' Jezmeen ordered. 'Rajni and I have some things to sort out.'

'No, stay where you are,' Rajni said, pinning Shirina's wrist to the armrest as if she might fly off otherwise. 'Jezmeen, if you want to talk, I'm sorry, I'm just not ready yet.' She shut her eyes and went back to breathing in and out. Jezmeen could tell from the way her face was squeezed that her mind was certainly not clear of angry thoughts. She waited until Rajni let out a long exhalation.

'It wasn't my fault,' Jezmeen said.

Rajni rolled her eyes. 'Sure, it wasn't.'

'The protest just happened. I was walking around Karol Bagh and I got on the Metro to join you two at India Gate—'

'You were supposed to be at India Gate with us from the beginning.'

'Sure, but that's a different argument altogether,' Jezmeen said. And not one she was keen on having. Nobody needed to tell her that she overdid the drinking occasionally – she was aware of it and wasn't that the first step? She was planning on taking more control over her impulses. Eventually, when she had the time, space and wherewithal. A trip across India involved too many variables without adding a sobriety challenge to the mix.

'If we came here to find ourselves—' Jezmeen began, not quite knowing where her argument would end up. She wanted Rajni to know that being arrested had frightened her. Although she was acting nonchalant about the whole thing now, she hadn't been able to sleep last night, and the thought of that cell still made her stomach turn. But that didn't mean she had been wrong to go to the women's march in the first place.

'We came here to remember Mum and to do service,' Rajni said.

'Isn't protesting a service? Fighting for women's rights? Did you know that there are women in the villages whose husbands share them with their brothers because female infanticide has resulted in an alarmingly low ratio of women to men?'

This got Shirina's attention. She looked up at Jezmeen, alarmed. 'It's true,' Jezmeen continued. 'It's something like six men to one woman in some of the poorer states here. It's disgraceful.'

Annoyance twitched across Rajni's features. 'Trouble just seems to find you, doesn't it? Since the day we started this trip, you've been sabotaging it.'

'I have not.'

'You have. You've been contrary from the beginning. Even Shirina agrees with me.'

Jezmeen stared at Shirina. 'Is this true?' she demanded. Shirina squirmed in her seat. 'Is it?' Jezmeen asked.

'I think you could have avoided drinking that much if you knew it was going to make it difficult for you to wake up the next day, that's all. I made a passing remark to Rajni on our way to the temple. I didn't say "contrary",' Shirina said defensively.

'Well, nobody says "contrary" unless they're over seventy,' Jezmeen said. To Rajni's credit, she let the comment slide. 'But I don't understand why you think I'm sabotaging the trip. Shirina's the one who's not even coming along to the last half of it. Somehow that's acceptable? While we're making an arduous trek up a mountain and sleeping on straw mats, she's going to be eating sweets and receiving newlywed gifts from her in-laws' extended family in the village. She'll probably even have WiFi access. That's not very fair, Shirina.'

'I'm sorry you feel that way,' Shirina said.

Jezmeen groaned. For once, it would be nice if Shirina didn't defuse every argument. It was so unsatisfying. From the corner of her eye, she noticed the toddler's head popping up again.

'Yes, darling? Yes?' Rajni cooed, beaming. 'What's that you've got there? Hmm?' The girl was dangling something else over the seat. It was a bright-yellow Tupperware container plastered in Peppa Pig stickers. 'Can I have this?' Rajni asked. The girl smiled and trained her eyes on Shirina. She shook the container at her.

Shirina didn't acknowledge the girl. She looked down at her book, fiercely concentrating until the girl lost interest and disappeared into her seat again. It was strange – the sight of the girl seemed to really bother Shirina. Jezmeen noticed that Shirina hadn't gone past the first page of her book.

Then Shirina turned to Jezmeen. 'I never said you were trying to sabotage the trip, but when we went to your hotel room yesterday and you were drunk, I was very disappointed.' Her lips were a thin line. Jezmeen stared at Shirina, speechless. This voice coming from Shirina, it didn't even sound like her. Even Rajni looked surprised. 'What's so difficult about stopping after a glass or two? Hmm? It's what people do. Normal people have limits. They know how to behave.'

'Shirina—' Rajni began.

'Don't drag me into your arguments when you want somebody to take your side,' Shirina continued. 'I won't be a part of that.'

'Okay, okay,' Rajni said.

'And I won't be lectured about family obligations,' Shirina said. 'Not by my two older sisters, who got into a fistfight at our mother's deathbed. Does it ever occur to you that the last thing she witnessed before dying was the two of you bickering, as always? Maybe she died that night because she had nothing else to hang around for, if you couldn't even put aside your differences for one day. Nothing changed, even after Mum died.'

Jezmeen was stunned. She looked at Rajni, whose expression matched hers. If this was what Shirina really thought, how long had she been holding onto her anger?

Had the train carriage gone quieter since their heated exchange began? It seemed that the family at the front had stopped talking. The air was taut with anticipation. Jezmeen shrank in her seat, worried that somebody might have had their mobile phone camera out. The last thing she needed was another YouTube upload: *Jezmeen Shergill in row with sisters on a train in India!*

The toddler popped up again but her mother quickly dragged her down, whispering urgently to her, '*Leave them alone.*' Immediately, the little girl began to cry. 'Didi,' she sobbed. 'Didi!' Jezmeen was surprised by the tears that sprang into her own eyes.

When the train finally pulled into the station, Shirina was ready to get up and go. They had spent the remaining eight or so hours of the journey only exchanging cursory words, choosing to entertain themselves. For Shirina, this meant reading her book, although her mind didn't absorb much and she ended up drifting off to sleep. She had fragmented dreams about Mum sitting up in her bed, alert to the scuffle between her two older daughters outside her room. In the dreams, Mum got out of bed and pleaded with them to stop. As a warning, she shook her jewellery case at them, but they ignored her. Shirina had never told anybody before that she blamed Rajni and Jezmeen for the way Mum's final moments played out. Even Sehaj didn't know what actually happened – he was just aware that Shirina was more eager than ever to start a family with him after she returned from London. When the test showed up negative a few weeks later, the disappointment felt unlike anything Shirina had experienced before – heavy and hollow at the same time. She was still grieving over Mum, so the hot tears that flooded down her cheeks didn't surprise Sehaj. He reminded her that it could take a few tries, that they were still young and had plenty of time. But Shirina felt let down, and wished she could talk to somebody who knew this feeling. Ironically, Rajni was the only person who would understand but Shirina was still too upset about what happened at the hospital to confide in her sister.

Rajni stood up now and counted all of their suitcases. 'We have six pieces in total,' she said. 'Do we have all six pieces?' Shirina took some delight in ignoring her. Rajni frowned and picked up her bags. They shuffled down the aisle, past the family who had gone sluggish and sleepy after their feast but were now on their feet with renewed energy.

Porters stepped into their path, offering to carry bags, asking where they were going. It occurred to Shirina that she had no idea where their hotel was; Rajni had that information on her itinerary. Shirina waved the porter away and kept her head down as she moved along with the crowd from the sun-soaked platform to the sheltered station. Beggars slept here – not on the edges, but in the middle of the floor so she had to step around them. Shirina met the pleading gaze of one woman sitting up on a folded piece of cardboard, a threadbare sari wrapped around her bony frame. Shirina took care not to tread on her fingers, which extended from her open palm, a silent request for money. Like the other passengers leaving the station, Shirina quickly learned the art of stepping gingerly around a person while also not looking at them.

They engaged the first rickshaw driver who called out to them. He took their bags and piled them in the back, turning and wedging them like pieces in a puzzle. Shirina hurried to get in first; she was conscious again of how awkward she looked when she had to hoist herself up (getting up the steep stairs into the train carriage had been more challenging than she'd anticipated). She didn't want Rajni and Jezmeen seeing her struggling. Rajni was more concerned about the bags anyway; she kept frowning and counting them. 'Six pieces,' she said again, nodding.

The auto-rickshaw's engine rumbled beneath them and the smell of burning rubber filled Shirina's nostrils. Jezmeen began to cough. Rajni grabbed the railing at the side of the car but the driver turned back and told her not to. She withdrew her hand just in time for a truck to clip past, narrowly missing the rickshaw.

The air was supposed to be fresher up north, but from the rickshaw, Amritsar and Delhi felt one and the same. The sweltering heat had already hit its peak for the day but the residual humidity clung to Shirina's skin. On the road, the only difference Shirina noticed between the two cities was the spaces between the squat buildings here, where the green fields behind the main road were visible. They merged onto a major road, the rickshaw flanked on either side by large trucks and buses. All the clamour of the city overwhelmed Shirina's senses. She shielded her eyes from the dust and grit that flew into the rickshaw and peppered her hair and skin. At one traffic light, she pulled her hand away momentarily to see a man teetering on top of a tall ladder, fixing a telephone wire. The ladder, made of bamboo, bent like a weak sapling against the wind. Shirina covered her eyes again.

The roads became narrower and turned into small lanes. Every time the rickshaw turned, Shirina feared a dangerous teetering and tipping and she wondered what would happen if they got into an accident here. If their bags popped free from the ropes that constrained them, their belongings mixing with the grime and dog droppings on the ground. Would anybody help them? It was unlikely. Traffic wouldn't stop for them – it would continue running, flattening everything they had. Shirina thought briefly about the contents of her bag and realized she wouldn't miss anything. Let it all tumble away, it would make her travels easier.

Her passport case was in her pocket, of course. She patted it frequently, made sure it didn't fall out from all the jostling of the ride. More important than the passport at the moment was the card inside the case that Sehaj had given her at the airport.

They veered into a lane clogged with vehicles and shops jammed together. A young man on a rusty bicycle shot in front of them, making the rickshaw driver curse loudly. Their hotel, The Holy City Palace, was at the end of this lane; its sign stuck out like a friendly waving hand. They pulled up and got out, a frowning Rajni counting the bags again.

Two gilded mirrors on opposite walls of the hotel lobby made endless multiples of Shirina, Rajni and Jezmeen. Behind the reception desk, there was a magnificent backlit portrait of the Golden Temple at night, its reflection melting across the calm holy waters. An elderly turbaned man stood behind the computer, nodding as they entered. Rajni handed him the booking sheet. He asked them to take a seat.

Shirina couldn't believe she was willing to sit again after having spent the whole day sitting down, but she was relieved to rest once more. Rajni picked up a newspaper and became absorbed in an article. Jezmeen came and sat next to her, picking up a magazine from the table. 'Ooh, that's a nice dress,' she said, pointing to a lime-coloured gown that clung to the model's hips. 'Imagine asking to get one of those tailored.'

'Especially around here,' Shirina said. Most of the women she'd seen so far were dressed in salwar-kameez out of respect for the holy city.

'Madam,' said the front-desk man. He gazed at all three of them, not sure who was in charge. Rajni responded to his summons. If they had husbands with them, it would be easier, Shirina thought. On the train, the conductors had come around asking all the sirs for their families' tickets. She felt a pinch of longing for Sehaj. At the airport, he had carried her bags out of the car and placed his hand gently on the small of her back. The gesture made her feel protected.

'They want our passports,' Rajni called from the reception desk.

'Open up to the stamp page, please,' said the man.

'The stamp page?' Jezmeen asked.

'The place where your entry into India was stamped,' he replied. 'We need to see it.'

'Oh,' Jezmeen said. She flipped open her passport. 'Honestly, I can't even remember them stamping it.'

'They must have,' Shirina said. She had already located hers, an inked box announcing her entry date.

'If no entry stamp, we have a problem,' the man said. 'National security.' His gaze shifted from Rajni to Shirina to Jezmeen. 'Amritsar is very close to Pakistan. We don't want people coming in illegally from that side, causing trouble here.'

Shirina thought his eyes were lingering on hers for a second too long. She wanted to tell him she wasn't here to cause trouble; if anything, she had made this trip to eliminate more trouble for herself. But she wondered if she looked jittery, or suspicious.

'Found it,' Jezmeen said, springing up from the sofa. 'It's very faded,' she explained to the man at the desk, who turned his look of suspicion onto her. Relief washed over Shirina. The heat of his stare was gone. She realized how tense she was, that any question, any suspicion or doubts about her intentions here made her feel as if she was being interrogated. In truth, it was nobody's business. Sehaj had said the same thing to her when she told him she didn't think she could maintain this lie while spending so much time with her sisters, in such close quarters. 'They're nosy,' she had told him. 'They'll know something's up.' To her relief and disappointment, they hadn't noticed what was going on with her.

The desk manager typed furiously into his computer. 'This could take some time,' he said. 'We'll show you to your rooms and return your passports later.'

Rajni frowned. 'We can probably wait,' she said.

'It could take an hour,' the desk manager said.

'An hour?' she asked. 'Why do you need so much time?'

He sighed. 'Madam, do I have to explain India's security issues with Pakistan? Do I need to tell you about Partition? Amritsar has been a border city ever since Punjab was split into India and Pakistan,' he said with pride, as if he had overseen the splitting himself.

'You don't need to give us a history lesson, our parents told us all about Partition when we were growing up,' Rajni said.

Did they? They must have been Dad's stories and Shirina must have been too young to understand them. Everything she knew about Partition, she had seen on Hindi films that featured a lover on each side of the border, separated by cruel politics, their families unsympathetic to their plight as violence ravaged their communities. Those movies always made her cry.

'Then you'll understand why I need to scrutinize these documents very carefully,' said the desk manager. 'This is our policy for all guests. We can't take any chances.'

'But we've got British passports. We clearly didn't scramble across the border.'

'Let it go,' Jezmeen said. 'What's the big deal if they hold onto our passports for a bit? We'll get them back.'

Rajni looked uneasy. She eyed the man. His expression did not change. 'India's national security first, Madam. We are on the front lines here.' The way he talked, it was as if it was 1947 and the war was raging at his doorstep.

'Fine,' Rajni said.

A porter loaded their bags into a trolley and pushed it towards the service elevator, pointing Shirina, Rajni and Jezmeen to a smaller lift. An instrumental Kenny G ballad floated over the speakers, completely incongruous to the lush palatial décor in the lobby and the reception staff's militancy. The sisters' rooms were next to each other, as if the hotel was aware of their birth order – 301: Rajni, 302: Jezmeen, 303: Shirina.

As soon as she entered her room, Shirina collapsed into her bed. This fatigue was a nightmare – and even worse that she had to dismiss it as a side effect of travelling. She took her phone and checked the time. Sehaj would be finishing dinner now, maybe watching some television. They hadn't actually spoken to each other since she arrived in India; just messages, the banal, perfunctory types to let each other know they were still alive. Today she needed to hear his voice. She entered the WiFi password and found Sehaj's number on her overseas calling app. He picked up on the third ring.

'Shirina?' he asked. The concern in his voice nearly melted her. 'Are you okay?'

Of course he loves you. It was a thought that surprised Shirina. She didn't realize that she'd doubted him until she heard him speak.

'I'm fine.' All of a sudden, her voice was thick with tears.

'I can't hear you, sweetheart,' he said tenderly. 'Speak up.'

'I'm fine,' she said loudly. It sounded more convincing with more volume. 'We just got to Amritsar.'

'How is it?'

'I haven't seen much yet. We were just on a hair-raising rickshaw ride and then checked into our rooms.' She smiled, remembering the taxi driver picking them up from Istanbul airport and chattering away in Turkish, pointing to various landmarks as he wove through traffic and entered the Old City, where their hotel was. The sun had glinted off the Bosphorus river and everything seemed possible; she was giddy with the mysterious romance of the city and she even thought she understood the driver after a while, the cadences of his language and the odd Hindi word – *subah*, *kitap* – catching in her mind.

The memory softened Shirina and she could sense Sehaj was thinking about their honeymoon too. She wanted to tell him how she was really feeling. 'I'm scared,' she said.

His voice overlapped with hers. 'Work's been really crazy.'

'Oh,' she said. The tears came up again. She listened as he told her about an unreasonable client, and the late hours he was spending at the office going through some contracts with a fine-toothed comb. The business was expanding to Europe, where tax regulations in certain countries were a nightmare to deal with from overseas. Her mind wandered as Sehaj spoke. Notes from the Kenny G elevator tune drifted in the back of her mind.

'. . . And I'm having to fix everybody's mistakes for them. Not that I want to wish my days away, but I'm really looking forward to the next long weekend.'

'That's months away,' Shirina murmured.

'Yeah, I know,' Sehaj said with a sigh, and then he said nothing. *Ask me again if I'm okay,* Shirina thought. *Ask about the train journey.* She wanted to tell him about the little girl on the train and how purposefully she had ignored her, even when she cried out and called Shirina 'sister'.

'Sehaj, I'm scared,' she finally said again.

This time, he heard. The distinct silence on the other end wasn't caused by a delay.

'Shirina . . .' he began.

'Don't,' she said. 'Don't say it.'

'I'm not saying you *have* to do it.'

She wanted to throw the phone across the room. It was so unfair, being told the decision was hers to make, when it wasn't, not completely. She wouldn't be allowed to have regrets or doubts if she was the one who had come up with the plan.

'What if I don't go through with it?' Shirina asked. 'I really can't come back?'

Another pause. 'It's something we need to discuss then,' Sehaj said finally.

'We – you and me? Just the two of us?'

'And my mother.'

Shirina groaned. 'How does she factor into this decision, Sehaj?'

'You married my family,' Sehaj said. 'We talked about this. We make our decisions together, we sacrifice things for each other. This is what families do.'

Shirina couldn't fault Sehaj for reminding her how families were supposed to behave – in the early days of getting to know each other, she had been so impressed with Sehaj's family. They had big gatherings, and took holidays together. They did what families did.

'But she doesn't have to be involved in *every* decision we make,' she insisted.

'She's my mother.'

'I'm your wife,' Shirina reminded him.

'Shirina—' With his lips too close to the receiver, Sehaj's sigh sounded like a roar. 'You're making this more complicated than it needs to be.'

'I'm allowed to say no, then?' she asked, emboldened by Sehaj's softened tone. He didn't want to fight; he just wanted the problem to go away. They had hardly the space to argue in his house, with his mother always in the shadows, but this long-distance phone call was allowing more privacy. 'This isn't a trivial thing like choosing curtains or—' She paused at the sound of shuffling in the background.

'Hang on,' Sehaj said. His voice became distant and then muffled because – of course, as if they conjured her just by speaking about her – his mother was now in the room. How did she manage to always do that?

Moments later, Sehaj came back to the phone. 'Sorry about that,' he

131

said, but his voice was already different. Shirina felt the shift. There was something business-like in his tone; all the tenderness was gone.

The distance gave Shirina courage. In the silence and the emptiness of her hotel room, she shut her eyes. 'Is she still there?'

Either Sehaj registered her steely tone and was taken aback, or the slight delay meant that it took him a second or two to hear her. Either way, Shirina felt emboldened. She opened her eyes.

'She just came up to get something,' Sehaj said.

'She came up, did she? All by herself? She must be well then,' Shirina said. She heard a warning voice – *Stop, stop it, you're going too far* – but she ignored it.

Again, the delay seemed to stretch. Shirina thought about the day she had handed in her resignation, saying that she had to stay at home to take care of her mother-in-law who needed help climbing the stairs at home after her hip surgery. 'There's nobody else there,' Shirina explained. 'It could be a long recovery.' The reluctance must have been apparent in her voice because her supervisor took her out for coffee that afternoon. 'You have such potential,' she said. 'Can't you take some time off? Can't you and your husband work out an arrangement? There are chair lifts if she can't move.'

Chair lifts became the single image in Shirina's mind every time she thought about the difference between Eastern and Western values. Indian daughters-in-law took care of their families. They made necessary sacrifices. They knew what it took to preserve the peace in their home. Westerners installed chair lifts.

'Shirina,' Sehaj said. And then he said nothing. There was more shuffling, more movement and voices. She recognized the sound of the door opening and shutting. He was leaving the room. 'Sweetheart,' he said. The tenderness was restored in his voice. He had left his mother and found some privacy. 'I know you're upset, baby,' he said soothingly. 'I know.'

It was all she wanted, or at least this was what she thought. An offer of understanding. She thought about the little girl on the train, holding her hand out to play. She hadn't stopped thinking about her and she could still hear the girl calling her 'sister', so disappointed when Shirina refused to play along. Throughout the journey, during all the bickering between Rajni and Jezmeen, Shirina hadn't flipped the page of her novel once. She had read the same line over and over again until the words lost their meaning.

Rajni needed the newspaper. She had left it in the lobby because the man at the reception desk was watching their every move, but an advertisement had caught her eye and the porter had whisked them away to their rooms before she could take down the information – discreetly, of course, she didn't need Jezmeen and Shirina knowing that she was considering hiring a private investigator. How would she explain that to them?

She stepped out of the room and entered the lift with the stealth of a thief, looking left and right. The lobby was empty. The desk manager caught her eye and nodded. 'Just another few minutes,' he said, thinking she had come for the passport. She was pleased for the excuse. 'I'll just wait here if you don't mind,' she said haughtily. Once his gaze returned to the screen, she took a seat on the plush lounge chair and pulled up the newspaper. There it was, the ad in the corner:

PRE-MATRIMONIAL INVESTIGATIONS
'Better pre-nup than post-nup'

Getting married? Want to know your future spouse's history? We can do a thorough financial and moral check-up. Our experienced and highly skilled investigators are discreet and detail-oriented. They will not let you down! With a network of dedicated pre-matrimonial specialists spanning across India and the diaspora, we are now specializing in inter-state and overseas marriages* and offering competitive rates. Call us now for a free consultation!

Next to the asterisk, there was a list in tiny print of territories where their detectives could reach. London, UK was third after Toronto, Canada and California, USA. Rajni glanced at the reception desk and pressed the newspaper to the table with her palm. Then she slowly ripped the ad out, careful not to make a sound. She had a feeling that even a small transgression like this could make the hotel owner revoke their right to stay in this holiest of cities.

Stuffing the torn piece of paper in her pocket, Rajni headed back to the lift. 'Ma'am,' the desk manager called as she passed him. She felt her heart leap in her throat and then realized how silly she was being. Ripping a newspaper was hardly vandalism, although after the visit to the police station yesterday, she didn't want to take any chances. Just the thought of getting into trouble made her break out in a sweat.

'Yes?' she replied, trying to sound casual.

'Your passport,' he said.

'I can take the others if you want,' Rajni said, feeling overly generous because now she felt bad about defacing his newspaper.

He paused to consider this and then handed all three to Rajni.

She returned to her room and read the ad again, considering what the detectives might do. What did she want them to uncover? She wasn't certain, but she knew that it was worth having a look around. Judging from the way she and Kabir left their last conversation, she was certain that he wasn't thinking the worst of Davina – that she could be a con artist. It would be ideal, Rajni thought as she dialled the number, her confidence building, if Davina was already married. Rajni didn't want to devastate Anil. She certainly didn't want the investigators to uncover something dangerous that might have an adverse effect on her son – like a serious STI or a violent criminal history (worse yet, if Davina's husband was in jail for violent criminal behaviour and was out on bail and could come after Anil). But she also welcomed the thought of handing over a dossier to her foolish, naïve son and saying, 'HAH!'

'WELCOME TO BHARAT INVESIGATORS,' blared a pre-recorded message that gave Rajni a jolt. She held the phone half an arm's-length away from her ear to listen to the menu options. 'PRESS ZERO TO SPEAK TO ONE OF OUR QUALIFIED PROFESSIONALS.' She pressed zero and waited again, this time through a staticky old Hindi song that she vaguely recognized – it was a classic about love.

'Hello, welcome to Bharat Investigators, how may I help you?'

The young male voice was a pleasant surprise. For some reason, she had pictured a matronly auntie type sitting at a cluttered desk serviced by a single fan that blew dust around the room. The detective's worldwide networks would be no more sophisticated than a community of wives and sisters-in-law who were migrants in other Indian enclaves in multicultural cities, and the work would be a side-hobby, no different from anything they were already doing, but now it earned them a bit of pocket money.

'Hello,' Rajni said. 'I'm considering engaging an investigator to do a background check on a woman.'

'No problem, ma'am. Can I know how to address you, please?'

'My name is . . .' Here she hesitated. If the investigator had networks in London, how likely was he to blab to a friend who might tell another friend about her family secrets? There was no harm in giving a false name. 'Meera,' she said.

'Ma'am, your real name, please,' the man responded.

'How did you—'

'Almost every woman who calls uses the name Meera,' he said.

She knew she should have picked a less common Indian name, or at least one that sounded authentic, like . . . . Rajni. It was like telling the detective that her name was Jane Doe and expecting not to raise any suspicions.

'I'm Rajni,' she said a bit sheepishly. 'Sorry.'

'No problem,' the man was breezy. 'We just need to be honest with each other in order to do this right, okay?'

'And your name?' she asked.

'Nikhil Ahuja,' he said. 'We're a pair of brothers running this company.' He prattled on for a while about the company's history – started in 2003 when a new generation of young Indians abroad began demanding pre-matrimonial checks after hearing horror stories of friends being deceived. (Those marriages were the result of a boom in Indian matrimonial websites, which made Rajni think of Shirina. Did she ever consider getting some-body to look into Sehaj's background? But of course, why would she? There was nothing suspicious about Sehaj – it was as if Shirina had typed 'perfect Indian male companion' into a machine and 3D printed the ideal husband.)

'And we recently expanded to territories in Southeast Asia, such as Malaysia, Singapore and Thailand,' Nikhil said.

'Alright,' Rajni said. She was feeling a bit overwhelmed by Nikhil's enthusiasm. 'And you handle, uh, cases where people want to just check somebody out because they have suspicions?' In Rajni's private opinion, a thirty-six-year-old woman getting pregnant by a young man half her age deserved a stronger description than 'suspicious' but for brevity's sake, she felt it was important to downplay it.

'Certainly,' Nikhil declared. There was that enthusiasm again. It made Rajni just the slightest bit queasy. 'I'll give you an example of a case we worked on recently – very successful, in fact it was even publicized. A young doctor in Singapore agreed to an arranged marriage to a woman in the Sikh community. Both boy and girl liked each other, decided to get engaged. However, the girl's mother had some suspicions about the boy. Not really any evidence, but he was a doctor – you know, high income and handsome. Why was he still available? Her family told her not to be silly; she was being overly cautious, they said. Then the unthink-able happened!'

Nikhil had a flair for the dramatic, Rajni noted.

'It turned out that the mother was trying to draw everybody's attention away from the daughter, who had a boyfriend in New Zealand, where she studied. Some pictures were beginning to surface. The boyfriend felt betrayed that after five years together, she was just leaving him for an arranged marriage. He had called the house several times to speak to the parents during the engagement. The doctor's parents were aware of it – the New Zealander had managed to contact them somehow as well, Facebook, I think – and the mother-in-law was already considering rescinding the marriage offer.'

'So the marriage wasn't going to go through, and the girl's mother was pre-emptively spreading the rumour that it was the boy's fault?' Rajni asked.

'Yes,' Nikhil said. 'Turns out the girl was the one doing shameful things.'

Shameful things. But really, all she did was have a boyfriend outside the community, didn't she? Rajni was uncomfortable with Nikhil's moralizing. When he posed his next question, she found herself stumbling and considered hanging up because surely he knew what she was hiding:

'So can you let me know the nature of your case?' he asked.

'Uh . . . yes. See, my son – he's going out with, he's about to marry this woman,' Rajni said. It was not strictly the truth, but if she told Nikhil that Anil had got Davina pregnant, he might not be very sympathetic. Worse yet, he would wonder what kind of mother she was – a question that had been turning in her mind ever since she awoke from her fainting spell back in London.

'Okay,' Nikhil said. 'And you have doubts? Some feelings that it is not right?'

'Yes,' Rajni said. That was putting it mildly. 'She's a bit older than him.'

'Okay,' Nikhil said. 'How much older?'

Rajni had done the maths as soon as Anil told her, but she couldn't bring herself to say it aloud. 'She's in her thirties. My son is . . . he's in his twenties.' Did it make a difference if she added a few years to his age? She decided not. 'Look, the thing I'm suspicious about is that he seems very . . . influenced by her. He had career plans that he's suddenly putting on hold because of this woman.'

'Could she be pregnant?' Nikhil asked.

Dammit. 'Yes,' Rajni said. 'She could be.'

'Could be, or she is?'

'She . . . she is,' Rajni said. 'They're getting together in a bit of a rush because of this whole thing, but I'm wondering if she's roped him into it.'

'It's a bit difficult for us to determine the circumstances around a woman's pregnancy,' Nikhil said after a pause. 'He's certain it's his baby?'

Anil still had that annoying teenager habit of filling every minor pause with 'uh' and 'like'. Rajni could not imagine him being certain of anything.

'He is,' Rajni said. 'But I think he's being fooled.'

There was a pause again. Rajni heard Nikhil repeating the facts under his breath, and a keyboard clicking away.

'I'd like to know . . . other things about her as well,' Rajni said. 'Her background. Any skeletons in the closet.'

'Of course,' Nikhil said. 'A woman like that, she's bound to have a few stories, or people who can tell us a few things.'

Once again, Rajni felt uneasy but she suppressed it. *That's not fair.* She tried not to think of Mum and the family who abandoned her after rumours started circulating about Rajni.

Nikhil gave her a basic game plan: he would discuss the case with his partners in the UK and do a comprehensive background check on Davina. These things were perfectly legal, he assured Rajni with a chuckle that indicated there were less legal methods to follow. 'If nothing comes up in the background check – no major debt, no current spouse, etc. – then I will assign somebody to follow her for a week. Details often emerge from this part of the investigation.'

'Alright,' Rajni said.

'Mrs Rajni, I have one more question,' Nikhil asked.

Here was where he was going to ask if she had been one hundred per cent honest with him. *Is there anything else I should know?*

'Yes?' she squeaked.

'Will you pay your deposit by Visa, Bank Transfer or Paytm?' Nikhil asked, his voice smooth as honey.

The tone in Cameron's email sounded genuinely excited. **'Have some roles that are perfect for you.'** The word 'perfect' had a line through it because Cameron had been so excited, he forgot how to underline.

'Jezmeen!' he answered the phone. 'How are things? How's India?'

How was India? She could not sum up her experience in an easy sentence. 'It's incredible,' she said. 'Just like the advertisements.' *And the consular guidelines, which I'll take more seriously from now on,* she thought.

'I backpacked through Uttar Pradesh myself, you know,' Cameron said with a hint of pride. 'Twenty years ago.'

'Did you?' Jezmeen asked, not because it was her first time hearing it (it wasn't) but because Cameron seemed to think that this was part of their connection somehow. He understood the Indian experience because he had stayed in a filthy flea motel on a mountain and got a parasite from a dodgy curry.

'Oh yes,' Cameron said. 'Really went off the beaten path. Incredible country. Such lovely people. So warm and welcoming to travellers.'

Men who backpacked or did cycling tours around India often said this of their experience. Such a great place to travel. They had made their way around solo, reliant on the kindness of strangers who invited them into their homes to share a meal. Travelling as a woman in India was an entirely different thing. Even with her sisters at her side, Jezmeen felt vulnerable.

'So tell me about these roles,' she said.

Cameron drew in a breath. 'Two possibilities, very strong ones – the first is for a new television series called *The Disgraced.*'

'I like the title,' Jezmeen said. She had an instant image in her mind of a strong female character, not unlike the one Polly played in *The Boathouse,* her backlit profile against the dark and mysterious waters of the Thames. 'What's the premise?'

Cameron cleared his throat. 'A promising young British-Asian woman looking for a match online becomes slowly radicalized by her lover, who is a fundamentalist and a skilled recruiter for a global terror network.'

'Very interesting,' Jezmeen said. There was some promise there. She didn't want to get too excited, and she hoped that the script would portray the woman as a universal, identifiable sort of character, not one of those 'my fundamentalism has always been in me like some kind of genetic mutation which has now been activated!' people.

'I thought you'd be intrigued by that. I have to tell you, before we go any further; you won't be considered for the main role.'

'Oh,' Jezmeen said, feeling a flutter of disappointment. 'What's the role then?'

'It's a smaller role,' Cameron said.

'Like a sister?' In a moment of sheer horror, Jezmeen thought he might offer her the role of this woman's mother.

'Like a wife,' Cameron said.

'Oh,' Jezmeen said. 'That's not so bad. The wife of another character then.'

'Yes,' Cameron said.

'Go on then, tell me about her,' Jezmeen said.

Somebody was knocking on the door. As Jezmeen walked over and pressed the phone between her tipped head and a raised shoulder, she heard Cameron's response but did not think she heard it correctly.

'Wife of Terrorist Number Seven,' Cameron said as Jezmeen threw open the door.

'WHAT?' she shrieked. The porter was at the door, holding a large silver tray.

'Ma'am, you ordered room service,' he protested.

'You want me to be the WIFE OF A TERRORIST?'

The porter looked very alarmed.

'Sorry,' Jezmeen said to him, opening the door wider to let him bring the food inside. It was a more elaborate meal than she thought she had paid for, and her mouth watered at the smell of the paneer masala and steamed rice. Still, she was not done with Cameron yet. *Focus.*

'Let me take a wild guess, Cameron. This character doesn't have any lines, does she?'

'No,' Cameron admitted.

The porter was setting her meal carefully on the table and laying out the cutlery.

'And she probably wears a hijab the whole time? A burqa? She's basically a pair of simpering brown eyes?'

'I think you'll need to discuss costumes later, but . . .'

'Oh, come on, Cameron,' Jezmeen said with exasperation. 'I know what Terrorist Number Five's role is – an angry brown man screaming things in incomprehensible Arabic and waving a giant rifle around, threatening the Western world when what he's actually saying is closer to "Can I have fries with that?"'

'Seven,' Cameron corrected her. 'He's Terrorist Number Seven.'

'So he's that low in the rankings. I can't even be Terrorist Number One's wife?' Once again, the porter looked dismayed. He glanced nervously at the door as if he might be taken hostage. Jezmeen tried to give him a reassuring smile and held her hand up to say, *I'll get your tip*, as she crossed the room, but he backed away and – she was certain she wasn't imagining this – edged closer to the butter knife.

'Would you consider that? A higher-ranking terrorist?'

'Is it a speaking role?' Jezmeen wasn't sure if this was a serious conversation any more.

'She might have a few lines, I suppose,' Cameron said. Jezmeen could picture him sitting at his desk in London, wiping the sweat off his brow and using one hand to type an email to the producers.

The porter was lingering at the door. 'Hang on,' Jezmeen said to Cameron, reaching for her purse. She gave the porter a few rupee notes which he touched to his forehead in a gesture of gratitude before backing out the door.

'So it's a no then?' Cameron asked when Jezmeen returned to the conversation. 'You realize that your options are narrowing, right?'

'I don't think Terrorist Number Six's wife is going to be my big comeback role, Cameron,' Jezmeen retorted. 'I'm sorry, but we're just going to have to work harder on this.'

'Seven,' Cameron corrected her. Jezmeen wanted to reach through the phone and club him on the head.

'You mentioned a couple of roles,' Jezmeen said. 'What are my other options?'

Cameron hesitated. With a sinking feeling, Jezmeen realized that Mrs Bin Laden was the good news.

'There's a movie which is being shot in India,' Cameron said. 'A sort of . . . train journey story.'

'Really?' Jezmeen asked, her interest piqued. Maybe Cameron had been trying to warm her up. 'Tell me more.'

'A family goes on a trip across Northern India to reconnect with their missing son,' Cameron said. 'It's a road-trip story with a bit of a twist.'

Jezmeen smiled. She could imagine the press junkets now: *I was on a similar journey — both spiritual and physical — with my sisters, and I can tell you, there were lots of unexpected twists and turns, haha.*

'. . . it's a cross-genre sort of thing,' Cameron said. 'Quite unusual. Fitting for a niche audience but maybe not limited to them, if done right.'

'What's the role?'

'Shruti,' Cameron said. 'The family's eldest daughter. Unmarried, a bit of a concern for the parents. Unbeknownst to her, they're taking her to the village to meet a suitable man.'

'Right,' Jezmeen said. She could work with that. 'Sounds like a good role then.'

'She's not in the story for very long,' Cameron said. That hesitation had returned to his voice. 'But her character makes a real impact, you know? We think about the consequences of everybody's actions long after.'

'What happens to her?' Jezmeen asked, already slightly involved and therefore grieving for Shruti.

'She catches a . . . uh, virus.'

'Okay,' Jezmeen said. 'A tragic heroine?'

Cameron cleared his throat. 'I suppose you could say that.'

'Cameron . . .' Jezmeen began.

'It's a very physical role,' Cameron said.

'What, she's leaping off buildings and rooftops in her condition?'

'She's undead.'

'WHAT?'

'She has a virus which makes her . . . you know, dead but not quite—'

'She's a zombie? You're offering me a role in a Punjabi zombie film?'

'Yes,' Cameron said miserably.

'How far into the film does she die?' Jezmeen asked.

'About ten minutes.'

'What the hell, Cameron!'

'It's a very physical death,' Cameron said brightly. 'You know how zombies are – lots of spasms and buckling. You'd get to display a range of emotions, which could come in handy for something else.'

'For another Indian monster road-trip film?'

'I'm not the one who writes these scripts,' Cameron protested. 'Don't shoot the messenger.'

'Who can I shoot then?' Jezmeen asked. 'Who wrote this movie?'

Cameron gave her a name that she hadn't heard of. Jezmeen sighed. 'It's disappointing, Cameron,' she said.

'We've talked about this, Jezmeen. The lack of roles and your current reputation.'

'I know, I know,' she replied. 'I'm disappointed in the scripting as well. The unmarried daughter is disposed of within ten minutes in what is – I'm guessing – a three-hour Bollywood spectacle with zombies, like some extended version of the "Thriller" video. They can't even keep Shruti alive to dance a little bit?'

Cameron clearly had no words. 'Hmm,' he said, as if he was considering sexism and all its complexities when it was just as likely that he was using one hand to type into the Google search engine: 'how to calm down angry brown actress'.

'Those are my two options then?' Jezmeen asked.

'For the moment,' Cameron said. 'I'm sorry, Jezmeen. You know that I'm advocating for you in every way that I can, but—'

'I know,' Jezmeen said. The pleading tone in Cameron's voice made her feel guilty. She thought of Rajni sitting in the police station, surrounded by men and wringing her hands, and she felt a pang of regret for putting her through all of that. 'Listen, I'll think about it, alright?'

'You will?' Cameron asked brightly.

'Give me a day or two?' Jezmeen asked. 'Send me the info.' Ever since the Arowana incident, she was aware that she couldn't afford to be choosy, but these choices truly depressed her. Her thoughts flashed back to the make-up counter. Was it worth doing that gig until another breakthrough happened? She was going to go into arrears in her rent; the only thing that would tide her over for a little while was the bit of money Mum had left them from the sale of the house.

After hanging up, Jezmeen ate her dinner of paneer masala and basmati rice, scraping her spoon across the bottom of the bowl, and then using her fingers to wipe up the last traces. She hadn't noticed how hungry she was until she started eating, but when she was done, she realized how quickly she had eaten. Immediately, the sensation of fullness turned into queasiness. The room was filled with the smell of spices now; she called room service to ask them to take her tray. 'Right away, Madam,' the porter said, probably terrified that she'd orchestrate a militant ambush on his family if he didn't obey her. The thought made her realize that she didn't have her passport back yet. After the police station yesterday, she felt naked without her identification – although she had played it cool, she'd actually been uneasy when the man behind the reception desk took her passport. *I'll need that back,* she had to refrain from saying because it sounded too much like something her haughty older sister would say.

'Could I come down to get my passport back, please?' she asked.

'Madam, we just returned all three of them to Mrs Chadha,' the desk manager said.

'Thank you.'

She sighed and hung up. She supposed she'd better go over to Rajni's room to talk to her anyway, try to clear the air. She wanted to be better at this pilgrimage thing – she did – but it was also occurring to her that she was going to need a lot more strength and patience to get through this leg of the journey. Amritsar was a holy city; alcohol was difficult to find here and she wasn't keen to wander the outer edges of the city in search of a cold bottle of beer.

She went out into the hall and knocked on Rajni's door. 'It's me,' she called. 'Just wanted to get my passport back.'

The door opened. 'Can I come in?' Jezmeen asked.

Rajni left the door ajar and turned her back to Jezmeen, busying herself

144

with unpacking. Her suitcases were neatly lined along the wall and open, her clothes categorized in those packing cells that she had bought for Jezmeen and Shirina years ago after seeing them in a sale. 'Your bras don't go missing,' she'd said with amazement, as if this was the worst possible consequence of travelling. Because of all her meticulous organizing and contingency plans, it probably was.

The passports were sitting on the bedside table. 'Raj, I'm really sorry,' Jezmeen said as she entered the room and shut the door behind her.

Rajni dismissed her apology with a wave, as if to say, 'Too little, too late.'

'Listen, I feel terrible. I know I made a joke of it on the train, but I was actually really scared. I didn't know what they might do to me in there.' She hesitated, because it was hard to talk about what could have happened. 'Rajni, I've never felt fear like that before – my skin crawled with it. Every time a guard walked by the cell, I held my breath until he passed because I was terrified he'd come in and do something to me. I realized I had no idea what the law permits police officers to do here, and they'd already decided we were rioters. The men at India Gate, they looked like they were ready to pounce on us and rip us to shreds – then the police had us in little cages and could do the same.' Jezmeen stopped when she realized her voice was shaking.

'Think about how worried I was,' Rajni said, extracting her toiletries kit from a tight space between two neatly pressed pairs of trousers. 'Me and Shirina. Why can't you think about other people before you plunge yourself into stupid things?'

'Rajni, we've been over this. I wasn't courting trouble out there. It just happened.'

'You and Anil,' Rajni said, shaking her head. 'You don't think about other people.'

'What does Anil have to do with this?' Jezmeen asked.

Rajni pursed her lips. 'Nothing,' she said quickly. Her gaze flitted away from Jezmeen's. 'He's just selfish sometimes, that's all.'

'He's just a teenager,' Jezmeen said. 'He's going to grow out of it.'

'What's your excuse then?' Rajni countered.

'I'm not self—' Jezmeen began, but she noticed the muscles tensing in

Rajni's jaw. There was no point arguing. This was how their problems at the hospital escalated. 'I was really, really glad to see you,' Jezmeen tried again. 'And more grateful than you'll ever know.'

Rajni's gaze softened. 'Good,' she said quietly. She paused her unpacking and rose to her feet. Her knees snapped and she winced.

'Ouch,' Jezmeen said.

'It didn't hurt,' Rajni said. 'I just hate that sound.'

'I get it too sometimes, especially if I've been sitting all day.'

'It gets worse. More frequent. I spend all this time trying to outsmart these little signs of my body wearing down – stretch, eat more flax seeds, get eight hours of sleep. But what can you really do?'

She sounded like Mum, lamenting that her years of balanced eating and recommended daily walks had taken her nowhere. 'After Mum's diagnosis, she started saying: "At least prayer is helpful,"' Jezmeen recalled.

'I don't know where she got that idea from,' Rajni said.

'Have you ever tried it?' Jezmeen asked.

'What – praying?'

Jezmeen nodded.

'No,' Rajni said.

'Not even after – you know, when Mum told us about the jewellery pouch? You didn't . . . I don't know . . .' She struggled to find the words. 'Check with God?'

'Did you?'

'No,' Jezmeen said quickly. She felt silly admitting now that after storming out of Mum's room and thinking *I need a drink,* she had found the hospital chapel instead and decided it was as good as any place to get some answers. She remembered sitting in that quiet room, shivering as an icy wind blew through a crack in the stained-glass window.

'God, I can't believe how much I wish she were here,' she whispered to Rajni.

Rajni took Jezmeen by the shoulders and guided her to sit down on the bed. 'I know,' she said.

'I just feel so untethered now that she's gone. Both our parents are dead. We're orphans, did you realize that?'

'I know,' Rajni said again.

'And we're next.'

'What?'

'I mean, we were children, we were that generation that was supposed to outlive the adults. Now that they've died, another entire group is going to outlive us. We're the next to die.'

'That won't happen for a long time,' Rajni said, stroking Jezmeen's back. 'It's decades away.'

'It's easy for you to say because you've got a legacy. You have a life established – your career, your home, your family. I'm still stuck where I was ten years ago. Virtually nothing's changed.' A sob escaped Jezmeen's throat. She saw her future in an endless list of insignificant roles, that woman who flashed across the screen in a rabid frenzy and perished from a zombie virus before the audience even knew her name.

'Shh,' Rajni said, holding her. 'It's okay.'

'It's not okay,' Jezmeen said. 'Even Mum thought my life wasn't headed anywhere.'

'She was just concerned about you,' Rajni said.

Jezmeen shook her head. 'After the doctors told her the cancer was terminal, and she didn't have much time left, she said, "How can I die knowing that you're not settled?" I thought she was referring to marriage, but it was other things too. She said I had no commitments. "You need to *settle*, Jezmeen," she kept saying. It just made me feel worse about my career and everything.'

'When was this?'

'A couple of weeks before she wrote that letter.' Jezmeen shut her eyes, remembering the way her voice and Mum's had escalated. She had dropped in at the hospital to see Mum on her way home from an audition for a small speaking role on a two-part BBC drama series. 'It went pretty well,' Jezmeen said hopefully. 'I'll know in the next couple of days.'

'How many of these things are you going to do, Jezmeen?' Mum asked

147

impatiently, surprising her. Although Mum had never been an enthusiastic encourager of Jezmeen's fledgling acting career, this outburst gave her the impression that Mum had been waiting a long time to tell her off. The ensuing lecture about settling down and being more responsible made Jezmeen feel even worse, and when the producers didn't call her back by the end of the week, she cheered herself up by polishing off a bottle of wine on her own before Mark came over for dinner that Saturday.

A few weeks later, when Mum talked to all three of them about the pilgrimage, Jezmeen had been the first to grasp her hand. *Don't leave,* she was saying, even though she had known for a while that the end was near. Mum's fingers were icy; her blood circulation had already become poorer but the shock of those familiar hands feeling so foreign had made Jezmeen recoil. It took her a while to grasp Mum's request, because she was still frightened by the thought of Mum's body rapidly deteriorating.

'We need to call a truce then,' Rajni sighed. 'You and me. No more of this. You saw how upset Shirina was on the train. We need to stop arguing.'

Jezmeen gulped back a sob and nodded gratefully. She had known from the start of the trip that a conversation with her sisters about Mum's death was inevitable. For the first time, the thought of it didn't seem so awful.

Chapter Nine

Day Five: The Golden Temple, Amritsar

At this stage of the journey, I trust that the three of you are feeling closer and more connected to each other. Visiting the Golden Temple is about recognizing the oneness of humanity. You should enter the temple's grounds with an open heart, and think about leaving the past behind. You must also take a bath in the sarovar to cleanse yourself of all burdens. As you do this, remember that purification is not just about water washing away grit. It is also about your thoughts and actions becoming simpler and more purposeful.

This part of the journey was about purification, Mum had said in her letter, and so in the morning, Shirina considered calling Sehaj and telling him that she was sorry. She felt a bit foolish for making such a fuss during their phone conversation last night. In the shower, she shut her eyes and let the water pour over her body, rivulets running down the curves of her breasts and thighs, the roundness of her abdomen. The light floral fragrance of the hotel body wash filled the small cubicle. She felt cleaner as the water pooled at the spaces between her feet and the foam circled down the drain.

As the days crept closer to her 'visit to the ancestral village' – the cover that Shirina was still sticking to, even though her sisters might wonder who these relatives were and why they'd never heard of them – Shirina felt a combination of dread and relief. She wished there were a different course of action that would make everybody happy, but she had gone through all the ideas and scenarios in her mind. Everything pointed back to Shirina. This wasn't easy for Sehaj either. Mother was adamant, and Shirina of all people knew what she was like when she dug her heels in. If she could come to terms with doing this one thing for the family, the tension in their home would melt away.

So every time the panic seized Shirina, she reminded herself of the future: returning to Melbourne, seeing Sehaj, starting over. She'd even lose this excess weight right away, beginning a mid-year new year's resolution. The future unrolled like a carpet before Shirina, and she saw an entirely new life where she and her mother-in-law had the kind of closeness that she had always craved from Mum. *Soon, soon,* she reminded herself as she stepped out of the shower. The creamy white body lotion smelled like lilacs, springtime. Soon, the obstacle that stood between her and her new family would be gone.

According to Google Maps, the Golden Temple was a straight line from their hotel. In practice, the sisters had to edge their way in single file along the narrow road, dodging rickshaws, potholes and stray dogs. The rattling aluminium doors of shops were just being raised for the day as Shirina, Rajni and Jezmeen made their way to the temple. Shirina had never seen so much Sikh paraphernalia in her life: T-shirts with glittery 'SIKH WARRIOR' slogans embossed on them and screen-printed images of the gurus, as if they were rock stars. One roadside stand was dedicated to selling karas, the silver bangles that Sikhs wore. A mother of two young boys made them hold out their wrists so the vendor could gauge their size. The older boy was reluctant. He shrugged when the vendor asked which kara he liked. 'No opinion?' the vendor asked, laughing. He picked through the bangles displayed on a crate draped with velvet cloth. 'Don't you want everybody to know you're a Sikh boy?' He held out a chunky kara, the kind Shirina had only seen on men, and the boy's eyes widened a bit with interest.

Shirina felt the coolness of her thin bangle against her wrist. She had worn the same one since she was a teenager. Mum had helped to remove her previous kara from childhood, which had grown so tight that soap and hand lotion were required to ease the removal. It hurt, Shirina remembered, especially at the point where her wrist bone jutted out and then widened to become her hand. 'Make a fist,' Mum kept saying, tugging the bangle. 'Good girl, good girl.' Praise worked on her and reduced the pain to an irritation. Shirina made a fist so tight that her fingernails dug into the soft flesh of her palms and drew blood. She was doing it now, clenching her fist just at the memory.

'Cool,' Jezmeen said as they passed a shopfront window with a gleaming display of knives and swords of different sizes. Mum had had a medium-sized kirpan with an intricately carved handle and a blade that curved at the tip. It was purely decorative, the symbolism more important than the function, but Shirina still remembered feeling protected by it.

Jezmeen pointed at the largest kirpan, which stretched across the table in the shop window. 'Imagine bringing that back to Britain and trying to explain it to Customs.'

'Mum's was about that size, wasn't it?'

Jezmeen shook her head. 'I think she had one of those necklaces,' she said, nodding at the small sword-shaped pendants that hung from long silver chains. Noticing their sudden attention on the pendants, the vendor plucked a few from the display case and came out of the shop to offer them to Shirina. She shook her head. 'Mum had one just like that,' she insisted, pointing at a dagger with a glinting tip. It looked like a prop from a play.

'You're probably thinking about Auntie Roopi's house,' Jezmeen said. 'She had lots of decorative stuff from trips abroad.'

In her memories, Shirina saw the kirpan sitting next to a carved vase on a mantel and realized that Jezmeen must be right. Their own house had been sparsely decorated – a commemorative glass ornament here, a few picture frames there. She remembered the plastic lilies that Mum had brought home from the supermarket once, cloudy blobs of glue attempting a dewy freshness in the dead of winter. The curtains were always drawn anyway, so the lilies did nothing to brighten up the shadowy room. Since Jezmeen mentioned Auntie Roopi at the market in Delhi, Shirina found herself confusing memories of both places. That cat wasn't theirs, but if she recalled her childhood now, she saw it creeping between the furniture of their house and stretching lazily at the foot of her bed. Auntie Roopi's house had been more welcoming than her own – the kitchen pantry over-flowing with packets of biscuits, the countertops clear of those bills with angry red letters at the top that sometimes made Mum cry.

The sisters ambled down two more lanes, politely declining offers of chai and roti from the vendors, and emerged into the main square, where the skies were open and the vehicles were barred from entering. Rickshaws crowded at the edges of the square, their drivers calling out prices to passengers. 'Wow, this has changed,' Rajni said as they stepped into the square. 'It's so civilized now.'

Shirina hadn't been here before but even she was impressed. The town square was neatly paved in reddish brick. The surrounding buildings all had a uniform exterior and they stood in tidy rows, unlike the jutting houses and shops everywhere else in the city. The blaring of horns and sputtering motors already seemed a world away. Two sculptures side-by-side caught Shirina's attention: a wedding dancing scene. One sculpture depicted the men, their legs raised high and their arms framing the sky above them. The women on the other platform were huddled closer together. Their dupattas were caught in the wind of their movements, trailing behind them as if they were softer than the iron and concrete materials that composed them.

'Looks like your wedding, Shirina,' Jezmeen said, nodding at the statues. 'I think our outfits were a little more up-to-date though.'

The women looked young, like sisters and cousins of the bride. Shirina remembered Rajni and Jezmeen dancing with her, and the photographer circling like a vulture, freezing the moment just like these statues did. In the pictures, the unbridled joy in their smiles gave them the strongest resemblance Shirina had ever seen. They looked like three sisters that had spent their whole lives laughing together like this.

'Do you remember all those old women who wanted to sing those dreary songs about brides leaving their home?' Jezmeen asked. 'And I kept turning up the music?'

'Those songs are horrible,' Rajni said. 'They did them at my wedding and Mum didn't let me stop the women. They sounded like cats dying.'

The songs were designed to stir up the bride's emotions and deepen her great sadness at leaving her family for the unknown. Shirina had been dreading them as well, and was glad that the festive mood continued despite the elders' insistence that traditions needed to be respected. Those women didn't have much say anyway; they were part of that hodgepodge of guests that Mum invited from her temple crowd to make up for their distinct lack of relatives compared to Sehaj's voluminous family. The mournful songs just weren't relevant to Shirina, and she was afraid she wouldn't be able to feign the appropriate bridal sadness. Once she found Sehaj and her new, perfect family, she was so prepared to jump ship that she would have done away with the goodbyes altogether.

Jezmeen and Rajni were recalling the words of those songs now, as they walked along the square, passing more souvenir shops, dhabas, tour booking agencies and a double-storey McDonald's. 'There was one verse which went, "Make sure you do all the cooking and cleaning to the utmost standards, you don't want to anger your mother-in-law",' Rajni said.

Jezmeen pulled a face. 'They need an update,' she said. 'Make sure your husband does his share of the work and tell your mother-in-law to bugger off if she interferes.'

Shirina had an image of her mother-in-law hovering around the background yesterday while Sehaj spoke to her on the phone. It was easy to say, wasn't it? Before getting married, young women always went on about how they wouldn't put up with this or that. The arranged marriage message boards were full of such threads. *HELP!! MIL wants to move in with us!* and *Any advice on how to say no to MIL without upsetting hubby?* The women who posted these frantic messages irked Shirina because by posting their private problems to a group of strangers, they were indulging in drama that they could have foreseen by marrying traditional men. *You should have known,* Shirina was tempted to say. It wasn't just to chide the women – it was a useful reminder to herself as well that she had wanted a traditional marriage. Although she hadn't exactly gone searching for a live-in mother-in-law, she welcomed the idea once she noted the size of the house, with enough rooms between them. Compromises were necessary. It was easy as well to declare, 'I would never quit my job' or 'I'd tell my husband that my needs came first.' But what women really did, the ways in which they bent and adjusted their values – that was reality. The women on those message boards should know better than to complain about a simple fact of life like overbearing mothers-in-law.

Across the square, a massive flat screen imposed on one of the heritage buildings showed the inside of the Golden Temple. The prayers boomed across a public address system. On the screen, a bearded granthi sang the hymns dutifully, the camera so close to his face that Shirina could see the creases lining his skin. She felt small, in that way that Mum probably intended for them on this leg of the pilgrimage – insignificant. The weight of Sehaj's request for Shirina faded away. It was just a moment, a speck in her history. There was so much to look forward to. She would tell Sehaj this when she had the next chance, echoing what he had said all along. 'I just have to get through these next couple of days and then I'll be home,' she would say.

At the stairs that led to the entrance of the grounds of the Golden Temple, a tour guide held court for a group of tourists who wore backpacks and used their hands to shield their eyes from the bright sunlight amplified by the pure-white stone of the walls and buildings that made up the surrounding complex. 'We go down these stairs and descend into the grounds,' he explained. 'This is intentional. The motion of going down rather than up instils humbleness and eliminates arrogance from our minds.' Two turbaned warrior guards wearing regal-blue garments stood on either side of the entrance. Shirina dipped her feet in the trough of water and climbed the stairs, leaving wet footprints on the marble surface. She listened to the tour guide as if she was part of the group. He went on about the Golden Temple's history – its significance as the most sacred place of worship for Sikhs, the entrances which could be seen from every angle, inviting people from all faiths. 'The fifth Sikh guru, Guru Ram Das, excavated a tank, which is this large pool of water. It became known as Amritsar, the Pool of the Nectar of Immortality. The holy city grew around it and took on the same name. The shrine was built in the centre of the pool and became the centre of Sikhism in the world.' The tourists nodded and uttered small acknowledgements of wonder — 'Ahh!', 'Oh!' Their phones captured snapshots of the unsmiling guards holding their tall spears and staring straight ahead.

Then the tour guide stopped talking. Shirina understood why — the sight of the golden shrine literally took his breath away. She wondered if this was a performance. Surely after visiting every day, it would grow old? But that blissful smile on his face seemed to reflect the stunning vision of that majestic golden jewel which appeared to float on the calm water. White marble floors and a complex of low-pillared buildings ran across the edges of the palatial grounds which surrounded it on all sides. The temple's intricately carved gilded domes glinted in the sun. Here, the sky seemed wider and bluer than anywhere Shirina had been, and it seemed like some divine trick that the temple was both immense and welcoming.

Shirina had only ever seen the Golden Temple in pictures, but they couldn't do justice to this view. In their home, Mum had a framed poster of the temple on the living-room wall — the only thing that hung on the wall besides a portrait of Guru Nanak surrounded by garlands and votive candles. Shirina was only about five years old when she had asked Mum, 'Whose house is that?' Mum had laughed. 'That's God's house,' she'd said. 'God lives there.' And then she looked at it with such yearning, that Shirina saw what she saw. Compared to their old couches and cracked windows, God's house was much better. Shirina had always understood Mum's longing for another home — it was a powerful sentiment that they shared but never spoke about. When Shirina announced to her family that she had met somebody and was going to marry him, she sensed the questions brewing in her sisters' minds. *Why didn't you say anything? Why are you going so far away?* Mum was the only one who didn't seem surprised.

* * *

Rajni led the way, barefoot, along the edges of the water. A long strip of carpet ran along the path to the temple. If she stepped off the carpet, her feet would make contact with the heat-soaked tiles. Ahead of her there were two children playing, nudging each other off the carpet as they tried to maintain their balance. From their play, Rajni understood that the marble floor took on the heat of lava in their imaginations. They stepped on and off, giggling and squealing. She felt an ache in her chest, thinking of Anil, and how much she had wanted him to have a sibling. How strangely incomplete her family always felt, as if there was a ghostly presence of something that never existed. Was that why he was so eager to start a family of his own? Had he always been lonely? She couldn't ask him those questions now. This morning, she trawled through her social media pages and found that they had been scrubbed clean of any traces of Anil. He had deleted and blocked her. It was strange how visceral and effective the pain of an online snub could be. Any small amount of guilt or doubt that Rajni felt over hiring that private investigator was gone now.

They continued their slow walk towards the temple, passing the men's bathing area of the sarovar. A screen blocked off the view but when the men emerged from the pool and stood up to put their clothes back on, their heads and feet were visible behind the screen. There was an air of celebration to the whole ritual – they patted each other on the back and called out.

'We're not going in there, are we?' Jezmeen asked.

'There's a separate bathing area for women,' Rajni said. 'I think it's over there.' She pointed at a bath-house ahead under the shade of a tree with outstretched branches, where women were lining up with their belongings neatly tucked under their arms. Another stream of women exited the bath-house, their actions not quite as congratulatory as the men's. Rajni wondered if this was because their bath was private whereas the men – save for the screen – were out in the open. Their purification was on display for the whole world to see.

As they got closer to the temple, the line of people thickened and the spaces became narrower. From what Rajni could see, there were two or three rows for lining up. One line seemed to move much faster than the others but it was the slow line that most people wanted to be in. 'I don't get what's going on,' she muttered.

'Feels like we're at a nightclub,' Jezmeen said.

A grey-haired woman in front of them turned around and explained: 'This line is for tourists. The people who just want to come inside, see the temple, and go. You move right through. The other line is for devotees to sit down. It takes longer to get through.'

'So . . . the express line then?' Jezmeen asked. 'We don't have to sit in there, do we? We just want to pay respects.'

'I guess so,' Rajni said, although she bristled slightly at being called a tourist. Tourists enjoyed themselves and brought home useless plastic souvenirs. They were here for spiritual purification – nothing about this trip felt like a holiday to her. She was beginning to feel the weight of returning to the past. Fragments of memories of her last trip with Mum here were surfacing and becoming more difficult to ignore now they were in Punjab, where it all started.

They moved into the quicker line. It was managed by a man at the front who counted bodies, let them in quickly, and then suddenly snapped the bar back in place. The people moved like floodwater rushing into every little space. The sudden crush of bodies alarmed Rajni; instinctively, she reached out for Jezmeen and Shirina, grabbing their hands.

'Can everybody just relax?' Jezmeen said irritably. Nobody appeared to hear her. Rajni felt the pressure of the crowd behind her and the barrier ahead. It was getting hotter; sweat broke across her upper lip but her arms were pinned to her sides by the other pressing bodies. She tipped her head up and took a gulp of air.

When they were eventually allowed into the temple, the procession was calmer. The desperation that Rajni felt from the crowd seemed to dissipate once they were let through. She checked over her shoulders to make sure Jezmeen and Shirina were following behind. Jezmeen was looking out over the water, its calm and glassy surface. Shirina's forehead was set into a deep frown.

It's not supposed to be this way, Rajni thought. She had known better than to come into this pilgrimage with too many expectations, but she thought Amritsar would be different. It was beautiful, certainly; the temple was nothing short of breath-taking. But now she and her sisters were being shuttled into the prayer hall, a room dripping with ornate gold trimmings, the sounds of hymns reverberating against the high ceilings. And all she could think was: *How long do we have here?*

It was like a theme-park ride where the wait was infinite but the ride itself only lasted under a minute and left everybody wondering why on earth they had anticipated it so much. They were ejected from the room almost as soon as they entered. 'Can't we sit?' Rajni asked. The current of the crowd carried her and her request out of the hall. Shirina and Jezmeen looked just as dazed when they emerged.

'Is that it?' Rajni asked.

'I suppose so,' Jezmeen said. 'Unless you want to go back and line up again.'

Rajni barely heard her. She was remembering saying those same words to the doctors when they told her that there was nothing left to do in Mum's case. 'So that's it?' she'd asked, over and over again until they could give her a different answer. She wasn't just talking about the cancer; she was shocked that Mum's life would just . . . end. After all those arguments, all those conflicts, she would cease to exist.

Jezmeen and Shirina stepped in front of Rajni and led the way back to the women's bath-house. Rajni was still deep in thought, this time recalling a visit to the hospital and seeing the anguish on Mum's face. 'Rajni, please press play on the iPad,' Mum had whispered when the pain passed and she could speak again. Anil had helped her to stream the daily prayers from the Golden Temple and their messages rang across the room from the tinny iPad speakers. 'I've got the Bluetooth speakers at home,' he'd said anxiously to Rajni. 'I can go get them and then she'll have, like, surround-sound and it'll be more relaxing or whatever.' Rajni had told him to go ahead, what a lovely idea. She needed time alone with Mum that day.

The line of women outside the bath-house hummed with excitement.

158

In front of Rajni was a teenage girl with a long rope of hair that hung to the base of her spine. Handing her belongings over to the girl next to her, she pulled her hair into a bulging bun and pinned it in place. Rajni touched her own short hair, which ended at the nape of her neck. The line inched forward at a much more peaceful pace than the line back at the temple.

'I'll be glad to have a dip in the water,' Jezmeen commented, fanning herself.

'We don't have to take all our clothes off, right?' Shirina asked as they made it through the threshold. There were several bare bottoms here and Rajni felt just as alarmed as her little sister sounded.

'I don't think so,' Rajni said. An attendant was sitting on a low wooden stool next to the pool's edge and ushering women in. Some were stripped down to their underwear and others were wearing light cotton tunics that reached their knees.

'Screw it, I'm getting naked,' Jezmeen declared. She set her belongings down on a bench and peeled her clothes off. Instinctively, Rajni looked away but she noticed how other women were drawn to Jezmeen's body art and her long limbs as she hopped into the pool and strode through the water. Two large orange carps shot off like fireworks as they saw her approaching.

Shirina kept her clothes on and found herself a corner and lowered herself down the stairs into the water. Rajni took in a deep breath and did the same. The water lapped at her feet and rose up as she descended, making her tunic billow about her like a tent. She pressed it down and waited for the weight to render it limp against her thighs.

The water was still, despite the women wading through it. Some would call this a miracle, Rajni thought, recalling everything she'd read and heard about these restorative baths in the lead-up to this trip. Mum had told her all kinds of stories that day as well, repeating that she wanted to go to the Golden Temple. A bath in the sarovar would take all her pain away, she insisted. 'Mum, Anil's going to bring his speakers later,' Rajni had said stupidly, knowing the futility of her response. Here her mother was, asking for a spiritual experience, and all Rajni could offer up was better sound quality on her electronic prayer program. All her life, Mum had told her stories of men and women who bathed in the water and had their health restored – eyesight miraculously regained, tumours dissolved, wombs suddenly fertile and hospitable to new life. But it was just water, Rajni would argue, the pragmatist in her unable to see anything beyond this argument.

'Rajni, listen to me,' Mum had said urgently, her features contorted with pain. *Here we go,* Rajni thought, knowing that she was in for another lecture about miracles, about things that happened without rhyme or reason. But what Mum said instead surprised her.

'You'll help me, right?' Mum asked. 'You'll make sure I don't suffer?'

'Of course,' Rajni said. Mum's expression was wide with trust. Her skinny fingers dug into Rajni's palms and brought tears to her eyes. She couldn't bear the thought of watching Mum whittle away, pain and suffering slowly dissolving her dignity. Rajni didn't realize what a heavy responsibility she had accepted though, until she began helping Mum research options over the next few days. *We can't do this,* she thought, looking at those websites. *Not like this.*

What a relief it was then, to arrive at the hospital one day to find that Mum had a letter written. She had this pilgrimage planned. She had a jewellery pouch tucked in her drawer and as she unzipped it to show her daughters the pills she had stashed away inside, Rajni was still nodding, still promising to do anything.

Chapter Ten

Our fifth Guru, Guru Arjan Dev Ji, said that bathing in the sacred waters of the sarovar washes away all of our sins. Water rids people of diseases, nourishes our bodies and brings clarity to our thoughts and actions. Your body's immersion in the nectar of immortality will bring eternal strength and fulfilment to your spirit.

Jezmeen cupped the water into her hands and raised them over her head. The water poured down her face, pooling at the shelf of her collarbone. It smelled like summer rain; earthy and fresh. She really felt as if she could stay here all day – if not for the spiritual release, then the refreshment of being out of the heat. With her eyes closed and the echoing women's voices fading into a singular din in the background, she thought there was something quite peaceful and otherworldly about this bath.

Next to her, a woman had rolled the cuffs of her white salwar up to her knees and was wading through the water with a toddler's legs anchored around her hips. She chanted into the little girl's ears and crouched to scoop up some water to toss on her small feet. 'This is God's water,' the woman said, loose strands of her fringe falling over her eyes. 'Its holiness will protect you.' The toddler kicked and squealed with delight.

Jezmeen had read those tales of lepers' wounds disappearing upon contact with this miracle water. Of course, some measure of exaggeration had gone into creating those stories. Wasn't it more convenient for the story that the lepers were cured instantaneously rather than a gradual process over weeks and months? When children were told those stories, could they really be trusted to listen patiently while the leper noticed tiny improvements in his scarring or strength gaining in his muscles? No. She bent at the waist and took another handful of water. As it cascaded over her shoulders, she became certain that the point of the spiritual bath was to start a slow progression of healing.

When she opened her eyes and blinked away the droplets, she noticed a large orange carp near her feet. It was impossible to know if this was the same one that she saw when she entered the water, but it seemed to be aware of her. It hovered at her feet, still and watching. Jezmeen stared back at it, wondering if some divine intervention had brought this fish to her. She recalled the Arowana's glossy eyes, its mouth moving as if speaking an ancient language.

'Go tell your friends I'm working on being better,' Jezmeen said to the carp. A middle-aged woman nearby looked at her in confusion and then also nodded at the fish. Jezmeen swayed her foot gently to create ripples so the fish would swim away. Watching it leave, Jezmeen felt sorry, more sorry than she had been when the Arowana had died, and she didn't know why. The pressure of tears built in her throat. Being in this pool for purification made her think about Mum sitting in her hospital bed, holding the edges of that letter in her frail hands as she read it out. *Cleanse yourself of all burdens,* she had said, holding her daughters' attention. Did the room tense up then? Jezmeen remembered thinking that she was the only one of her two sisters who really had burdens – every rejection and every passing year slimming her chances of a breakthrough.

Once Mum had got through her explanation of the itinerary, she paused and began to whisper. Rajni, Jezmeen and Shirina huddled closer to Mum. There was something else she wanted her daughters to help her with. Her voice was so full of hope that she didn't seem to even notice how horrified Jezmeen was when she explained the pills.

'I've been storing them for a while now,' she said, her eyes shining. 'I'll take them all at once tomorrow morning. I'm telling you because I think you should know, but also because I need you to keep a lookout for nurses. I don't know their schedules well enough to know when somebody will pop in to do a test or bring a meal. If somebody is coming, you need to distract them.'

'What you're asking us to do is illegal,' Jezmeen said, looking to Rajni and Shirina. 'Right?' Shirina nodded in agreement. 'There must be another way,' she said, but Jezmeen heard the uncertainty in her voice. Rajni, probably knowing that Shirina would give in to Mum's requests eventually, took them both out of the room to discuss it.

Back in the present, a commotion erupted behind Jezmeen and shook her out of her thoughts. She heard a sharp gasp and turned to see Shirina sitting on the edge of the pool with her legs splayed before her. A stout elderly woman with rosy cheeks crouched next to her. 'Shirina,' Jezmeen said, wading through the water. 'Are you okay?'

The woman's expression was etched with concern. She took Shirina by the elbow and gently helped her up. Then she said something to Shirina – it looked like a question or a comment, but it seemed to startle her. Shirina shook her head and turned her back to the woman.

'I'm fine,' Shirina said. 'I just – I slipped.'

Jezmeen glanced at the rosy-cheeked woman. Now she appeared confused. She stared at Jezmeen for a few moments and then returned to her family, two little girls wearing matching swimsuits and long tracksuit leggings.

'What did that lady say to you?' Jezmeen asked.

'Oh, you know,' Shirina said. 'Just to be careful. I'm fine though. A fall on your bum hurts a lot more when you're an adult, doesn't it?'

That rush of words and the forced smile didn't hide Shirina's embarrassment. Jezmeen wondered for a moment what it would be like to be her little sister, so prim and perfect that a fall in a bath-house would be the humiliation of a lifetime. *Have you read my Wikipedia entry?* she wondered. 'Don't worry about it,' Jezmeen said. 'Nobody saw.' They gathered their belongings and stepped out of the bath-house gingerly together. But as they passed the woman and her two daughters, her stare lingered on Shirina. It was more curious than unfriendly, but Shirina seemed to make it a point not to look back.

The hot tiled floor stung Jezmeen's feet. She spotted Rajni sitting on a bench, squinting against the glare of the sun.

'What happened?' Jezmeen asked. 'You were in there for all of five minutes.'

Rajni shrugged. 'I didn't feel like staying.'

'Why not?' Jezmeen asked.

'I couldn't stop thinking about Mum.'

A trickle of water made its way down Jezmeen's forehead. She wiped it away with the back of her hand. 'I thought the bath would make me feel better,' she said. 'That was the whole point.'

'Do you feel better?'

Jezmeen nodded. 'I feel like something changed in there. I don't think I believe the water has miraculous healing properties, but . . . I don't know. Haven't you ever taken a bath to forget a stressful day? That's how it was for me.'

'Jezmeen, this isn't as simple as forgetting a bad night out.'

Jezmeen felt a scrape of irritation with Rajni. Of course it wasn't so simple, she knew that. But the bath also gave Jezmeen clarity about some-thing that she hadn't admitted until now: she resented Mum for putting them in this situation. They wouldn't be in India if not for her – they'd have nothing on their consciences. Jezmeen wouldn't be having those recurring dreams. The sequence of events in Jezmeen's life played out in reverse, as if a tape was swallowing them back. If Mum hadn't written that letter, none of this would have happened.

They sat together in silence for a while, watching the worshippers fall into line and emerge from the dark bath-house into the bright white temple grounds. 'Where did Shirina go?' Rajni asked.

'She's around,' Jezmeen said. 'She said something about taking a picture for Sehej's family.'

'She probably went looking for her in-laws' tribute,' Rajni said. 'They made a donation to the temple recently and there's an engraved dedication to them.'

'How big a donation?' Jezmeen asked. On their way in, they had passed all manner of tributes, names of prominent families engraved into the grand marble walls.

Rajni raised an eyebrow. 'A *big* one.'

So Shirina wouldn't have trouble finding her in-laws' plaque then. The significant donations took up more wall space and attracted their own followers. Earlier, Jezmeen had seen a murmuring crowd standing around a towering tribute from a prominent Sikh hedge-fund manager from New York.

'They've got lots of money to spend, haven't they?' Jezmeen asked.

'They certainly didn't spare any expense on those wedding celebrations.'

Jezmeen remembered feeling overwhelmed by all of Shirina's in-laws and their glittery outfits, and by how many of them had taken the not-small decision to fly all the way from Australia for the wedding. They wore their success in brand-name shoes and designer suits. The only person who stood out was Shirina's mother-in-law. Her clothes, though tasteful, were simple to reflect her widow's status. Sehaj's father had died when he was a teenager. Jezmeen imagined this was something they had in common when they first began chatting online.

Is it the money? Jezmeen had wondered when Shirina announced she was engaged to Sehaj. She had never known her sister to be a gold-digger but who wouldn't be impressed with all that Sehaj's family had to offer, especially after growing up in that old semi-detached house with taps that sputtered and a hole in the fence big enough for the neighbours' incontinent German Shepherd to visit their yard to relieve himself? Jezmeen too had spent her childhood imagining a glamorous life, but her fantasies were of stardom. *The whole world will know my name,* she promised herself, shaking away her fears of insignificance.

Rajni was fiddling with her phone. 'I really wish this thing would work,' she grumbled, shaking the phone as if this would make it function properly. 'The FindMe app keeps showing Shirina in the same spot as we are.'

'Maybe her phone is off,' Jezmeen suggested.

'I really don't want to lose one of my sisters in Punjab,' Rajni said, frowning at her phone.

'Relax,' Jezmeen said. 'It's the Golden Temple. Only good things happen here.'

'Right,' Rajni said with a sigh. She stared at her phone as if she was willing it to start ringing.

'Do you use the FindMe app to track Anil's movements as well?' Jezmeen asked. 'He's off at a pub somewhere and you know exactly when he's leaving?'

Rajni looked insulted. 'I don't keep track of my son's movements,' she informed Jezmeen haughtily.

'I was joking. Did I tell you I saw him recently?' Jezmeen asked. 'In the mall?'

Rajni's face seized. Jezmeen could tell from the pinched look on her face that she was hiding something. 'I think he was buying you a birthday gift. I thought it was quite sweet.' *Quite unlike Anil,* she thought, but she kept that observation to herself.

'Oh yes,' Rajni said with a forced laugh. 'Bless him. Such a thoughtful one, isn't he?' She held up her phone and shook it once again. 'Would you believe this useless thing?' she cried. 'Now it's saying that Shirina's on some back street. Honestly.' She chucked the phone into her bag with more force than necessary, suggesting to Jezmeen that she did not want to discuss Anil's thoughtfulness any further.

Shirina alternated between cursing to herself and gulping in breaths of air as she power-walked towards the hotel. This narrow lane connected the two major streets and she needed all the shortcuts she could find. There was a dull ache in her belly, followed by a cramp, and in her panic, she couldn't remember if it started before or after she had fallen. She was furious with herself for not recording the relevant information in her phone, choosing instead to keep it on that card that Sehaj had given her.

Back in the hotel room, Shirina took a moment to sit on the edge of her bed and catch her breath. Room service had already come through and replaced her sheets – soaked in sweat, she was ashamed to think of it, but last night had been hot even with the air-conditioning on at full blast – and now there wasn't a single wrinkle to be seen on the flat, white sheets. The bed was vast like the Golden Temple grounds, and there was that same sense of freshness, of starting over.

She picked up the phone and pressed 0. 'Yes, how can I help you?' asked the young man that she had seen manning the reception desk. 'Madam Shirina, is it?' he asked. 'Room 303?'

'Yes – uh—' She cleared her throat. 'I was wondering if you could give me the number of a nearby hospital?'

'Are you unwell, Madam?'

'Not – no, I think I might be injured. I'd just like to know where the nearest hospital is, just in case.'

'Just one moment, Madam.'

Why didn't she watch where she was going? Then she wouldn't be in this situation now, this panic. She closed her eyes and took in a deep breath and waited for the pain to return. There it was, a cramp that spread like fingers across her sides and radiated across her belly. She'd felt something like that before after a conversation with her mother-in-law and later, she realized that it was the beginning of a panic attack. Could that be it? Just a panic attack? No need to see a doctor then, just take a few deep breaths and return to the temple as if nothing had happened.

The young man's voice returned to the phone. He recited a list of hospitals and their addresses. Shirina murmured the names back but she didn't write anything down. A doctor who didn't know her situation would ask too many questions and she couldn't have that.

Then again, it was better to be on the safe side. If the pain intensified and she was back at the temple, how would she explain herself to anyone? It was bad enough, what that woman said to her when she was helping her up, and the way she looked at her – suspicious, Shirina thought, although she knew that it could just as well have been concern. She wrote down the name of the last hospital the bellboy mentioned.

'Madam, if it's an emergency, we can arrange for transport to take you there right away,' he said.

Tears stung her eyes. 'I'll be fine. Thank you,' she said, and then she hung up. She wanted to talk to Sehaj again but she couldn't imagine what she'd say or what he could do to make her feel better. She got to her feet and paused, waiting for the pain, but it was absent. Maybe it was just a panic attack. Then she went to the safe where she'd kept her passport locked away after Rajni returned it this morning.

She opened the passport case and realized with a jolt that the card was not in the little pocket where she'd kept it neatly folded in half. This was strange. She bent the cover of her passport to ease it out of the case and flipped the case over, shaking it over her lap. Nothing. Fishing through the slit pockets, she found a faded fast-food receipt stubbornly wedged into the leather, the Turkish writing with all its additional accents itemizing a bistro meal they had at the airport at the end of their honeymoon. She felt the pain again, this time tightening in her chest. It was definitely panic.

A huge extended family was checking in at the reception desk when Shirina came down the stairs. 'Excuse me,' she said, elbowing past their overflowing suitcases and two grandparents in wheelchairs. 'I'm very sorry, but I need to talk to you,' she said to the desk manager.

He raised an eyebrow. 'Yes?'

'My passport,' she said. 'There was a card with very important information on it. Did it slip out, by any chance? Maybe you threw it away?'

'I don't remember it, Madam,' he said, returning to his typing.

'It just had a name and a number on it but it's very important,' Shirina repeated. The man probably caught the hint of urgency in her voice. He stopped what he was doing.

'I really can't recall seeing a card in your passport case,' he said. 'If it fell on the floor, it was swept up long before you got your passport back.' He pointed at the framed certificate on the wall congratulating them for steadfast cleaning service. 'We don't like litter on our floors.'

'Okay, thanks,' Shirina mumbled, returning to the room. It wasn't a huge problem, she told herself. She could call Schaj and ask him for the info again, and he'd tell her and it would be fine. It was late afternoon in Australia now. Although the pain from her fall was gone, she didn't want to take any chances.

Back in the room, she paced the tiny length of floor between the bed and the bathroom door and took in a few deep breaths. As she picked up her phone from the dresser, she noticed that her ring finger was still bulging around her wedding band and engagement ring. The heat made her feet swell as well; she could feel the beginnings of a blister forming on the side of her big toe where it rubbed against the strap of her sandals. She pressed Sehaj's name in her contacts list and wriggled the ring off. The call connected just as she placed it on the dresser.

'Hello? Sehaj?' she asked.

'Who is this?' replied a croaky woman's voice.

Mother. What was she doing answering Sehaj's phone?

'Hello, Mother,' Shirina said. Her manner was always formal with her mother-in-law, even at this distance. She sat up a little bit straighter. Her heart began to patter in her chest. What was going on?

'Hello, *beti*,' Mother replied. There was little affection in the way she greeted Shirina, even using a term of endearment. 'Everything is going smoothly?'

'Yes,' Shirina said. 'I just need to talk to Sehaj.'

'He's not around. He went for a run.'

Sehaj usually left his phone in their bedside table when he went running along the creek near their home. One of Shirina's earlier memories of their marriage – the honeymoon period – was standing on the newly built deck and watching him pass, his limbs cutting through the air like machinery. Now she shuddered to think of what else she had left in that dresser drawer that her mother-in-law felt so free to rummage through: a half-empty tube of lubricant, an illustrated pocket copy of the *Kama Sutra* that a co-worker of his had given as a cheeky engagement present.

'Can you ask him to call me back when he returns?' Shirina asked.

'I don't think that's such a good idea,' Mother replied.

Her response felt like a punch in Shirina's stomach. 'What do you mean?'

'You heard me, *beti*,' Mother said. If it was possible, the word felt even colder this time, devoid of affection. 'It's not such a good idea.'

'Why not?' Shirina demanded. 'He's my husband.'

There was a long sigh on the other end of the phone that sounded just as familiar as when Shirina was standing head to head with Mother in their home in Melbourne. It was strange what the long-distance lines picked up. Shirina knew what Mother was going to say next; it was as if she read from a script, yet Shirina fell for it every time. 'You don't have to get so emotional.'

'Emotional' was like a first warning. 'Rude' was the second warning. No matter how politely Shirina said something, no matter how many pleases and thank-yous and with-all-due-respects she used, as long as she said no, she was being rude. The final strike wasn't clear. Shirina hadn't gone that far yet.

'You called him yesterday, didn't you?' Mother continued.

'Yes,' Shirina said, already knowing where this was going. 'I thought he should know that we were in Punjab already.'

'But was it necessary to make such a fuss? To create such hysterics? He was beside himself after that phone call.'

'What do you mean?' Shirina asked.

'I found him in tears in his bedroom, babbling about how sorry he felt for you.'

Sehaj was upset on her behalf? He hadn't sounded that way over the phone, but maybe he was putting up a tough façade. This information buoyed Shirina. She could still go through with what the family wanted her to do, but she just needed to know that Sehaj understood how hard it was to hide and lie and pretend that it wasn't happening.

'I didn't mean to upset him,' Shirina said. 'I was having some doubts and I was scared. Surely you'd understand that, Mother.' *Remember when we used to understand each other?* Shirina wanted to ask. In the first few weeks, when she was still adjusting to her new life, she and Mother would walk to the shops together and they'd both pull shawls around their shoulders, shocked by the sudden biting Melbourne wind when it had been sunny only moments before. 'It's so nice having a girl around the house,' Mother said so approvingly whenever she saw Shirina wiping down the kitchen counters or rearranging the shoes in the doorway that Sehaj carelessly kicked off.

Then Shirina found a job and she had less time for housework during the week, so it piled up for Saturdays and Sundays. Mother's comments changed focus to what needed doing – the dust-coated windowsills, the loads of washed and dried laundry waiting to be folded and put away. 'I didn't think having a daughter would be as messy as having a son,' Mother would say with a laugh that told Shirina she didn't actually find it funny at all.

Mother let out a laugh now as well. 'My goodness, so much *drama*,' she said. Shirina could picture her shaking her head. 'Since you came into our lives, it's been up and down, a rollercoaster. Sehaj kept going on about how it wasn't your fault. Nobody said it was your fault. Did I? Did I say that?' She chuckled again, how ridiculous!

'No,' Shirina said through gritted teeth.

'That's right,' Mother said triumphantly. 'In fact, I was very hurt by what Sehaj told me after that. You made a comment about how I was able to make it up the stairs.'

'I was simply wondering where you got the strength from all of a sudden,' Shirina said. 'A week ago, you needed a wheelchair and you needed my assistance to go anywhere.'

'Well, with the help of God's blessings, my hip is healing very well, dear. It must be all that service you've been putting into the temples in India. It is very kind of you. You're doing a good thing there, Shirina, and I'm very grateful.'

This was said with no malice and Shirina felt herself softening. Beneath her tough exterior, Mother loved her. Sehaj had told her this many times: 'She loves you, Shirina. Sure, she can be a bit overbearing but it's how she shows her love.' You couldn't have closeness with family members without aggravating each other once in a while. She had to remind herself that Mum's distant parenting had left her feeling like an afterthought. Even when Mum read out that letter, Shirina could sense that it was addressed to her older sisters, because her response didn't matter.

In her new family though, it was different. There was a chance to have a close relationship with Mother, if she just did this one thing. Shirina realized that up until this moment, she had been undecided. There was clarity and immediate relief in having her feet firmly planted on one side, rather than tiptoeing around the border, afraid to commit.

'Can you please ask Sehaj to call me? I lost the information for the driver and the address and everything.'

'Oh,' Mother said. 'Then why didn't you say so? I have all of that information written down. Just give me a minute, *beti*.'

There it was, that word again, this time infused with tenderness. Shirina felt the tension in her chest melting away as she sank back into the clean, cool sheets tautly stretched across her bed. She'd allow herself some time to lie down here and then she'd wash all of that water out from her hair. The sarovar did not do much to cleanse her, and the fall felt like a terrible omen. She had to start all over again.

The main square in the centre of the holy city was brimming with tourists now that it was afternoon. A group of men and women in backpacks huddled around a statue commemorating the Jallianwala Bagh massacre. Rajni only had a rudimentary knowledge of the massacre; it wasn't covered in her school textbooks and it happened so long ago that it wasn't relevant to her. But the captivating statue could represent any horrific incident: the faces of men and women rising from a viscous smoke, their faces forlorn and some mouths twisted in anguish. She was a little girl when another massacre took place in the Golden Temple, and she remembered Mum watching the news non-stop, her hand hovering over her heart. Rajni was too young to know the details at the time but years later, the story became woven into her own history: Prime Minister Indira Gandhi had ordered her soldiers to storm the Golden Temple to remove a militant leader. There were more raids on the Punjab countryside to round up suspects, and there were protests and violent fights between Sikhs and Hindus in the cities.

She glanced at Jezmeen and Shirina, who were looking at the statue with a different sense of curiosity – more removed, more as spectators of the events than Rajni. So much had happened before Jezmeen and Shirina were even born. Rajni remembered watching the news with Dad and seeing him nervously patting his beard, his eyes full of worry for the first time. Sikhs were being hunted down in India, their beards and long tresses cut to humiliate them. 'It could start happening here,' Dad had warned Mum, looking out the window as if the thugs were clamouring at their door. 'Keep a low profile around your Hindu friends,' he'd told Rajni. But at school, brown was brown, and everybody was too busy worrying about being bullied for being Indian to start turning on each other.

A small group of tourists began to wedge their way into the crowd to take pictures near the statue. Shirina stepped closer to Rajni. Rajni caught a whiff of the hotel's floral-scented body wash and noticed that Shirina's hair was nicely fluffed. Had she left the Golden Temple to return to the hotel for a shower? Something about this irked Rajni. They had waited for over an hour for her to come back, during which time the lunch service was almost finished and all that was left to eat were the charred pieces of roti from the bottom of the stack, and some dal which had gone cold.

Just thinking about it made Rajni's stomach rumble. She placed a palm on her belly, embarrassed at the noise, but Jezmeen clearly heard it.

'I could go for a snack too,' Jezmeen said. 'Was it just me, or was the temple food a little light?'

'It was,' Rajni agreed. The problem was, she was a little bit sick of Indian food. She should have eaten more variety in Delhi, where there was Chinese and Western.

'There are a couple of dhabas over there,' Shirina said, pointing at a strip of restaurants that led back out to the main road. 'I saw a Trip Advisor sticker on one of them.'

'It's going to be more of the same though, isn't it?' Jezmeen said. 'I don't know about you guys, but I'm getting tired of Indian food.'

'Me too,' Shirina admitted.

'Well, if that's how you two feel,' Rajni said with a shrug. She didn't want to seem too obvious but she could kill for a burger. Ever since they arrived, she'd been eyeing the two-storey McDonald's and the new McFlurry advertisement that took up an entire window.

Jezmeen and Shirina led the way. Rajni tossed a glance over her shoulder at the statue. Some people had their eyes shut and they were praying to it. A middle-aged woman wearing jeans and a loose cotton top dipped her head, kissed the tips of her fingers and touched the foot of the statue. Rajni wondered if she should do the same – it seemed wrong to turn her back on this tribute to pursue an ice-cream sundae – but her sisters were marching ahead, already having forgotten about the dead and suffering. Another pang of hunger struck Rajni. She noticed the soft bounce of Shirina's hair and felt another tickle of irritation.

Right outside the restaurant's entrance, men were circulating and holding boards with photographs of nearby tourist destinations. 'Himalayas,' a man called. 'Very pretty drive.' He waved his board featuring snow-capped mountains against wide blue skies. 'Wagah Border,' another man called. 'Wagah Border Wagah Border Wagah Border,' he continued frenetic-ally as he saw the three sisters approaching.

'No,' Rajni said right away but Jezmeen took a brochure from him before they entered the restaurant.

'I've heard it's quite a show,' Jezmeen said, flipping through the brochure as they stepped into line at the counter.

'The India–Pakistan border?' Shirina asked. 'There's a show there?'

'The changing of the guards. That's what these guys are advertising. You go there at the specific time that the guards switch duties. It's a bit of a spectacle. I've seen it on YouTube.'

Rajni had seen it in real life, during her last trip to India with Mum. Some relatives had suggested the day trip and they had all gone together in a noisy, crowded car. Rajni remembered the dusty road on the drive there and the stern military guards at each checkpoint. She remembered how frighteningly passionate everybody on the India side of the border became during the pre-show. 'Why aren't you cheering?' an uncle had asked her. She'd been shocked to silence by the booming music and the feverish wave that swept over the crowd, bringing her to her feet and dropping her back down again. The uncle nodded and smiled knowingly. 'Ah, you're an English girl, that's why.' It wasn't said kindly. By then, Rajni was already aware that her relatives viewed her as a foreigner, and it was with a mix of amusement and distaste that they pointed it out to Mum, who responded with stern words to Rajni. 'Didn't I bring you here to learn about your culture?' she asked loudly for everybody's benefit, while Rajni seethed with rage.

Shirina didn't look too keen to go either. 'How far away is it?'

'About an hour's drive,' Jezmeen said.

Shirina shook her head. 'I really don't want to do any more travelling than we have to,' she said.

Jezmeen turned to Rajni. 'Raj? Come on.'

Rajni looked at Shirina, already ordering her ice cream. *She* didn't want to do any more travelling? It was Rajni and Jezmeen who were going to be completing the most difficult part of the pilgrimage. Shirina just had to visit relatives – her husband's *rich* relatives. They were sending a chauffeured car for her. Who was she to complain about travelling?

'You know what, maybe I will go,' Rajni said. 'It's a very comfortable drive and it's something we can do together.'

'Oh good!' Jezmeen said. 'I'll go book in with the guy now.'

Four McFlurries arrived on a tray. 'We only ordered three,' Rajni informed the woman at the counter, who presented the receipt to her. Four McFlurries.

'Two for me,' Shirina said.

This irked Rajni as well, although she couldn't quite explain why. It was greedy to have more than one ice cream but Shirina didn't seem to notice. She let Rajni take the tray and they made their way up the stairs, finding a quiet table by the window. Below them, the street was busy with touts and tourists. Rajni watched Jezmeen negotiating the trip with a man wearing a sandwich board. His arms waved about enthusiastically. When Rajni turned back to face Shirina, she was taking a huge mouthful of ice cream. Rajni noticed that her wedding ring was gone.

'Did you take your ring off?' Rajni asked, nodding at Shirina's hand.

'Yeah,' Shirina said. 'In the interest of being humble and everything.'

Was she being smug? It came across that way to Rajni now. That ostentatious diamond ring had always bothered her but the absence of it, and Shirina's reason for taking it off – *I don't want to flaunt what I have in front of all the poor people* – bothered her even more.

'This hits the spot,' Shirina said, scooping her spoon into the ice cream.

Rajni said nothing, edging her spoon into her ice cream to take a tiny portion, just out of spite. 'I've never seen you indulge so much in sweets before,' she said.

She expected Shirina to look a bit self-conscious about her two ice creams, apologetic even. Instead, she nodded and took another scoop. 'When on holiday, I suppose.'

The words burst from Rajni's lips: 'You are not on holiday.'

Shirina's spoon hung between the cup and her open mouth. She looked like she was posing for a commercial, except the expression on her face was puzzled. 'I know, Rajni.'

'I don't think you do know,' Rajni said. 'We came here with a purpose. It's not some holiday where we meander from one thing to another.'

'And eating in McDonald's was part of Mum's spiritual plan, was it?' Shirina shot back. Rajni was taken aback by Shirina's retort. It was like arguing with Jezmeen all of a sudden.

'You're not taking this trip seriously,' Rajni said. 'Right from the start, you've made it clear that you'll be dodging the difficult stuff.'

'I told you, this was all arranged at the last minute. I've got obligations. You know how hard it is to say no to the in-laws.'

Rajni ignored Shirina's appeal to her experience with Indian in-laws. Kabir's mother had sewn her the most hideous cushion covers – turquoise beading on sunny yellow fabric – and expected her to have them on display every time she visited. Rajni remembered stuffing her cushions into those covers with such rage that one of the beads popped off and hit her in the eye, momentarily blinding her. 'It's literally an eyesore,' she complained to Kabir, who shrugged and said, 'Is it really such a big deal, Rajni? What's wrong with just giving in once in a while?'

Rajni understood obligations, but Shirina's lack of remorse felt inexcusable. Look at how she was wolfing down that ice cream. 'And what happened today? Jezmeen and I had a lovely time reflecting on Mum's life by the water, but you went off on your own.'

'I told you, I was finding Sehaj's family's—'

'I know you were, but that's the point. Since when did your husband's family's needs come before ours?'

Shirina stared at her. The ice cream was beginning to melt from her spoon. Rajni wanted to hear her say it: Sehaj's family was better. They were richer, they were more sophisticated, they showed up to the wedding and whisked her away into a life of comfort that she never had, and she was loyal only to them. But Shirina said nothing, and this was even more infuriating because it made Rajni feel petty.

Jezmeen came bounding up the stairs, waving a pamphlet at them. 'We get picked up in an hour,' she said breathlessly. 'He'll stop at a good dinner place on the way back.' She looked at Shirina and then Rajni, whose gazes were locked in a staring contest.

'I hope you didn't pay for me, because I'll be spending the evening in the hotel,' Shirina said. She stood up and left, taking both her ice creams with her.

Chapter Eleven

I also want you to experience the familiarity of our ancestral state. You girls are British, yes, but all the previous generations of our family lived in India. It is in your blood – the language, the food, the way things are, these things are not erased just because you grew up elsewhere.

'It's about making time for your family, isn't it? How often do we get to see each other? Never,' Rajni said.

They had been on the road for twenty minutes and it was Rajni's third rant about Shirina's poor participation in the pilgrimage. Jezmeen still didn't know what to say. She was used to Rajni railing against her; Shirina never got into trouble. It was clear that Rajni's feelings had been festering for a while.

'It's those in-laws of hers,' Rajni said. 'She's like their puppet.'

'Isn't that how it always is?' Jezmeen asked. 'Especially in the first few years of marriage. She's got all these people to pay respects to. Surely you had to do the same thing.'

'I travelled with Kabir. Where's Sehaj? Why are his family visits encroaching on our time together? It's bad enough that she left so quickly after Mum's funeral. She went running back to Sehaj as if spending any more time with us was that unbearable.'

Maybe it was, Jezmeen thought, remembering Shirina's outburst on the train yesterday. Although Jezmeen and Rajni had managed to put aside their differences about the funeral arrangements, the resentment over their fight had still hovered over their interactions.

Rajni wasn't through with venting. 'And you should have seen how she said that thing about being humble when I asked her about her wedding ring. It was a backhanded brag.'

Jezmeen looked out the window. It wasn't as enjoyable as she'd thought, being on Rajni's side. Her mouth was twisted in that expression of distaste like she'd just sucked on a lemon. Fragments of a dream Jezmeen recently had about Shirina floated in her mind. They were talking, but the distance between them became wider as the conversation continued and eventually, one of them hung up.

They passed a wide expanse of fields dotted with farmhouses and live-stock. The highway was coated in golden dust. On the side of the road, there was the occasional canteen or restaurant with plastic outdoor furni-ture. Away from the city of Amritsar, the sky did seem bluer and less smoggy. Jezmeen could feel the warmth of the afternoon sun on the window, which made her grateful to be in this air-conditioned car. Their driver had given them his card earlier: Tom Hanks, he said his name was. 'What's your real name?' Jezmeen had asked. He shook his head solemnly and told them he wanted to be known as Tom Hanks.

'Uh, excuse me,' Jezmeen said now in Punjabi, leaning towards the driver's seat. 'Could you pull over at a rest stop in the next ten minutes?' She looked out the window at a filling station with a rusted and gutted car propped up on breeze-blocks. A dark and blurry cloud of flies hovered over something in the hollow where a wheel had been. 'Maybe a restaurant?'

The driver nodded. 'Tom Hanks will bring you to the cleanest rest stop,' he said.

'Thank you,' Jezmeen said. 'You know, you could really tell us your Punjabi name. We're not complete foreigners. We can pronounce it.'

'Tom Hanks,' he said.

'Tom? Thomas? That's what your parents named you at birth?' Jezmeen asked.

'Tom *Hanks*.'

'Okay,' Jezmeen said, defeated. She sank back in her seat and glanced at Rajni, who was still fuming. 'Raj, maybe Shirina's just not feeling so well. Travel does different things to people. She might just want to be on her own.'

'She's been on her own this whole time,' Rajni pointed out. 'Hasn't she had enough time to rest?'

The car switched lanes and slowed down as it approached a restaurant: Ravi's Punjabi Dhaba. 'One of the best,' Tom Hanks said with a flourish as he yanked back the hand-brake.

'Good food?' Jezmeen asked. The restaurant was set back behind a fountain and two tents for outdoor seating. Children chased each other between tall potted plants in the front garden.

'Food is not bad. Seven-out-of-ten rating, if you ask me. Toilets, however, are excellent,' Tom Hanks said.

'That's alright with us,' Jezmeen said.

Tom Hanks was not exaggerating about the bathrooms. They were spotless, with hand-soap dispensers and gleaming sinks. The lock on the door clicked right into place, a luxury that Jezmeen had already started to think she could do without, considering the times she had used toilets with flimsy or non-existent locks in the temple and on the train from Delhi. 'Our driver sure knows how to keep his customers happy,' Jezmeen remarked to Rajni at the sinks as they both washed their hands.

'He probably carts around people like us all the time,' Rajni said.

'I wonder what that's like,' Jezmeen said. 'He's aware that we have different standards but somewhere inside he must be thinking that we're a bunch of prats.'

'We haven't been so bad,' Rajni protested. 'I only gasped that one time when he overtook that bullock because I thought we were going to run the poor animal off the road.'

'Not that,' Jezmeen said. 'Don't you think about it sometimes? About how different our lives would be if we had grown up here? We wouldn't be tourists. We'd be . . . I don't know. I'd be married off to some eligible guy in the village by now. If you find a husband with lots of land, he's a catch, isn't he? I'd like to think I would have been matched with a man with a few acres to his name.' She fluffed her hair in the mirror and fluttered her eyes at her own reflection.

Rajni didn't play along with the joke. Her expression hardened, a look Jezmeen recognized from earlier when they were at the Golden Temple. Something was upsetting her about this trip and it was more than Mum's death, more than Shirina's attitude. 'Raj, are you alright?'

'Hmm? Yeah, fine,' Rajni said. She became busy all of a sudden with drying her hands. The automatic dryer roared and drowned out all of Jezmeen's thoughts.

As they left the restaurant, a busboy dressed smartly in a white and gold-trimmed kurta came running up to them. 'Madam, please, your bill.'

'Bill?' Jezmeen asked. 'You're charging us for using the toilets?'

The busboy shook the bill at Jezmeen and she had a look. One aloo paratha, one small cup of chai. Tom Hanks was sitting at a table near the fountain, taking a luxurious sip. 'That's fine,' Jezmeen said. She paid the bill and they returned to wait in the car while he finished his meal. The air-conditioning was left on at full blast and a bhangra beat pulsed from the stereo speakers. When Tom Hanks returned, he thanked Jezmeen and Rajni for the meal.

'Not at all,' Jezmeen said.

'It would have been nice if he'd asked though,' Rajni pointed out in a whisper.

'It's not a big deal,' Jezmeen whispered back. She could feel herself bristling again at Rajni's constant suspicion of Indian people. How did she live her life, thinking that everybody was out to rip her off?

'Is he going to do that at every rest stop then?' Rajni asked. 'Order himself a meal and charge it to us?'

'So what if he does?' Jezmeen asked. 'He probably had to anyway, because the restaurant wouldn't let us use their toilets if we weren't customers.'

Rajni was dissatisfied with this response, but she dropped the subject, leaving Jezmeen to focus on the landscape. Along the edges of the dual carriageway, large patches of farmland were fronted by sprawling gated properties, the types of homes that she'd mostly seen in photographs that aunties and uncles would pass around at family functions. 'This is the house we built, cost a fraction of a flat here in London,' they'd say with equal measures of pride and scorn, as if the Indian economy should really know better. The houses were furnished with Italian leather sofas that ran along the living room's edges, and the kitchens were taken straight from the catalogues, down to the crockery sets and the 'Home Sweet Home' embroidered onto tea towels. They were English homes in India, unlike their distinctly Indian homes in England. Everywhere people went, they had to remind themselves that they were somebody else. The houses sat empty all year until the summer visits, when some servants could be hired to grease the hinges and dust off the counters, and the families would live in the luxury that they had left this country to afford.

'We still have family in Punjab, don't we?' Jezmeen asked. 'On Dad's land?' She only had a vague understanding of where Dad's ancestral village was. Mum had brushed off her questions when she tried to ask about it for a history project for school. 'Choose a different topic,' Mum replied. 'So many things have happened in the history of the world, and you want to talk about some farm in India.' Jezmeen was disappointed. From the way Mum dismissed her question, it was clear that Dad never owned sprawling acres of land in India like the patriarch of a Hindi drama that Jezmeen had been following at the time.

'Did you ever get to see Dad's village?' she asked Rajni. There it was again, Rajni clenching her jaw. It seemed that nothing Jezmeen said was right.

'Not sure where it is,' Rajni said.

It wouldn't be too difficult to find, Jezmeen thought. They just needed to contact one of those aunties or uncles in England – they weren't blood relatives, but they would be able to provide a village name or a phone number. 'We probably won't get another chance to see it again,' Jezmeen said.

'It's really not something Mum would want us to do,' Rajni reminded her.

'Why not?'

Rajni turned to face her. 'Mum expressly didn't mention any of Dad's relatives in her letter. Why would we go and seek them out then?'

'I don't understand that,' Jezmeen said. 'Did they fall out?' Jezmeen remembered that brother of Dad's being unpleasant when he visited them all those years ago. Sensing the tension in the house, she had asked Rajni when her uncle would leave, but she didn't know what happened. It was all between the adults and Rajni, who was a teenager then and understood more than she did.

'I guess so,' Rajni said.

'What falling out could be so terrible that Mum wouldn't want us speaking to Dad's family?'

'Only Mum knows the answer to that question,' Rajni said, but Jezmeen didn't buy it. Rajni knew something, even though she acted as if she didn't. The trip that Rajni got to take here as a teenager while Jezmeen and Shirina were left in Auntie Roopi's care – she had known Dad's family, dined with them, seen them.

'They're the only family we have left,' Jezmeen pressed. 'Wouldn't they welcome us? Let bygones be bygones and all that?'

'It's probably not that simple,' Rajni said.

Jezmeen pictured herself venturing through the villages with a crumpled piece of paper bearing a pencilled map and a scribbled address. She'd knock on doors and eventually come upon her ancestral home. They'd embrace her; they'd have to, after she came all this way and seemingly travelled across time. While she sat and exchanged stories over tea with her long-lost aunts and uncles, a withered old woman would appear, bearing Jezmeen's very features beneath layers of wrinkles. 'You look like her,' the others would say. And Jezmeen would have a reference point, a prototype of sorts. 'I take after my paternal great-aunt,' she would tell people. 'I have her eyes. People say she had a sense of theatrics as well, but the dementia has taken that away now.' It was a story that gave Jezmeen roots; it would be harder to keep criticizing her as shallow and callous if she had an ancestral connection.

Jezmeen was rudely jolted from her reverie as the car swerved to avoid grazing another car that had wandered into its lane. She grabbed the sides of the passenger seat in front of her. The other car, a gleaming black mini-van, was racing ahead now.

'Mother fucker,' Tom Hanks muttered. He glanced at Jezmeen and Rajni in the rear-view mirror and gave them an apologetic smile. Then his foot hit the accelerator so hard, Jezmeen and Rajni were thrown back against their seats.

'What are you doing?' Rajni asked, panicking.

'Madam, that driver needs to learn a lesson,' Tom Hanks said.

'No, he doesn't,' Jezmeen said firmly. 'We don't want to get in an accident – just ignore him, please.'

'You don't understand, Madam,' Tom Hanks said, still focused on the car. 'He did it on purpose.'

'I know we all take these road incidents personally, but—' Before Jezmeen could finish placating Tom Hanks, he made a sharp and sudden swing into the black van's lane. Rajni let out a long, operatic shriek.

'STOP IT! STOP IT NOW!' Rajni shouted. Jezmeen's words were frozen in her throat. 'TOM HANKS, YOU ARE GOING TO GET US ALL KILLED!'

The car slowed down. Jezmeen looked behind her and saw that the black van was meekly following behind now, having learned its lesson. 'Why did you have to do that?' she asked. 'It was very dangerous.'

Tom Hanks did not reply. His lips were set in a grim line and his eyes stared straight ahead. 'These people think they own the roads,' he finally said.

'Which people?' Jezmeen asked.

He didn't answer her question. *People like us?* she wondered. People who came back to India from abroad and pulled up to their empty mansions in their fancy cars and treated everybody like they were servants? People who could afford drivers to transport them to be entertained by a show of power between two countries that had actually cost lives and spilled blood? Jezmeen looked over at Rajni. Worry lines had appeared on her forehead. She could tell they were thinking the same thing.

* * *

Nothing had changed. Rajni drew this conclusion as she stepped out of the van and her feet hit the dusty ground beneath her. Unpaved and rocky, bits of gravel flicked her ankles and rolled into her sandals as she and Jezmeen walked away from this dirt-road car park.

'Take my card,' Tom Hanks told them. 'In case you can't find me on the way back.'

'You'll be in this same spot though, right?' Rajni asked. She heard the sternness in her own voice and she didn't care. He had nearly killed them just now, so she felt justified in making everything sound like a pre-emptive reprimand.

'I'll be here, Madam,' he said. 'Don't worry. But there are lots of cars and it gets confusing when everybody is wandering around afterwards. You don't want to get into the wrong car.'

No, she certainly didn't. All around her, drivers leaned against their vehicles, their eyes following the tourists. Rajni took the card and tucked it into her purse. It was suddenly the most important thing she owned.

She felt a flash of cold on her hand and looked down to see a boy with a palette of paints and a brush. In one quick stroke, he had given her a streak of orange, one third of the colours needed to create an Indian flag. 'I don't want this,' she informed him. 'No, thank you.'

'Oh, come on, Raj,' Jezmeen said. 'It's less than fifty pence and it's fun.' She was squatting next to another boy and tucking her hair behind her ear, letting him paint the flag on her cheek.

'You look like you're at a carnival,' Rajni said when Jezmeen's face-painting was finished.

'It feels like a carnival,' Jezmeen remarked. Popcorn vendors and drinks carts were scattered along the crooked boundary between the car park and the wide main road. The little boy with the paintbrush persisted, following Rajni and Jezmeen and repeating his prices. When he started humming the Indian national anthem Rajni decided to give up.

'Just a small one,' she said, putting out her hand. 'It'll wash off right away, yes?'

'Of course,' the boy said. With a flourish, he swept the brush across her hand in three confident strokes: orange, white, green. They were wavy, as if the flag were caught in the wind.

She paid him and they continued, following the crowds towards the main security entrance. Here, they were separated by gender – 'Men here, women there,' a guard called out, waving his arms to indicate each designated line. Everybody was patted down but the women were allowed to have it done in a curtained booth, by a female guard. When Rajni's turn came, she watched the guard poke her torch in her purse and raised her arms to let her feel for weapons. She remembered the story of an elderly relative who came to London from Punjab, her first ever visit on an aeroplane. During the routine airport security pat-down, she thought they were hugging her farewell.

The cheering and chanting started as Jezmeen and Rajni advanced towards the stands. It was like a football game, and it was exactly as Rajni remembered. She could feel Jezmeen's excitement radiating off her. 'Look at all these people,' she gushed. She nudged Rajni. 'I know you've seen it before, but don't you think it's exciting?'

'It's fine if you like a spectacle,' Rajni said. She didn't even enjoy school assemblies – those skits the senior students created, always with some vague innuendo and inside-jokey reference to the teachers they didn't like. She hated the raucous applause, the way everything felt like it was going out of control, and when she saw the faces of the other teachers – especially the young ones who didn't mind, who joined in sometimes – she thought: *You're not in charge, that's why.* Moving towards the towering stands with Jezmeen, Rajni realized that this was the motto of her entire life as the eldest sister. She was in charge. Nobody else had that responsibility, and – at least according to Mum – nobody else had managed to screw it up as much as she had. Jezmeen and Shirina had no idea what Rajni had sacrificed.

Jezmeen led the way up the concrete steps. An usher pointed out a spot and urged people to move in. Rajni and Jezmeen scooted along the row and ended up on the far end of the bleachers, overlooking the

Pakistan side. The boundary had puzzled Rajni the first time she saw it – she had expected a river, or a deep, cavernous valley separating both countries, but it was a track of dirt, only a few metres wide. Along the border, tall iron fences and storm clouds of barbed wire sent a clear message.

The music on the India side was a deafening boom, so loud that the speakers' static drowned out the lyrics. The show of patriotism began shortly after Rajni and Jezmeen sat down, schoolchildren racing along the bleachers and to the stage area with Indian flags. When they reached the stage, they danced and clapped in a circle, waving to the audience who cheered them on. People began to leave the stands to join them and soon the stage was crowded with spectators cheering for their country. A woman who was sitting one row ahead turned to her husband and said, 'Come on then, we're only here once.' She had a crisp British accent but she pumped her fist in the air and chanted slogans along with the crowd.

On the Pakistan side, no dancing. There was some faint music, subdued and drowned out by the bass on the Indian side. The bleachers were only half full. Rajni remembered the uncles so smugly commenting on Pakistan's lacklustre turnout back then too. 'Look at them. No pride,' he said. 'And they have all these restrictions against women. They can't even dance in front of the men like our women can.' And then he nodded appreciatively at the women half his age who were shaking their hips for the love of India.

Rajni turned to say something to Jezmeen and noticed the space next to her was empty. She spotted her sister running down the steps to join the dancers. 'Raj!' she called, tossing a look over her shoulder. 'Take a picture.'

Rajni waited for Jezmeen to reach the stage area and then she pointed the phone and shot. All the pictures were slightly blurry because Jezmeen was in motion. She tried for a video. Jezmeen sashayed across the screen in miniature, throwing her hands into the air. Two little girls took her hands and she fell in step with them, laughing and mouthing the chorus that she had only just heard moments ago.

A similar video existed in their family's history. It was long gone now, tossed out with all the other VHS tapes that had more or less disintegrated. Nobody had been organized enough to salvage the tapes and convert them to DVDs when some electronics shops were offering this service, and so they gathered dust and mould and became obsolete. Rajni had only seen it once after that childhood trip. Mum was the star of the video. She was dancing just like Jezmeen. There was that same abandon in her moves – hips shaking, palms open as if she was trying to grasp a piece of the sky. Years later, in the lead-up to her wedding, Rajni anticipated seeing Mum dancing like that again but she didn't. She stayed in the background during Rajni's wedding, still hurting from the fact that Dad's older brother chose not to come. Rajni hadn't wanted to invite him, but Mum felt that it was the proper custom for him to stand in for Dad. It was an important gesture too, to show people that all had been forgiven.

Rajni pressed the stop button on the phone and put it back into her purse. Once the changing of the guards ceremony started, she knew she'd take it out again and record the whole thing – the marching, the high kicks, the theatrics of guards flinging open the gates to protect their land.

Jezmeen's cheeks glistened with sweat when she returned. 'You looked great,' Rajni said. 'Just like Mum. She danced here too.'

'She did?'

Rajni nodded. 'She was sitting right next to me, and when the music started, she started bobbing her shoulders like this.' Rajni did an impression of Mum, shutting her eyes and letting the music course through her.

Jezmeen laughed. 'Mum couldn't resist a good song. Remember how she kept on going at Shirina's wedding? The women on Sehaj's side couldn't keep up.'

Rajni remembered how pleased she had been to see Mum celebrating, but also the twinge of envy she felt towards Shirina. Shirina got to have Mum dancing at her wedding because so much time had passed since that falling out with Dad's family, and Mum had moved on.

'Like one of those battery-operated bunnies in the advertisements,' Rajni agreed. 'That's how she was here too, except twenty-five years younger and in the best health. Dad had died and she hadn't danced or celebrated anything in ages.' Rajni felt a lump growing in her throat. She could feel the warmth of Jezmeen's attention on her face and she swallowed hard, pushed the memory down into her chest and the pit of her stomach, where all of these old fears resided. 'She danced exactly like a woman at her peak,' Rajni said. 'It was one of those moments where you're sitting in a crowd and so much is going on around you – the drinks sellers are calling, the music is throbbing, everybody's cheering and chattering, and it feels like it all stops because there's this woman dancing her heart out and just rejoicing.'

'I can picture it,' Jezmeen said with a wistful smile.

Rajni smiled back. It was a nice memory to leave her sister with, and one that she didn't have to embellish, unlike so many others. She knew Jezmeen was becoming curious about their roots – her mention of Auntie Roopi had startled Rajni yesterday because until now, Rajni wasn't aware that her sisters even remembered being sent to live there while she and Mum took that last trip to India. There was no reason to tell Jezmeen about the fight that happened, and all the events that led up to it. There was no need to tell anybody about the guilt Rajni couldn't help feeling, even though it had been so many years since they came back from that trip. 'I can never go back there again,' Mum had said to Rajni. 'You realize that? You understand what you've done? Because of you, I can never return to India again.'

Chapter Twelve

The messages sign was blinking on Jezmeen's phone. *'YOUR CREDIT IS VERY LOW – PLEASE CALL 8801 TO TOP-UP NOW.'*

That made no sense. Jezmeen had hardly even used her phone here, besides that recent conversation with Cameron and the call she made to Rajni from the police station. The hotel's wireless internet was a bit patchy and she had been in the middle of downloading her emails when she lost her connection. There was an email from Cameron, the subject line reading: *'Have another potential role for you . . .'* But when she clicked on it, a notice popped up reminding her that she was no longer connected.

She dialled the number and fished her credit card out from her purse, tapping it against the dresser as she sat through the recorded options. Her heart thrummed in her chest. Cameron's email could mean something, or it could be another dead end. It was the hope that kept her going. The slightest flicker of interest from a producer, or a role that might just be the one – this was why Jezmeen hadn't quit yet.

'For recharge, please wait while we connect you to an operator.' Jezmeen sighed and picked up the remote control. She flipped through the channels on the television, settling finally on BBC Lifestyle. A woman wearing a yellow-and-green caftan strolled across a pebbled path cut through a sprawling garden lit with tiki torches before the camera zoomed in on a table that looked as if it had been carved out of a felled tree. The host

picked up a glass of white wine. Jezmeen's throat felt parched – the wine looked so deliciously refreshing. The host nodded at the camera, her brilliant smile flashing at Jezmeen before she took a small sip and closed her eyes in appreciation.

'I hate you,' Jezmeen muttered.

'Ma'am?'

'Oh sorry,' Jezmeen said to the operator. 'Not you. The woman on the telly.'

'You are calling for a recharge, Ma'am?'

'Yes – but I also want to know why my credit has run out so quickly?'

There was some typing in the background. 'Ma'am, you've used up all your data in four days.'

'Yes, I know that. I'm wondering how? Is there a breakdown of how much I've used?'

'For that, I have to connect you to our usage specialists. Please hold—'

'Ugh, never mind. Can I just get a recharge?'

It was too late. She was placed on hold. A recorded advertisement in Hindi blared into her ears, followed by an upbeat chorus singing about upgrading to a family package.

'Hello, this is Krishna, how can I assist you?'

'Hi. I'm curious as to why my phone data has run out so quickly,' Jezmeen said. 'I've only had it for four days.'

'Let me check. Your name, please?'

'Jezmeen Shergill. Father's name is Devinder Singh Shergill.'

'Your identification number?'

'What would that be? My passport number?'

'Yes, Ma'am.'

Jezmeen reached for her passport and flipped open the case. A small card flipped out and fell to her feet. She recited the numbers to the man on the phone.

'I will check for you, Ma'am, please give me one minute.'

The recorded chorus burst into life again. *Save more time with family time,* they sang. Jezmeen picked up the card. It was folded neatly in the centre and when she opened it, she had a distinct feeling that she was infringing on somebody's privacy, even though the card contained just a name and an address.

Tejpal 'Lucky' Singh, ACC Car Hire
Dr Wadhwa, Restoration Road Clinic
S.CO. 01-36, Sector 9-C, Madhya Marg, Chandigarh

It was written in a careful hand, each letter round and deliberate. Jezmeen flipped it over. It was blank. She looked at the words again. Clearly, this was important to someone.

'Madam Jezmeen Shergill?'

'Yes, I'm here.'

'I'm looking at your records and it appears that your internet usage is very high.'

'I don't think it is,' Jezmeen said. 'I'm only checking emails and surfing the internet . . .' Her voice trailed off when she remembered downloading the first three episodes of *The Boathouse* during her drunken evening in the hotel in Delhi. She had fallen asleep with the crushing realization that Polly Mishra was indeed a fine actress.

'Okay, never mind. I think I know where it's gone.'

'Anything else I can help you with?'

'Yes. Can you recharge my credit, please?'

'Ma'am, please hold while I reconnect you to the recharge department.'

Jezmeen sighed and sat through another string of recorded advertisements. She looked at the card again and decided there was no point in trying to find its owner – she didn't know how it had got into her passport case in the first place but it seemed this whole trip was about things going missing and reappearing. After returning from the border, she had taken a foamy, luxurious shower only to realize that her hairdryer wasn't in the depths of her suitcase. Good thing it was just a cheap travel hairdryer. Her salon dryer with seven settings and possibly the same horsepower as a small car remained in London.

After the loop of recorded ads timed out, the line disconnected. 'Thanks for the service,' Jezmeen said sarcastically. She took out her frustration on the card and ripped it up. Just as she tossed the pieces into the bin, her phone rang and Cameron's name appeared on her screen. Jezmeen wasn't sure if she had the energy to hear about another Asian cliché that Cameron thought she'd be perfect for, so she let the phone ring while she took a deep breath. She was channelling the wine lady on BBC Lifestyle, who was now carrying a wicker basket and wandering down a cobblestoned path somewhere in France.

'Hello, Cameron.'

'Hi there, Jezmeen, how are things?'

He sounded very upbeat, a good sign. 'I'm well,' Jezmeen said.

'I'm glad,' Cameron said. 'Not Googling yourself too much then?' He laughed a bit too hard at his own comment while Jezmeen stayed silent. He cleared his throat, 'Actually, you'll be happy to know that the backlash is dying down now.'

'Really?' Jezmeen said. Cameron probably considered it good news that the online Jezmeen-bashing had tempered down to only a few 'off-with-her-head' comments a day.

'Oh yes. There's that scandal in America right now about that singing contest finalist searching for Simpsons pornography. Did you hear about this? The internet's ablaze.'

'No,' Jezmeen said.

'Presumably he was drunk while searching, because he put all the search terms – raunchy fantasies about Marge Simpson in particular – into Twitter, and just kept on pressing enter. There were about seventeen tweets before he realized what he was doing.'

Jezmeen wanted to feel sorry for this man, but she was too relieved that the internet's focus had shifted away from her. She was even just the tiniest bit offended to be forgotten so quickly. *If Polly Mishra kicked a fish to death, I bet people would hate her for weeks!* she thought, before turning her attention back to the conversation with Cameron. 'So you might have something for me?' she asked hopefully.

'I think you'll be pleased with this one. It's not a definite role, it's a meeting with a casting director for a film he's shooting in India.'

'A meeting?' Jezmeen asked. 'Not an audition?' This could suggest that the director was so certain about Jezmeen's potential casting that he was willing to bypass auditions altogether. The meeting could just be a formality to check that she wasn't insane. Or it could be nothing, a noncommittal chat over coffee: let's think about working together in the future, and then she'd never hear from him again.

'A meeting,' Cameron confirmed. 'But he's very keen to have you in his next project. The director's name is HC Kumar. Not sure if you've heard of him but his next project is a bilingual Hindi and English series set in Mumbai. A noir crime thriller with a strong female lead – I thought it would be right up your alley and he's very interested in you as well.'

Jezmeen barely heard anything after 'HC Kumar'. She wanted to toss the phone into the air and scream. Had she heard of him? She'd only seen all of his films growing up. 'When does he want to meet?' Jezmeen asked.

'I told him you're in India at the moment, and willing to meet. Can you make it back to Delhi on Tuesday?'

'Tuesday,' Jezmeen said. Her mind raced. She and Rajni would be in the mountains on Tuesday. 'Can he do Wednesday instead?' She squeezed her eyes shut, aware that she had just asked if her dream director could wait two days to meet her.

'I'm not sure, Jezmeen. He's got quite a busy schedule. I've got Tuesday at 4 p.m. written down here.'

Jezmeen Shergill in HC Kumar's latest film. She allowed a moment's indulgence in the fantasy and in a flash, she was transported to a bright and exciting future. Her face printed on glossy posters, audiences wondering where she came from and why they hadn't noticed her before. *Move over, Polly Mishra,* the critics would declare.

'You still there?' Cameron asked. 'I'll need to let him know quickly. If you can't make it, then—'

'I'll be there,' Jezmeen said quickly. She didn't want Cameron to finish that thought.

Somebody was knocking on the door. 'Coming,' Shirina called. Room service was very prompt at this hotel. She had only placed her order five minutes ago. She scrambled to find clothes to put on. Since returning to the hotel after her fight with Rajni in McDonald's, Shirina had moped about the room in various states of undress, wishing the heat would seep away from her body. Anything against her skin, even a cotton nightie, felt oppressive.

'It's me.'

Shirina found a T-shirt and threw it on. She opened the door to see Jezmeen standing in the hallway. 'Can I come in?' she asked.

'Sure,' Shirina said, stepping aside. Jezmeen came in and stood awkwardly near the bathroom door. 'You can sit over here,' Shirina said. She pushed aside the pile of clothes that she'd rejected earlier when she returned to the hotel. Nothing fitted the way it used to and it bothered her even more after ordering two ice creams and watching Rajni's eyes widen as she ate them.

'You wouldn't believe who wants to meet me,' Jezmeen said.

'Who?' Shirina asked.

'Movie director. I'll give you three guesses.'

Shirina was too tired to guess. She just wanted answers. 'Umm . . .' she said, pretending to think about it. Jezmeen bounced impatiently on her feet.

'HC Kumar!' The name burst from Jezmeen's lips.

'Wow. Really? That's wonderful.'

'I know, I know. I just got off the phone with my agent and he wants to schedule a meeting. No guarantees, of course, but it's still a huge step in the right direction.'

'He's not the one involved in that actress scandal, is he? The guy who was caught on tape bragging to a production assistant about promising roles to young actresses if they slept with him?'

Jezmeen's face fell for a moment. 'Where did you hear about that?'

'It was all over the news. The guy who directed that blockbuster that came out recently.'

'Oh no, no. That's HR Sharma. Different director.' Jezmeen laughed. 'Phew, Shirina, you were starting to make me nervous. So anyway, he thinks I might be suitable for his next film, and he wants to meet me. Isn't that amazing?'

'So amazing,' Shirina said. Her mind was still on the director she had read about. Shirina recalled seeing a story that somebody had re-posted from a Bollywood celebrity news site about the scandal. The post on the message board attracted many views and comments – the reply rated most popular was: *'A) do you believe everything reported on this trashy site? B) it's not exactly unheard of in the industry. C) did she get the role in the end? I've never heard of her. Could be sour grapes. D) what constitutes "feeling up" anyway?'*

The last question started a heated debate about what was considered inappropriate touching, and the moderators eventually turned off comments, putting up a strict notice about community standards and the purpose of the message board. Shirina hadn't commented, but she was most curious about the posts that claimed that the world was becoming too sensitive these days. *'Everything's abuse or assault these days,'* one person had written. *'Where does it stop?'*

Hearing the exasperation in that woman's tone, Shirina felt strangely relieved. Only the day before, her mother-in-law had given her a hard jab in the rib for letting a pot of pasta boil over. While wiping the starchy liquid off the stove, Shirina's eyes had filled with tears, more from shock than anything else. By bedtime, she managed to convince herself that Mother meant no offence – it was an attempt to alert Shirina, not hurt her. She was lucky that Mother's reaction had been so swift.

Jezmeen had let herself into the bathroom and was examining her pores in the magnified round mirror. She raked her fingers through her wet hair. 'Hey, can I borrow your hairdryer?' Moments later, the dryer was roaring.

'How was the border?' Shirina asked when Jezmeen was done.

'It was fun,' Jezmeen said, helping herself to a generous dose of Shirina's leave-in conditioner. 'They put on quite a performance out there – beating their chests and kicking their legs. I did some dancing for the motherland.'

'That's very patriotic of you,' Shirina said.

'Well, might as well get into the spirit of things,' Jezmeen said. 'It would have been fun if you'd been there too.'

Shirina nodded. 'I just didn't feel like being in another huge crowd, that's all.'

'I know,' Jezmeen said.

'Is Rajni still upset?'

'She'll get over it.'

'I'm taking this trip as seriously as she is,' Shirina said. 'I hope she realizes that.'

'She knows. She just gets on her high horse sometimes – I wouldn't worry about it.'

'Okay,' Shirina said. She wasn't worried exactly, but she did not want to leave for Chandigarh tomorrow on bad terms with her sister. Who knew when they would see each other again? She didn't have any visits planned to London for the near future, and having her sisters visit her in Melbourne was out of the question. They'd know in an instant that she had left her job and that her marital home was her world. They would judge her for it.

Somebody knocked on the door. 'Room service,' the bellboy's voice called. Shirina opened the door and let him in. He brought the tray to the small coffee table in the corner of the room and lifted off each lid with theatrical flourish – fluffy basmati rice, a bowl of vegetable korma, a small serving of raita and two gulab jamuns, courtesy of the hotel.

'I hope the dessert makes you feel better, Madam,' he said, nodding at the gulab jamun bowl. 'The manager informed me that you were unwell – were you able to get through to the hospital?'

'No,' Shirina said quickly. 'I mean – yes. No. I didn't need to go after all. I'm fine.' She was aware that Jezmeen had gone quiet in the bathroom and could hear the conversation. 'Okay then, thank you,' Shirina said, ushering the bellboy out the door. She grabbed some notes from her purse and pushed them into his hand – far too much for a tip but she didn't want him to say another word.

Jezmeen stood in the bathroom doorway, surveying the platter of food. 'Want some?' Shirina asked. 'There's plenty.' She was aware that it was a bit early for dinner but if they all went out tonight, she'd probably be hungry enough to eat again.

'No, thank you.'

Shirina avoided Jezmeen's gaze and sat down on the armchair. As she scooped the rice into the bowl and topped it with a generous serving of korma, she wondered how she'd explain the hospital to Jezmeen.

'I overreacted,' Shirina said, trying her best to look embarrassed. 'You know how I fell in the baths today? It hurt so much, I thought I had broken my tailbone.'

'Oh,' Jezmeen said.

'I get nervous about falls,' Shirina continued. 'Especially the older we get. When we were little, it was like our bones were made out of rubber. But now I think about Dad and how he slipped in the shower and then walked around for days without knowing that it had begun to kill him.'

This, Jezmeen would understand. After Mum's funeral, she had confided to Shirina that she had been losing sleep obsessing about the hidden dangers that could kill her before her time was up.

Jezmeen nodded but she still looked concerned. She looked around the room as if searching for the next thing to say. Shirina might have just imagined it, but she thought she saw Jezmeen's gaze flick at her stomach, which protruded slightly beneath the T-shirt. She drew her shoulders back and tucked her tummy in. Warmth rushed into her cheeks.

'I've had a hard couple of months,' Shirina said. She decided she had to say something, or Jezmeen wouldn't leave her alone. Anyway, what would Jezmeen be able to guess from a small admission that Shirina was having trouble settling into her marital home? Maybe it was good to be a little honest, so her sisters thought that all her problems were just a matter of adjustment. Sometimes Shirina could still fool herself into thinking this way too.

'Work has been stressful and I have a lot waiting for me when I get back.' If only Jezmeen knew how Shirina was counting the days till she was on the plane again to Melbourne. By then, everything would be done and she could go back to her life as planned.

'And things at home?' Jezmeen persisted. 'Things with Sehaj, your mother-in-law – all good?'

'Yeah,' Shirina said. 'Of course.' She said it too quickly though. Jezmeen looked at her with curiosity. 'I mean, there's always an adjustment period, right? We've been married a few years,' she said lightly. She thought about the American sitcoms – the mother crinkling her nose at her daughter-in-law's casserole dish and offering a sugary *Thank you, dear,* as the audience giggled. *It's funny,* Shirina told herself when Mother tipped her roast chicken into the rubbish bin because there were a few burnt patches and Shirina had suggested just scraping them off. The memory stung. Sehaj hadn't thrown his meal away but he had only eaten half of it, his loyalty divided.

'It's hard sometimes, you know?' Shirina said. She decided she could afford to say this much. It had been a long time since she spoke to Lauren about what it was like living with Sehaj and Mother in that huge, quiet house. 'My mother-in-law isn't always the easiest person to get along with.' Even this admission made Shirina feel guilty. *You should be grateful.*

'She seemed quite reserved,' Jezmeen offered. 'I only met her once at the wedding though.'

Shirina nodded. 'She means well, but she's got some old-fashioned ways about her. And it's really not her fault.' This was where Lauren would raise an eyebrow and say something about everybody taking responsibility for their own actions. She was half expecting this reaction from Jezmeen as well, but to her surprise, Jezmeen just listened. Shirina pushed away the guilt, the voice telling her that she was disrespecting her in-laws.

'It's little things, like she expects me to get the cooking just right and the laundry has to be pressed a certain way.' *And she hurts me.* This, Shirina would never say, because it was going too far. It was alright to complain about the little things. On the message boards, there were threads dedicated to abuse, but Shirina never let herself go there. It was indulgent, calling her problems abuse. She didn't have bruises, she wasn't living in a small village hut with a mother-in-law who beat her.

'What does Sehaj say about all of it?'

'He doesn't really get involved.'

'He's aware of what's happening and he chooses not to get involved, or he doesn't know?'

'He doesn't know,' Shirina lied. She thought about Sehaj glowering while Mother prattled on at the dinner table about another girl that she'd liked on the matrimonial websites. *Of course, in the end, it's up to your son to choose, isn't it?* she had said, reaching across the table to pat Shirina's hand. *And he chose you.* She'd said it so sweetly, so kindly, that Shirina wasn't certain if she was right to be insulted until later, when she was lying awake and the words churned in her mind. *Why didn't you say something?* she asked Sehaj, shaking him by the shoulders. He sat up, startled, his eyes glassy from being woken so abruptly, and then mumbled something about how it wasn't worth the fight.

'Is it something you can talk about with him?' Jezmeen asked.

'Not really,' Shirina said carefully. 'It's difficult getting in the way of a man and his mother, especially when he's the only person she's depended on for so long.'

'It's unfair to you though,' Jezmeen pointed out. 'And to him.'

'I know,' Shirina said, closing her eyes. If Jezmeen knew how much she was sacrificing for the sake of keeping the peace, imagine how outraged she would be. The concern had already evaporated from her face and been replaced with anger on Shirina's behalf. 'It's a delicate thing. She's been ill, you know.'

'Has she? What's wrong?'

'She had surgery on her hip,' Shirina said. 'The recovery has been slow and painful. I've had to help out a lot. She needs me to help her up the stairs, and she can't stand for very long, so there's a lot of housework that piles up.'

On top of your full-time job you're also playing nurse to your mother-in-law?

This was what she expected Jezmeen's response to be. Incredulous, outraged, positioning her as the fool for accepting so much responsibility. Lauren had looked at Shirina with pity and everything she said afterwards sounded so patronizing, as if Shirina wasn't aware that she had options, that she didn't have to do this.

But Jezmeen nodded and waited for Shirina to say more. The room was so quiet that Shirina could hear a suitcase being wheeled down the hallway, and the murmurs of new guests as they entered their room. 'It's nothing I can't handle,' Shirina said to assure Jezmeen. 'It's been stressful, that's all, but this is a good break.'

'It's hardly a break,' Jezmeen reminded her. 'We've got this itinerary to follow and we're sequestered in the hotel most evenings because it's not exactly the friendliest environment for female travellers. This is why I really wanted to take that side trip to Goa – lie on the beach, feel free. It's not going to happen though.'

Shirina shrugged as if the idea of lying on a beach didn't make her want to pack up all her things and flee this instant to the airport. 'There will be other holidays. This one is for family,' she said.

'You're looking forward to meeting Sehaj's relatives then? There's going to be a big welcoming committee and you're not going to be stuck doing housework with all the other good daughters?'

'It'll be fine,' Shirina said. 'They're nice people.' In her head, she had invented these extended relatives of Sehaj's in the same way that she had built up his closer family when they were still getting to know each other online – warm and welcoming, eager to include another one into the flock. Each time she felt a flutter of nerves or anticipation at what awaited her at the doctor's office in Chandigarh, she replaced the clinic with an image of the family standing outside a sprawling multigenerational home on acres of lush farmland as the car pulled in. They were all waving hello. They couldn't wait to welcome her home.

Chapter Thirteen

Day Six: Amritsar, Punjab
Awakening the Guru

Before the sun comes up today, you should be at the temple to witness an important ceremony. The Guru Granth Sahib, *our Holy Book, is also considered the eleventh and final guru in Sikhism. Every morning, it is awakened and transported to the temple, where volunteers have already cleaned every inch of the shrine and washed the floor with milk. Watch this ceremony and recite the Lord's name along with your fellow Sikhs here and everywhere else in the world. Afterwards, please do some seva in the kitchen to prepare food for all the people at the temple who have woken up early with you to participate in our Guru's awakening.*

It was so early in the morning that Rajni felt caught in the space between sleeping and waking up, while her consciousness remained under that blanket of nothingness which would eventually dissipate to reveal the day ahead. Packed in a crowd with Jezmeen and Shirina at the temple's entrance, she waited for the procession to arrive. The atmosphere was solemn yet festive – Rajni could feel the anticipation in the excited whispers surrounding her. 'Is it coming? Do you see it?' Jezmeen asked a few times when trumpets blared and the crowd stirred. Shirina tipped her toes and tried to look past the sea of people that seemed to stretch across the city.

The temple, adorned with golden lights and radiating against the dark sky, was even more stunning before the sun rose. Jostling with the other worshippers and edging closer to the sarovar, Rajni found herself facing the temple's smudged, upside-down reflection. The water caught something indistinct – the essence of the place. She liked it better in this blurry, shape-shifting form. The temple itself was too vivid, like a memory that became sharper and stronger, the more you tried to forget it. In the water, it was just an illusion of lights.

Mobile phones on selfie sticks shot up into the air like eager hands volunteering an answer. The chorus of chanting was approaching. Jezmeen was the tallest of them, and had the advantage of her long arms for taking a photo, but she didn't. Neither did Shirina. Rajni realized that the only person for whom she would photograph this ceremony, was Mum. In her absence, there wasn't anybody she needed to show this to. She patted her phone in the bag that hung from her waist, and just focused on the chanting. All around her, worshippers had formed a chorus, repeating God's name, *waheguru*. Although she only considered herself a spectator, she found her lips moving to the shape of a word which had such history in her household as she was growing up. Mum would sigh *waheguru* if her backbone cricked as she stood up. She uttered the word after every sneeze and prayer, every misfortune or perceived divine intervention from God. If you were in trouble, all you had to do was say *waheguru* and God would answer.

Mum explained the eleventh guru to Rajni when she was a little girl, before Jezmeen and Shirina came along. It was the tenth guru of Sikhism, Guru Gobind Singh, who decided that the final guru would be a book containing all the hymns and tenets of the religion. The hefty book sat on a special canopied platform in every temple and prayer room, wrapped in layers of shimmering embroidered and tasselled cloth. Only years after Mum told Rajni about the eleventh guru did she wonder about it. 'Why didn't he want another person after him?' she asked. 'He probably knew what people were like,' Mum replied. It was no secret at that point that Mum had little faith in people. Dad's land in Punjab had been sold and the share of the property which belonged to Mum, was being withheld by his family. There were conditions, they claimed, but they only hinted at what these were. Mum decided to make a trip to India. It would be easier to negotiate in person, rather than over brief and expensive long-distance calls. They were already starting to struggle financially with Dad gone.

The chanting grew louder and more excited. Trumpets blasted to herald the book's arrival. 'Here it is,' Jezmeen said, tugging Rajni's sleeve. A turbaned man with a little boy propped on his shoulders stepped in front of them. Rajni caught only glimpses of the book as the people drew closer, straining their necks and phones to record the view. The book was bound in gold cloth and nestled in the palanquin, every edge of which was propped on the shoulders of men who travelled through a crowd that shifted and parted for each of their steps. The chanting became louder and more jubilant.

The pushing began as the book came closer. People scrambled for the best view, shouldering through and inching forward along with the book. The chanting grew uncomfortably fervent. Sweat poured down Rajni's back and she became unsteady on her feet. She grabbed her sisters by their elbows and tried to link arms with them but there was suddenly no space to even stretch her arms. 'Excuse me,' she said, knowing it was in vain. The crowd swayed and Rajni felt the danger of tipping over and becoming lost under this sea of people. She pressed her feet into the ground and as she tried to push back against the crush of bodies, a sharp and swift pain shot into her ankle. She cried out but nobody heard her. The chanting just continued, *waheguru, waheguru,* that word that was supposed to heal everything.

The crowd only began to loosen when the book was out of their sight. The moment there was room to move again, Rajni pulled her sisters away from the current of people. 'Shouldn't we stay to hear which hymn the priest reads?' Jezmeen asked.

'It'll be broadcast everywhere,' Rajni said, still wincing from the pain in her ankle.

'Why didn't Mum ask us to take part in the ceremony?' Jezmeen asked.

'You wanted to take part in that?' Rajni asked. 'It looked pretty intense.'

'We couldn't anyway,' Shirina said. 'Only certain Sikhs are allowed to prepare the shrine. All the people who cleaned it and bathed the floor in milk at two in the morning are baptized.'

'Mostly men, I suppose,' Jezmeen said. 'It was only men that carried the palanquin.'

'And it's mostly men here anyway,' Rajni said, looking around. 'There's either a rule about it or men just pushed their way in.' Mum wasn't allowed to scatter Dad's ashes when he died. A couple of distant uncles and cousins in India carried out the final rites instead. 'It's a good thing nobody tried to tell us we couldn't scatter Mum's ashes because we're women.'

'It's not right,' Jezmeen agreed. 'There can't be any valid reason for it either.'

'Those are the rules though,' Shirina said. Rajni noticed she looked more tired than yesterday, but her insistent response made her seem more awake all of a sudden.

'That doesn't mean the rules make any sense,' Jezmeen said.

'Maybe it's just how it's always been done,' Shirina said.

'You're saying that if somebody told us we couldn't scatter Mum's ashes just because we're women, it would be okay?' Rajni asked.

'It wouldn't be okay, but it would be the thing to do,' Shirina said. 'Some things just are what they are.'

Jezmeen looked taken aback. 'But—' Rajni said.

'We respect traditions, don't we? Or do we just pick and choose the ones we like?' Rajni hadn't seen Shirina speaking with such passion before. 'What do you want?' she challenged Jezmeen. 'Do you want to start looking for inequalities in every little thing? Because it's a very long list and you'll never get through it.'

Rajni and Jezmeen exchanged a look. What had got into Shirina? They walked in silence for a while. A loud announcement broke Rajni's thoughts. It was the daily hymn being read and broadcast. An echo reverberated strongly with each syllable, making the words unclear. Mum used to turn on the radio to listen to the broadcast every morning. Like Sikhs all over the world, she waited for this daily guidance on how to go about her life. The Golden Temple was the beating heart at the centre of the Sikh world, sending a vital message into thousands of homes in Britain and elsewhere. As the pain in Rajni's ankle went from a niggling sensation to something more noticeable, she wished making the pain vanish was as easy as reciting the Lord's name. It didn't hurt to try. With the next few steps she took, she said his name. Despite her doubt, she thought the steps were a little easier to take.

Preparations for breakfast had started before the sun came up, so by the time Jezmeen arrived in the Golden Temple's kitchen with her sisters, it was crowded with volunteers. Elderly ladies sat on mats and split garlic with their thumbs, discarding the papery skins onto a spread of newspapers. A circle of men tended to the massive machinery that took balls of dough through a conveyer belt and flattened them into rotis. Jezmeen, Shirina and Rajni stood on the edges of the kitchen like new students in the cafeteria, unsure of where they were needed. It was only when a group of European backpackers descended on the kitchen and scattered amongst the different stations in a flurry of sandalwood-scented dreadlocks that Jezmeen realized nobody expected anything of them. She joined the women who were washing dishes that were already piling in from the early morning crowd. Rajni followed her. Shirina went to the furthest corner of the kitchen – as far away from the two of them as she could manage.

As they settled into a routine, Jezmeen turned to Rajni. 'Something's going on with our little sister,' she said. 'What was that outburst about?'

Rajni peered at Shirina, who was settling on a stool with some women peeling potatoes. She smiled and nodded at the women who made space for her and handed her a peeler and pushed a pile of potatoes in her direction. 'Don't know. It was strange though.'

'She seems unhappy – she started confiding in me yesterday but I could tell she was holding back. I think she's really dreading going on that trip to the village. She looks tired too, doesn't she? She seems preoccupied all the time.'

Rajni dunked a steel plate into the soapy water and handed it to Jezmeen to rinse. 'Family visits to the village are never fun,' she said. 'The novelty wears off after a couple of hours when everybody stops parading you about. At least she's not single. I was fifteen, and every other day, some auntie or another was remarking on how I would be a good bride.'

'What did Mum say to that?' Jezmeen asked.

Rajni hesitated. 'She didn't object, let's just say that.'

'You were *fifteen*!'

'Yeah, and Mum was desperate to please her relatives.'

'Why?'

Rajni hesitated again. 'The usual pressures to impress the family in the old country, show them that we're not that far removed from our culture.' Rajni concentrated very hard on scrubbing a spot off a steel cup. It looked as if there was more she wanted to say but she was refraining.

'Should we talk to Shirina?' Jezmeen asked. 'Sit her down and ask her what's going on? Maybe she'll be more honest with you.'

'Why would she be more honest with me?' Rajni asked. 'You two are closer in age.'

'But you're married,' Jezmeen said. 'Didn't you deal with all this in-law stuff when you married Kabir? You had some visits and obligations, didn't you?' She just remembered Rajni having to touch the feet of Kabir's relatives when she entered their home for the first time, and standing behind her sister, Jezmeen had felt a rush of indignity. She would never touch anybody's feet. 'I'm never getting married,' Jezmeen had declared to the laughter of Kabir's relatives. Mum was positively aghast with her statement.

'I didn't do anything I didn't want to,' Rajni informed Jezmeen. 'I could always say no.'

'I'm getting the sense that Shirina doesn't have that luxury,' Jezmeen said. She watched Shirina sitting with her legs crossed, her head bent to her task. She was methodically peeling potatoes and setting them aside in a neat pile instead of tossing them into a basket like the other women.

Every movement of hers seemed slow and calculated, like she was attempting a role.

'What do you think of Sehaj?' Jezmeen asked Rajni.

Rajni looked at her curiously. 'Why are you asking?'

'I just never got a sense of who he was. The whole engagement and wedding happened so quickly.'

'That's how Shirina wanted it though,' Rajni pointed out. 'I'm sure she had to adjust to a few things but everyone does that in marriage.' Rajni dunked her hands into the soapy water, thinking. 'Although there was something weird the other day in the café.'

'What was it?'

'Probably nothing, but I told her about how Mum used to prescribe all these fertility remedies for me, and she was really interested. Your message came soon after that, so I didn't really follow up on it – and maybe there's no reason to – but I did wonder if she and Sehaj are trying to have a baby? Maybe it's not going so well. I gained weight and was pretty depressed as well after my miscarriages, you know.'

'Should we ask her about it then?'

'I certainly didn't want to be asked about it,' Rajni said. 'It's such a sensitive subject, infertility. See if she brings it up first.'

Rajni shifted positions and winced visibly. 'Is it your ankle again?' Jezmeen asked. On the walk, Rajni had paused twice to massage her ankle. She grimaced and nodded at Jezmeen. 'I don't know why it's hurting so much. I've landed on it heavily plenty of times before.'

'We're in a different place,' Jezmeen said with a shrug.

'I don't see what that has to do with it.'

'Doesn't your body just change when you're in a new environment? Your hair becomes coarser or softer, your eyes are drier, your dreams are weirder and more colourful?'

'Maybe,' Rajni said. 'I guess it'll just heal by itself when I get back to London then.'

'Or you could try bathing in the sarovar again,' Jezmeen said. 'I'm going to go back in later. I'm starting to think it really does have the power to heal.'

'Oh, please, Jezmeen.'

'What?'

'You know it's not going to help. It's just water.'

'Go in there with a little bit of faith and maybe you'll see some results. The water is called the nectar of immortality, after all.'

'Figuratively.'

Jezmeen rolled her eyes. 'I *know*, Rajni. I don't think a dip in a pool is going to magically make my life eternal.' But as she said it, she felt a little sad that this was the truth.

'All your gushing over the benefits of a healing bath makes you sound like Mum,' Rajni said. 'She would have convinced herself to will away the cancer if we'd let her. Honestly, I thought you were a bigger sceptic than this. Has the pilgrimage changed you?'

'It's nice to have something to believe in,' Jezmeen said. 'Otherwise, I don't know what we're all doing here. Do you?'

'We're here because Mum wanted us to be.'

'I don't mean here, as in the kitchen of the Golden Temple. I'm talking about *here*. Our existence. What's the meaning of it all?' Jezmeen surprised herself with the question. She had never articulated it before but it had been nagging at her since the Arowana incident. She'd always hoped to be immortalized through her work; instead, she was best known for her biggest mistake.

'Oh, I don't know. I just want to get through each day at this stage.'

Now Rajni was the one who was beginning to sound like Mum. All that sighing, all that lamenting about how life was not how she'd expected it.

'Aren't you curious at all about what happens after all of this? Don't you do things and wonder why you're doing them at all?' Jezmeen persisted.

Rajni turned and gave her a very sharp stare. 'If I thought about the higher purpose of everything I did, I'd get nothing done. I'd go through all my days like Mum, doing rituals that made no difference, and making a hobby out of prayer because she was so convinced that the afterlife held more promise and less disappointment than this world.'

'You make Mum sound so bitter,' Jezmeen pointed out. 'She wasn't eager to die just so she could escape this world.'

'Why did she ask us to help her to die then?' Rajni asked.

'That was because she was suffering,' Jezmeen said. Tears welled up in her eyes. 'And as I recall, you didn't exactly hesitate.'

'I wanted to help Mum in whatever way I could,' Rajni said. 'I didn't think I'd have nightmares about her death for this long.'

Jezmeen stared at Rajni. So she dreamt of Mum too? Rajni had gone back to scrubbing plates. Her face was tense with anger and she was putting too much force into her motions. This was how she had looked that day in the hospital, when Mum had shooed them out of the room and Jezmeen marched towards the nurses' station, insisting that they inform somebody. Rajni caught Jezmeen by the shoulder, and told her to stop. 'Let go of me,' Jezmeen shouted, jerking away. She waved down a nurse who was passing by. 'Excuse me,' she said. Then Jezmeen saw Rajni's fist coming almost in slow motion, and then the bolt of pain soared across her cheek and time sped up rapidly. Shirina backed against the wall, her hands clapped over her mouth and her eyes wide with shock. The nurse rushed to separate them and then they were ordered to leave the hospital.

The next day, Jezmeen didn't answer any of Rajni's calls. A purple bruise shone just under her eye, and as she tenderly patted concealer over it, the calls kept coming until her phone battery died. *Get the hint,* she thought. An apology was not going to fix this. Finally, when she went to plug in her phone charger, she saw a message from Rajni: *'Pick up the phone. It's about Mum.'*

When they went to take Mum's things, Jezmeen was still hoping that she had just passed away in her sleep, her prayers answered. Yet she still had dreams of Mum opening that jewellery case and taking those pills, one by one, like small pieces of candy.

Chapter Fourteen

Back in November

Sita is sitting upright in her hospital bed, having just read the letter to her daughters. She folds it up neatly and sets it on her lap, satisfied. There is nothing more to say, but she clears her throat, only to fill the taut silence.

As she expected, Jezmeen is staring at her in horror. If it were up to that girl, everybody would live forever and growing up would be unnecessary. Jezmeen belongs in a movie, preserved within the confines of a screen and replayed over and over again, so that in ten, twenty years, she won't have aged at all. Rajni, on the other hand, is nodding. Sita takes this as a good sign. Even though she and Rajni have discussed this option privately before, she has been nervous about how Rajni would react once it became a reality. Shirina's forehead is creased with worry lines and she's looking back and forth between her sisters.

'You're sure you have enough?' Rajni asks. She is speaking very softly, although Sita is quite sure that the woman in the next bed is partially deaf. She can tell from the volume of her radio every afternoon at 6 p.m., when she listens to the BBC news.

Jezmeen turns to Rajni. 'You're not actually going to let her go through with this, are you?'

Rajni and Sita exchange a look, which Jezmeen catches. 'Jezmeen, she's suffering,' Rajni says. 'She wants to put an end to it. We – she – has clearly been thinking about this for some time.'

It's that small slip that Jezmeen catches. Sita winces, but not with pain. She knows now that Rajni will have to explain what she meant by 'we'. She will have to explain that once Sita was given the diagnosis, she knew what kind of suffering lay in store for her and she was not interested in clinging on to this life while her body deteriorated. 'What can I do?' she had asked Rajni, and Rajni had pulled up some websites, did some research on places in Europe where Sita could go to end her life with dignity. They downloaded brochures and made a hopeful project of Sita's assisted suicide, until reality sank in. The costs would be astronomical. The small sum from the sale of her London home that Sita wanted to leave behind for her daughters and her grandson would be swallowed up by this final act, and she didn't want that. She had spent so much of her life scraping by, and there was no reason to splurge on her death. 'Isn't there a simpler way?' Sita asked Rajni. How did people end their lives peacefully if they couldn't book into a clinic in Switzerland? Even before her diagnosis, Sita had always thought of death as a wave washing over the person, lulling them to sleep. The thought of settling into her bed and sinking into a deep, tranquil state was even more enticing now that the pain kept her awake most nights.

Then she remembered the sleeping pills. The nurses gave them to her before bed each night. Sita stockpiled them, and put up with a few agonizing sleepless nights for the eventual reward of eternal peaceful sleep. She is only telling her daughters about it because she doesn't want it to come as a shock to them. She also needs them to keep a lookout for anybody who might stop this from happening. It's important that they are uninterrupted.

'Try to understand, *beti*,' Sita says. She reaches a trembling hand out to Jezmeen, hoping to connect with her. 'I'm not getting any better.'

'They haven't said all hope is lost. Nobody actually said that you're going to die,' Jezmeen says.

Sita and Rajni share the same sigh. It surprises Sita and she can tell that Rajni has noticed too, how they responded with an identical action. 'They've given every indication that Mum's not going to recover. The cancer is spreading and chemo has stopped being effective. That means—'

'It means there's a chance of a miracle happening,' Jezmeen said. 'You hear about people springing to recovery from the most dire illnesses – cancer, comas. There are people with paralysis who start walking again. It can happen.'

'It's not going to happen,' Shirina says quietly.

Sita is thankful for her youngest daughter then, even though she has only just flown over, having been warned by Rajni that Sita's days are numbered. Nevertheless, even she understands that Jezmeen's hope is naïve and it's not based on any faith. Jezmeen doesn't think God is going to help Sita. She's hoping for a medical miracle, some unexplained glitch that works in Sita's favour at the last minute. This is a foolish way to look at things, but wasn't Jezmeen the one who struggled with her father's death in the same way? Even though Sita explained repeatedly that he was with God, Jezmeen spent years convincing herself that her father hadn't actually died. At age twelve, she devoted herself to a great deal of research about people who faked their own deaths for various reasons. Sita remembers getting upset with Jezmeen for telling her about a man in America who staged an accidental fall off a cliff during a family camping trip. Years later, his wife's friend living in another town spotted him in the background of a picture in a news clipping about a local school fundraiser. He had been alive all that time, and enjoying life very much with his new family. 'Don't be so stupid,' Sita snapped at Jezmeen. It was bad enough to be saddled with her husband's unfinished business – it was quite another thing to imagine that he might be in another town somewhere, enjoying a re-do of his life while Sita tried to figure out how to make ends meet.

'Why tell us then?' Jezmeen asks. 'If your mind is made up.'

'I don't want it to come as a shock to you,' Sita says. 'And I want you to be by my side when I do it.' She hesitates. 'You need to make sure you do the pilgrimage in my letter, you take that bath in the sarovar, and you do a lot of seva.'

The wave of shame covering Sita is all-encompassing. What she wants to do, God will not be pleased about. Suicide is frowned upon in their religion. What kind of person throws their life away? She thought about this every time she put away another pill and she did her best not to let the guilt overcome her. Life is meant to be cherished, not carelessly wasted or ended, and she knows that, but isn't her life already being wasted? Isn't waiting to die as good as dying, and actually even worse because she's simply taking up space on earth? She has many arguments to present to God when they eventually meet, and none fully satisfy her, but this she knows: her daughters will have time to absolve themselves. If they help her by keeping a lookout, they can spend their whole lives redeeming themselves in the eyes of God. They can start with the pilgrimage – service to others, cleansing themselves, taking an arduous journey to a spiritual peak. It's all outlined in her letter.

'Come on, you guys,' Jezmeen is saying. 'This is ridiculous. She must be loopy or something.'

'She's not,' Rajni insists firmly. 'She's in pain but she's got her senses about her. I don't think it's a bad idea.'

'But we'll be—'

'We won't.'

'—abetting a suicide.'

The word hangs in the air like a thick plume of smoke. Rajni crosses her arms over her chest. 'And what are we if we stand by and let Mum suffer? I don't think it's that easy to decide what's wrong and right any more, Jezmeen. There are circumstances . . .'

'Don't you want Mum's suffering to stop?' Shirina asks Jezmeen. 'It's a humane and dignified way to go, if this is what she wants.'

Jezmeen looks cornered. Her eyes flit back and forth between her sisters and Mum. 'Of course I do,' she says. 'But this is wrong. It's not the right way to go about it.'

'What's the right way then?' Rajni asks.

'Didn't the doctors say they'd make you as comfortable as possible?'

'Does she look comfortable?' Rajni retorts. 'She's suffering. There's only so much they can do when cancer is spreading through a patient's body. It's excruciating – they'll give her enough morphine to stop the pain but that will be the quality of her life: depending on a drug to numb her just enough without killing her.'

'Jezmeen, please try to understand,' Sita murmurs, but she is half-hearted in her attempt to placate her daughter. The pain is beginning to build again and soon it will be surging through her like an electric current. She braces herself for it by clutching the sheets. All three of her daughters notice this movement.

'Mum?' Rajni says. She reaches out to stroke Sita's hand but before she can make contact, Sita flinches. The worst thing somebody can do while she's anticipating this pain is touch her.

'Leave me alone,' Sita whispers. 'All of you, just go away for a while.' She shuts her eyes and listens to her daughters' feet shuffling against the linoleum floors. A memory comes to her — little Jezmeen and Shirina creeping around the house in the early hours of a Sunday morning, trying not to wake anybody. Sita would hear the muffled noises and debate whether to get out of bed or simply stay where she was. It was always tempting to stay in bed, especially in those dark days after her husband died and then afterwards, when rumours began to circulate. *They're not true, they're not true,* she wanted to scream, but who would hear her? Eventually something, like an invisible string, would draw her out from under the sheets and lead her down the stairs, where Jezmeen and Shirina would be giggling on the sofa or prancing about the kitchen.

Sita's memory is interrupted by a short, sharp scream. She knows right away that it is Jezmeen, but she doesn't open her eyes because the pain is roaring now, and about to shut out all of her senses. She twists and whimpers and presses the call button to summon the nurse. There is the pounding sound of shoes down the hallway but they stop outside her room. *Hurry,* Sita thinks. *Help!* She doesn't know whose assistance she is invoking here — her daughters, the nurses or God himself. The jewellery case is in her dresser. Jezmeen had shut the drawer as soon as she understood what Sita was asking of her. It is agonizing for Sita to lean towards the dresser and pull open the drawer, but after cancelling the call for the nurse, she is able to do it. She touches the case with her fingers, and says a prayer for her daughters.

Chapter Fifteen

Rays of morning sun caught the gently rippling water of the sarovar and held it to Rajni's eyes. Miracle water. She limped towards the bath-house. Jezmeen and Shirina were still serving but Rajni needed a break. The heat and clamouring noise in the kitchen, just like the one in the gurdwara in Delhi, had become stifling and standing at the sink was making her ankle worse. She told herself that she just wanted to dip her feet into the water for the cool relief. There was no need to hope that the sarovar would take her swelling away and fix her old injury.

It was only 7 a.m. but women were already lining up outside the bath-house when Rajni joined them. There was some excited chattering, just like yesterday, but this morning there were many more teenagers. There was a group wearing matching white T-shirts with blue lettering, their long rope-like braids hanging down their backs. One girl shook her head and her braid swung, revealing the title on her T-shirt: *Youth Leader: International Sikh Youth Summer Camp*. Rajni caught the accents then – some Americans, some Australians and a few that she could not distinguish, probably from Southeast Asia and Africa.

The line inched forward. The girl in front of Rajni began to roll up her track-suit bottoms, revealing her sturdy ankles. Rajni felt the pain throbbing in her own leg. It was starting to travel to her knees and her hip now, signalling that something worse was happening. Of course, of course, she thought about Mum's pills. They clattered in a metal tin in her mind, even though the jewellery case had soft sides and was silent like the secret Mum wanted them to keep. Rajni looked over her shoulder in the direction of the langar hall where she had left Jezmeen to deal with the dishes. Did Jezmeen really think she was the only person who suffered from guilt? That it had been easy for Rajni to sit with Mum and look through the brochures for those fancy facilities in Switzerland where terminally ill patients checked in to die? Every conversation had exhausted Rajni. She'd come home to talk to Anil and Kabir and realize that they had gone to bed, their lives so easily continuing without her. On some nights, she'd return home and see the slice of light under Anil's door and she'd hesitate outside, wanting to knock and say hello but also afraid of being rejected. He was always so eager to get back to his phone, to leave the house.

Once they stepped into the bath-house, the noise and excitement of chatter became amplified. Voices bounced across the walls. Rajni's own silence felt out of place here – everybody else was celebrating but she was alone. She glanced around to search for other solitary women and spotted one older lady methodically peeling off her garments and folding each one – first the tunic, then the salwar. The old lady winced at the piercing noise of the girls' high-pitched giggles but once she stepped into the water, a look of calm washed over her.

Rajni rolled up the cuffs of her salwar, knowing that it wasn't possible to be healed by water. As her feet made contact with the water, she breathed out a sigh nonetheless. It was involuntary – the cooling of her soles after they had been pressed against the hot tiles outside. Rajni inched her way to a wall to keep herself steady as the girls began to pile into the pool. Some were completely unclothed, others had just stripped down to their tunics and were wading across the length of the pool. Rajni's ankle still ached but the water was distracting her. She shut her eyes and was even able to shut out the voices of the girls. She wanted to block out everything, to see a black canvas of nothingness, but all she could see and hear were Mum, Kabir and Anil. The three people whose expectations she had spent her entire adult life juggling.

The images kept coming back to her of the fight with Jezmeen that evening. She didn't know what overcame her – at one moment, they were arguing in heated whispers, and the next, her hand was clenched in a fist and knocking her sister's cheek so hard, her head snapped back and nearly hit the wall.

Why did she do it? Jezmeen had said to her: 'You're crazy if you think this is going to work.' Rajni had replied, 'Just think about it, just for a moment. You'll see how much sense it makes.'

The water lapped at Rajni's feet, a ripple created by another stream of pilgrims. These women were not part of the Youth Camp – they had arrived separately and they were older. Completely stripped of their clothes, they heaved their hefty bodies into the water and strode confidently through, creating their own current. One woman submerged herself completely and broke through the surface after what seemed like minutes, although it was probably seconds. She made eye contact with Rajni. It was the briefest contact, but Rajni felt self-conscious immediately about how she was standing so stiffly.

'Raj.'

She turned to find Jezmeen standing at the edge of the pool. 'What are you doing?' Jezmeen asked.

'I just wanted to cool off,' Rajni said. The truth was, her ankle was feeling better. The gentle waves had soothed the swelling and distracted her from the pain. She didn't want Jezmeen to know this though.

Jezmeen began rolling up the cuffs of her salwar as well. As she waded into the water, the elderly woman who had glanced at Rajni looked up and gave her a nod. 'You were here yesterday,' the woman said.

'Yes,' Jezmeen said.

'Was that your sister with you? The girl who slipped and fell?'

Jezmeen nodded.

'She's okay now?'

'I think so.'

The woman rubbed some water over her face and said, 'Good. She should take care of herself.'

'Who is that?' Rajni asked, watching the woman wander off.

'That's the woman who helped Shirina up yesterday,' Jezmeen said. 'She said something that seemed to spook Shirina.'

Rajni shrugged. 'She seems nice enough. Just watching out for her.'

Jezmeen bit her lower lip and watched the woman for a while. 'I guess so,' she said.

'Is Shirina still in the kitchen?'

'Yeah. I told her I was going to the sarovar but she wasn't interested.' Jezmeen swished her feet in the water a few times. 'You know, your ankle still looks a bit swollen.'

Rajni looked down. 'Well, I wasn't expecting to find a miracle cure here.' She regretted her words instantly, or at least the volume of her voice. A few women looked up sharply. Clearly, everybody else was here for a miracle.

'I'm just saying that you shouldn't put too much weight on it.'

'I'll try not to.'

'Do you think you'll need to see a doctor or something?'

The concern in Jezmeen's voice seemed overwrought. 'I'll be fine,' Rajni said.

'Because if you need to see a doctor, or . . . I don't know . . . take it easy over the next few days—'

'Okay, what's going on?' Rajni asked irritably.

'What do you mean?' Jezmeen asked. She was all wide-eyed innocence but Rajni was already able to figure out that Jezmeen was looking for a way out of the next leg of their journey.

'I plan on continuing with this pilgrimage no matter what,' Rajni informed her.

Jezmeen swallowed. 'Do you know HC Kumar?'

'Is he an actor?'

'He's a director. My agent has set up a meeting with him for tomorrow. In Delhi.'

'You're not going to be in Delhi tomorrow. We're doing a trek to Hemkund Sahib to meditate about Mum and scatter her ashes in a lake,' Rajni said calmly.

'No, but I was thinking . . . we've done most of the pilgrimage already. We've connected with each other, we've spent time together and I know I've thought about Mum throughout this journey. Is it really necessary for us to do the trek? And um . . . all bodies of water lead to the same source, so really, if we just scattered her ashes in a river, it would be the same thing in the end, wouldn't it?'

Just the thought of that arduous walk intensified the pain in Rajni's ankle. But they could hire transport, improvise the pilgrimage a little bit. Cancelling an entire two days was out of the question. They had to finish what they'd started, or this trip would be another botched effort to bring a resolution to Mum's existence. Where were they going to find another river? Was Rajni going to have to bring Mum's ashes back to London and bury them in her backyard?

'It's necessary because it's what we came here to do,' Rajni reminded Jezmeen. 'You didn't come to India to go for auditions.'

'But Shirina? She's not coming.'

'What do you want me to say? Go ahead? Shirina decided to make her own plans so you should, too?'

Jezmeen straightened her shoulders. 'I'm not asking for permission, I hope you realize that. I can go wherever I want.'

'Then why are you here?' Rajni asked. 'Why try to make it sound like I'd be better off abandoning our plans?'

'I don't want this trip to end with us fighting again,' Jezmeen said. 'I'm tired of that. It's not what Mum would have wanted.'

Rajni snorted. 'I think we're well past the stage of considering what Mum would have wanted. Do what you want.' She turned around and began to wade out of the water, when to her surprise, Jezmeen caught her by the arm.

'Rajni, this could change everything for me.' Jezmeen's eyes were bright with hope. 'It's that important.'

'So go then, Jezmeen. You don't need me telling you what to do.' Who listened to what Rajni wanted anyway? Anil certainly didn't care. Kabir wasn't interested. Sometimes she felt like she was underwater while the rest of the world carried on above, oblivious to the fact that she was drowning in expectations and responsibilities.

A look of anger flashed across Jezmeen's face. 'You know, sometimes you can be so—' She appeared to struggle to find the word she was looking for, and instead let go of Rajni's arm. With both hands, she drew a square frame around Rajni's face. '*Rajni*,' she said triumphantly. 'You can be so bloody Rajni that you actually out-Rajni yourself.'

'I don't even know what that means.'

'This passive aggression. You say everything's okay and your face betrays an entirely different emotion. It's transparent. Everyone can see that what you say is not what you think.'

'That's because when I say how I feel, I get told off for it. Suddenly I'm the uptight one, the one who can't be flexible or take a joke.' How many times had she noticed work colleagues looking skittishly in her direction before making jokes? 'Oh go ahead, I'm not going to be offended,' she'd say breezily, but her head throbbed from the sound of their laughter after somebody made a comment about female bosses or immigrants running England into the ground.

'What's going on with you?' Jezmeen asked. 'You've been on edge ever since we came to Punjab.'

'I'm fine,' Rajni said. It was an automatic response. 'None of this is easy. Coming here to honour Mum while not wanting to actually think too hard about why we're here.'

The water rippled at their feet. The women were wading out of the pool and drying themselves off. Another stream of women entered the bath-house – tourists from some East Asian country; either Japan or Korea, Rajni decided. Their reverent whispers and tentative steps made Rajni self-conscious about speaking at all, let alone discussing Mum's suicide in this holy place.

Jezmeen peered at Rajni. 'Do you still think it was the right thing to do?' she asked softly. 'Leaving her in the room like that?'

'We didn't have a choice. We were asked to leave the hospital right away,' Rajni pointed out. 'I was so shocked by our fight that I didn't even think to go back to Mum. I just wanted to get out of that building and drive home.'

'Start over the next day,' Jezmeen said. 'That's what I thought would happen. We'd come to the hospital at the same time the next day. The letter, the jewellery case, all of it would be a silly story from the day before.'

Rajni nodded. What she never expected was for Mum to wait for the lights to go down and the nurses to do their final checks for the evening. She never expected Mum to ask for a tall glass of water to be placed at her bedside, and for the inexperienced nurse to cede to her request despite the fact that most of her fluids were being given intravenously. She could picture it now, almost as clearly as if she had been there – Mum waiting, just to be sure that nobody was around, and then gently reaching over to pull out the jewellery case. She unzipped it and stared at the accumu-lated pills, hesitating perhaps to say a prayer. Her first few sips were dainty, one pill reserved for each intake of water. Then she became more daring and began popping three, four into her mouth. How many could she swallow? She didn't want this to go slowly any more.

'I didn't think she'd take the pills either,' Rajni said. 'When I found out, I thought she did it because she was afraid you'd tell the nurses what she was planning to do.'

Jezmeen's eyes widened with surprise. 'You think it was my fault?'

'I didn't say that. I said—'

'She probably wouldn't have gone through with it if you hadn't agreed,' Jezmeen retorted. 'She was seeking permission from us, not just telling us to stand guard. It didn't even matter in the end that we weren't there.'

Rajni held up her hand. 'I don't want to argue about this, Jezmeen. It doesn't matter whose fault it was. Anyway, from Shirina's outburst on the train, it looks like she thinks Mum took the pills because she didn't want us to fight any more.'

'Why does it have to be anybody's fault then?' Jezmeen asked. 'Mum died. Whether she died because of us or despite us – it doesn't matter, does it?'

Rajni saw Jezmeen's point but she couldn't help feeling guilty. In her dreams, she saw herself feeding the pills to Mum while Jezmeen stood behind the locked door of the hospital room, shouting and banging her fists.

I should have been a better daughter, she wanted to say. All of her efforts to help Mum to put an end to her misery were about making up for another loss many years ago. Jezmeen wouldn't understand it because she wasn't there when Rajni and Mum came to India together. She had no idea how different things could have been for her and Shirina if Rajni had just stayed out of trouble.

Chapter Sixteen

As you prepare to leave Amritsar, I hope that you girls are feeling strong and ready to support each other on the next stage of the journey. The climb to Hemkund Sahib requires individual resilience, and cooperation. You need to stick together, and support each other more than ever during this final stage.

Shirina folded the last of her clothes and pressed them neatly into her suitcase. Next were her toiletries, and after that, her shoes. Then the hotel room would be as empty as she found it. Out of habit, she even made the bed. She never understood those people who said that the pleasure of staying in a hotel was leaving the sheets rumpled and having somebody else straighten them for you. Just tucking the corners and plumping the pillows made the whole place look tidier, and she needed that. Her mind was cluttered with information – the driver's name, the name of the clinic, which she kept on the tip of her tongue, afraid that she'd lose it again. She even had the address memorized – that complex combination of numbers and letters that felt a bit like a secret code, or coordinates on a map.

It was strange though, how the idea of cancelling the whole thing flickered temptingly at the edges of her consciousness. It was like standing near an open flame or leaning out of the window on the top floor of a skyscraper. Somewhere in her mind, she was aware that she had a choice. Her upbringing in England, her education – these were not for nothing. She was not some silenced village bride being shuttled from one appointment to another, her every move under the careful surveillance of her in-laws.

You can't come back unless you do this.

There it was, the reality of the situation. Shirina simply didn't have a choice, unless she wanted to throw away her marriage. She had never been given an ultimatum before, and sometimes she wondered why she let it get to this point.

She had spent her whole life listening rather than speaking, accepting rather than objecting. Even though she didn't think Sehaj was being fair, there was no reason to start fighting now.

Shirina knocked on Rajni's door first. 'I'm going to head downstairs,' Shirina said.

'You want us to come with you?' Rajni asked. 'I'm done packing myself.'

Shirina shook her head. 'That's okay,' she said. The last thing she wanted was to make small talk with Rajni while watching the clock, nervous that those words on the tip of her tongue would spill out and she'd reveal everything.

Rajni looked a bit hurt. 'Alright then. Enjoy. Send our regards to Sehaj's family.' There was a hint of sarcasm in her voice and a twitch in her lip. Although she couldn't possibly know where Shirina was actually going, Shirina felt a flash of worry.

From the hallway, Shirina could hear clattering sounds coming from Jezmeen's room. She stepped closer to the door and knocked tentatively. 'Jezmeen, I'm heading off,' she called.

Jezmeen flung open the door, her face looking slightly flushed. 'It's my phone,' she said. 'I think I've lost it.'

'Do you want me to locate it?' Shirina asked. She'd meant to disable the FindMe app but it was still on now. She opened the map and saw a bright light signalling Jezmeen's phone at the temple. 'Looks like you left it in the sarovar,' she said.

Jezmeen cursed under her breath. 'I'll walk out with you then,' she said. 'I swear, if I keep losing things at this pace, I'm going to have a very light suitcase to take back to London.'

In the lobby, a tour group was checking out. They formed a long line from the desk to the door. The bellhops were working in overdrive, picking up the suitcases and hauling them to each other in a frantic assembly line. Shirina glanced at the clock. A few minutes to nine, nearly time to go. She wondered if she should have spent a bit more time saying goodbye to her sisters, but what was there to say? They had all done their part by coming on this trip, this pilgrimage they did not want to take, and what did it achieve? Arguments, ugly memories and none of the healing that Mum had wanted for them. Why prolong the trip any further? It was time to step into the next phase of her journey, and then return home. Shirina did not know when she'd see her sisters again – there were no plans to return to England regularly to visit; there was nothing she missed about London that she could not find in Melbourne. Would they come to see her? She doubted it. It would take another major event for them to be together again. A wedding, maybe, if Jezmeen found someone. Or a funeral. Shirina shook away the morbid thought, surprised that it entered her mind. The person in her life most likely to die in the near future would be her mother-in-law and she didn't want to think of that. If she thought of it, she might will it to happen.

Rental cars were parked along the road outside. The bus for the tour group was parked at a diagonal, blocking the way. 'Is your driver going to call you?' Jezmeen asked.

'I guess he'll have to,' Shirina said.

'We had a guy called Tom Hanks taking us to the border yesterday, did I tell you that? He wouldn't tell us his real name.'

Shirina smiled. 'I think they do that to make you feel at ease. You know you're going to have a reliable journey with someone named Tom Hanks.'

Jezmeen snorted. 'Tell Rajni that. She was certain he would kill us before we got to the border. So what's your driver's name then? Mr Speed Limit?'

'Lucky Singh,' Shirina said.

Jezmeen turned to Shirina. There was some confusion in her expression. It wasn't that uncommon a nickname, Shirina thought, but Jezmeen looked taken aback. 'Okay,' she said. The bellhop was holding open the door for her now. She gave Shirina a hug and said, 'Safe travels,' and hurried off towards the temple, glancing back once before being swallowed by the crowd.

Shirina's phone dinged in her purse. She picked it up. *'Notifications: Updates needed for FindMe app.'* She ignored the notification, and opted to disable the app before throwing her phone back in her purse. Nobody needed to find her; Sehaj and Mother knew where she was headed.

Rajni was in the midst of packing her bags to leave Amritsar behind her when she heard the faint ringing of her phone. She reached for it and realized it wasn't on the side table. 'Coming,' she said, as the muffled ringing persisted. She must have packed it with her clothes. It had rung out by the time she'd tossed aside all the contents of her suitcase. 9.27 a.m.: one missed call from Nikhil, the private investigator. When she pressed the button to return the call, her heart began to beat a bit faster.

'Hello, is this Nikhil?' she asked.

'Yes, is this Rajni, ma'am?'

'Yes. Sorry I missed your call earlier.'

'Not a problem. Is this a convenient time to talk?'

Rajni glanced at the clothes strewn all over the hotel-room floor. Check-out wasn't for another half hour and the hotel could bloody well wait if Nikhil had some good information for her. 'Yes,' she said.

'Ma'am, we had one of our network investigators in London do a search on this woman, Davina. We found nothing out of the ordinary in her history – no previous husbands, no children. She does have an outstanding loan and took a second mortgage last year—'

Ah-hah! Rajni thought triumphantly. *Gold digger!*

'—but our records show that her payments are on time and she's not at risk of going into any further debt. There's no money-seeking motive there, which should be a relief to you.'

'Yes,' Rajni muttered. 'What a relief.' Disappointment sank like a lead ball in her stomach. 'So you haven't really found anything on her then?'

'No,' Nikhil said. 'But we're still in the very early stages of investigation here. There could be much more to uncover about this woman, but our protocol is to keep you continuously informed.' He had become officious again. Rajni could hear clicking in the background. Her phone pinged in her ear. 'Ma'am, I've just sent you a folder of pictures that we found on her private social media accounts. Nothing incriminating there, but if you want a record of what she's up to and who she's with, these things are useful to have.'

Rajni suppressed her feelings of queasiness that were emerging again from talking to Nikhil. A mother had to be sure, she reasoned with herself. 'Thank you,' she said, eager to get to the photos. Maybe there were things that she would spot that Nikhil wouldn't know to look for. Her intuition had to be good for something.

The attachment took a little while to download. Rajni tapped her fingers against the dresser impatiently and began to throw her clothes back into her suitcase, this time caring less about her system of packing cells. They would all get rumpled again anyway. Her heart thrummed in her chest.

The first picture popped up. So this was Davina — more diminutive than Rajni had expected, with narrow shoulders and a refined, aristocratic nose. In the first photo, the stem of her wine glass dangled between her fingers. She smiled, leaning towards her dining partner. There was no mistaking who he was. If the picture were grainy, or taken from much further away, Rajni would still know those broad shoulders and that sly grin. Anil.

There were more pictures and screenshots in the folder. Rajni skipped past the individual photos of Davina and focused instead on the pictures with friends or Anil. She didn't know what she might be able to uncover but once she knew what Davina looked like, she wasn't interested in seeing her selfies at a concert, or a holiday photo from several years ago in skiing gear with powdery-white mountains rising behind her. There were a few chains of comments with the screenshots from Davina's social media accounts — *'Lookin' good!' 'Thanks dear, you're so sweet!'* she always replied. Rajni had to admit, she was an attractive woman.

Finally, Rajni came across another picture with Anil. He and Davina were sitting together on a park bench. From the focus and clarity of light, it was obviously a professional photo. Rajni clicked on the next one — they were a series of engagement shots, she realized. Davina's head rested on Anil's chest in one picture. Anil kissed her on the cheek in another one. Rajni grudgingly allowed herself to notice that they looked like a happy couple.

She looked through the comments on the screenshots to see what other people were saying.

'Congrats you two!'

'Dav, he's one lucky guy! You are GLOWING!!'

'Enough pictures of you two, where's the ring??!! LOLLL!'

Davina had dutifully responded to all of the comments, with the usual *'Thank you'* and *'You'll meet him soon enough.'* Always followed by a winking face. In response to the comment about the ring, she said, *'Had to get it resized already, would you believe it? Fingers already swollen.'* This was followed by two winking faces. The friend replied: *'Starting early I see! I know how that goes! By four months preggers, I was wearing Steve's slippers. Feet never came back to normal size!!'*

So people knew. Rajni wondered how long it had been public knowledge that Davina was pregnant. The comments were clearly from friends of hers but this meant that the information wasn't being kept between them. Maybe it had never been a secret. Maybe Rajni was the last to know. She certainly didn't have any way of finding out what Anil was broadcasting since he'd blocked her on social media.

Rajni looked back at the pictures. Davina hardly looked pregnant, but she was in the early stages. Rajni remembered those days well – not just in her pregnancy with Anil, but the next pregnancy that ended so early that she vowed that next time she wouldn't tell Kabir and Mum until she was certain – telling them about the miscarriage had devastated everyone.

Then after the next pregnancy ended again before she had a chance to tell anyone, Rajni hoped for another chance. If she got pregnant again, she wouldn't dare even *think* about it until it was safe to do so. Her promise didn't make any difference – the miscarriage still happened and it still broke her heart, although Rajni liked to think that by keeping it a secret, even from herself, she was able to dull the pain. You couldn't feel loss for something that you never had, after all. After the doctor told them to stop trying, Rajni didn't allow herself to think about pregnancy at all. At work, she was the last person to guess that a colleague was pregnant, often only noticing the woman's weight gain or increased sick days after she'd made the announcement. It pinched Rajni each time, just a little bit, when somebody was expecting a child. She always thought she had come to terms with her infertility but those moments reminded her of the grief that was always waiting in the wings.

It was easier to pretend that it wasn't there.

Rajni looked at Davina's pictures again. Knowing that she was pregnant, Rajni could make out the faint outline of a bump pressing against the tight fabric of her dress. In that picture where Anil was kissing her cheek, she was facing the camera and smiling, a hand resting on his shoulder. A bare hand, the fingers already too big for a ring.

Like Shirina's hands.

Rajni squinted at the photo. She returned to her phone menu and searched it, not knowing what she was looking for at first. It was crazy to think that Shirina was pregnant, and hadn't told them. Why would she do that? She remembered her conversation with Jezmeen this morning about Sehaj.

Rajni tried calling Shirina first and got no answer. She looked her up in the FindMe map and found that Shirina was no longer on it. Not just inactive, but completely disappeared from the map. Now Rajni began to panic. The certainty of Shirina's pregnancy began to grow in her mind – how she was ill on the way to the police station. Rajni had been so occupied with Jezmeen's problems that she had ignored Shirina. And what Shirina had said to her in the café about having daughters.

Sehaj's name was just above Shirina's in Rajni's contact list. Rajni pressed on his name. It was probably afternoon in Melbourne now.

'Hello?'

'Hi. It's Rajni.'

There was a pause. 'Rajni. Hello. How are you?'

'I'm fine. And yourself?'

'Good. What's the weather like over there?'

He wasn't wondering why she was calling him? It struck Rajni as strange, but she played along.

'Oh, you know India. Hot hot hot,' she said.

'It's freezing over here,' Sehaj said. 'Take whatever sunshine you can get.'

'Yes,' Rajni said with a small laugh. 'Listen, Sehaj, I was—'

'And Kabir and Anil are good?' Sehaj asked.

'Yeah,' Rajni said. 'Sehaj, when did you last speak to Shirina?'

'That would be . . . yesterday, I think. Is she there?'

'No. She's gone off to visit your family. We said goodbye earlier.'

'Oh. Alright. Is everything okay then?'

'Yeah, I think so. I just—'

Somebody knocked on her room door. 'Raj, Raj! It's Jezmeen. Open up quick!'

Rajni dropped the phone and ran to the door.

Jezmeen stood in the hallway, her face ashen. 'It's Shirina,' she said. 'We have to go and get her.'

Chapter Seventeen

Tom Hanks was the first driver Jezmeen spotted at the end of the lane when they hurried out of the hotel. He was polishing his wing mirrors while bobbing his shoulders to the beat that thumped from his speakers. Jezmeen flung open the door and buckled herself into the back seat. 'We need to get to Chandigarh as soon as possible,' she said.

'Your price, Madam?' Tom Hanks asked, poking his head in the open window. 'There is a last-minute booking fee—'

'Anything,' Jezmeen said. 'Just get us there as soon as possible. I'll give you the address in a minute.' The tattered pieces of the card were in her pocket. She took them out and began fitting them together on her lap while Tom Hanks put her bags in the boot.

'Jezmeen, hold on,' Rajni shouted. She was hobbling along the lane and wrestling to release the wheel of one of her suitcases, which had got stuck in a gutter. Two turbaned men sitting on a low bench outside a juice stand got up to help. 'Hurry, hurry,' Jezmeen said through gritted teeth as she watched them pull the suitcase free. Tom Hanks got into the driver's seat and shot the car out of the lane like a rocket.

Jezmeen screamed, 'Tom Hanks! Wait for my sister!'

'Oh, sorry,' Tom Hanks said, peering over his shoulder. 'I thought we were trying to get away from her.' He pulled the car into reverse. They flew backwards down the lane and arrived at Rajni's feet. The men leaped out of the way and hollered at Tom Hanks, who apologized with a wave. 'Just get in, Raj,' Jezmeen urged. Tom Hanks threw Rajni's suitcases into the boot, got back into the driver's seat, and off they went.

'We didn't even check out properly. Did you take anything from the mini-bar?' Rajni asked once she was buckled in.

Jezmeen didn't answer her. She was reading the address on the card. 'Restoration Road, Women's Clinic,' she said to Tom Hanks. 'Do you know where that is?'

'I'll find it, Madam, no problem. Have I mentioned that using the GPS service requires an additional fee?' The car hurtled out of the lane and onto a major road. Jezmeen gripped the sides of her seat.

'We're trusting this guy with our lives again?' Rajni asked under her breath, and then she cleared her throat. 'Tom Hanks, I know we need to get somewhere urgently but we also need to get there alive, understand?'

'Yes, Madam,' Tom Hanks said. The car slowed down and Tom Hanks resisted overtaking the truck in the next lane. A cow at the back of the truck stared balefully into their window.

'Thank you,' Rajni told Tom Hanks. She turned to Jezmeen. 'Now what the hell is going on?'

'Shirina's on her way to that women's clinic and I think I know why.'

'She's pregnant, isn't she?'

'Did she tell you?'

'No,' Rajni said. 'I just put it together. Her swollen fingers, the nausea, the weight gain. Honestly, I can't believe we didn't notice it before. Sehaj didn't exactly deny it.'

'You talked to him?'

'I was on the phone with him just now. He didn't seem to think Shirina's pregnancy was any of my business though.'

'That's because it's a girl, and they're making her terminate it.'

Rajni swallowed and stared at Jezmeen. 'How do you know?'

'You remember that older woman from the baths, the one who was with me and Shirina when she slipped yesterday?'

'You said she said something that freaked Shirina out.'

Jezmeen nodded. 'I left my phone in the baths this morning, so I went back to get it. She was there. She saw me and said, "Tell your sister she should be careful. When I was expecting my third child, I slipped in the kitchen and they had to bring the midwife over right away because they thought I was going to give birth right there." I said to her, "My sister isn't pregnant," and she just gave me this look like I was completely daft. I said, "She can't be pregnant. She would have told us." The woman said, "Must be a girl then." So then I asked her what she meant by that, and she sort of waved me off like she didn't want to talk about it any more. It only took me a moment after that, and then I wondered how the hell I didn't see it before.'

'I didn't figure it out either,' Rajni said. 'And I spent years looking for every little sign of pregnancy in my own body when we were trying for another baby. I guess I just thought that if she was pregnant, she'd be shouting it from the rooftops like I would have wanted to.'

All of Shirina's strange behaviour made sense. All those moments during the trip: Shirina avoiding the little girl on the train, which was weird because she was usually so nice to children. That stricken look on her face as well, when Jezmeen mentioned the statistic about female feticide in the villages. Then there was that strange outburst after the awakening ceremony. 'Do you think she wanted to talk about it to us at any point?' Jezmeen wondered aloud.

'She did ask me if Mum regretted having daughters,' Rajni said. 'Honestly, I didn't know what to say. All those years of wanting another child, sometimes I'd break down and confide about it to Mum and she'd flippantly say things like, "Just be thankful – the next one could have been a daughter." Or, if I said we wanted to try again, she'd say, "Make sure you don't have a girl." As if I could control the outcome! It frustrated me, but Shirina must have grown up hearing things like that and thought her whole existence was a burden.'

Jezmeen sighed. 'I wish we'd paid more attention. We spent so much of this trip wondering if something was up with Shirina but not actually addressing it with her.'

'I thought everything was fine,' Rajni admitted. 'She was just being Shirina – uninvolved with us and wholly devoted to her in-laws.'

A thicket of bushes was coming up, and in the far distance, a cluster of blocky new houses – an extended family building their empire, Jezmeen thought. 'What was it that bothered Mum so much about us having daughters though?' she asked. 'She couldn't inherit her father's land, but that's kind of irrelevant for us, isn't it? It's not like we were denied any land. Dad didn't have any, and the rules about inheriting land were different when she was young anyway.'

The question made Rajni shift uncomfortably in her seat. She looked out the window, suddenly disinterested in the conversation. Jezmeen followed her gaze. In a clearing between the straggly trees on the edge of the road, there were scattered patches of sunburnt farmland. Ploughs and livestock dotted the horizon. The hottest afternoon hours were approaching, and even though they were speeding through the Punjab countryside, Jezmeen had a sense of everything slowing down.

'Madam, the air-conditioning is alright?' Tom Hanks called. Before waiting for an answer, he turned it on full blast. Air burst from the vents and scattered Jezmeen's cards onto the floor. Rajni was too distracted by her thoughts to notice.

What was she being so secretive about? Jezmeen picked up the pieces of the card and stacked them together. It seemed she understood very little about her sisters, even though the purpose of this journey was to bring them together. She couldn't remember a recent time when she and Shirina banded together the way they used to when they were little. Even their trip to the market in Delhi together had the feeling of two old friends reluctantly reacquainting.

'You know, I never told anybody this,' Jezmeen said. The memory, even though it happened so long ago, still hurt to recall, but if Jezmeen wanted the truth from her sisters, she had to start with herself. 'When I was about eight and Shirina was five, there was one Saturday that we really wanted to go to the park. You were out at some university thing. It was the first warm and lovely day of the year, and we had this idea that we'd have a picnic. I think I'd seen a family on television sitting on a checked blanket and eating baguettes and I thought it looked very sophisticated. We kept pestering Mum to take us, and she was tired. She had just started commuting to that hotel housekeeping job in Central London, and she was always exhausted when she got home. So I came up with the idea to go by ourselves. We took a couple of slices of bread from the pantry, and the two spotted bananas on the fruit bowl, and we sneaked out the back door. It didn't last very long – the woman who worked at the newsagent's noticed us wandering around on the main road and she marched us back home. Mum's reaction was so extreme though.'

'What did she do?' Rajni asked.

'She didn't speak to us for the rest of the day. Like she literally didn't acknowledge us – no food, nothing. We were gone for all of twenty minutes, but something about us leaving like that really upset her. She didn't even seem angry. It was more like she just . . . gave up on us.'

'How did you manage to eat then?' Jezmeen noticed that Rajni was listening closely. Her hands were clasped tightly together.

'We didn't. We waited for ages, and searched the fridge, but we didn't know the first thing about cooking, so we couldn't eat whatever was in there. Eventually Auntie Roopi came around to hand us some mail that had been delivered to her place by accident,' Jezmeen said. 'We told her Mum was sick, and we needed something to eat. She didn't ask any questions but she had a quick chat with Mum and offered to have us over for lunch. She said she had ordered fish 'n' chips because her daughter was going to have friends over, but she'd decided to go to a movie or something, so there was extra. Mum just went straight back to bed.' Jezmeen sighed. 'Mum had other breakdowns like that, where she suddenly just switched off and didn't want to deal with us. Any time Shirina and I got into trouble, it was because of some scheme that I had cooked up. Sometimes she told you what we had done, and then you'd lay into us as well. After a while, Shirina started distancing herself from me and just focusing on being a good daughter so Mum wouldn't neglect her any more.'

Jezmeen shut her eyes. The truth had been bubbling beneath the surface for a long time, and it was finally coming out. 'It was because of me that Shirina wanted to get out of our home, and distance herself from all of that tension. She was advertising for a new family when she put her profile up on the matrimonial site. It's my fault she ran off to Australia and . . .' She blinked back tears. 'I should be saying all of this to Shirina.'

'It wasn't your fault,' Rajni said. 'Listen—'

'I know, you'll say she made her own choices,' Jezmeen said. 'But I could have looked out for her more. I spent the past decade focusing so much on my acting career that I completely forgot about my sister. No wonder Mum probably thought having daughters was a burden.'

'For the record, having *children* is difficult,' Rajni said.

'I didn't exactly make it easy. It was my fault that Shirina grew up hearing Mum saying things like that.'

'That wasn't your fault.'

'It was.'

Rajni shook her head. 'No, it wasn't. Jezmeen, listen. The way Mum felt about having daughters? That was because of me.'

Chapter Eighteen

Twenty-eight years ago . . .

There was a drought in Punjab the summer before Dad died. The Punjabi community in West London was rife with speculation about weather patterns, the news having travelled all the way from India to England through networks of friends and relatives who had one foot in each country. Rajni's parents agreed that the poor farming conditions back home were another reason to be grateful that they lived in England, although they waited anxiously for the overdue rains to revive the dying crops and heal the cracked soil. To Rajni, it didn't always feel like they were in England. Sometimes it seemed that a huge tornado had uprooted her parents' home from Punjab and plunked them down in London – the smoky scent of spices in the kitchen and the morning prayer broadcast from Amritsar serving as constant reminders of where home really was. The atmosphere in their house certainly felt more jubilant the day the rains returned to their ancestral land thousands of miles away.

Dad wanted to sell the land then. It had been stressful hearing about farmers driven to suicide because of their dwindling livelihoods. He brought it up with Mum at the dinner table, and it led to arguments. Although it wasn't hers to give up, she was reluctant to let go of their place in Punjab. 'If we don't have that, we have nothing to go back to,' she said. It bothered Rajni that Mum saw India as a place to go back to. She remembered walking home from primary school once, and a group of girls had cornered her and pointed to a murky puddle of water they named Paki-land. *That's where you belong.* Rajni hated the idea that they might be right. Where Rajni belonged was Britain. But sometimes she had trouble proving this to Mum, who had stern rules about her hemlines and her music, her preference for Western food and her disdain towards Punjabi community gatherings where all the aunties and uncles compared their children and reminisced about India. *It's irrelevant now,* Rajni always wanted to say when they became nostalgic about the past. They were in England and it was time to move on.

That October, Dad's older brother, Thaya-ji, came to visit. From her parents' conversations about the land in Punjab, Rajni was aware that Thaya-ji had made some poor business decisions and had to sell his portion of the land at a loss during the drought. He and his wife also had to move to Delhi to live with their elder son, who had just got married. It was shameful, having to depend on his son, and allowing Dad to pay for his ticket to England because he couldn't afford it himself. The trip was long overdue though, because Dad had not seen his brother in many years. Rajni noticed how excited Dad became as the day of Thaya-ji's arrival approached. The long-distance phone calls over the years hadn't allowed much room for telling Thaya-ji about his daily life, and he was keen for his older brother to see England. 'We'll take him to all the tourist sites,' Dad said. 'But also, he will want to go to the temple, see how close-knit our community is here.'

Instead, from the moment he stepped off the plane, Thaya-ji made his disdain clear. 'Our people come all the way here to clean toilets?' Thaya-ji asked, referring to a Sikh man he had seen mopping the toilet floor at Heathrow. Rajni could tell the comment stung Dad, who worked gruelling shifts in a factory because his university qualifications from India hadn't been transferable.

Thaya-ji spent most of the visit reiterating how unimpressive he found Dad's life in Britain. 'All of these things can also be found in Delhi,' he said when he accompanied them on a trip to the shops. 'The weather is so damp and dreary – you enjoy shivering like this all the time?' he scoffed. Dad didn't argue, out of respect for his older brother, even when Thaya-ji made comments about Mum's cooking ('too bland') and Rajni's rusty Punjabi language skills ('she sounds like a *gori*'). Jezmeen and Shirina were just little girls then, and they weren't held to the same standards.

One night, as Mum was clearing the table, Thaya-ji mentioned to Dad that Mum had spent a while chattering with a red-faced Englishman who came to their door. 'You mean the man who checked our water meter?' Mum asked. 'He had come back from a family holiday in Norfolk and I was just asking him how it was. It's only polite small talk.'

'It's just that you have daughters,' Thaya-ji said. He liked bringing this up as a mild warning. 'You don't want them learning to talk in such a familiar way to strange men, do you?'

Rajni noticed Mum seething afterwards as they rinsed the dishes together, but if Dad noticed that Mum was upset, he didn't say anything. It was probably better than agreeing with Thaya-ji, Rajni thought, although she wished he'd stood up for Mum. The next morning when the postman arrived just as Rajni was heading out the door for school, Mum said quietly in Punjabi, 'No need to smile and say hello, alright?' Rajni pretended to be distracted by something in the distance as she walked past the postman. She reminded herself that Thaya-ji would only stay with them for another week, and then she hoped never to see him again.

But the next day, Thaya-ji found something else to criticize. Mum was finally learning how to drive, having put it off for years by taking buses and walking to the market. Her instructor was a man from the community who was recently divorced. Seeing Mum pull up to the driveway after her lesson with the man, Thaya-ji was not pleased. 'It's inappropriate,' he said. 'It's after dark. What will people say?'

'They will say that I'm learning to drive,' Mum said. Her voice was calm but Rajni could see a hint of uncertainty in her expression. Mum shot a look at Rajni, Jezmeen and Shirina sitting at the dinner table. *It's just that you have daughters.* Maybe if they were boys, Thaya-ji wouldn't meddle so much.

Thaya-ji's laugh was short and unpleasant. 'You don't have to turn everything into an argument. I was simply saying—'

'You've said enough,' Mum snapped. Thaya-ji was so stunned that he didn't reply.

Rajni was filled with admiration for Mum for speaking up. It was about time. Although Dad looked a bit embarrassed, he simply shifted in his seat and didn't say anything. That night, Rajni heard her parents arguing in hushed voices. Their words were indistinct, but at one point, Dad's voice rose sharply and the conversation was over. In the morning, Mum was distracted and irritable. She threatened to take Jezmeen's breakfast plate away if she didn't finish eating on time. As Rajni swung her bag over her shoulder and left for school, Mum said, 'You come straight home after school today – no hanging around in the shopping centre with Nadia afterwards.'

'But—' Rajni protested.

'Oh, you want to argue?' Mum challenged. 'Come home right away.'

The rest of Thaya-ji's visit was filled with tense smiles and stiff silences. Mum didn't seem triumphant after talking back to her brother-in-law. Knowing that she had crossed a line, she was careful not to enter any more arguments with him or Dad, and she became stricter with her daughters. Rajni was told off most often – for rolling her eyes, for playing her music too loud, for doing anything that Thaya-ji might consider too English. The general sense of unease in the house was enough for little four-year-old Jezmeen to notice. 'When's he going back?' she whispered one night, when Rajni was putting on some glittery eyeshadow for her. She had been begging to look just like Madonna on the cover of Rajni's album.

At dinner the night before Thaya-ji was due to leave, Dad tried to defuse the tension with a joke. He had fallen in the shower that evening and hit his head – not really hard enough to be concerned, but his fingers kept returning to the spot, checking for swelling. 'You really shouldn't have pushed me,' he said to Mum with a grin. Mum, filling Shirina's plate, looked up in surprise and then retorted, 'Don't think I haven't thought about it.' Thaya-ji didn't laugh. He gave Mum a hard look. *Come on, lighten up,* Rajni thought. It was the kind of joke that always passed between her parents, and she was relieved that things would get back to normal after Thaya-ji left.

Dad's death was nobody's fault. He couldn't have known that the impact of the fall was more severe than it seemed, especially since he wasn't dizzy or throwing up afterwards. The slow bleeding in his brain only caught up to him four days later while he was clocking off from his factory shift. A supervisor found Dad slumped near his car but there was nothing anybody could do at that stage. The doctor made sure to explain what was called an acute subdural haematoma to Mum, who was already taking responsibility. 'My fault,' she kept sobbing. 'Now, Mrs Shergill,' the doctor said firmly, 'this was just an unfortunate thing that happened.' But misfortune, rather than the accident itself, was what Mum was blaming herself for. Rajni knew how Mum's superstitious mind worked. It was checking all of her transgressions that invited the evil eye. She shouldn't have celebrated so much when the rain returned in Punjab, tempting fate by saying aloud how lucky they were to live in Britain. She shouldn't have argued with her brother-in-law. She certainly shouldn't have made that disrespectful comment about pushing Dad.

After Dad's ashes were flown to India and scattered by his brothers, Mum's superstitious behaviour went into overdrive. Rajni and her sisters were grieving too, but Mum's concerns were wrapped up in rituals to protect them from suffering any more unexpected tragedies. The rules were the same as before but more strictly enforced, and attached to consequences by tenuous links the logic of which only Mum could see. Leaving the windows exposed invited evil spirits into their home, so Mum kept the curtains drawn at all times, and the house was shrouded in darkness. 'I am just trying to protect you,' Mum insisted when she lined up the girls and circled their heads with fistfuls of dried chillies and birdseed to ward off bad luck. Prayers from the Golden Temple boomed from their speakers throughout the day now, drowning out the beats from Rajni's radio.

Mum implemented more house rules too, as if taking on the roles of both parents meant she had to be doubly strict. She implemented curfews and constantly asked Rajni to consider what people would think about their family if they saw her chatting with boys on the bus, or trotting around in those skin-tight blue jeans. Mum explained that they had to be more careful about how they appeared now, because with Dad gone, a family of only females was more vulnerable to gossip. 'God knows how I'll get you all married off now,' Mum sighed. 'People will say, "Those girls raised without a father? We don't want our sons getting involved with such a family."'

Rajni responded with rebellion. She hiked up her skirt as soon as she disappeared from Mum's view, and she skipped classes and smoked cigarettes. On Saturday afternoons, she danced her frustrations away with her friend Nadia at the daylight discos for hours until her clothes were soaked in sweat. With pop music still ringing in her ears, she returned home before dark and made sure to mention just enough details about that afternoon's study session at the library to keep Mum's suspicions at bay.

It was little Shirina curiously rifling through Rajni's things one day, who found a pack of cigarettes. Not knowing exactly what they were, she carted her new find around the house until Mum spotted her. Rajni came home from school that afternoon to find her bed covered in a display of everything she had kept hidden – the short skirts and tube tops borrowed from Nadia's older cousin, the cigarettes, a coaster she had nicked from the club and photographs of scenes Mum would never allow: Rajni with a boy's arm casually slung around her shoulder, Rajni in a low-cut top, pouting her painted lips for the camera. Those pictures were proof of another life. Rajni took some pride in them because they reminded her that she wasn't what those mean girls said she was.

The trip to India afterwards had two purposes. The first, Mum had already suggested a few weeks before uncovering Rajni's double life. There had been problems communicating with Dad's family over the sale of his land. Mum was entitled to the land Dad had owned, but every time she called Dad's relatives, it seemed they were occupied with something else, or the person Mum wanted to speak to wasn't there. Soon, whatever savings Dad left behind would not cover the costs of running a household. The sale of Dad's land in Punjab would be helpful. If Dad's family were avoiding her, she needed to go to India in person to sort things out. The trip would also be a good opportunity for Rajni to reconnect with her culture. Buying another ticket at the last minute was an additional expense but worth every penny, by Mum's calculations. The price of letting her daughter spend the whole summer going wild in Britain was much steeper.

They started off in Mum's brother's house in Punjab, where the days were filled with rounds of visits over samosas and steaming cups of tea. Rajni spent every afternoon in the sitting room of some cousin or uncle she'd never heard of, politely nodding to questions and squirming under their curious gazes. The female cousins had unplucked eyebrows and wore their hair in thick plaits. Rajni prided herself in taking better care of her appearance. Whenever she was allowed to use the house phone, she called her friend Nadia, who was stuck on a similar visit in Delhi. They jokingly made a plan to break Rajni out of this house. 'We could say you got kidnapped. British citizen abducted abroad!' Nadia giggled.

Meanwhile, Mum was making little progress wading through the bureaucratic nightmare of inheriting her husband's land. Dad's relatives rarely answered calls. They had never been kind to her anyway – after she had three daughters, they had even less reason to involve her in family decisions. When Mum did manage to get in touch with Dad's relatives, they were aloof and rude to her. Rajni witnessed her throwing the phone down in anger several times after yet another conversation which brought her no closer to getting what was rightfully hers.

Mum's presence in India wasn't helping her at all. She started looking into getting lawyers involved, but everything had to be done through family-member networks there, and her brother was reluctant to let people know that there was a family conflict brewing. 'It's starting to get embarrassing,' Rajni overheard her uncle saying to Mum. 'You're looking desperate, and hard-up.' It wasn't the image that they portrayed to their neighbours, of their sister who was doing well in England.

Image had become more important to Mum than ever. Again, she began to fret about what people would say about her, and whether she was ruining her chances at getting her daughters married one day if word travelled from Punjab to London that she had returned to India to scrabble for loose change after her husband died (the land was worth more than that, but by the time the rumours reached London, Mum would be portrayed as a scheming, calculating widow).

The stress took a toll on Mum and she grew impatient with Rajni, who wore her foreignness in Punjab like a badge of honour. Rajni's eyes glazed over when her cousins spoke rapidly in Punjabi. She made a face when her aunties joked that she'd be ready for marriage in a few years. 'In England, people get educated before getting married,' she replied pointedly, knowing she was being condescending. They took a trip to Amritsar and the Wagah Border to watch the changing-of-the-guards ceremony one day, and all Rajni could do was sulk and refuse to participate.

'Do you think you're too good for all of this?' Mum asked that night, as they got ready for bed. 'Is this what I raised you in England for, so you could come to India and look down on everyone?' Moonlight spilled through the window and gave her face a sickly, bluish tint. At the border, Mum had joined the dancing and looked happier than Rajni had seen her in a long time. Rajni blinked back tears but made sure Mum didn't see her getting upset. Of course she felt guilty for being difficult but she just wanted to be back in London. The whole stupid trip was Mum's idea anyway – hadn't this punishment gone on long enough? She was dying to get back to a nightclub again, to dance away her pain. Instead, they still had one more visit to get through, and Rajni was dreading it.

The visit to Delhi on the way back to London was more about Thaya-ji's family saving face than anything else. Despite the unpleasantness of his stay in London, they had to reciprocate Mum's hospitality by hosting them for a few days. Mum saw it as her last opportunity to claim Dad's land. Thaya-ji of all people would understand how devastating the loss would be, having had to sell his portion cheaply to pay off debts. 'We might have to offer him some of our land money to persuade him to help us,' Mum said to Rajni as they settled into their seats on the train out of Punjab. 'But it's worth a try.'

Thaya-ji and his wife were polite at first, but it quickly became clear that the tension from his visit had not dissolved – Rajni noticed them frequently exchanging glances and making smug comments about Mum's return to India. The payback was obvious one night when Thaya-ji started talking about his time in London. 'It's funny, isn't it,' he said to his wife, within earshot of Mum and Rajni. 'I arrived in England and the first thing I saw was one of our own men holding a mop and bucket. It made me think about all the success these people brag about from miles away, when the reality is quite different.'

'Don't say anything,' Mum warned Rajni.

The atmosphere in the flat was suffocating. Rajni hated being nice to an uncle who treated them so poorly but Mum warned her not to talk back to him – all he wanted was for them to be remorseful, and then he'd probably help them out. Mum recalled a more generous time, when Thaya-ji supported Dad's education, and even sold some of his property to help Dad get started out in England. 'It's his duty to help,' Mum said. 'That's why he seemed so arrogant during that visit – he was uncomfortable taking any charity from his younger brother.'

Rajni thought Mum was being naïve, but Mum insisted that Thaya-ji wouldn't let his younger brother's family languish. It wouldn't be the honourable thing to do, and one thing Thaya-ji repeatedly made clear was the importance of honour.

They had three days in Delhi. Rajni found a chance to talk to Nadia again one afternoon, and found out that Delhi had an exciting nightlife, none of which she would have any exposure to if she spent the entire trip with her relatives. She lamented to Nadia that she was going to return to England having spent her whole summer indoors, being a dutiful Indian daughter. 'All bloody day, I'm just sitting here with my mouth shut, bored to tears,' Rajni said. 'At least you've got your cousin to hang out with.' Nadia's cousin, a first-year fashion design college student, had taken her shopping in Khan Market and brought her to a store in Karol Bagh that had the most genuine-looking knock-off handbags.

'Just another couple of days and you'll be back in London,' Nadia said. 'You have a sweet sixteenth party to look forward to at the end of August, don't think I haven't forgotten!'

'I don't think I can take another minute of this,' Rajni said. She paused as a shadow passed in the hallway – one of the adults walking by. A moment passed, and then Mum called out to Rajni from the kitchen. 'Come and help make the rotis, Rajni. Rajni? Where are you? Are you on the phone? Calls aren't free, you know.'

'Did you hear that?' Rajni asked Nadia between gritted teeth. 'I have to go, but seriously. Save me.'

'Come out and meet me tonight,' Nadia said. 'We'll celebrate your birthday a little early.' She gave Rajni some directions, and assured her that she would get her home before anybody noticed she was gone. After hanging up, Rajni kept the directions in mind, but she knew it was too risky to try to sneak out of the apartment. *Only a few more days,* she reminded herself as she headed to the kitchen to help Mum.

'Blend the dough,' Mum instructed, handing Rajni a bowl of flour. 'Don't put too much water in there – it was too sticky last time. *Hai,* what are you doing? Didn't I just say not too much water? What kind of daughter-in-law will you make, not even knowing how to cook proper rotis?'

The kind of daughter-in-law who would tell her husband to make his own dinner if he's going to criticize, Rajni thought, but she didn't say anything. Nadia's offer to take her out that night became more tempting. A plan began to form in Rajni's mind – her relatives usually went to sleep early and from sharing a room with Mum on this trip, Rajni knew that she was a deep sleeper. The blare of traffic outside the window didn't stir her, and it would take a lot for her to wake up in the middle of the night and notice Rajni was gone.

Dinner seemed to drag on that night. There was an agonizing wait for everybody to go to bed, but Rajni knew that once they were asleep, she had to move quickly. Under her pillow, she had hidden a tank top and the pair of tight jeans that Mum forbade her to wear here unless she wore a loose and long kurti top over them. She grabbed these clothes and her small make-up pouch, and slipped to the bathroom to change. Before tiptoeing out of the house, she checked Nadia's directions again. It looked like it would be a quick walk to the main road, and then Rajni would be able to find her way from there.

Just stepping out into the night air made Rajni feel free. The lane was crowded with discarded polystyrene cases from a nearby warehouse and shadows seemed to swallow up the path, but Rajni was carried along by the thrill of her escapade. Finally, she was doing things on her own terms. She dodged a motorcycle as it came hurtling down the street with no warning. The driver looked at her suspiciously and called out something as he passed. Rajni hurried along towards the lights of the main road in the distance. Adrenalin fizzed through her bloodstream. She couldn't wait to see Nadia. *They've been keeping me like a bloody prisoner,* she'd shriek when they reunited.

As Rajni approached the end of the lane, she realized that the main road was further away than she thought. A crumbling brick wall with shards of broken glass glued to the top blocked her from going any further. Beyond it was another neighbourhood of low-slung apartment buildings, lined crookedly like old teeth. Lights shone between the buildings but now Rajni wasn't sure if they were coming from the main road at all. She had to hurry – Nadia was probably wondering where she was.

Rajni made a turn, and then another turn, and when it seemed like she was getting somewhere, she found herself heading towards a dead end again. The neighbourhood seemed walled in by darkness, and there were spaces she was afraid to enter. At this time of the night, only men were out. Rajni's presence was noticeable – conversations stopped as she hurried past, keeping her head down. The catcalling was loud and ugly. Some men followed her, chuckling as she picked up her pace. Stray dogs stretched their limbs lazily and stared at Rajni with indifference as she searched for a way back home.

Somehow, Rajni finally emerged from the neighbourhood and onto the main road, but Nadia wasn't anywhere in sight. It had been nearly an hour since their set meeting time and they had agreed that if Rajni was late, it meant that she'd been caught. Now the chance of getting caught didn't seem nearly as dangerous. At least she'd be indoors.

Instinct told Rajni that the convenience stores – those that were still open at this hour – weren't safe places to enter or ask for help. She trained her eyes on the way ahead to avoid the grins that gleamed from men's faces. She wished she couldn't hear the things they were saying. *How much? What will you do for me?* The panic was making her knees shake but she kept walking, almost breaking into a run when she spotted the police station.

It was early morning when Rajni arrived back at the apartment with two officers at her side. She had had to wait in the station for another hour and answer questions even though she hadn't done anything wrong. The officer who questioned her took pleasure in giving her a hard time. His eyes roamed across her bare arms and lingered at the hint of cleavage that her tank top exposed. Her make-up was smudged and she had her arms crossed over her chest when she walked into the door of the flat, aware of how she looked and what everybody thought. Her relatives stood like chess pieces, waiting for somebody to let them move. Mum's pale, stricken face at that moment never left her memory. She pulled Rajni by the elbow into the bedroom and began shouting at her. 'What the hell were you thinking?' she cried. 'Going out like that. You shouldn't have bothered coming back!'

Those were the words that hurt most. Mum had no idea how frightening the experience had been for Rajni. She didn't think she was ever going to make it back to the apartment. Tears burned her eyes as Mum continued to berate her. Everything Rajni did was wrong, disappointing, shameful. What kind of example was she setting for her little sisters? What would her father say if he knew what she had become? The mention of Dad struck a nerve, and she responded before she really understood what she was saying.

'Oh, and you're such an upstanding person?' Rajni cried. 'You probably pushed Dad and killed him because you were sleeping with that driving instructor.'

The room froze. Rajni's uncle and auntie had been shadows in her periphery during this argument, but now she was very aware of their presence. She could practically hear the questions forming in their minds after hearing her accusation. It wasn't true. Rajni knew it, and Mum knew that she knew it. But once the words flew out of her mouth, they took on a meaning that would haunt Rajni for years to come.

For Thaya-ji, it was all the proof they needed that Mum wasn't worthy of the land. 'I wanted to help, but if this is the truth, then I cannot,' he said with a dramatic sigh. His sad reluctance was exaggerated – Rajni could see his eyes shining with excitement at the excuse to get Mum off their backs. This had been her last chance – once they returned to London, Thaya-ji would see the lawyers and make the calls to claim the land for himself. With Mum's reputation in tatters, nobody would dispute him.

By the time the word spread to Dad's and Mum's families, the story took on mythic proportions. In their imaginations, Rajni had sneaked out with a boy, several boys, there was alcohol on her breath, she stumbled into the house, she was incoherent, she had had to do a few favours for those police officers before they would bring her home. Mum's chances of getting the land were ruined.

Chapter Nineteen

As Rajni recounted all of these memories aloud, she was aware that Jezmeen was paying close attention. This was what Jezmeen wanted to know.

'I always blamed myself for all the hardship that you all endured afterwards,' Rajni said. 'I know Mum got back on her feet eventually, but you and Shirina had to deal with having very little. Mum was always so stressed out, and I felt like I had caused that. The whole situation was enough to scare me straight.'

'That's when you changed,' Jezmeen recalled. 'I was too young to really question it but I remember that when you returned from the trip, you were more stern. You threw out all of the make-up I used to nick from your room.'

'The make-up, the outfits, everything. It made me feel like I was doing something to help. I told myself that I was still me, but I just needed a break. My rebellion against Mum had really hurt our family. Then,' she sighed. 'Then I went to university, met Kabir, and married him as soon as I graduated. I didn't miss the fighting with Mum.'

'Raj, you didn't hurt our family,' Jezmeen said. 'Those relatives did. They spread hurtful rumours and they withheld something from Mum that she badly needed. They're the immoral ones, not you.'

'I know that now,' Rajni said. Her eyes were filled with tears. She fumbled for the packet of tissues in her purse. 'I know it and I don't know it. I know in my head that it's not fair to feel responsible for all of that loss, but things could have gone differently for Mum, and for you guys.'

'Or not,' Jezmeen said. 'That brother of Dad's probably never intended to give up his land. And so what, Raj? We all survived. It wasn't the worst childhood. We had a roof over our heads. Auntie Roopi looked out for us. You looked out for us.'

'I didn't. I just nagged and hovered over you to keep you from letting Mum down the way I had.'

'It didn't work though,' Jezmeen said with a grin. 'I spent most of my life telling you to shove it.'

'What about Shirina? She had such a rotten time growing up that she ran away and into the arms of another family.'

'Also not your fault,' Jezmeen said firmly. 'You said yourself that Mum took way too much responsibility for Dad's death – the evil eye and all that. You're doing the same thing. You're making connections between something that happened years ago as if you're the only reason those things were possible. We've all made our own choices. You're the one who always reminds me of that. You tell your students and Anil the same thing as well.'

Anil. Rajni shut her eyes and tipped her head back. 'Anil's certainly made his choice,' she muttered.

'What do you mean?'

She might as well tell Jezmeen. Those engagement pictures would probably be up on his social media sites soon. 'He's engaged.'

'What? I didn't even know he was seeing someone.'

'Me neither. She's thirty-six.'

Jezmeen's eyes grew wide. Rajni took in a breath. 'They're having a baby.'

'Fuck me,' Jezmeen said. Rajni flinched as Tom Hanks' ears perked up at the swear word. 'Sorry!' Jezmeen called to him. He waved back to show that he wasn't offended. 'Rajni, what the hell?'

Rajni wiped her tears away with the back of her hand. 'He's forgoing university and everything we've worked for, so he can start a family with this woman.'

'I mean, why didn't you say something?' Jezmeen asked. 'You've known this the entire trip?'

'Yeah, but I don't think I was really admitting it to myself.'

'It's a lot to come to terms with,' Jezmeen said.

'I don't think I listened to what Anil really wanted,' Rajni said. 'He's completely locked me out of his life now.'

'There you go again, blaming yourself,' Jezmeen said. 'Listen, if Anil's cutting you out, that's his choice. You didn't push him to do that. You didn't push him to make any of his choices. I guess . . . the thing is, does he seem happy with the way things are turning out? Are you okay with that?'

'No,' Rajni said. 'How can I be okay with Anil throwing his life away?'

'He might not see it that way,' Jezmeen pointed out. 'It's not the life you imagined for him – that doesn't mean it's the wrong way to live.'

'But—'

'Look, Raj. You just said you're sorry for breathing down my neck, and for being such an uptight, morally righteous prig. You deeply regret wasting all those opportunities to be a cool big sister because of that massive stick lodged up your bum.'

Not quite how Rajni would have phrased it, but she let Jezmeen continue.

'It hurt when Mum forced convention on you, didn't it? Wasn't it infuriating to have to live up to her standards? What mattered more to Mum than your safety that night was how it looked to other people. Don't tell me that this isn't the same thing.'

'It's not,' Rajni said. 'I don't care what people think.'

Jezmeen snorted. 'Fuck fuck fuck fuck fuckity fuck,' she suddenly sang aloud. Tom Hanks looked up in amusement.

'Stop it,' Rajni hissed. 'What will Tom Hanks thi—' She stopped when she noticed the smirk on Jezmeen's face. 'It's not the same thing, Jezmeen. He's my only child.'

'So this is about Anil being your only chance at parenting?'

'. . . Maybe,' Rajni said.

'Would it be different if you had more children then? If you had a daughter?'

If I had a daughter. It wasn't Rajni's first time pondering what life would be like if that sibling for Anil had materialized. She didn't have an answer for Jezmeen. What she knew was that all of this felt terribly unfair, but so did Dad's death, and the land being taken away, and Mum's cancer and Mum dying. It was unfair that Shirina was in Chandigarh right now, doing something she thought was necessary to save her marriage. Looking out the window, Rajni saw that they were still deep in farmland and it was impossible to avoid thinking of what they had lost.

But maybe Rajni could avoid losing anything else. 'Excuse me, Tom Hanks?' she asked.

'Sorry, Ma'am,' Tom Hanks said. Rajni only addressed him to chastise him for speeding.

'Can you go faster, please?' she asked. 'We need to get to Chandigarh urgently.'

'Ma'am, you're asking me . . . ?'

'To hurry up,' Rajni said. 'Get us there as fast as you can.'

With that, Tom Hanks slammed his foot on the accelerator and the farmland around them stretched into an infinite green blur.

Chapter Twenty

There was a close-up photograph of a blossoming pink orchid in the waiting room. It looked identical to the one that was mounted on the wall of the clinic that Shirina had been to in Melbourne five months ago. Surely that was a bizarre coincidence. It wasn't as if one flower photographer had a monopoly on obstetrician clinics around the world. But it was a comfort to know that Sehaj had taken some care to find a clinic of the standards she was accustomed to – the leather-upholstered couches and the lilac-scented air freshener were also consistent with the atmosphere of the Melbourne practice. Not one of those Third World clinics she had in her imagination, with a dim low-hanging bulb over bare steel tables, where blank-faced women waited for their turn to reverse time.

She wondered how long Sehaj had taken to research options and find this place – maybe his family was connected to the doctor in some way? He had handed her the card so quickly at the airport that there wasn't time for questions. They had only ever discussed this procedure in abstract terms. *Going through with it. Doing what's necessary. Handling the situation.* There was no chance for nuance when every conversation escalated and ended with sharp words, and then a lengthy silence during which all the other sounds of the house became amplified – water slipping down the pipes, windows shuddering against the chill.

The receptionist called her name. The weight pulled at Shirina's centre as she pushed herself to her feet. There was no need to pretend she wasn't pregnant here, but out of habit, she took casual strides, as if unencumbered by the bump. It was still carefully concealed – thank goodness she was one of those women who could reach the second trimester without it being too obvious.

At the counter, she gave her name and was asked to select a method of payment. 'Visa,' she said, handing over the credit card that she and Sehaj shared. The receptionist handed her a clipboard with a stack of forms to fill out. *Details of your medical history.* She ticked the boxes mechanically. No, no, no to nearly everything. A couple walked into the waiting room and sat down across from her. The woman was much further along, her belly a swollen moon under a long and elegant turquoise kurti. She complained to her husband about her ankles – 'Just look at them,' she muttered, pointing out two blocky feet. 'It doesn't go away right away either. Drima told me that her feet went up two sizes and remained that way. That's why she stopped at one.' The husband said something inaudible and the woman gave him a playful shove on the shoulder.

Shirina handed the clipboard back to the receptionist, who gave it a quick glance and nodded. Out here, they were still doing something proper and completely legal. She was an expectant mother going in for a routine check-up – like the couple in the waiting room, who were too cheerful to be here for any other reason. Behind closed doors, she would wait for the doctor to tell her that there were options. They would have to keep their voices low, and the doctor might even ask her to turn off her phone, to make sure she wasn't recording the conversation. Shirina had read a CNN exposé where a journalist posing as a pregnant woman visited a clinic like this in an upscale Mumbai suburb. She had placed her iPhone on the table to gain the doctor's trust but sneaked another one in the seam of her purse.

It was ironic, doing this procedure in India, where sex-selective abortions were illegal. Doctors here weren't even allowed to notify women of the sex of the baby. But there was nothing that money couldn't buy, of course, and Shirina wouldn't be here if she hadn't delayed it so long, if she had just admitted the truth to Sehaj and Mother when she first found out she was having a girl. She thought about Mum setting the date for the pilgrimage in the summer holidays to make travel more convenient for Rajni. She wouldn't have known that this trip would also coincide with the cut-off date for Shirina to terminate her pregnancy. Maybe on some level, Shirina kept putting off telling the truth to Sehaj in Melbourne, thinking that the trip would save her. She'd go to India, return to Melbourne and say, 'Whoops, too late.' How naïve she was, to think that it would be so easy.

The pregnancy test instructions stated a wait time of five minutes for an accurate reading but Shirina was too excited to wait. They had been trying for a few months, but this time felt different: her period was a week late and she felt the strong undertow of fatigue. Only a minute after she peed on the stick and placed it on the edge of the sink, she returned to it. The pink control line appeared and darkened right away. As Shirina impatiently drummed her fingertips and stared at the stick, another line appeared. 'Sehaj!' she squealed, rushing out of the bathroom. It was a Sunday morning, and he was lazing in bed. 'You're going to be a father.'

Sehaj's expression. Shirina wished she'd had a camera. His eyes lit up and a grin spread across his face. Shirina crawled back into bed and gave him a kiss. She knew she had carried her sadness around each time another test came up negative. Still recovering from Mum's death and the ugliness of her sisters' fighting, becoming pregnant was an attempt to replace her loss with some hope. Now she and Sehaj were going to start their own perfect family.

'If we're having a boy, we'll name it after your father, and if we're having a girl, we can name it after my mum,' Shirina said. The hormones made her feel sentimental. She had fantasies of Sehaj being the kind of doting father who fought back tears when his child went off to school. As a child, Shirina sometimes daydreamed that her own dad was still alive, and he made up for all of Mum's shortcomings. He was protective and attentive. He didn't let her feel forgotten.

Sehaj's reply surprised her. 'The first one has to be a boy.' Shirina had smiled at his definiteness but she was also unnerved. *Has* to be? It was one of his mother's views, of course. Since joining the family, she had heard Mother use the same tone when explaining the way she liked the house to be run. Dinner had to be ready by seven, it didn't matter if Shirina's boss kept her back late or the tram was delayed. Shirina had to take time off work to look after Mother during her recovery from hip surgery, and then she had to take more time, until it made more sense to quit. Shirina had avoided thinking of these obligations as anything but duties, the sorts of things daughters did for mothers, and wives did for husbands – but the sex of the baby was a different thing altogether. 'What do you mean, it has to be a boy?' she had asked, laughing. 'I can't control these things.'

After a beat, Sehaj laughed as well. He told her he was kidding, doing a bad impression of a more conservative man. 'We'll see anyway,' he said. It wasn't exactly what Shirina expected to hear from him but she pushed her fears out of her mind. Surely nowadays nobody insisted that a woman was responsible for determining the sex of her baby, or that a girl baby should be terminated. Maybe in villages, but not in Melbourne or London. Out of curiosity, Shirina searched for the topic on her bridal forum. The number of posts that came up stunned her. '*In-laws prefer a girl!*' '*Am pregnant with first and it's a girl, anyone been through this?*'

Shirina thought it was ridiculous, but she also found herself hoping she could avoid the conflict altogether. *Please be a boy, please be a boy,* she found herself thinking as she lay down on the table for the sonogram three months later. She was so distracted by her wishing that when the ultrasound technician asked where her husband was, she simply said, 'No.' The technician smiled and repeated the question. 'Oh, sorry. He's got an important work meeting, so I'm here on my own,' Shirina said.

'Baby brain,' the technician said knowingly. 'I had it with all three of my kids. I put the laundry in the fridge instead of the cupboard one day!'

She nodded along impatiently as the technician chattered away and began running the probe along her belly. 'You might be one of the lucky ones, like my best friend,' she continued, nodding at Shirina's flat belly. 'She only started showing after six months – before that, nobody would believe she was pregnant.' Shirina kept her eyes trained on the black screen. There was a flicker of movement, and the underwater sounds of an echoing heartbeat. Shirina bit her lip to hold back tears. The technician continued to guide the probe along her belly, and pointed out the wobbly vision of the baby's arms and legs, the scanner showing a tiny reptilian spine, the nose and chin briefly visible in profile as the baby turned. The technician paused for the big announcement. 'Would you like to know what you're having?' she asked with a smile. Shirina began to cry as soon as she found out she was having a daughter. The technician thought they were tears of happiness, and gave her an extra tissue to wipe her eyes.

Driving home from the hospital, Shirina wished that the scan had been inconclusive. The technician had warned her before the scan that this could happen sometimes, if the baby's legs were crossed. It would be out of Shirina's hands then, for the time being. When she walked in the door and saw Mother's expectant face, Shirina felt a fierce sense of protection over the baby. 'They couldn't tell,' she said. She wasn't usually a very convincing liar, but she found herself recreating the scene for Mother – the screen showing the spine, the nose, the chin, but those legs firmly crossed, revealing nothing.

Mother accepted the answer. 'You can find out at the next test then,' she said. 'But you can't wait too long, *hanh*? When is the next one?'

'In a few weeks,' Shirina said. Thankfully, Mother was unaware that there were blood tests that could determine the sex of the baby too, or she would have sent her right back to the hospital to do that.

That evening, Shirina looked through her wedding album. It had become a habit since Mum died because the best photographs of her were there – her face glowed with happiness and health. Sehaj walked in the door at 7 p.m., and came upstairs to freshen up before dinner. He was greeted with the sight of Shirina poring over the pictures. 'Remember this?' she asked, pointing to a surreptitious look between them that the photographer had managed to capture. Their smiles were mirror images of each other. As Sehaj crouched on the floor next to the bed and kissed Shirina in that tender spot behind her ear, she wished she didn't have to lie to him.

'So how was it? All the fingers and toes present and correct? And does my boy take after his father?' He puffed his chest out.

'It was great,' she said, wincing inside. 'But the gender bit was inconclusive.' She closed the wedding album. 'But it doesn't really matter, right? Whether it's a girl or a boy? Why do we even need to know?'

Sehaj's body tensed beside her.

'Aren't you just happy that we're going to have a baby?' Shirina pressed.

Sehaj sighed and kissed her forehead, and said, 'It's not necessarily about what I want. It's what my mother—'

'But she'd adjust, wouldn't she? You've said that about her before, that there are some things she just has to get used to.' Like marrying me, Shirina thought. Mother didn't think much of the girl from a working-class family in England, but Sehaj had put his foot down. He could do it again. Mother didn't need to have her own way in everything.

'Think about how much happier we'd be if you just listened to her once in a while,' Sehaj said.

'I do listen,' Shirina said, feeling a lump rising in her throat. Mum had told her to listen to her in-laws, to do as they pleased, and she had tried so hard to obey. How much harder did she need to try to appease them? When was it going to be enough?

The moment Sehaj noticed Shirina's voice wobbling, he reached out and clasped her hand. She thought he'd say something to comfort her. Instead he said: 'I've got a lot of stress at work these days, Shirina. You have no idea what it's like.'

'No, of course I don't. I left my job, didn't I?' Shirina snapped. She pulled her hand away like he had scalded her.

Sehaj stood and walked out of the room. Shirina stayed in the room that night and skipped dinner. The nausea that was supposed to abate by the end of the first trimester was still persisting, and she didn't feel like facing Sehaj and Mother anyway. She was angry with herself, although it wasn't clear why. In the pit of her stomach, perhaps bred into her for years, was the secret shame of having done something wrong.

The silence that followed that evening was the worst Shirina had experienced since marrying Sehaj. Every creak in the floorboards and hiss from the vents became trumpet-loud in the absence of conversation. It followed her everywhere – breakfast, the car ride, the waiting room – and even when Sehaj did begin speaking to Shirina again the next morning, his words were measured and terse. Every sentence contained the same obvious message: *If you're going to question things around here, you're alone.* It recalled the clawing anxiety of those days after Mother found her on the doorstep leaning against the taxi driver's shoulder – but this time Mother didn't just wilfully ignore her; she behaved as if Shirina had never existed in the first place. It was chilling, feeling like a ghost, and it was disturbingly resonant of Shirina's own childhood. She couldn't live like that again.

Things eventually thawed with Sehaj, and Shirina worked hard to maintain the peace. Although she still had questions about what she was expected to do if they found out the baby was a girl, she buried them. They wouldn't order her to terminate the pregnancy . . . would they? Sometimes Shirina found herself looking at Sehaj across the table and wondering if he would come right out and say it. This was also something she didn't want to think about, so she decided to just wait. It wasn't a problem yet because as far as everybody knew, she could be having a boy. The ultrasound technician had given her an estimated due date, and from a quick calculation, Shirina realized that her trip to India with her sisters would end at the twenty-four-week mark, when it would be too late to have an abortion.

Why *did* she call Lauren then? Shirina wasn't in any trouble. Was she just hoping that somebody would sympathize with her? Or was Lauren her only friend? Maybe it was because she was afraid of the thoughts that ran through her mind late at night, while Sehaj snored lightly next to her. Thoughts about just telling Sehaj and Mother the truth, and doing what was necessary to restore peace. *You're young. You can try again. People make sacrifices for their families all the time.* At one point, she considered calling Rajni or Jezmeen, but the embarrassment stopped her. After fleeing her family in London for greener pastures with Sehaj, she couldn't face her sisters knowing that things weren't ideal. She could barely admit it to herself.

The first thing Shirina blurted out when Lauren answered the phone was, 'I miss work.' Not even 'Hello,' or 'Help,' but Lauren heard what she was saying right away.

'What's wrong, darl?' she asked. 'Where are you? Stay where you are, I'll come and get you.'

Shirina knew she should hang up, but she clutched the phone to her ears, unable to speak or move.

'Are you still there?' Lauren asked.

'Yes,' Shirina managed, and then she gave Lauren a meeting place. She usually had a free hour after dropping Mother off at St Vincent's for her weekly physiotherapy session. The Kitchen Hand café on Gertrude Street wasn't very busy, and it wasn't a likely hangout for any of Sehaj's family members, but Shirina still looked over her shoulder whenever she mentioned Sehaj's name to Lauren.

'This is abuse,' she said plainly. 'If you're keeping the sex of the baby from them because you're afraid they'll force you to have an abortion, it's abuse.'

Shirina suppressed a familiar impulse to defend her husband and mother-in-law. It was a cultural thing, it was just a preference, hadn't she heard Western women say they wanted a boy too? These excuses flooded like a rush of adrenalin in her veins – defensive, indignant, *you just don't understand* – and for the first time, she let them go.

'You need to get out of there,' Lauren said.

Her determination made Shirina nervous. 'I don't think leaving Sehaj is the right step to take,' she said carefully. 'I just need someone to talk to. My thoughts rattle around, keeping me up at night. Sometimes I think it would be easier if . . .' She couldn't complete the sentence, but Lauren knew what she was saying.

They talked until Shirina had to be back at the hospital, and agreed to meet the following Wednesday in the same café. 'I'm so glad you called,'

Lauren said, giving Shirina a tight hug before they parted ways. 'Stay strong, alright? Remember, you have a choice.'

Over the next few days, Shirina received messages from Lauren:

'Just checking in. How are you feeling today? Remember, they can't make you do anything against your will!'

Shirina replied, *'Okay'* and then deleted each message. She deleted Lauren's name from her contacts as well, committing to memory the first four digits of her phone number. It was better not to have Lauren's name popping up all the time – if Mother looked at her phone, she would get suspicious. Lauren was the bad influence, after all, the one who led Shirina astray by enticing her to drinks after work. As the messages continued, they began to bother Shirina. *'It would be okay if you want to be away from Sehaj for a while. There are resources to support women in your situation.'* While Shirina appreciated Lauren's concern, she felt she was blowing things a bit out of proportion. There was no need to suggest that Shirina leave her family.

'This isn't his fault,' Shirina texted back. *'He's under pressure too.'*

'That's called brainwashing,' Lauren replied. Moments later, another message came through: *'Sorry, insensitive thing to say. But I think he's controlling you more than you realize.'*

Shirina didn't reply. Wednesday rolled around. After dropping Mother off, Shirina walked in the opposite direction of Gertrude Street, ending up in the gardens behind the Parliament building. Newlyweds loved having their photos taken here, the brides' white gowns spilling like cream down the steps of the stately building. Shirina watched an East Asian couple posing. The air was chilly and heavy blue clouds hung low in the sky. Although she'd lived in Australia for nearly a year, Shirina was still getting used to the idea of winter in July. The groom held a black umbrella over the bride to protect her elaborate hairdo from a wind that whipped up suddenly, upturning umbrellas and whirling leaves on the footpath. The world felt upside down in a lot of ways now.

There were seven missed calls from Lauren by the time Shirina returned to the hospital to pick up Mother. Shirina figured Lauren would give up eventually, but as she walked back out into the blustery air, her phone continued to buzz in her purse. 'Who keeps calling you? Why aren't you answering?' Mother asked with narrowed eyes as they got into the car. *Great,* Shirina thought. All she needed now was for Mother to become suspicious about her having a secret. 'Just an old work friend,' Shirina said. She wanted to turn the phone off, but that would make Mother even more suspicious, so she blocked Lauren's number and dropped the phone in the compartment between their seats.

When the phone rang again, Shirina was merging the car onto the freeway. It couldn't be Lauren, so she didn't mind Mother picking up. The only calls that came on weekday afternoons were from telemarketers anyway.

'Hello,' Mother said. A pause. 'No, Shirina is driving. Do you have a message?'

Shirina heard a bubbly voice chattering on the other end. 'Just hang up if it's one of those survey people,' Shirina said. 'They don't take no for an answer.'

Mother's face was stony with concentration. 'Yes, I will let her know. Goodbye.' She pressed 'End' and put the phone back in the compartment. Rain had begun to dot the windscreen and the cars ahead were slowing down. 'That was the hospital confirming your next appointment,' Mother said.

'Okay, I'll call them back when I get home.'

'She referred to your baby as "she",' Mother said.

Shirina clutched the steering wheel. She flicked on the windscreen wipers and tried to think of a lie but knew the tension showed on her face. 'What did she say?' she asked, to buy some time.

'She said, "I hope the little girl is doing well, and she's not giving Mummy too hard a time with morning sickness."' Shirina could feel the heat from Mother's stare. 'Do you have something to tell us, Shirina?'

Shirina's cheeks burned with shame. For a split second, she considered lying but that would just prolong the inevitable. Mother was watching her like she could read her thoughts.

'Yes,' Shirina whispered. Her instinct was to apologize, but the words didn't come out. 'I should've told you,' she said, her voice heavy with regret.

At home that evening, Shirina heard Sehaj and Mother talking in low voices in the kitchen. Sehaj's voice rose at one point, but it quickly became quiet again. Shirina couldn't make out what either of them were saying but when he came to bed, he wouldn't look at her. Every day after that, the quiet was so punishing, and the house was so still that Shirina thought she could hear her blood coursing in her own chest at one point.

Things only felt normal again when they had that tender moment together at the airport. *It's over now*, Shirina remembered thinking as she rested her head against Sehaj's chest. She wished the memory could end there, but then he had given her a card and an ultimatum, and walked away.

The receptionist called Shirina's name again and told her to go into room 4C. Shirina knocked on the door before entering. A nurse opened the door and wordlessly gestured for her to take a seat.

'Mrs Arora,' said Dr Wadhwa. Behind the frames of his wire-rimmed glasses, his eyes lit with recognition. 'You are here from Australia.'

'Yes,' Shirina said.

The doctor ran Shirina through a list of familiar questions. How many weeks had she been pregnant, and how was she feeling? 'Fine,' she said, because over this trip, she had got used to pretending that the bouts of queasiness that had followed her into the second trimester were just her body's response to the soupy heat of India.

'Good,' Dr Wadhwa said. Then they discussed the procedure. Shirina nodded along numbly as the doctor explained in a low, gentle voice about the sedation, and the discomfort she might feel afterwards. 'Since we are removing a very' — he cleared his throat — 'developed foetus, the recovery time might be longer. Now tell me, do you have any history of blood clots? Cysts?'

'No,' Shirina said.

'Allergies to any medications?'

Shirina shook her head.

He wasn't making any notes – avoiding a trail of evidence, Shirina supposed. This office was cramped compared to the bright and airy waiting room. A slumping potted plant on the windowsill looked like it had seen better days. The nurse was also apparently an air-conditioning repair person; she tapped at the yellowed unit and declared, 'It's the filter that needs to be replaced' in a tone that suggested she and the doctor had had a lengthy argument about which part of the air-conditioner's anatomy was riddled with disease.

Was the doctor going to ask her why she was getting rid of this baby? Shirina itched for somebody to give her a chance to explain. He was avoiding her gaze now though, calling for the nurse to take a moment away from office repairs to take Shirina's blood pressure. A small machine was wheeled to Shirina's side, a tray pulled out for her to rest her elbow. The nurse wrapped a band around Shirina's arm.

'I'm not so sure about this,' Shirina blurted out.

The doctor's expression didn't change. Shirina thought maybe he didn't hear her, but the nurse looked up. The band around Shirina's arm squeezed itself tight, a snug embrace first, and then an uncomfortable one. There was a ripping noise from the Velcro as the nurse pulled it off Shirina's arm.

'I need more information,' Shirina tried again. 'What – what will happen exactly?'

Don't read up about the procedure, one website supporting women who wanted abortions warned. *It will make you more anxious. On the other hand,* it continued, *if knowing the details gave you a sense of control, then it could be helpful to talk them through with the doctor.* 'Do you have a lot of experience in these?' Shirina asked.

Dr Wadhwa and the nurse exchanged a look. *It's normal to have cold feet,* the website assured.

The doctor didn't answer Shirina's question about his experience. He didn't look insulted either, just a bit bored. Maybe other women did this, Shirina thought. They made the appointment – or their husband's families made it for them – they arrived at the clinic, they filled out the forms, and then they started second-guessing their decision. 'I don't mean any disrespect,' Shirina said. 'It's just that this is quite risky, isn't it?'

'No procedure is without risks,' Dr Wadhwa replied. He looked at the clipboard that the nurse had handed to him when Shirina walked into the room. 'We will take good care to make sure that any potential problems are minimized.' He paused and looked up. 'Your husband's family and mine go way back. We'll take care of you, don't worry.'

Although Dr Wadhwa probably meant to reassure her, it also sounded like a warning. He returned to his clipboard before she could read his expression further.

'You're planning on conceiving again soon?'

Shirina nodded. 'What if the next one is a girl?' she asked. 'And the one after that?'

Dr Wadhwa said, 'Some women try five or six times before they're successful with a boy.'

Five or six more pregnancies, five or six more lengthy arguments with her husband and mother-in-law. Or maybe it would get easier, and Shirina wouldn't be so hesitant the next time around. Or maybe she'd have a boy next, and this first pregnancy would fade into the history of their relationship, a tiny blip on an otherwise ideal marriage.

Shirina didn't know what would happen if she turned back now. What was a marriage without compromise? Rajni had sent her a few articles about the secrets to a happy and peaceful marriage – 'SO TRUE', she wrote just above the link – and 'giving in' featured consistently in all of them.

There were consent forms to be filled in before they could proceed. 'Understandably, the forms will officially state that the pregnancy is not being terminated due to gender preference,' the doctor droned. The nurse handed Shirina the clipboard again.

The procedure was due to start soon. She'd be sedated, and wouldn't feel a thing, the doctor assured her. Afterwards, there would be bleeding, and she was advised to take things slowly for a few days. Sehaj had booked

Shirina a five-star suite at the Hilton. She'd be there for three days, recovering with room service, a hot-water bottle and all the Hindi television dramas she wanted.

Peace. Normality. A return home. *You can't come back unless you do this,* Sehaj had said to her in the airport, pressing the card into her hand. *I'm sorry,* Shirina thought, as she signed the consent forms. She didn't know who she was apologizing to any more.

Chapter Twenty-One

How many roundabouts did a city need? Jezmeen wondered as Tom Hanks shouldered the car around another island of landscaped grass. If she weren't paying such close attention to the street signs and landmarks, she would've thought that Tom Hanks was simply caught in an eternal orbit of traffic. Jezmeen didn't know what good it did to name the street signs as she saw them — she had no sense of orientation in this city, or anywhere else in India, but Chandigarh's neatly planned streets and landscaped gardens were reassuring. Shirina couldn't be lost in the depths of this place for too long.

Rajni was watching the city as well. They hadn't said much to each other for the rest of the journey, and Jezmeen was itching to get out of the car. She needed some distance from all of this history that Rajni had laid bare between them in this tiny space. The news about Anil was taking a while to digest as well. She wondered: if Rajni was going to be a grandmother, then what did that make her? A great-aunt? The title made Jezmeen want to vomit.

'Madam, I think it's in that shopping centre over there,' Tom Hanks said, just as a bus wobbled into their lane. Tom Hanks made a hard right, and the shopping centre disappeared into the distance.

'Hang on, I'll make the turn on the next go,' Tom Hanks said. The road was teeming with vehicles though.

'We need to get there quickly,' said Jezmeen. 'Can you just let us hop out here?'

'Where?' Rajni asked. 'He can't just let us out in the middle of the road.'

'He's going to spend an eternity trying to get back to that side,' Jezmeen said. 'We'll walk and the cars will stop. Look, people do it all the time.'

'No,' Rajni said. 'Absolutely not.'

'Rajni, we have to get to Shirina before she goes through with this thing.'

'Your suggestion is that we plunge headfirst into speeding cars on a roundabout in India?'

'It's all about confidence,' Jezmeen said. 'Tom Hanks? We're getting off here, thank you.'

'No, that's a very stupid idea – you will both die,' Tom Hanks said calmly. 'Just give me a moment.'

Ten minutes later, they had only moved a few feet. Jezmeen sighed and squirmed. 'Try calling her again,' Rajni suggested.

'It goes straight to voicemail,' Jezmeen said.

'Just try again. You never know.'

Jezmeen tapped on Shirina's name and listened to the phone ring once before the automated voice recording politely informed her that Shirina was not available. She wasn't expecting anything different, so she was surprised to feel a heavy sinking disappointment. Suddenly, she wasn't so sure any more if Shirina would be so easily retrievable, even in this neatly planned city.

'What if we find her, and she doesn't want to come with us?' Jezmeen asked Rajni quietly.

'What do you mean?'

'She came all this way,' Jezmeen said. 'She spent the entire trip hiding her pregnancy from us, and then she got into a car and headed here on her own. Maybe she doesn't want to be rescued.'

Rajni frowned. 'Why not, Jezmeen?'

'I'm afraid Shirina thinks this is the only way to fix her marriage,' Jezmeen said. 'You know how she's always taken the path of least resistance when it came to any sort of conflicts with family or friends.'

'It won't be the last sacrifice she makes for them though,' Rajni said.

'That's just not how it works. If they can get Shirina to do this for them, they'll keep expecting her to bend to their rules.'

The shopping centre came into their view again as Tom Hanks focused on making a precisely timed exit. He cut through a stream of screeching motorcycles and delivered Jezmeen and Rajni expertly into a space that was definitely not for parking. 'I'll wait right here for you,' he said, as the car juddered to a halt. 'And Madam, it's going to be okay. Your sister will be relieved to see you. Remember what happened at the end of *Captain Philips.*'

All Jezmeen could recall from the end of that movie was Tom Hanks' character splattered with blood from the Somali pirates who had hijacked his ship. In this analogy, perhaps she and Rajni were the Marines who shot them dead. 'Thank you,' she said nevertheless as she threw open the door. They were about to storm an obstetrician's office – any words of encouragement were welcome.

The air was stiff with heat. Jezmeen scanned the shop signs – the bright blue of Domino's Pizza, the wedding-card business that took up two floors, and the crowded display windows of the kitchen appliances emporium.

'There,' Rajni said, pointing. Jezmeen's first feeling was relief. The clinic looked legitimate – at the very least, Shirina wasn't in some dingy tin-roofed shed.

The receptionist's desk was empty when they pushed through the glass doors and entered the air-conditioned waiting room. 'Hello?' Jezmeen called. She looked for a bell at the reception desk but it was bare except for a phone and a green glass penholder. An enormous black-and-white framed photograph of an eye took up half the wall.

'Shirina?' Rajni called. 'Are you here?' Her voice was calm but Jezmeen could see the panic on her face. 'What if they've taken her?'

'Where would they take her?' Jezmeen asked.

'I don't know,' Rajni said, looking around. 'SHIRINA!' she hollered. 'IF THEY'RE HOLDING YOU BACK THERE, MAKE A NOISE!'

The door of the clinic opened then, and in walked a harried-looking young woman wearing a creased salwar-kameez. 'Oh!' she said. 'Do you have an appointment?'

'Our sister is here,' Rajni informed her. 'Shirina Arora. She's here against her will and we're taking her back.'

The woman stepped around to the reception desk as if Jezmeen and Rajni were a puddle of spilled drink. She typed on her computer for a few moments and then said, 'I don't have a Shirina Arora here. Are you sure her appointment is today?'

'Yes,' Rajni said.

'Try Shirina Shergill,' Jezmeen suggested.

The woman glanced at her screen and shook her head. 'We only had two appointments today and they were both over and done with by lunchtime.'

Over and done with. The receptionist was so cavalier about the procedure. 'She was supposed to be in here now,' Jezmeen said. 'If something has happened, we need to know about it.'

'There was no Shirina here,' the receptionist insisted.

She had clearly been instructed to pretend that Shirina had never walked in through those doors. 'I know that certain procedures are off your books, but this is a very serious matter. She didn't want to do this,' Jezmeen said. 'Her husband's family made her.'

If it was possible to be both irritated and interested, the receptionist's expression was a perfect combination of the two. 'They *made* her? Why?'

'They're old-fashioned,' Jezmeen said. 'It's a stupid preference they have. Look, we know she's here and we know why she's here, so let's just cut the charade.'

'Or else we can go back there,' Rajni said, nodding to the glass doors.

'If you trespass, I will call the police,' the receptionist said.

'*We* should be the ones calling the police,' Rajni retorted. 'You have some nerve, performing an illegal procedure and then threatening to have us arrested.'

'What's illegal about it?' the receptionist asked. 'If it's more convenient for somebody to live the rest of their lives without—'

'More convenient?' Jezmeen said. 'Is that how you see it?'

'Yes, more convenient. Women especially are much more confident after undergoing this procedure. Their husbands are also happier.

Everything is clearer for them. That's probably why your sister's in-laws made her do it.'

Confidence? That was a new one. Jezmeen knew there were many reasons that women were convinced to give up baby girls but confidence was not one of them. The eye on the wall fixed her with an intense, singular stare. It was a strange choice of portrait for a gynaecologist's clinic, where patients awaited being uncomfortably exposed.

'That's it, I'm going in there,' Rajni said. She marched past the front desk, ignoring the receptionist's protests, and pushed the glass doors.

The receptionist went after Rajni, shouting about trespassing. Jezmeen picked a name card off the desk.

Dr Chopra Eye Centre
Vision Care and LASIK Surgery

Jezmeen was about to call out Rajni's name when she saw her being led back out the glass doors by the elbow. Rajni shook the woman off. 'It was a bit excessive, grabbing me like that,' she huffed after they made their apologies and scurried out of the clinic. 'I would have left of my own accord after I saw the vision-testing chart.'

In the car park, Tom Hanks was wiping down his mirrors. He didn't notice them emerging from the building. The traffic was so heavy now that the roundabout looked like another car park.

'What do we do now?' Jezmeen said. Rajni could sense her panic as she paced the footpath outside the shopping centre.

'Let's try the FindMe app again,' Rajni suggested. Maybe Shirina had enabled it.

'Did we just get the address mixed up?' Jezmeen looked at the card pieces again. 'I think the numbers go up in that direction. Thirty-two . . . thirty-four . . .'

'Thirty-six!' Rajni shouted, spotting the clinic sign at the end of the row. 'Let's go.'

She hurried, ignoring the throbbing pain in her ankle. *Mum, I'm sorry it turned out to be such a disaster,* she thought as she and Jezmeen arrived at the clinic's entrance. She had wanted at least one trip to India – if not with Mum, then in her memory – to go as planned. She knew that Mum wanted this for her as well. Although it wasn't written anywhere in the letter, Rajni believed now that Mum wanted her to remember India differently from that place where bad memories were buried.

At the glass doors, Rajni and Jezmeen hesitated. Neither knew how to do this again. It was as if they had spent all of their energy on that last public scene. 'Go on,' Jezmeen said, nudging Rajni.

'We're sure this is the right place?' Rajni asked, looking up again. There was the sign: *Restoration Road Women's Clinic*. Through the glass, Rajni eyed the receptionist who sat under a large framed photograph of a pink orchid. There were a lot more people in this waiting room, and Rajni didn't want to disturb them. For some reason, she decided to knock on the door. The receptionist looked up and beckoned them in.

'Uh, hi, hello,' Rajni said when they entered. She nodded at all of the people in the waiting room as well, as if they were part of the conversation.

'We're looking for our sister,' Jezmeen said, marching to the front desk. 'Shirina Arora. She's here against her will and WE'RE NOT LEAVING TILL SHE'S OUT OF THERE! SHIRINA, COME OUT! SHIREEEEENAAAA!'

Too much, Rajni thought, but she had to support what Jezmeen was doing. She knocked a pen off the desk and scowled at the receptionist.

'Madam, there is no need to shout,' the receptionist said, standing up. 'You are scaring the other patients. Have a seat and calm down, or I will call security.' She glared at Rajni. 'And pick up my pen, please.'

'Yeah, sorry about that,' Rajni mumbled. She picked up the pen and replaced it on the desk, next to a nameplate which read *Manjinder Bhatti*. There was a couple sitting on the couches who huddled together, watching the scene unfold. The woman held her round belly protectively and her husband stood up for a moment, then sat down, then stood up again. 'Look, we're very worried about our sister, and we need to speak to her right away. I think she's with Dr Wadhwa. Would you please give him a call and let her know that we're here?'

Manjinder regarded Jezmeen and Rajni as if she was trying to decide if they were from a prank television show. The husband took a seat again and clasped his wife's hand reassuringly.

'Your sister's name?' Manjinder asked.

'Shirina Arora,' Rajni said.

'Oh, that patient has been and gone already.'

'Left? Like she walked out of here?'

'About ten minutes ago, yes.'

They were too late. Rajni gripped the edge of the receptionist's desk to steady herself. Jezmeen buried her face in her hands. Rajni heard a sob and wanted to comfort her, but she was too filled with disappointment to offer any words of solace. She thought about the last time she saw Shirina in Amritsar. In her memory, that round belly was so obvious, now that she knew what Shirina was hiding.

Manjinder cleared her throat. 'When you see her, can you give her this form, please? She was supposed to sign it and I think she forgot. She was out of here so quickly.'

'Pardon? Does that mean . . . ?' Jezmeen asked. She turned to Manjinder. 'Wait, did she have the procedure?'

Manjinder shook her head. She pointed at her screen. 'It was a very quick appointment. She left within fifteen minutes.'

They clutched each other's hands and Jezmeen let out a little whoop of joy.

'Where did the taxi go, do you know?' Rajni asked.

'No idea,' Manjinder said apologetically. 'You can't call her?'

Rajni shook her head. That image of Shirina saying goodbye to her at the hotel stayed in her mind as she and Jezmeen walked out of the clinic. What would she say to Shirina the next time she saw her? Would they see her again, or was this Shirina's final gesture to shut the door on their family? The pain that accompanied this thought felt all too familiar – it was like Anil saying that nothing could keep him and Davina apart. Whatever happened next, Rajni knew she had to fix things with Anil. She wished she could board that plane now and just see her family again.

Tom Hanks was nowhere to be seen, but the car was parked. Rajni took out her phone to text him. 'Why do you think she left? Do you think she knew we were coming?' Jezmeen asked while they waited on the kerb.

'What do you mean?' Rajni asked.

'Do you think she knew we were on our way, and she decided to back out before we showed up to stop her from doing the procedure?'

'I don't know,' Rajni said.

'Or maybe she walked out and decided not to do it?' Jezmeen asked hopefully.

'Maybe,' Rajni sighed. 'But either way, she's not coming back here. Let's just look for a hotel in Chandigarh and stay here for a day. We can wait for a call from Shirina, or I'll try calling Sehaj again.'

She was about to put her phone back in her bag when it buzzed. *FindMe: Shirina is online.*

'Oh my god,' Rajni said. She tapped her screen and saw Shirina's little dot on the screen. It hovered over Rajni's and Jezmeen's dots. She was here? Rajni spun around. At her desk in the clinic, Manjinder was sitting very still, watching them.

'She's in there,' Rajni said. 'She's in there, Jezmeen, quick!'

As they wrenched the door open again, Manjinder stood up and backed herself against the door that led to the doctor's room. 'Madam, we are under strict orders from the Arora family—'

'I will call the police,' Jezmeen warned Manjinder. 'I will tell them that you are holding my sister against her will. Open the door now.'

Manjinder pressed her back against the door and began to shout for help. The couple in the waiting room hurried out of the clinic, leaving Rajni, Jezmeen and Manjinder alone. They tried to push past her but she was surprisingly strong despite her lithe figure.

'SHIRINA!' Jezmeen shouted, still struggling to get a grip on the doorknob. 'SHIRINA, COME OUT!'

'Madam, I'm just doing as I'm told,' Manjinder pleaded as Jezmeen tried to pry her fingers from the doorknob.

'What exactly were you told?' Rajni asked.

'The doctor said Mr Arora called after he heard that you two were coming, and he said not to let you in under any circumstances. He said you were dangerous, and that your sister doesn't want to see you.'

Sehaj must have heard Jezmeen when she burst into the hotel room while Rajni was on the phone with him. 'Look, if you let go of the door, we'll take full responsibility. We'll say we charged in and you didn't have a chance.' They'd probably say that anyway, Rajni thought, because they weren't getting anywhere with trying to overpower this woman.

'I can't,' Manjinder said. 'Please, I'll lose my job.'

There was some movement in the hallway. Rajni saw it first – the opening of a door, a head peeking out curiously and disappearing. *That's enough,* she thought. After hitting Jezmeen in the hospital that time, Rajni had been horrified and disgusted with herself, but this was different. She lowered her shoulder and barrelled into Manjinder like a bull chasing a waving flag, startling her enough to make her lose her grip on the doorknob. Jezmeen flung open the door and they hurried inside. Manjinder chased after them, shrieking and grasping the belt loop of Rajni's jeans to pull her back. Jezmeen got ahead first. She tried the doorknob frantically and then pounded on the door with her open palms. 'SHIRINA!' she shouted. 'SHIRINA, CAN YOU HEAR US?'

Rajni felt the weight of Manjinder's entire body toppling her to the ground. Her face smacked hard into the floor and a ringing noise filled her ears. All she wanted to do was try to shout encouragement to Jezmeen, but the fall seemed to have knocked the sound out of her windpipes.

She watched helplessly as Jezmeen continued hollering and banging on the door. Manjinder scrambled to her feet to try to pull Jezmeen away, but it was too late. The door opened and out came Shirina, her eyes wide with surprise. When she collapsed into Jezmeen's arms, Rajni burst into tears.

Chapter Twenty-Two

Day Seven: Trek to Hemkund Sahib

This will be the most difficult and rewarding part of your journey. I never had a chance to trek to Hemkund Sahib when I was healthy, and it was the first place that came to mind when the doctors told me that I was terminally ill.

The temple at the top of the mountain is the most elevated Sikh gurdwara in the world. People who have been there have described it as a trek to heaven. Walk steadily, and meditate on the knowledge that your ability to move, climb and connect with nature, are all temporary. What's left, as your body and mind slow down, is your spirit. You will feel an appreciation for your body, for each other's support as you undertake this physical and mental challenge.

Hemkund Sahib sits near the calm and sacred waters of Lokpal Lake. Encircled by seven snow-clad peaks, this glacial lake is where our tenth guru meditated and achieved spiritual unification. This is the place where my journey will end. I would like my ashes to be scattered in this lake so that I can rest in the same place where our guru became one with God.

The view from the hotel window was of short, flat-topped apartment blocks. Satellite dishes bloomed out of their windows. Below, the muted whir of constant traffic circulating.

If Shirina had gone on the trek, if everything had been completely different, she'd be stepping cautiously along a pebble-strewn path, the view ahead misted by the mountain fog. The thin air and the jagged mountain peaks would certainly feel like another realm. Instead, here she was in Chandigarh, in a hotel suite that Rajni had booked for the three of them on her phone as Tom Hanks drove them away from the clinic yesterday, offering platitudes from films like *Forrest Gump* and *Big*. Anything to stop Shirina from crying, he probably thought, as he reminded her that life was like a box of chocolates. She hadn't stopped crying for nearly the whole journey – it was a release of all her bottled-up outrage and fear from the past few weeks.

This hotel was situated in a central part of town cluttered by shopping malls and billboards. The suite had adjoining rooms for each sister, but Shirina noticed that Rajni had deliberately opened the door that connected her room to Shirina's, and left it ajar. 'Call if you need anything,' Jezmeen said anxiously, after wandering into Shirina's room to borrow her hairdryer. She had lingered at the doorway for a while before leaving.

'You're okay, right?' she asked, eyeing Shirina's place on the chaise longue near the window. Shirina nodded and waved her off, trying not to let her annoyance show. She understood why her sisters were concerned, but they didn't have to tiptoe around her. Now that they knew about Shirina's pregnancy and her marriage, they acted as if she was full of untold secrets.

'Did Sehaj ever . . . ?' Rajni asked at one point in the drive over here, before blinking and looking away.

'He never hit me, no,' Shirina said. 'His mum sometimes jabbed me though. She snatched my phone from my hands as well.'

Jezmeen was furious for Shirina. She wanted to call Sehaj and have a word with him. 'How could he put you through this?' she asked. 'He had some bloody nerve, warning the doctor about us like that. I'm not afraid of him, you know. I could call him right now and tell him what I really think about him.'

But Sehaj was full of fear too. Shirina knew that if Jezmeen called him, he'd nervously excuse himself and hang up. Sending her to India to have an abortion was like every other move he made – staying at the office late to avoid hearing about Shirina and Mother's latest conflict, staring at his phone at the dinner table when Mother was giving Shirina a hard time about the quality of her cooking. He was too afraid to deal with Mother's disdain for Shirina, so he distanced himself from Shirina, as if she was the problem. After handing Shirina that card at the airport, and telling her she couldn't come back, he had walked away quickly to avoid another argument.

Shirina supposed she had once mistaken Sehaj for a person with more power over her as well. She only began seeing things differently after the receptionist knocked on the doctor's door and told him there was a call from Australia. 'She says it's urgent,' the receptionist said before the doctor threw a quick look at Shirina and hurried out of the room. Knowing it was probably Mother calling, Shirina stood up then, clutching her bag to her chest. She had been asking every question she could think of, hoping Dr Wadhwa would understand her doubts and sympathize, maybe call the whole thing off. Returning from the phone call, the doctor mentioned again being friends long ago with Mr Kamal Arora, Sehaj's father. He clearly wanted Shirina to know he couldn't say no to them. There were obligations and favours that undoubtedly extended beyond the moral code of his profession.

Although Shirina was standing at that point, she couldn't bring herself to walk out. She still felt that she needed somebody to tell her it was okay to leave. She reached for her phone and noticed a window had popped up: *Are you sure you want to disable FindMe?*. She hadn't confirmed it. She pressed No and made herself Visible, for whatever that was worth. Dr Wadhwa began talking to the nurse in a low voice. They glanced at Shirina a few times, and she realized with a chill that if she wanted to go, it wouldn't be so easy. Fear flipped her stomach and kept her rooted to the seat, squeezing her hand around her phone. It was really only when Shirina heard the commotion outside the doctor's office that she sprang into action and rushed to the door. It didn't occur to her that the voices outside were Jezmeen's and Rajni's, just that somebody was providing a distraction outside.

Somebody was knocking on her adjoining door now. 'Come in,' she called. Rajni poked her head in. 'You alright?' she asked for the hundredth time that day. 'Do you need anything?'

'I'm okay,' Shirina said. Perhaps she shouldn't be sitting so close to the window – it probably made Rajni nervous even though it was sealed shut. 'Thank you for organizing this room again, by the way. It must have cost a fortune at the last minute.'

Rajni waved the comment away. 'It's fine,' she said. 'The more important thing is that you're comfortable. How's the nausea?'

'Comes and goes,' Shirina said.

Rajni stepped into the room and sat on the edge of Shirina's bed. She smoothed out the covers even though they were stretched taut over the mattress. The room smelled faintly like rosewater from the honeymoon suite on the same floor.

'What would you like to do today then?' Rajni asked brightly. 'We should start with brunch – you must be starving. I saw that there are some nice restaurants nearby.'

'Rajni—'

'Or room service? You're probably tired. Room service would be better then.'

'You don't have to behave like this,' Shirina said.

'Like what?' Rajni had an exaggerated look of surprise on her face.

'Like I'm a basket case. I could do without you and Jezmeen acting like I'll fall apart any moment.'

'Shirina, you've just been through something really huge,' Rajni said. 'You've made a really big decision, and you're coming to terms with what it means for your marriage.'

Shirina shook her head firmly. 'I'm fine. Sehaj and I will be . . . we'll be fine.' Tears welled up in her eyes. She didn't want to think of the alternative. Shirina's flight back to Melbourne was a day away and she still had no idea what to do.

She had called him from the car and left a message to say that she had left the clinic with Rajni and Jezmeen. 'I'm not doing it. I'm keeping our baby,' she said and then she stayed on the call until it timed out. She didn't want to hang up abruptly but she wondered what Sehaj made of the minute or so of indistinct background noise – the purring car engine, the tune that their driver hummed to himself.

'If you and Sehaj are not fine, that's alright too,' Rajni said. 'You can come back to London. Or go back to Melbourne if you want, but move out of his home. It's up to you.'

Shirina felt an apology coming. It was her fault that Rajni was so concerned, and the pilgrimage had been altered. What would Mum think of all of this? 'I know I've put you through a lot,' Shirina said. 'I was hiding this from you, and I nearly went through with . . .' She looked down at her round belly and placed a protective palm over it.

'What's important is that you're safe,' Rajni said firmly. 'Nobody is judging you for having a horrid old-fashioned mother-in-law. I wish you'd told us what you were going through, but Jezmeen and I weren't exactly paying attention to anyone but ourselves lately.'

There was another knock on the door. 'Hey Granny,' Jezmeen said brightly to Rajni as she breezed into the room, holding the hairdryer. 'Just returning this, Shirina. Also, I was wondering about the plan for today. Sightseeing? Sitting by the pool?'

'Let's stay in and put some movies on,' Shirina said. Now that she was no longer hiding her pregnancy, she just wanted to lie down and put her feet up. 'I saw on the TV menu just now that there's this old HC Kumar film playing.' She sat up suddenly. 'Hey, weren't you going to meet him at some point?'

'Yeah,' Jezmeen said. 'But things changed. There will be other chances.' Her smile, like Rajni's over-enthusiastic tone of voice, didn't seem genuine. Shirina waited for Jezmeen to say more, but she simply shrugged and began coiling the wire around the hairdryer.

Jezmeen had given up her opportunity so she could be with her. 'Jezmeen, you should have gone to meet him,' Shirina said. 'Is there still a chance?'

'I asked my agent if we could reschedule, but HC Kumar is a pretty busy guy. He didn't get back to us. It's fine.' Jezmeen was trying to brush it off, but Shirina caught the pain in her voice.

'Is there a chance of seeing him tomorrow before we head off? Or if you stick around in India for a bit longer, maybe you can arrange something?'

'I was thinking about it but I can't afford to just hang around here on the slim chance of breaking into the Indian film industry. It's very competitive here,' Jezmeen said. 'But it's alright, Shirina. Mum said I had to start being more realistic, and maybe she was right. At best, this meeting was going to lead to a small role, but time's running out. It could take years to establish myself, and by then, the number of available roles will shrink again because I'll be close to forty.'

She sounded convinced, but Shirina wasn't buying it. 'Why don't we go there tomorrow?' she asked. 'On our way to the airport.'

'Go where?'

'His office, or his studio, or wherever,' Shirina said. 'If he's there, surely he'll give you a few minutes of his time.'

Jezmeen shifted her weight from one foot to the other and appeared to be thinking about Shirina's suggestion. 'What if he doesn't like me?' she asked in a small voice. 'People said some pretty horrible things about me online – why would HC Kumar think any differently?'

'He's already impressed with you, Jezmeen. He wouldn't have asked for a meeting if he wasn't at least thinking about giving you a role,' Rajni said.

'So, we'll do it then?' Shirina asked.

'We have to leave early then, to make sure we don't miss our flight,' Rajni said.

'Okay, Granny,' Jezmeen smirked.

'Why does she keep calling you that?' Shirina asked Rajni. 'Is it because of your ankle?' She had noticed that Rajni was hobbling a bit, and she'd asked for a bucket of ice as soon as they checked in.

'You haven't told her?' Jezmeen asked Rajni.

'Anil and his girlfriend are having a baby,' Rajni said to Shirina. 'I'm going to be a grandmother.'

Anil was going to be a father? Shirina stared at Rajni. 'Sorry, I think I misheard you.' She looked at Jezmeen for confirmation, who began to snicker. 'Isn't he only eighteen?'

'Thank you, and don't feel obliged to hide your surprise. I didn't see it coming either.' Rajni shot a glare at Jezmeen. 'Let's order whatever we want from the menu tonight and do some proper catching up.'

'And champagne for me and Granny here,' Jezmeen said. 'We haven't actually properly celebrated all these pregnancies.'

'Jezmeen, if you call me Granny one more bloody time—'

Jezmeen giggled and pointed the hairdryer at Rajni like a gun. Rajni picked up a pillow and aimed it at her head but Jezmeen ducked and it missed. 'Nice moves, Granny,' Jezmeen called as she bolted out of the room. Rajni went after her and their shrieks travelled through the walls.

Shirina patted her belly. Some movement from the baby kept her awake last night, and she felt a determined kick this morning. *My daughter.* She looked out the window again. This was a greener city than Delhi, with trees and flowered bushes appearing in manicured strips between the roads and in carefully arranged bouquets on the landscaped roundabouts. There was a sense of order here that calmed Shirina, even though it wasn't the spiritual place Mum had envisioned for this stage of their journey. One day perhaps, she and her sisters would complete this pilgrimage the way Mum had intended it. Her daughter would be there too.

Chapter Twenty-Three

Day Eight: Flying home

Jezmeen grinned into her pocket mirror to check her teeth for lipstick stains. She tucked her hair behind her ears, decided it looked too bookish, tossed her hair, decided it looked too messy, and then checked her teeth again. This time there was a tiny red smudge on her incisor. 'I can't do this,' she declared, dropping the pocket mirror into her lap.

'You can,' Rajni assured her from the front seat of the car. 'Did you visualize the best possible outcome?' This was one of the self-help tactics Rajni had found in a quick internet search on her phone. 'Or how about this one: *Top Ten Mantras for Success.*'

The GPS on Tom Hanks' dashboard indicated that they were five minutes away. On the entire ride from Chandigarh to Delhi, Jezmeen wondered if they were doing the right thing. HC Kumar hadn't bothered getting back to Cameron about an alternative time to meet, so maybe he had moved on to another actress, somebody more reliable.

'What if he saw the Arowana video and he's decided that I'm a scumbag?' Jezmeen asked.

'He probably set up that meeting in spite of the video,' Shirina reminded her. 'Everybody's seen it by now, so it's a good sign that he wants to meet you regardless.'

'Wanted to,' Jezmeen corrected. 'Then I didn't show up and now he's like, "That's what I get for giving a chance to a fish murderer."'

'That's not what he's saying,' Shirina said calmly. 'Oh!' She grabbed Jezmeen's hand and placed it on her belly. A moment passed, and then there was a tiny bump against Jezmeen's palm. 'She's wishing you good luck.'

'Thanks, little lady,' Jezmeen cooed.

'Isn't it "Break a leg"?' Rajni asked.

'That's theatre,' Shirina said. 'Or can it be used for film?'

'Not sure,' Rajni said. 'It's a funny thing to say in any case, isn't it?'

While Jezmeen appreciated that her sisters were trying to be encouraging and supportive, she was drowning in doubt. Last night, she couldn't sleep, and it probably showed. She found herself scrolling through her IMDB page, clicking on all the little roles that she'd had, some so small that they didn't link to a description. She was a passing body, just filling the background while the lights and cameras focused on bigger stars. Of course, then Jezmeen went where she had been repeatedly warned not to go – the comments under the original Arowana video. Although the furore had died down in recent days, some of the ugliest sentiments against her had still been 'up-voted' to the top of the comments section. *Can't believe that there are people fleeing wars in other countries, and we have people like this in ours,* one commenter had lamented. Another, to whom Jezmeen was tempted to respond with a string of expletives, had said: *Looks like a publicity stunt – she's probably desperate for attention. Bet the producers from that crap show of hers arranged the whole thing.* Scrolling through a bottomless feed of other people's unbridled opinions was as addictive as it was self-destructive. Jezmeen's mind kept wandering back to Mum, and what she would have made of all this.

'I wish Mum had a little more faith in me,' Jezmeen told her sisters. 'All I can think about is how she died thinking I still had a lot of growing up to do.'

'She probably thought that about all of us,' Rajni said. 'A mother never stops thinking of her children as children.'

They didn't say much else to each other until Tom Hanks announced that they were arriving at Connaught Place. At the sight of the Georgian columns and arched windows of the imperial-white buildings, Jezmeen's stomach lurched. *You're ready for this. You've been waiting for this to happen for a long time.*

'I need a minute,' Jezmeen said when they pulled up. Rajni and Shirina nodded and stepped out of the car. HC Kumar's office was in a tall tower with tinted glass windows that dwarfed the historic shophouses. Jezmeen closed her eyes and tried to visualize the best possible outcome. She saw herself coming face to face with HC Kumar, and shaking his hand. He told her he was impressed with her and wanted her to be his new leading lady. Then he turned into a giant Arowana. Jezmeen's eyes flew open. She looked out the window and watched Rajni and Shirina approaching the building. Whatever happened next, Jezmeen was grateful for her sisters, who had helped her to brainstorm ways to get into HC Kumar's office.

The plan was to try to get past security by saying they had an appointment. If that didn't work, Shirina was going to ask to use the toilets. Nobody would deny a pregnant woman access to the loos. Jezmeen would go with her, and they'd try to find HC Kumar's office. It was not an airtight plan, and there was the possibility of many things going wrong, but Rajni and Shirina insisted that Jezmeen had to at least try. Jezmeen considered this the final effort of her career. Her plane would leave for London tonight, and if this didn't work out, she would either continue searching for roles or start seriously thinking about a different career.

Jezmeen noticed Shirina waving her over, and she got out of the car. 'I'll be parked just over there,' Tom Hanks called, and not actually indicating where 'there' was, he drove off down the wide avenue.

'The doors are locked. There's an intercom,' Shirina said as Jezmeen approached. 'Maybe you should talk to them.'

Jezmeen looked at the little box on the wall. There was a small camera that would magnify her face on the screen. She pressed the button for HC Kumar's production company's office and waited.

A voice buried in the heavy roar of static called, 'Good afternoon, HC Productions.'

'Hi!' Jezmeen said. 'I have an appointment with Mr HC Kumar?' She shrugged at Shirina and Rajni, who gave her a thumbs up.

'You are?'

'Jezmeen Shergill.'

There was some rustling. Jezmeen shut her eyes, hoping that her trick would work.

The voice returned. 'Ms Shergill, there is no appointment listed here.'

'Okay, uh, that's weird,' Jezmeen said. 'Because . . . listen, Mr Kumar and I were supposed to meet yesterday, but I couldn't make it because of a family emergency. I was wondering if – hello?' The small light next to the button had stopped blinking and the static noise was gone.

'I think she just hung up,' Jezmeen said.

'Try again, explain that he wants to see you,' Rajni urged.

Jezmeen pressed the button again. 'Hi there,' she said as soon as the light came on. 'If there's any way that I can see Mr Kumar now . . .'

'He's in a meeting,' the voice said. 'He has a very packed schedule and—'

'I have to use the toilet,' Shirina blurted out, peering into the camera.

'There are toilets in the shopping mall just across the road,' the voice said kindly.

'Look,' Jezmeen tried again. 'This is very important.'

'I understand, but he is busy, and then he's getting on a flight to Mumbai.'

'Couldn't you just knock on his door or something?'

'I'm pregnant,' Shirina declared. Rajni led her away. Jezmeen made a mental note to never involve Shirina in a plan to get past security again.

'Ms Shergill, we get actors showing up out of the blue, asking to see Mr Kumar all the time. That's why we have a strict screening system. I'm really sorry.'

A lump rose in Jezmeen's throat. She turned to Rajni and Shirina. 'That's it then,' she said. 'Let's just go.'

'I'm sure there's something you can do,' Rajni shouted into the intercom. 'We've come a long way.'

'Raj, you don't have to yell. I think she can hear you,' Jezmeen said.

The voice apologized again. 'If you want to leave your details behind, Mr Kumar can get back to you.' She didn't sound very convincing.

'My sister will never have a chance like this again. You work in this industry, surely you understand that?' Rajni hollered.

'Again, Rajni—' Jezmeen began. She knew Rajni was just trying to be heard but she sounded a bit unhinged.

'I'll need to call security,' the voice said.

'We're not afraid of that,' Rajni said. 'We were threatened with security twice in Chandigarh.'

'Not helping,' Jezmeen said. 'It's over, Raj. This is a sign.'

'I did not like her tone of voice,' Rajni muttered. 'Very snobby.'

'I can still hear you,' the voice said.

They had a few hours to kill now that Jezmeen wasn't going to meet HC Kumar and Tom Hanks was nowhere to be seen. She realized that she had been setting herself up for disappointment – her fears weren't about her odds at getting another shot. They were about getting that shot and still not succeeding. What if HC Kumar met her and decided she didn't have what he was looking for? Casting calls and auditions and the long waits for callbacks had taken up too much of her adult life. 'Let's go,' she said firmly to her sisters. This was where her career would probably end.

'Rajni?' A male voice rang out behind them. Jezmeen and her sisters turned around.

'Hari!' Rajni said. 'What are you doing here?'

'I work here – there was a call for security because some people were trying to get into the building, so I looked out the window and saw you.'

Jezmeen's first thought was that the man was the spitting image of HC Kumar. He had the same silver-streaked hair and broad smile as the director she had seen on those behind-the-scenes videos she liked watching. *What are the odds, that a lookalike works in the same building?* she mused.

Then it hit her. This was him. Rajni knew him. Rajni knew him? So many thoughts and questions rushed through Jezmeen's mind that she felt light-headed.

'Shirina, remember this lovely man that we met in the uh . . . that day when Jezmeen was at the protest?' Rajni was asking. Shirina smiled and nodded. Rajni glanced at Jezmeen. 'Why do you have such a weird look on your face?'

'I'm Jezmeen Shergill,' Jezmeen said. 'I believe we were supposed to meet today.'

'You're . . . ?' Rajni said.

'I'm HC Kumar,' he said. 'You can call me Hari.'

Chapter Twenty-Four

'I hadn't heard of you until a few days ago,' Hari admitted. 'My daughter Parvana was rounded up at the women's march at India Gate too. She said that an actress who everyone thought was Polly Mishra gave a very powerful speech about what it felt like to travel in India as a woman.'

Jezmeen beamed. It was probably the first time Rajni saw her brushing off the comparison to Polly Mishra. 'And that's why you got in touch with my agent?'

'Yes, I had no other way to reach you and just hoped you were still in India. When you cancelled for a family emergency, I just assumed you had to go back to London.'

'I'm really sorry about that – I'd appreciate it if you could take the time now though.'

'Yes, come on upstairs. We'll have to be quick because I have a flight to catch later.'

'I actually really do have to pee now,' Shirina whispered to Rajni. 'Do you think he'll let us into the building?'

'Why don't we leave you two to chat?' Rajni suggested to Jezmeen and Hari. 'Shirina and I will do some window shopping in Connaught Place, and then we'll meet back here.'

'Sure,' Jezmeen said, already heading back towards the building.

Hari smiled at Rajni. 'What a great coincidence. I'm so glad we saw each other again.'

'We didn't get to say goodbye, did we?' Rajni said. 'You were outside on a smoke break when Jezmeen was released.'

'And all the girls after her,' Hari said, with a wink. He followed Jezmeen back into the building.

It took a moment for Rajni to understand what his wink meant. 'I think he was responsible for getting Jezmeen and the others out of jail that day,' she told Shirina as they walked towards the shopping area. 'He probably used his influence to release them – that's why he was so chilled out about his daughter being there.'

'Maybe that's why his daughter continues to get involved in those protests,' Shirina said. 'If she gets into trouble with the authorities, her dad can make some calls. It's probably safer for the other girls without influential fathers to join her.'

Everything in this country is about who you know, Mum had said to Rajni one day, after hanging up the phone in frustration. She had been finding it impossible to get a lawyer to represent her about Dad's land without referrals from family members. A woman on her own in a country that was no longer hers, Mum had a hard time getting through to anybody.

Walking with Shirina towards the arched entrances of the colonial shophouses, Rajni couldn't stop thinking of Mum. The weary look on her face as she tried another phone number, how hopeful she sounded about getting the land from Thaya-ji. Mum had faith in people. She had faith in her daughters too, otherwise she wouldn't have sent her back here.

The urn was still in Rajni's suitcase. After Shirina returned from the toilet, Rajni said, 'We still need to spread Mum's ashes.'

'We're coming back here next year for that, aren't we?' Shirina asked.

Rajni shook her head. 'No. I mean, yes, we'll return to India and we'll make the trek, but I don't want to go back to London with unfinished business.' It would be too reminiscent of the way Rajni left India last time. Her head hanging in shame, the shadow of betrayal hovering over her. Shortly after she returned home, her sixteenth birthday came and went.

Mum didn't ignore the day out of spite – she really seemed to forget. She had found a cleaning job that would let her take extra shifts – backbreaking work that saw her leaving the house at dawn and coming back late at night, long after Shirina and Jezmeen had fallen asleep at Auntie Roopi's house. That was when Rajni decided things had to change.

What Jezmeen said about all bodies of water leading to the same place had some truth. 'Doesn't the Yamuna River run through Delhi at some point?' Rajni wondered aloud. It was a tributary of the Ganges, where ashes were more commonly scattered. In one of Jezmeen's early emails disputing every item on the itinerary, she had pointed this out.

'We could ask Tom Hanks,' Shirina said. Rajni took out her phone to call him and saw that he had sent her a message to say that he was parked behind the office tower.

They found Tom Hanks sitting in the car and watching something on his phone. When he noticed Rajni and Shirina approaching, he beckoned them closer. His eyes were glistening with tears. 'It's my favourite part,' he said. It was that scene from *Castaway* where Tom Hanks – the actor – was crying over the imaginary friend that he had conjured from an image of a bloody handprint on a volleyball.

'Yes, I've seen it,' Rajni said. 'Tom Hanks, we were wondering . . .'

Tom Hanks held up a finger to silence her. He nodded at the screen. 'WILSON!' cried Tom Hanks the actor. 'WIIILLLSONNN!' Rajni and Shirina exchanged a look, and Shirina shrugged.

The scene finished but it looked as if another one was about to load. Rajni caught a glimpse of the sidebar on the phone – *Tom Hanks' Greatest Scenes Playlist* still had several more videos in queue. 'Tom Hanks, we need your help,' she said.

This got his attention. He put the phone down and started to turn on the ignition again.

'We can't go anywhere yet,' Rajni said. 'We need to wait for our sister. But before you take us to the airport, can you drive us to a river? The Yamuna River goes through Delhi somewhere, doesn't it?'

'It does,' Tom Hanks said. 'But it might take a while to get there.'

'Is it far?' Shirina asked.

'Not far,' Tom Hanks said. 'I can show you on my phone. Traffic will be horrendous though. It will take ages to get to the outer ring of Connaught Place from here, and by then we'll have to contend with the rush hour.'

Rajni really didn't want to be in a panic over getting to the airport on time. 'Does the Metro go there?' she asked.

'Yes. Take the Metro from here to Indraparshtha Station and walk about five or ten minutes. You'll see the river.'

Rajni and Shirina looked at each other. 'You sure this is how you want to do this?' Shirina asked.

Rajni nodded.

Jezmeen walked out of the building, her heart pounding, to find Rajni holding the canister of Mum's ashes. 'How did it go?' Rajni asked.

'I'll tell you later,' Jezmeen said, keeping her eyes trained on the urn. 'What are you doing with that?'

'We're thinking of scattering Mum's ashes on the Yamuna River, which leads to the Ganges. Turns out it's not far from here, and we can get back in time for Tom Hanks to take us to the airport. Indraparshtha Station is only a few stops away.'

Take you *to the airport,* Jezmeen thought. She couldn't bring herself to say it though. In the last hour, an opportunity to star in a television series had been presented to her with one small catch: she had to stay in India. At first, Jezmeen had thought the choice was easy. *Of course!* she'd said. But Hari told her to think about it, and then the doubt crept in. This meant leaving London behind, which she had been so glad to do last week when she was leaving for a temporary trip, but there were so many different things to consider now. She had suspended her frustrations with India because she knew she was just visiting; would she survive here on her own?

Luckily, she didn't have to say anything yet. Rajni and Shirina were too busy trying to find the Metro station according to Tom Hanks' directions. Rajni clutched the canister to her chest as a surge of commuters went against their direction at the station's entrance. They paid for their tickets and made their way to the platform. The smooth tiled floors and air-conditioning muted out the noise from the city above.

'I wonder what Mum would say if she knew this was how we were doing this,' Shirina said, holding a protective hand over her belly as they jostled with other passengers through the doors of the women's section. A seat was quickly cleared for Shirina, who thanked the woman and sat down. Rajni and Jezmeen stood next to her.

'Mum's letter contained a lot of reminders for us to bond with each other and look after each other. I think she'd be happy enough to know we were doing this together,' Rajni said. The train jerked suddenly, the force knocking Rajni into Jezmeen, who reached out instinctively to grab the canister. Rajni stabilized and hugged the urn to her chest with one hand. With the other, she held onto a pole.

'Or she'd say, "I should have chosen a burial,"' Jezmeen said. Rajni and Shirina started laughing.

'So tell us what happened with Hari,' Shirina said. 'Is he going to follow up, or was it just a meeting to say hello?'

Jezmeen waved the question away. 'One thing at a time,' she said, nodding at the canister. 'I'll tell you guys after we're done.'

There was a muffled announcement and then the train pulled into the station. Jezmeen couldn't help remembering that day at the protest, all the women pouring out of the station and into the white sunlight. They brimmed with energy and anger. Jezmeen had felt as if she was part of an exciting movement, and the injustice of being catcalled and harassed were so fresh from that walk from the hotel to the station. 'Your sister told me you couldn't stay out of trouble,' Hari had said in his office earlier, with a grin. He was joking, but Jezmeen's stomach knotted at the thought.

The noise of the street greeted them as soon as they emerged from the station. The river was visible in the distance, but they had to walk in single file along the wobbling stones of a pavement to a traffic junction. A bus teeming with people thundered past, trailing a long black puff of exhaust. Jezmeen wasn't sure if the sheen of being in India had worn off, or if she was just thinking about it more because of the dilemma she was in, but she missed London. She missed it even more knowing that she might not go back for a while.

The river was clogged at the banks with rubbish. Empty plastic bottles and scraps of wood bobbed along the water. Poking between the debris were weeds, clumped and blackened with oil. This was all to be expected, but when Jezmeen saw the look of uncertainty on Rajni's face, she wondered if they had come here for nothing.

'We don't have to do this now,' Shirina reminded Rajni. 'There's always time to come back.'

'You'll have a baby then,' Rajni said. 'Anil and Davina will have one too, and I'll be busy helping them. I don't have much time off except during school holidays. Life will get in the way and we'll keep putting it off.'

Jezmeen looked around. 'If we walk a bit further, we can find a better spot,' she said. She had no idea if this was right, but Rajni and Shirina took her advice. They walked in silence along the edges of the river, which curved away from the road. There was a row of boarded stalls on the embankment. The people in the shops looked curiously at them as they walked past.

'Here,' Rajni said, nodding to an area where the water was clear. All of the rubbish had floated and collected together on the other side – there was a small sanctuary. Jezmeen felt the sun prickling her skin. The sky was a blur of pale yellow, like parched grass. It wasn't Lokpal Lake, but there was beauty in searching for a space like this for Mum too. Shirina clasped her hand.

Rajni twisted open the lid from the canister and hesitated. 'Shall we take it in turns?' Jezmeen and Shirina nodded, so Rajni lowered herself slowly to a squat and began to tip the ashes into the water. They sprinkled out and peppered the surface. 'You're home now, Mum. Rest well.' Rajni stretched her arm and shook the canister again, spilling more ashes.

'Your turn,' she said to Shirina, wiping the tears from her eyes.

Shirina stayed standing. She held onto Jezmeen's hand and took the canister from Rajni with her other hand. She whispered, 'Thank you Mum. Thank you for bringing us together. Thank you for our lives.' After she shook some of the ashes out, she waited and watched them floating on the water's surface.

Tears blurred Jezmeen's vision. A part of her wanted to run away from all of this. It was too difficult to put an end to Mum like this. She felt that familiar choking, that need to turn time back. 'Go on, Jezmeen,' Rajni said gently. 'You can do this.' Jezmeen shook her head, refusing the canister from Shirina.

Rajni and Shirina waited for her. They stood quietly on the banks of the river, looking out at the horizon, lost in their thoughts. Jezmeen gathered up the strength to say goodbye to Mum. She didn't have anything to say aloud, like her sisters did. She felt as if she had too many things to say, that there were so many conversations she wanted to have with Mum in place of all the arguments they had over trivial things. *You have to take more responsibility.* This was why Jezmeen was so afraid to stay in India. What if trouble found her again and she didn't have anybody to bail her out?

The clouds shifted, letting in a shard of sunlight that made Rajni and Shirina blink and look away. Jezmeen closed her eyes. Light danced in the darkness and then materialized into familiar shapes. She saw Mum sitting up in her hospital bed, nodding a greeting as Jezmeen walked in. It was just like that day when Jezmeen visited her on the way back from the audition, except Jezmeen had different news now. *I have an opportunity,* she said. *It could be amazing.* Mum listened, her expression unchanging. In the fantasy, Jezmeen heard herself telling Mum that she had worked very hard for a long time, and it was time she had a break. *I need you to have a little faith in me,* she said.

When Jezmeen opened her eyes, the sunlight was defining every ripple in the water. She shielded her eyes and held out her other hand for the canister. Shirina placed it in her grasp. Jezmeen clutched it fiercely to her chest, remembering how strange it felt to hold Mum's limp, bony hands.

Unlike her sisters, Jezmeen had no parting words for Mum. What she resolved to do then was more powerful than anything she could say.

She turned the canister over and emptied it into the water. The ashes drew together to make a floating shadow on the surface before the water shifted and they broke apart.

Chapter Twenty-Five

My daughters, the completion of this journey should bring you peace. I'm sure travelling together was not easy, but perhaps this trip to India has taught you something that you couldn't have learned in England. I cannot command you to spend any more time together, or to cherish each other's presence in your lives. I can only leave you with hope that the lessons of this journey will continue after you return home.

Goodbyes had to be quick at the entrance of Delhi airport. Passengers poured from every direction towards the sliding doors, their trolleys piled high with wobbling luggage. A tour bus pulled up on the kerb and began a deafening series of honks to clear the cars parked ahead. Jezmeen and Shirina were locked in a tight embrace. Tears spilled down Shirina's cheeks and darkened Jezmeen's blue cotton peasant top.

'You take care of yourself,' Rajni said briskly, when it was her turn to part with Jezmeen. She was almost tempted to just give Jezmeen a pat on the back and dive into the crowd of passengers to avoid any more wrenching emotion. Instead she gave Jezmeen a quick hug. She could feel her eyes welling up, so she turned her attention to her suitcase and said, 'Right, off we go.' She sensed rather than saw Jezmeen wandering off into the crowd. Shirina waited and waved, and caught up with Rajni as she entered the airport.

After checking in and putting their bags through the scanners, Rajni and Shirina were to give their father's name for the last time at Customs. The immigration officer scrutinized Rajni's passport photograph and gave her a hard, unblinking stare. It hadn't been that long since the photo had been taken, but Rajni was conscious of how different she probably looked. With each passing year, her cheeks sank a little bit more and her laugh lines deepened.

'Look here, please,' the officer said. Rajni didn't realize that her eyes were wandering. At the next counter, Shirina was having a conversation with the immigration officials. It was probably because of the last-minute change in her ticket.

But Rajni still worried. She had not stopped worrying since they found Shirina in that clinic, even though she was working hard to stay upbeat for Shirina's sake. In the car on the way here, Rajni asked Shirina, 'What's the first thing you want to do when we get back to London?' Shirina shrugged. 'Come on, tell me,' Rajni urged. 'We'll go wherever you want. Maybe that new Ottolenghi restaurant? I haven't tried it either, but I heard it's got rave reviews. Or a West End show? Did any good musicals come out while you were in Melbourne?' Rajni realized that she was selling the tourists' version of London to a person who had lived there all her life, but she wasn't sure if Shirina thought of it as home any more.

Last night, while her sisters were watching a movie in the hotel suite, Rajni had called Kabir. They hadn't spoken since that late-night conversation early on in the trip, and their conversation now was careful, with pauses that Rajni knew could only be filled when they saw each other in person again. After telling Kabir about Shirina, and deciding together that Shirina should stay with them for a while, she asked after Anil. 'He's well,' Kabir said. 'He and Davina have started flat-hunting.'

Rajni had felt the twinge in her gut, but accepted that it would always be there. This was her son after all, and he was starting adulthood far earlier than she'd wanted. She was allowed to grieve while also supporting him. She took in a deep breath and said, 'I'd like to meet her. Maybe we can have her over for dinner when I come back?'

'That would be really nice,' Kabir had said. Rajni could feel his relief over the phone. Her next phone call was to Nikhil, the private investigator. She thanked him for his services and told him to close the investigation. After assuring him she didn't want a refund, she hung up and deleted his number from her phone.

Now Shirina was nodding at something the official was telling her. Her gaze flickered at Rajni, and she nodded again. There was a sign on the wall that instructed passengers not to wait in this area, but nobody had shooed Rajni away yet. All sorts of travellers trailed past Rajni, lumbering under the weight of backpacks and dragging suitcases which bulged with excesses from their journey. Rajni realized she hadn't bought a single thing in India to take home. The contents of her bags were the same as when she left London, but so much had changed. She had a new relationship with her sisters – that and a throbbing pain in her ankle.

Rajni had been worried too when Jezmeen announced to them that she had decided to stay in India. Rajni knew staying in India was the best thing for Jezmeen's career, and she couldn't wait to see her sister succeed, but she also wished they were returning to London together. She remembered taking Jezmeen and Shirina to the shops when they were little girls. She'd link arms with her sisters, one on each side. Sometimes, if Rajni picked up her pace, Jezmeen would stumble and ask her to slow down. Rajni would smile, and say, 'I forgot your little feet.' The comment made Jezmeen take long, quick strides, an imitation of a fairytale giant. When Mum first told them to take this pilgrimage, Rajni had had a mental image of racing against her sisters across India, out of sync and gasping for breath. Rajni wished that Mum could see what the journey had done for them. She imagined Mum waiting for them at Heathrow, expecting three bickering women who couldn't wait to get away from each other, but instead finding her daughters chatting amicably, making plans to see each other again soon.

Rajni's phone buzzed in her bag. As she pulled it out, a border officer marched towards her, wagging a finger. Rajni dropped the phone back in her bag and cast a glance over her shoulder. Shirina was holding up the stub from what looked like her Melbourne-to-Delhi boarding pass.

The security officer waved Rajni along. She walked as far as she could while still keeping Shirina within her sight. Outside a Duty Free lounge, Rajni picked up her phone. It was a message from Jezmeen:

'It was very hard to say goodbye but you should know that I have all the love and respect in the world for you. I gave you a hard time while you were organizing this journey but it was only because you were so sure of where we were going while I still had to figure it out. Give my love to Kabir and Anil – they're lucky to have you back.'

Rajni bit her lip. She went into the Duty Free shop and busied herself with perfume samples to keep the tears back but they came anyway, and now she smelled like peonies and musk. She read the text again and pressed REPLY but before she could compose a message, there was another one from Jezmeen. A picture of three grandmothers with their grey hair in curlers, clinking their full wine glasses. *'So much to celebrate soon!'* she had written. Rajni laughed and let the tears fall.

Shirina was finally being waved through the Customs counter, and she was walking towards Rajni. A smile bloomed across her face, and she looked more rested than she had been on the entire journey.

'Everything okay?' Rajni asked.

'Yeah, they just wanted to know why I changed my destination,' Shirina said. She tucked her passport back into its case and put it in her handbag.

'What did you tell them?'

'Same thing I told Sehaj on the phone this morning. I just want to go home.'

Epilogue

Shirina had just finished feeding Anaya in the small back room meant for wedding presents, when her Skype ringtone began to sound. Jezmeen was a few minutes early. Shirina adjusted the neckline of her dress, propped Anaya on her lap and pressed the green answer button.

A ghastly version of Jezmeen appeared on the screen, with a bloody gaping wound on the side of her head. The minute Anaya saw her, she began to shriek. It took a few minutes of jiggling and hushing to calm her down. 'Shh,' Shirina said. 'It's your Auntie Jezmeen, calling from India. She's just wearing make-up, darling. She's playing.'

Rajni popped her head into the room. 'Everything alright?' Her eyes narrowed when she noticed the screen. 'Oh for heaven's sakes, Jezmeen, why would you scare a baby like that?'

'I didn't know she was going to see me,' Jezmeen protested. Behind her was a whirl of activity – crew members hurrying by, talking into their mouthpieces, a large camera on a trolley being pushed. Jezmeen's hair was pulled back and piled high, making the gash on her head even more obvious.

'I'll take her out to see the ducks,' Rajni said to Shirina. 'You two catch up.' Anaya stretched out her arms with gratitude and threw the screen a scowl as Rajni took her away.

'Some warning would have been nice,' Shirina informed Jezmeen. 'You look like a murder victim.'

'A murder attempt survivor,' Jezmeen said. 'If you'll remember, at the end of the last season, I was bludgeoned by that mafia boss who left me for dead in a house he set on fire, but I got rescued at the last minute by the undercover guy.'

'I do remember,' Shirina said. She and Rajni had been on the edge of their seats watching the finale a few months ago. Shirina had trouble sleeping afterwards, and left a message with Jezmeen just to confirm that her character would make it. She thought Jezmeen might laugh at her for not knowing the difference between fiction and real life, but in their conversation the next day, Jezmeen was delighted to know that her show was giving viewers nightmares. 'It's the realism of *Lawless* that's making it so addictive,' Jezmeen said. 'Hari is a genius with that stuff.' This was also the reason the show was being picked up by major networks in the US and the UK.

'How's the party then? I'm sorry I'm missing it,' Jezmeen said. After the show's unprecedented success, shooting of the second season had to begin immediately.

'It's really nice,' Shirina said. 'Kabir and Rajni rented out this lovely restaurant which opens out onto a pond, so there'll be some great pictures of the bride and groom.'

'How are they? I want to talk to Anil later to convey my congratulations,' Jezmeen said.

'They're glowing. Davina looks beautiful.' In a simple white summer dress with a lace-trimmed shawl, Davina was an understated bride, but she was radiant. Their three-month-old son Arjun was the real show-stealer, wearing a tiny tuxedo romper complete with a red bow tie.

'And how's mother-of-the-groom?' Jezmeen asked.

Shirina checked behind her to make sure the door was shut all the way. She lowered her voice. 'You missed it. There was almost *an incident*.'

'Oooh, share,' Jezmeen squealed. Behind her, a hair stylist sprayed something in her hair and walked off.

'Okay, so earlier, they were doing family photos near this big weeping tree outside. Very picturesque, the weather's cooperating, and then the photographer announces he wants one of just Rajni and Davina together. You know the type of photograph where they say, "Just converse with each other. Act natural," and you become really self-conscious.'

Jezmeen snorted. 'Especially when Rajni's natural stance towards Davina is probably an icy stare at best.'

'Exactly. He has them standing near the pond and he keeps calling out things for them to talk about – all those memories you've shared over the years, how happy you are that this day has arrived – and then it dawns on all of us that he's thinks they're sisters.'

'HAHAHA. So what happened?'

'Rajni informs him that she's actually the mother-of-the-groom, and he starts to backpedal, and tells her it's a compliment because she looks so young.'

'When really we know it's because they're so close in age.'

'Yeah, but then it gets worse, because the photographer decides he wants one with Rajni and her grandchildren.'

Jezmeen let out a hoot. 'Children, plural? He thought Anaya was her granddaughter?'

Shirina nodded. 'And another child – this toddler who was just feeding the ducks with his parents. He went from thinking Rajni was the sister of the bride to The Old Woman Who Lived in a Shoe.'

Jezmeen was convulsing so hard with laughter now that a tendril of her hairdo came loose. The stylist returned to reset it, jabbing more pins into Jezmeen's hair. 'Oh my god. That's too good, Shirina.'

'If you could have seen it! She launched into this lecture to the photographer about protocols and how he should have read the email she sent him expressly explaining the dynamics of our family. She had drawn up a family tree and everything, so he'd be able to call everybody by name and relation, and avoid the usual chaos of these things.'

'Why am I not there?' Jezmeen sounded genuinely sad then. Shirina had been disappointed too, to hear that Jezmeen was going to spend the summer in India.

'You are here,' Shirina said. 'You've been here a great deal.' She wasn't just saying it to comfort her sister – she really had showed up via Skype for every momentous occasion, no matter the time difference or her filming schedule. It even became something that an entertainment journalist picked up on in a recent profile about Jezmeen, which Shirina kept taped to her fridge:

The up-and-coming starlet prioritizes her family, even on days packed with shoots and publicity commitments. During this interview, she tells us that she's expecting a call from her sister in London, with whom she speaks once a day. But Shergill wouldn't describe their childhood as being particularly close. 'My sisters and I didn't always get along,' she admits. 'But as you get older, you recognize the importance of people you used to take for granted.' Getting older would be another sore point for most actresses, but Shergill takes it in her stride. Breaking into her first major role relatively late compared to other women in Bollywood, Shergill says her previous setbacks gave her the resilience for her role as Manika Kapoor, a female detective fighting corruption in the highest ranks of the police force in HC Kumar's acclaimed series, Lawless.

Shirina savoured a different line from that piece every day. She was so incredibly proud of Jezmeen, and so happy that she was finally being recognized. Whenever Anaya caught sight of the glossy image of Jezmeen staring boldly at the camera, Shirina pointed and said, 'That's your auntie. She's fearless.'

There was a knock on the door before Rajni hurried in, toting Anaya on her waist. 'Are the nappies in here?' she asked. 'I think someone needs a change.'

'I'll do it – you catch up with Jezmeen,' Shirina said, taking Anaya from her. She breathed in the scent of Anaya's skin. Shirina never missed a chance to bury her face in her baby's hair. She was born with dark wisps, which were curling slightly on the ends now.

'Hi Jezmeen, how are you?' Rajni said too loudly.

'I'm good. Just waiting to go on but it will be a while. We were supposed to start an hour ago, so it's still early.'

Rajni grinned. 'Ah, India.'

While her sisters caught up and Shirina carried Anaya to the changing table, she was struck by a feeling she occasionally had. It was the opposite of an out-of-body experience, and one that she considered uniquely hers until she read about it in Jezmeen's profile:

'Sometimes I just feel sort of captivated by this sensation of fully being, if that makes sense. I don't want to sound pretentious and say I'm fulfilling my life's purpose — it's probably simpler than that. It's just a profoundly gratifying feeling of being exactly where I want to be.' The actress claims she is not spiritual or religious, but a trip to India with her sisters last year, during which she was discovered by HC Kumar, taught her to accept the impermanence of life.

The speeches and toasts were all fairly casual, as Anil and Davina wanted. Anil's best friend Joshua told a memorable story about the times he and Anil did daredevil stunts on their skateboards and posted the videos online. 'Considering his aunt was the *DisasterTube* host, we should've known better,' Joshua said with a wink at Shirina. She shook her head to tell him he had the wrong aunt but he was too pleased with himself to make the correction.

Shirina sneaked a look at Rajni during the maid-of-honour's speech, which mentioned several times how Davina loved to keep her friends on their toes. 'We were not expecting Anil,' she quipped. 'Nor were they expecting Arjun. Full of surprises, our Davina!' The titter that went through the small crowd made Rajni visibly stiffen. She still wasn't fond of jokes about accidental pregnancies or age differences.

Anaya was bundled in Shirina's lap, her chubby legs dangling beneath the frothy bridesmaid dress that Davina had bought her. It was very sweet, and earlier, as the pictures were taken with Anaya and Arjun sitting together on the grass, Shirina felt a wave of sadness. It was an odd thing, grieving a marriage. Sometimes she didn't know what felt worse – Sehaj's unwillingness to fight for her, or his continued absence from their lives. By the time Anaya was born in November, Shirina had filed for divorce. Although she was relieved to find out that he wouldn't try to fight for custody, she was also deeply hurt for Anaya.

Her last message to Sehaj remained unsent. She had composed it so many times, in so many changing tones and questions and lengthy paragraphs that it became a conversation with herself. Over time, she was able to delete the lines that no longer mattered. Questions about why Sehaj married her at all if his family wanted so much control. Angry rants about his mother and all the damage she tried to inflict, just because she felt threatened that a woman would steal her precious son. Delete, delete, delete – it became easier, and even the sadness she felt now was muted. It was like the grief she felt for Mum, something that became a little easier to carry as the days passed. Now Shirina only had one thing to say, and it didn't matter if Sehaj knew it or not. *I named her Anaya. It means freedom.*

'Is she asleep?' Shirina looked up to find Davina standing over her, holding Arjun. He had Anil's round eyes and Davina's big smile. Shirina looked down to find that Anaya had drifted off to sleep. 'I must have been rocking her,' she said. 'Sometimes I don't even realize I'm doing it.'

'Same here,' Davina said. 'I was swaying back and forth in line at the supermarket the other day, while Anil was outside with Arjun. The checkout lady told me there were toilets out the back.'

Shirina laughed. Davina had an ease about her that Shirina really enjoyed, and having another new mother in the family had been a real blessing. They stayed in touch even outside the fortnightly family dinners that Rajni had started organizing after they returned to London. Shirina had lived with her and Kabir in Anil's old room for a few months before she found a place of her own nearby. Anaya came home in a bundle of fleece blankets to that modest little flat, where Jezmeen's picture smiled from the fridge and Rajni was only a few streets away.

Anil, Kabir and Rajni wandered over. 'Lovely ceremony,' Shirina said to Anil. 'You clean up nicely.' Anil smiled and straightened his jacket lapels.

'He takes after me,' Kabir said.

'You mean before the cleaning-up part, right?' Rajni scoffed. Kabir pretended to look wounded.

'We chose a great day for a wedding, didn't we?' Davina said. The summer sky was blissfully blue, with a light breeze picking up the ends of her shawl.

'For all intensive purposes, this was the best venue too,' Anil agreed.

'I'm sorry, what did you say?' Davina asked.

'For all intens—What? What's wrong with that one?'

'It's "For all intents and purposes",' Rajni said.

'That doesn't make any sense,' Anil said.

'This is the same thing he said about "irregardlessly",' Davina informed Rajni.

'He's still doing that? Anil, really, sometimes it's like you never went to school.'

'Hey Josh, come over here for a second,' Anil called. His best man came bounding over. For the second time, Shirina did not return the wink he gave her. 'How do you say it – "For all intents and purposes" or "For all intensive purposes"?'

'Neither,' Josh declared. 'It's "For all, in tensive purposes."'

'What?' Rajni and Davina asked in unison.

'Like, you know, for all people who are, like, in "tensive" purposes. Like something's tense, it's a tensive purpose.'

Rajni and Davina both had the same expression of disbelief on their faces. 'Do you want to explain it, or should I?' Rajni asked. Davina just shook her head slowly.

Shirina began to laugh. Anaya shifted momentarily from the vibration in her ribs, and then relaxed into slumber again. Tomorrow, when Shirina and Jezmeen spoke again, she had to tell her about this. She'd recount how Rajni and Davina teamed up to launch into a lecture that sent Anil and Kabir scrambling away together. She'd tell Jezmeen that she missed her but she was looking forward to her season premiere. She also couldn't wait to see Jezmeen in the flesh, but that was a surprise that she and Rajni had been planning together. Next month, once Rajni's school holidays started, they were taking Anaya to India.

Acknowledgements

It truly took a village to nurture this novel. My deepest gratitude goes to the following people:

My agent Anna Power for believing in this novel, even when I wasn't always sure what the Shergill sisters were getting up to, and where they were headed. Thank you for the pep talks that propped me up when I needed them most.

The wonderful team at HarperCollins who cheered me on: my editors Martha Ashby and Rachel Kahan provided valuable feedback and were always just a phone call away to work through the knots in my mind. Fliss Denham and Camille Collins worked tirelessly to promote my previous novel, and will no doubt champion this one.

My parents took me on a trip to India in 2016. Thanks for the excuse to drink chai and eat pakoras and call it 'research.' Thanks to all the kind people in Delhi, Amritsar and Chandigarh for your hospitality and your patience with this particularly clueless non-resident Indian.

Barrie Sherwood was only supposed to give me his thoughts on the first chapter but got roped into reading much more. Thank you for your positivity, your enthusiasm and your patience. I aspire to be the kind of mentor and teacher that you are.

My PhD mates at NTU. There are many of you, and although I didn't submit chapters of this novel to our workshops, I'm so grateful for your supportive presence in my life during this novel's creation.

Jim and Lucy Lee opened their beautiful, art-and-book-filled home in Virginia to help me kick-start this book. Thank you for holding me account-able to my daily word counts, but asking no questions if I lingered in the kitchen for two hours, clearly avoiding my laptop.

Members of my Hollins Village, the best village there could be: your moral support and virtual hugs meant everything to me. This book was written in a time of the greatest and most challenging transition in my life, and your parenting advice helped to put me at ease so I could get back to writing.

All of my friends with sisters. Too many over a lifetime to mention, and you probably didn't know that your sibling dramas would make their way into my book. I feel like I have absorbed many moments of complicated love-hate sister experiences from our conversations. I envy your sisters for having you in their lives but I'm grateful for the next best thing: your friendship.

The staff at Trehaus, a wonderful co-working space that also provides infant care. You gave me the space and time to focus on finishing this book. Thank you for welcoming us into your lovely community.

Paul, husband and father extraordinaire. Every time I say, 'I can't,' you shrug and say, 'Of course you can.' You make everything possible.

Asher, one day, if I manage to talk around the clichés, I'll tell you how you changed my world. How I thought I knew who I was until I became a mother, and how incredibly blessed I am to be yours. For now, all I can say is that I love you, and let's dance!